City of Oom

Book 3 of the War Bunny Chronicles

CHRISTOPHER ST. JOHN

Harvest Oak Press

Published by Harvest Oak Press, April 2024

Copyright © 2024 by Christopher St. John

All rights reserved. No part of this publication may be reproduced, distributed, or transmitted in any form or by any means, including photocopying, recording, or other electronic or mechanical methods, without the prior written permission of the publisher, except in the case of brief quotations embodied in critical reviews and certain other noncommercial uses permitted by copyright law.

First Printing, 2024

ISBN: 978-1-7368857-6-5 (ebook)
ISBN: 978-1-7368857-7-2 (paperback)
ISBN: 978-1-7368857-8-9 (hardcover)

Cover art by Belle McClain

For the animals

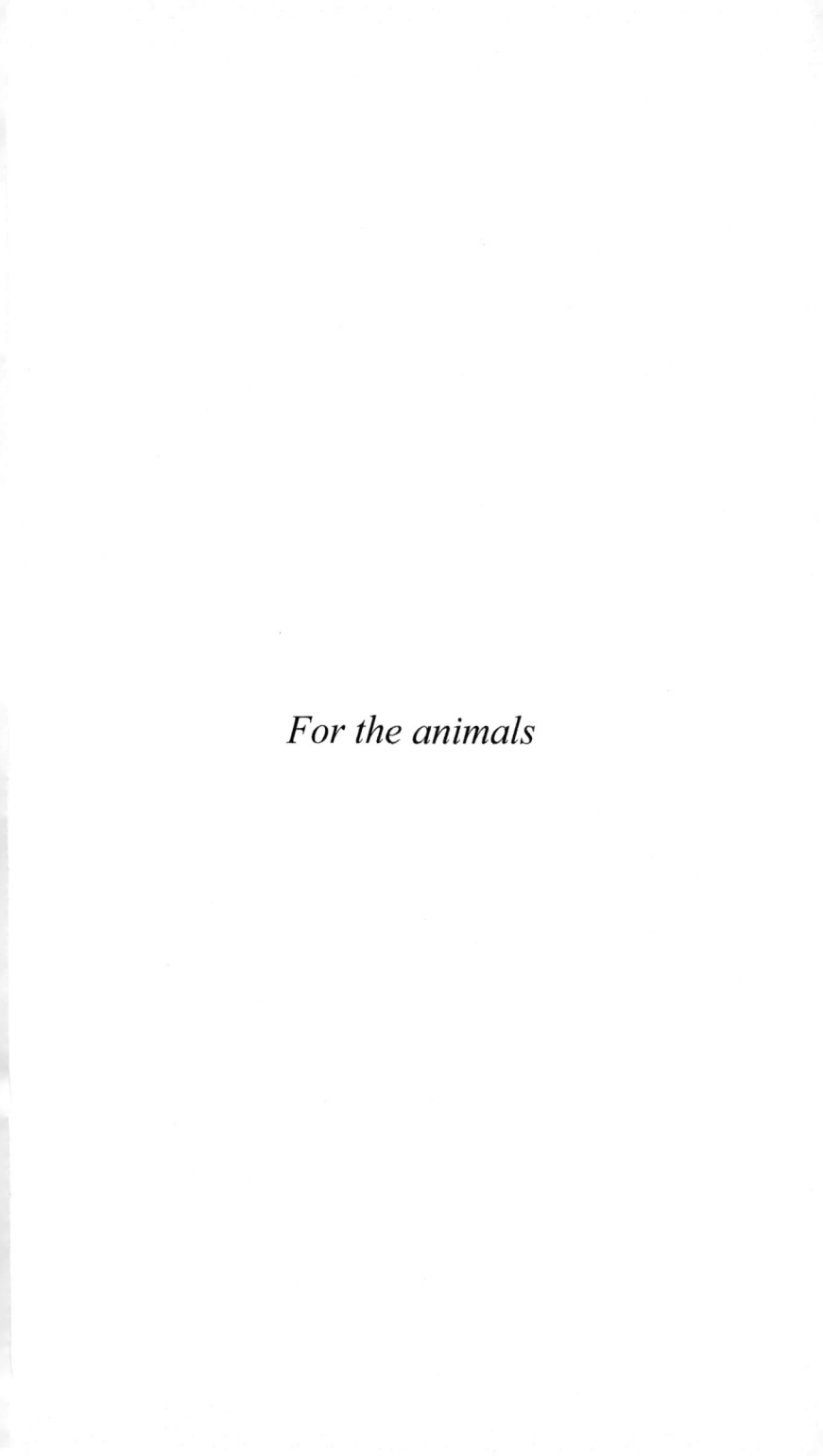

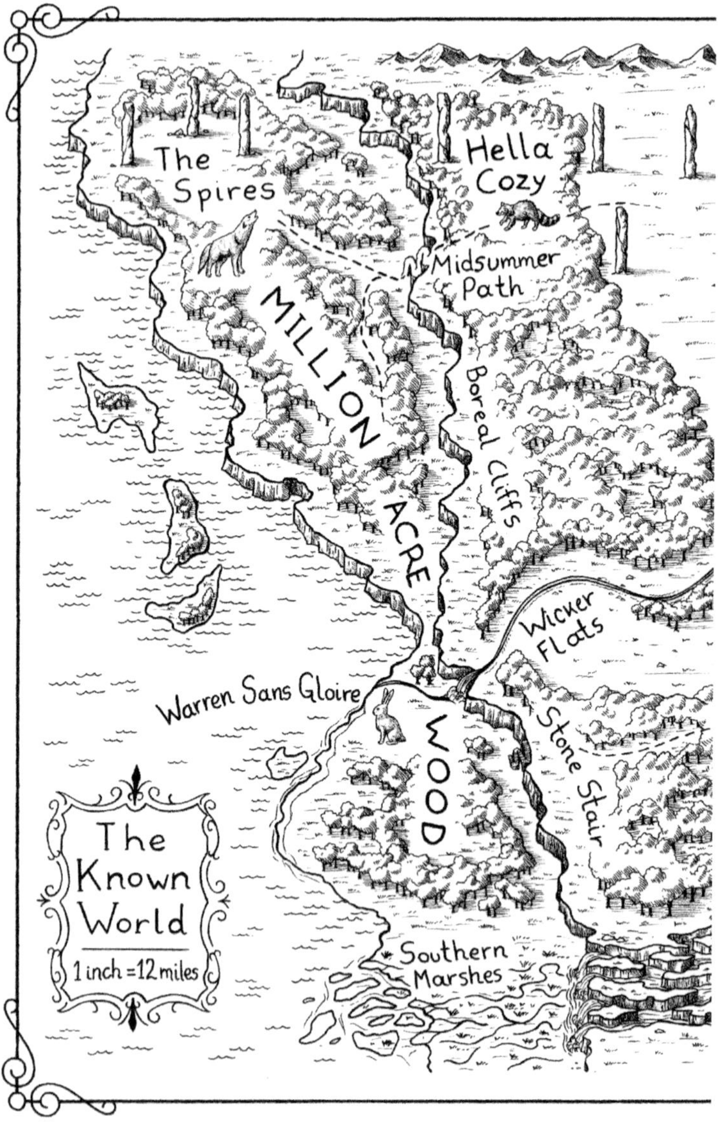
The Spires
Hella Cozy
Midsummer Path
MILLION ACRE
Boreal Cliffs
Wicker Flats
Warren Sans Gloire
WOOD
Stone Stair
Southern Marshes
The Known World
1 inch = 12 miles

Le Sanctuaire
Rime River
Sea of Grass
Shandy River
City of Oom
Delf River
Braided Gorges
Hills of Pi

Synopsis

City of Oom is the third book in the *War Bunny Chronicles*.

The first book, *War Bunny*, told the story of Anastasia, a plain brown rabbit living in the Million Acre Wood, doing her best to fit in with her warren and its deep commitment to the worship of Dah. Plagued by compulsions, she was already an underbunny before her imperious mother, Olympia, forcibly cast her from the warren. Scared and alone, Anastasia resisted the teachings that directed her to embrace "glorification," which would mean becoming food for predators. In a fateful encounter with a fox, she learned she could fight back.

Meanwhile, other bunnies were finding themselves thrust into the dangerous unknown. Studious Freddie, struggling with farblindness, barely managed to escape a weasel attack on his warren that seemed to be an inside job. And flirtatious Love Bug, flouting the rigid hierarchy of rabbit warrens, was violently kicked out of his home. These two wandering bunnies gravitated to Anastasia, who had begun to defend herself and her small burrow. She allowed them into this new kind of warren, in which the dream was not glory but life. One by one, more small creatures made their way to Warren *Sans Gloire*.

This affront to the world order wasn't taken lightly, either by the predators who enforced it or the upper echelons of rabbit society who benefitted from it. Word of prey animals fighting back spread through the Million Acre Wood, reaching the foxes, raptors, and weasels who experienced it firsthand, and then the coyotes who oversaw the domain. While most predators guffawed at these tales, the limping coyote Gaetan was smart enough to know when to bring in upper management—in this case, Aliyah, heir apparent to the Summerday Clan of golden wolves. And Olympia, seeing her daughter as a dangerous heretic, sought to undermine the new warren by any means necessary, risking the lives of young bunnies as "Dah's Flowers" in the process.

As the weeks went on, Warren *Sans Gloire* was bolstered by newcomers of diverse talents and species. Wood mice, led by the honorable Death Rage, lent their warrior prowess and tenacity. The craftrat Bricabrac created for Anastasia a blade she could wear—the Dragon Claw—and armor to keep her safe, along with weapons for other creatures. Rabbit Readers, none better than wise Nicodemus from Anastasia's home warren, provided knowledge gleaned from scraps of pages penned by the Dead Gods. But it was the arrival of the barbarian lop-eared rabbit Wendy that introduced a world-changing idea: hunting predators.

Anastasia could not stomach the thought of deliberately killing another living creature. She staunchly refused to sink to that, believing that only the defense of herself and her loved ones was justified. Her new community, however, could feel the pressure bearing down from the predators of the Wood. To maintain alliances with neighboring warrens, her friends decided to kill a coyote while Anastasia was away.

But before they could put their plan into action, a coyote found Nicodemus at a vulnerable moment and Anastasia, returning from her journey, was forced to intervene. To save her friend from danger, she struck the killing blow against the coyote. Word spread through the Wood that a coyote had been slain by a rabbit, and Anastasia wrestled with her faith and the future of this new power. By the end of the book, the predators had momentarily withdrawn, and Olympia was stunned. The denizens of Warren *Sans Gloire* came together to enjoy a party out in the open, free to live in peace, if only for an evening.

The second book, *Summerday*, picked up the story a few weeks later. Anastasia and her Warren *Sans Gloire* compatriots were working hard to prepare themselves for whatever might be coming next. Then reports reached them that the golden wolves of the Summerday Clan were coming to investigate the warren and its revolutionary ideas. Not long after, an assassination attempt with poison against Anastasia was almost successful. Animated by threats from all sides, the Free Warrens set out to gather every advantage they could, from Dead God secrets to long-lost survivalist caches.

The wolves, however, were making moves of their own. Troubling reports from crows indicated that the restless prey of the Wood were becoming braver, and the introduction of the upland wolf Tennyson, though of particular interest to Aliyah, was just one more mouth to feed in a pack that had seen too few deer lately. Driven by hunger to the criminal act of eating racoons, they decided to finally put down the revolt for once and for all, sending out a call for all the predators to join the fight.

Scheming also continued in the orthodox rabbit warrens, led by Olympia. Her spy in Warren *Sans Gloire*, Coriander, was proving less and less effective. And having been the originator of Anastasia's poisoning, Olympia was anxious to find another way to neutralize her growing power, because it was disturbing the natural order and attracting wolf-led reprisals.

Then Anastasia sent a spy into the wolf fortress, the brave warmouse Death Rage, and there she discovered that the wolves and crows together were manipulating the rabbit religion through turncoat rabbit priests, and the holy words of Dah were crafted to make rabbits easier prey.

Anastasia, now freed from the strictures of her religion, leaned toward a more aggressive stance. And the Free Warrens, seeing a mighty battle coming, threw all their efforts into fortifying themselves. The discovery of "farkillers"—crossbows—promised a tectonic shift in the balance of power. And the small animals and their new raccoon allies got to work building and practicing with these new machines.

As the impending fight neared, many smaller conflicts erupted. Bricabrac had helped his sister gain a commission with the wolves to build armor for them, and he was imprisoned by the rabbits for this act. He only escaped when Death Rage took pity on him. The Ascending Squirrels managed to save young bunnies from wolves out on a hunt. Later, Coriander sacrificed himself to save Sunbeam. And when Love Bug and Wendy came face-to-face with a Summerday wolf, they fought for their lives and just barely managed to kill him.

On the eve of the final clash, Olympia, coming to realize that the rabbit religion was a sham, called off another attempt on Anastasia's life. And Aliyah Summerday and Tennyson had a romantic encounter, fueled by dirty apples and night-before-action jitters.

When the day of battle arrived, Anastasia was captured and taken behind enemy lines. Her army rose to the occasion, and with the help of their crossbows and trenches, managed to hold off the onslaught of predators. Anastasia was rescued by songbirds, and when the Summerday alpha wolves charged, they too were killed by the crossbow quarrels. Aliyah, seeing her lover and her parents dying, fled the battlefield.

Anastasia allowed the surviving predators to go free, but warned them to never again harm a living creature while in the territory of the newly established Free Nation. She reunited with Freddie, recognizing him as the partner she had always needed, and they enjoyed a victory party while pondering what was in store for their new world.

City of Oom begins a few weeks later. It is now winter, and the rabbits are realizing that Free Nation faces two existential threats. One from within and one from without.

Chapter 1

Before the bears came to City of Oom, there was no life and no law. It was a wasteland carpeted with bones of the Dead Gods.

—Thimble Thimbalian
History of the Known World

Anastasia

"If the bears don't come down from the uplands and rip us apart, we will devour ourselves from inside," said Anastasia as the snow swirled around her. She shook the flakes off her long brown ears. "Unless we get this figured out, our little nation will die." She stood shivering on the embankment the rabbits had just finished building before the snows came, with fifteen crossbows spaced out along the top.

Freddie squinted into the breeze. "We've come so far," he said. "No animals have ever done what we've done." She could hear that he was trying to sound confident.

Christopher St. John

Anastasia pressed against his thick black-and-gray fur, her lean muscular form hungry for warmth in the January cold. "I wish it was the bears that scared me most," she said. "Who would have thought that our biggest enemies would turn out to be ourselves?" She started quietly murmuring strings of numbers again. *One, two, four, eight, sixteen…*

After a few moments, a brisk wind whipped up more snow flurries as the pale day drifted toward an early twilight, and the two bunnies continued on with their perimeter walk.

Anastasia touched the stock of each crossbow as she passed it. They were all aimed at the foot of the Stone Stair, a long staircase built into the Boreal Cliffs. It was one of two points of entry from the uplands, which made it the likely invasion highway for the grizzly bears from City of Oom, or their corps of enforcers, the Municipal Wolves.

She paused and gazed at the weapons, her forepaw resting on her owl claw necklace. Many of these crossbows had been hauled south from the Battle of the Narrows, where they had helped bring down the Landlords of the Million Acre Wood just two months before. It was because of these wooden machines that Free Nation existed today.

As they reached the end of the embankment, they came upon Stan, the bluebird Air Captain of the aerial wing of the *Armée Libre*. He was taking a turn on sentry duty, and had made a little snow cave for shelter from the wind. The two rabbits sat down near him with their flanks pressed together.

"Come and get warm," said Anastasia.

"Thanks, Godmother." Stan gratefully slipped in between the two rabbits and arranged himself with just his balding blue-feathered head sticking out of the snug rumple of rabbit fur. Anastasia could feel his cool little body squirming around as he settled in.

"Geez, it's frickin' cold out here," he growled. "Now I know why bluebirds migrate south. I'm freezing my tail off."

"Thanks for staying with us this year," said Anastasia.

"Next year, I'm going," said Stan.

For a few moments, all the animals sat in silence, looking out at the snow whipping past the crossbows, each with its stash of stone-pointed quarrels neatly stowed in a loading box nearby.

Then Anastasia glanced up at the top of the cliff, where some flashes of color showed that songbirds were foraging along the cliff edge, a hundred and fifty feet above. "Still having that problem?" she asked.

"Ya, ya," said Stan. "Our peeps are fierce, but we can't make any headway against the upland songbirds. And the swarming tactic that worked great against raptors doesn't work against birds our own size."

"What do you think's causing it?" asked Freddie.

"Songbirds have always been territorial, but someone has them convinced that *we* are the enemy," said Stan. "Dumb clucks, right? But there's no reaching them." He paused for a moment and cocked his head. "If you listen now, I think you can hear them singing their song."

Freddie and Anastasia swiveled their ears to point upward, and the faint sound of birdsong came to them from above.

"Birds of Upland, let us fly
Toward our future filled with glory
Praise our homeland, lift it high
Tell again the grand old story

Dirty ones came from away
Tried to harm our noble forebears
And then on our darkest day
We were helped by mighty warbears

Birds and bears in brotherhood
Bound in friendship now and ever
Swore a great oath in our wood:
Keep out dirty ones forever!"

Anastasia frowned. "Is that new?"

"It is, but it sounds like you've heard it before, doesn't it?" said Stan. "Plus it has just the kind of sing-songy melody songbirds like to learn and repeat. They sing it all the time now."

"Is this real?" asked Freddie. "I mean, are these real events? Dirty ones and bears and whatnot?"

Stan shrugged. "For songbirds, if a new song tastes good to learn—and sing—it's real." A big snowflake landed on his head. He shook it off. "Clearly, this is trouble. And not just that, a new *kind* of trouble. Somehow, the bears are making this happen."

"But we're still not at war," said Freddie.

Anastasia looked at him. "Yet."

Aliyah

Aliyah Summerday, the last golden wolf drawing breath in the world, stood on the edge of a strange country, dusted with snow.

After climbing the Midsummer Path two months before, she had drifted steadily south along the tops of the Boreal Cliffs, her gaze drawn constantly to the Million Acre Wood spread out below. She had crossed the peaceful blue Shandy, wandered through the spindly woodlands covering the Tikituk Hills, and finally arrived at the Braided Gorges of the fast-flowing Delf River.

The hot rage and grief that she had felt after the destruction of the Summerday Clan and her first days of exile to the uplands had now cooled to a heavy ache in her heart that never left her. The one bright spot in her existence was the litter of pups growing in her belly. They were the Summerdays to come, a new world waiting.

She gazed out over the deeply fissured Braided Gorges area. When the Delf River entered the soft limestone that underlay this part of the uplands, it splintered into many channels, all of which cut far into the earth.

Some streams ran through gulches only twenty feet wide, with steep walls that rose seventy feet or more up to the surface. The channels twisted back and forth, rejoining others and then dividing again, following the logic of what had once been random cracks in the limestone. All the watercourses eventually reached the Boreal Cliffs and poured out through steep-sided gullies, falling a hundred feet or more to the Downlands, creating the Southern Marshes that bordered the lower edge of the Million Acre Wood.

Gaetan the coyote appeared with two small kills in his mouth, limping on his injured leg. He laid the bodies in the snow. "For you, my Lady."

"Just two?" was all she said. Then she scarfed them down quickly, not asking if he had already eaten.

Over the past two months, Gaetan had accompanied her as she wandered, ever loyal, ever solicitous. They were bound together by their shared memory of what had happened at the Battle of the Narrows, when little animals with farkillers and dishonorable tactics had laid waste to the *ancien régime* of the Million Acre Wood. Now she was the heir apparent of a kingdom that no longer trembled at her name. And he was the lone retainer of a noble house that had recently joined the ranks of the wandering penny gentry.

"I need to find a place for a birthing den," said Aliyah, licking the last of her meal off her lips. "I've never done this before, because at the Spires, the birthing dens had all been in use for generations …" She trailed off and looked down, her breathing fast and thready. Gaetan came near her and nuzzled her side. "I'm fine," she snapped, raising her head.

Gaetan stepped back. "*Dois-je aider?*"[1] he asked.

Aliyah looked away from the Braided Gorges. "Let's go back. See if we can find a little canyon with a stream," she said. "Someplace beautiful. Someplace fitting—" her eyes took on the thousand-yard stare "—for the rebirth of Clan Summerday."

Anastasia

In the last days of autumn, Anastasia had supervised the digging of Stone Base, to house the Stone Stair garrison. It

---

[1] Shall I help?

featured several entrance ramps which began near the crossbow embankment and led down into a large open space. So if the crossbows were overrun and the wooden gratings at the entrances were breached by enemy, they would find themselves confronted by several hundred *Armée Libre* fighters all at once.

The entry tunnels and central space were sized for raccoons, and around the edges were alcoves designed as bunks for smaller animals. There were also working areas for craftmice and raccoons, lit by small skylights.

On this day, the cold and clear weather had dropped temperatures past freezing, even in the newly mild Canadian winters brought about by four hundred years of warming climate. So most of the animals were inside the base, working, dozing, gossiping, and telling stories to pass the time. All the body heat made the chamber toasty warm.

Anastasia snuggled with Freddie in her alcove as they talked quietly about their plans. He started singing a silly little song he'd made up recently as he nuzzled her ear.

"Who's the best pookie in the whole wide Wood?
Everyone loves the little bunny that could."

Anastasia scoffed and elbowed him. As always, it was hard for her to relax, but she was trying to take a moment before she started the trek north to Warren *Sans Gloire* to get back to the work of governing. Her new nation still stood on wobbly legs and she was determined that it would not fall.

There was much to be done. Some warrens were having food shortages. The efforts to exhort the citizens of Free

Nation to have fewer young needed to be amped up. The denizens of Musmuski Grove were demanding more representation. There were reports of raccoons making grabs at mice in the hinterlands that had to be looked into. And on and on.

Across the open space, Anastasia could see Lorazepam and Wellbutrin, the two kindly local raccoons who had helped her wrangle their fierce cousins a few weeks earlier. Apple growers by trade, they were here for their weeklong rotation on crossbow duty as members of the Free Nation militia. In the dim light, Wellbutrin held Lorazepam's paw clasped over his heart, and their tails were intertwined. They chatted drowsily with Dingus, the leader of the Ascending Squirrels, as he leaned into forward fox pose.

"Like this. Ah … chek," murmured Dingus as he settled into a deep stance.

"Sweet," chuckled Lorazepam. "You'll have to teach me that one, honey."

Nearby, Anastasia could see Nicodemus, the wise Elder Reader, playing a game of *Terre Soleil* with Mabel, the priestly party girl who was still trying to figure out the how to reinvent rabbit spirituality now that the rabbits' god, Dah, had been exposed as a fraud.

Nicodemus moved a large piece of earthy brown hematite forward and said, "Bear launches attack."

"What is the nature of bear?" asked Mabel, as she pulled a black ear down and cleaned it.

"The nature of bear is muchness," said Nicodemus.

Mabel moved a sparkly chunk of chalcopyrite to the side. "Fool finds a way."

City of Oom

A few feet away, Wendy, the lop-eared barbarian commander of the *Armée Libre*, was reclining in her alcove near one of the ramps. The doughty warrior Love Bug, first rabbit to kill a Summerday wolf, was lounging nearby. He was rubbing a fine oil scented with cedar and allspice onto the pads of Wendy's large back feet, while she sang a deep, rumbly song about Love Bug the Goldkiller that she had composed herself.

"Woof big like sky and gold like sun
Hoo hoo haroom!
Coineanaich[2] no place to run
Tha e fior[3] haroom!"

Death Rage and a group of warmice, all of whom loved both fighting and singing about fighting, were sitting nearby in a semicircle, clapping their small hands and chiming in on the *harooms*.

After a few verses, Death Rage slipped over to her bunk in the mouse alcove and came back with an ornately carved flute her father had made for her out of an ancient juniper twig. She began adding accent trills that extended the melody Wendy was singing.

"Wendy fly and cut woof bad
Hoo hoo haroom!
But mighty jaw make Wendy sad
Tha e fior haroom!"

---

[2] Rabbits

[3] It is true

Wendy nodded approvingly at Death Rage's contribution. So another warmouse ran and got a tiny gourd filled with cactus spines, and began to add a soft *shooka-shooka* under Wendy's rumbling voice.

Anastasia smiled. On some days, it was so good to be a rabbit.

"Then Love Bug pull his blade and say
Hoo hoo haroom!
Goldkiller come this very day
O seadh, a ghràidh,[4] *haroom!"*

Suddenly, three songbird sentries were racing into the hall shouting, "*Wolves! Wolves! Wolves!*" They circled the hall, feathers cascading behind them, calling, "*Stations! Stations! Stations!*"

Anastasia felt a hot smear of adrenaline burn down her back as she rolled out of her alcove with Freddie at her side. Wendy was already lunging up the ramp, raptor claw necklace jangling, Love Bug a step behind. And all the creatures of the garrison were pouring out of their alcoves and racing for their positions, the central space boiling with small, fierce animals in motion.

When Anastasia reached the embankment, she could see the silent forms of gray wolves slipping down the Stone Stair, ghostly in the late winter twilight flecked with puffy snowflakes. *Municipal Wolves*. She had never seen them before. She stood for a moment, watching them move, as Wendy

---

[4] O yes, my love

City of Oom

rapped out a series of rapid-fire orders and Love Bug threw paw signs to direct the Loving Auntie's Guard to form a perimeter around her.

The crossbow teams hurled themselves into the fight. Wellbutrin and Lorazepam, slipping in the fresh snow, scrabbled into place on their backs on each side of their crossbow, bracing their back feet against the stock and pulling the bowstring up to the catch-hook. Then Lorazepam slapped a quarrel into place, snugged it against the bowstring, and they both rolled away from the loaded weapon.

Now Dingus was leaping into position on his balancing platform, seizing his trigger string, and taking control of his machine by shifting his body weight. Within a few seconds, most of the crossbows were loaded, bow riders in place, sights sweeping the battlefield. As they brought the noses of their farkillers to bear on the wolves coming down the switchbacks of the long stairway, Dingus was calling out in his silvery command voice: "*Fire! Fire! Fire!*"

Thirteen of the crossbows snapped, and an instant later, snarls of rage from the dimly lit stairs proved that some had found their targets. Then, as the crossbow teams were reloading, a flurry of crows descended on them like a black rainstorm, pecking at the eyes of the raccoons and driving the squirrels off their platforms. Anastasia flicked out her Dragon Claw and leaped skyward, slashing at the dark flyers. Out of the corner of her eye, she saw Mabel bounding ahead, jabbing her bite blade into the midst of the crows. And a moment later, she heard Stan calling orders as he hurled his songbirds into the aerial scrum.

Some of the wolves had reached the bottom of the long stairs, but they did not come racing toward the embankment.

Instead, they stayed behind cover, flickering from tree to boulder to stump. Clearly, the forces from City of Oom had learned something from the destruction of Clan Summerday at the Battle of the Narrows.

Nine of the crossbows got off another shot. This time, there were no snarls or yelps from the wolves. Anastasia paused and crouched down, breathing hard, as a multicolored rain of feathers fluttered down from the aerial combat just overhead, stippling the pale snow. She could see more wolves arriving at the foot of the stairs. And they were dividing into two groups and moving to the sides, staying behind cover. More crossbows snapped. None seemed to find their targets.

Suddenly, there was a great crashing in the branches of the trees that grew near the cliffs. The sharp sound of large tree limbs breaking seized everyone's attention. *What is that?* A moment later, a large granite boulder several feet wide landed on the sloping ground at the foot of the cliffs and came spinning towards them, bouncing as it came. When it struck the ground, it landed with the force of a giant's fist.

Anastasia could feel the vibrations of each impact. It was coming straight towards the embankment, covering the ground in great leaps. *That's why the wolves moved out of the center.* She started to back away from the boulder's path, snow slipping under her feet.

Wendy was yelling orders at the fire teams, and the raccoons in the center of the embankment grabbed their crossbows and dragged them towards the sides, with the rabbits pushing. Anastasia threw her shoulder against a nearby crossbow, and for a moment found herself face to face with Wellbutrin, his eyes wide and scared in his dark mask. Love Bug and the

Guard joined in the effort, and even Nicodemus was doing his best to shove a crossbow along, rear claws sliding in the mush.

After a few more seconds, when the boulder reached the embankment, even the songbirds and crows disengaged from their aerial slugfest enough to move out of the way. The boulder bounced forward and landed halfway up the slope, then rolled upward, launching off the lip and flying over their heads. A moment later it was crashing into the shrubs behind them as it rolled over the top of Stone Base and on down the long slope of the hill.

The Municipal Wolves were coming toward them now, slipping through the trees, creating a two-pronged attack heading for the flanks of the embankment. Some of the raccoons were trying to drag their crossbows back to the center, crawling over the slippery mess of churned-up snow and dirt. "*No move!*" shouted Wendy over the raucous swirl of songbird attack melodies fighting for dominance with harsh crow calls. "*Load now!*"

Where had the boulder come from? Anastasia scanned the cliff top in the dimming light, trying to see through the jumble of leafless branches. At last she picked out several teams of raccoons, a hundred and fifty feet above, using levers to push against the boulders that dotted the cliff edge. A moment later, another boulder gave way and dropped straight down, smashing through a scree of small tree limbs. Three seconds later, it had reached the foot of the cliff and came hurtling forward, snapping the dry winter brush. It hit a large tree at an angle, then headed off to the side, away from the battle.

The wolves on each side of the embankment were getting closer. Anastasia could see that they each had a loop of metal in one ear. And their amber eyes seemed to glow in the frosty twilight. They were calling to each other now, quietly, sharing information, giving orders. She tilted her ears forward, trying to screen out the noise of the birds fighting just overhead. There were more than fifteen wolves on her side. *That's as many wolves as the whole Summerday Clan.*

The memory of her time at the mercy of the golden wolves washed over her, and the bitter, metallic taste of fear filled her mouth. She shook her head and flicked out her Dragon Claw. The rabbits still had some surprises in store, but it could get ugly quickly if everything didn't go according to plan. She felt her feet starting to shuffle backwards, and forced herself to hold her ground, as she knew her example was the most powerful weapon she wielded. Love Bug pulled the Guard closer around her. Death Rage and several other warmice ran past her, seizing positions of advantage among the jumble of boulders at the end of the embankment, leaving tiny tracks in the snow. "*Timent muram!*"[5] shouted Death Rage.

The raccoons on top of the cliff pushed off another boulder. This one fell through the branches and came straight down the center. It mowed through a stand of young trees, which slowed it down and set it rolling instead of bouncing.

Anastasia could see the wolves gathering for a charge. Some of the crossbows were firing, brushing the wolves back when they got too close. But many of the shots were wild. It was clear the crow attack was crippling the crossbow teams' effectiveness, and the wolves were making good use of cover.

---

[5] "Fear the mouse!"

Anastasia could hear Wendy shouting orders from the other side of the embankment. "*Hold fire! Wait til woof show!*" The number of quarrels was limited, and the antsy crossbow teams had already buried many sharp points in the trees and brush between the embankment and the cliffs.

The third boulder came rolling up to the embankment, moving more slowly, leaving a great gouged trail in the snow. Anastasia heard a terse order from the wolf captain. Then she saw the shaggy gray bodies dip down in preparation for the rush. An eyeblink later, the wolves were leaping forward, gray and silent, amber eyes hot. In the same moment, the third boulder reached the bottom of the embankment and fell through a thin layer of twigs and leaves covering the deadfall trap the rabbits had dug. It disappeared into the deep darkness of a long trench.

Anastasia was so close to the wolves that she could see their eyes track to the side at the sound of the boulder falling into the trap. The moment stretched out, the wolves' bodies curving gracefully in the air as they hurtled forward. Anastasia felt her heart bang against her ribs. Would the wolves understand what this meant? An instant later, the wolf captain rapped out an order and the wolves were suddenly thrusting forward with their forepaws to stop their rush. As they came sliding to a halt a few dozen feet from where Anastasia was crouched, their paws were already breaking through the top of the deadfall trap in front of them, triggering the collapse of the false ground. As the latticework of twigs and leaves fell away into the long dark hole, the wolves scrabbled backwards, back feet fighting for purchase in the churned-up snow.

A moment later, they turned and ran, yelping as the crossbows sank obsidian quarrels into their exposed flanks. Death Rage ran forward to the lip of the deadfall trap and shouted, "You better run!"

The crows, seeing their wolf comrades in retreat, hounded the crossbow teams for a few more seconds, until the wolves were in the cover of brush and trees. Then they abruptly flew off into the twilight, with the songbirds close on their tails, trumpeting an adrenaline-fueled victory melody in aggressive staccato.

Anastasia hunched down and started touching the stones near her in a complicated pattern as she focused on her breath. Freddie came near her and pressed against her flank. She tried to remember what she had learned from Dingus about Oga For Young Goats. *In, two, three, hold, out, two, three, four.* She had hoped for more time to get things sorted out, but City of Oom had spoken.

The war had begun.

Chapter 2

Outside you may hear the storm
Comfy snuggles keep us warm
Who has any place to go?
All hail the warren, ho!
 —Winter solstice song of the northern rabbits

Gaetan

Aliyah sited her birthing den in a lovely, steep-walled canyon, a mile or so from the Delf River. A cold clear stream ran along the bottom, which would provide easy access to water. She dug it in amongst a heap of granite boulders, so she could create a roomy space with lots of nooks and crannies, perfect for pups to explore. Now she was just finishing pushing out the last of the earth, which lay in a large dark sprawl across the white snow.

Nearby, Gaetan was digging himself a guard post and sleeping nook under an old maple stump. He knew he would not be allowed in the birthing chamber, of course, and he was looking forward to having someplace snug to curl up at night. Just a bit of space he could warm with the heat of his own body.

He was muttering to himself as he dug, claws scraping at the cold ground. Why was he still following Aliyah Summerday around like a lost puppy? It's not as though she treated him well. And his earlier crush on her seemed ridiculous.

He scratched at a hard chunk of earth tucked up amongst the roots of the stump. His affection for her was long worn away. He clung to her now as the last remnant of the world he had been born into and grown up in. A world in which wolves ruled by divine right, and coyotes were in a privileged, although very distant, second place. He chewed his lip as images of the before-time swept over him. *Plenty of food, some almost-friends, and Lilou with her kind eyes.* The memory of his older sister tore a deep sigh from him. Sure, there had been bullies, and he had definitely been middling-to-low status in the pack, but being a crippled coyote wasn't the worst thing in the world.

Aliyah's new birthing den reminded him of his own mother. He remembered her as kind and strong, until the chaos plague had rolled over them. He shuddered. He didn't like to dwell on that part.

His thoughts were interrupted by a loud cawing sound, and he turned to see an ancient crow landing in the snow nearby. Immediately, there was a delighted yelp, and he saw the fearsome Aliyah Summerday somehow transformed into a golden puppy, wagging her tail as she wriggled with joy.

"Grammy Kark! It's you! It's you!" Aliyah bellied down in the snow, nuzzling the old crow's worn black feathers.

"My beautiful shiny child," rasped Grammy Kark. She rubbed her face along the side of Aliyah's gleaming muzzle. "The Old Crows are smiling on me this day."

"Grandmother of my Mother," said Aliyah. "How I have longed to hear your sweet voice." Her eyes were wet as she tried to push even further under the crow's dark feathered breast.

Grammy Kark spread her black wing over Aliyah's muzzle and gently rubbed her fur. "You are the Summerday to come," she murmured. "I'm so happy I've found you. My heart feasts on exultation."

Gaetan, as was often the case, sat feeling awkward and out of place in the presence of such warmth of feeling. Not for the first time, he was envious of the wolves and their capacity for unselfconscious joy.

Later, after the three of them had a meal that Gaetan hunted up, they all lay on the dark earth at the mouth of the birthing den, now warmed by the weak sun, and talked at length about what had happened.

"My eyes were injured at the Battle of the Narrows," said Grammy Kark. "A speckled chickadee and a black-tailed gnatcatcher came at me. I gave them something to remember me by," she said darkly. "But still, they hurt me, and old ones heal slow." Aliyah tenderly licked her head. "After the fight, the murder was scattered and the songbirds were vicious. It was all I could do to make it to the Boreal Cliffs before I fell from the sky like a stone." She groomed some of the fur along Aliyah's jaw. "I heard a shiny golden wolf had come up the

Midsummer Path and I thought you might be staying near the cliff edge."

Gaetan nodded, remembering the many times he had seen Aliyah standing and looking out over the Million Acre Wood.

"It's my home," said Aliyah. "They can drive me out, but they can't stop me from loving it."

"Where will you go when the pups come?" asked Grammy Kark.

Aliyah looked down. "Don't know."

"Municipal Wolves will be making more sweeps once the spring comes," said Grammy Kark. "I've heard the bears want to expand Land of Oom all the way to the cliffs now. They won't be happy about a new freelance pack taking hold in their demesne."

"*Oui, nous en avons parlé*,"[6] said Gaetan. "It'll probably be a join or … or else … situation."

"Wolves are powerful there," said Grammy Kark. "Maybe there could be a place for you."

Aliyah shook her head. "I want to be free," she said. Her eyes drifted up to the pale white cirrus clouds drifting by overhead. "I have … unfinished business."

"You have much to offer the City," said Grammy Kark. "You could exact favorable terms."

Gaetan cracked a small bone. As usual, no one was asking him what he planned on doing.

Aliyah stood and stretched, shaking out her coat. "Grandmother of my Mother," she said. "You are my last

---

[6] Yes, we've talked about it

living family, and I love you with all my heart." She bellied down near the old crow and fastened her maple-leaf green eyes on her. "I am golden. I am strong. *And* I am bringing back the Summerday Clan. We are not defeated. We are just beginning."

The old crow nodded. "I see you, Clan Mother."

"There will always be a place for you in my Clan," said Aliyah. "I pray to the Old Crows that you will be there."

Grammy Kark looked at her for a long time. At last she fluffed her feathers and slowly beat her wings as she paced in a circle around Aliyah in the slow-stepping ceremonial walk of her people. "You are the golden fire that was, and is, and is to be," rasped the ancient crow. "Whithersoever you go, I will go also. Your Clan will be my Clan. And your children will be my children."

Anastasia

Three days after the attack at the Stone Stair, Anastasia walked up to the grand new wooden gate at the front entrance of Warren *Sans Gloire*. The sturdy branches that framed the entrance were alive with carvings of the little animals of Free Nation, showing them as strong in war and joyful in peace. It looked quite imposing, like the entry to an underground city. Which it was.

She paused for a moment and touched the left side three times, and then the right. All the animals near her paused respectfully as she did this and then sang her threshold couplet.

*"Brave little bunnies may want to roam
Smart little bunnies come right on home."*

Then Anastasia touched the earth twice and entered. Holly, the Home Steward, and Yasmin, Captain of the Home Guard were there to greet her.

Holly stepped forward, a little unsteady on her three legs, and nuzzled Anastasia's shoulder. "Welcome home, Loving Auntie," she said, her amber and white fur shining in the cool winter light. "Your people rejoice at the safe return of their sun and moon."

Anastasia nodded. Normally she might parry this with a joking riposte, but with a new war in the air, everything felt much more serious. She bowed. "I thank you, Home Steward."

Then Yasmin approached, her bearing stiff and formal, befitting the moment and her military station. "*Sans Gloire* is on high alert," she said, the dark rims around her eyes sharply contrasting with her cinnamon fur. "The city is safe and awaits your command."

Anastasia bowed again. "The command remains yours, Captain," she said. "And I thank you for your diligent protection of our people."

These formalities concluded, the two rabbits flanked Anastasia as she made her way down the main passage.

In a few steps, she reached the underhall, now grown to be quite large. Its arched ceiling was supported by a wide tangle of roots growing from the poplar tree above the warren. The thicker roots grew through the space and into the floor below, carefully left by the rabbits to both shore up the layer of earth above and keep the tree healthy.

On this day, the room was crowded with rabbits, mice, squirrels, and raccoons, with songbirds on perched on exposed roots.

City of Oom

The light that filtered down from the two skylights was pale and gray, but the space was warm from the heat of all the bodies within and the insulation of the good earth all around. Everyone was sitting around the edges of the room, leaving an empty space in the middle.

Elder Reader Nicodemus sat near the center, under one of the skylights, his silver fur bright. Anastasia stepped forward and sat down under the other skylight. Freddie placed a heavy bag of agave leather in between them, then took a seat in the shadows.

The Loving Auntie looked around the room at the gathering, filled with many people she knew well, and others not at all. She adjusted the *aluminum d'or* circlet on her forehead and spread her forepaws.

"*Citoyens*,"[7] she said. "Three days ago, City of Oom made its first attack on Free Nation. Our *Armée Libre* fought well and bravely." She touched both forepaws to her forehead and threw a wide *respect* sign. "And everyone lived to fight another day."

"Hooah," rumbled Wendy.

"Hooah!" roared the fighters.

Anastasia smiled and let the moment of celebration linger. Then she looked at Nicodemus.

The old bunny sat up tall and spoke. "We did not know for sure that the armies of Oom would come. But this attack proves that the bears will not abide any group of animals throwing off the yoke of the hunter and choosing to live freely. Because if it happens *here*, it can happen *there*." He looked at

---

[7] Citizens

the many small animals surrounding him, the splash of white fur on his forehead shining. "Our very existence puts their way of life at risk. The last thing the bears want is for their prey animals to start questioning the rules they live under." He nibbled a foreclaw. "We don't know exactly what the bears will do. But most likely, now that they have begun, they will come at us until we are gone. Or they are."

A quiet moan rose out of the assembled group.

Nicodemus stood. "Our fighters tell me this was not even a real attack. It was a probe, just an attempt to learn about our defenses." He took a deep breath and exhaled slowly. "And yet, in this minor excursion, I saw twice as many wolves as there were at the Battle of the Narrows."

A louder groan sounded from several in the crowd. Anastasia was not the only one who carried a special terror for wolves from that day.

"Their crows were disciplined and fierce," he continued. "They crippled our crossbows. And the wolves had upland raccoons fighting for them, throwing boulders down the cliff, which we've never even heard of. If they surprise us next time, that may be the last time."

Some murmuring began on the edges of the group and crept around the circle. Yasmin cast a sidelong glance at the raccoons sitting among them.

Anastasia raised her paws for silence. "There is more." She rested her forepaw on the bag Freddie had placed near her. "We have achieved the most extraordinary blessing any group of small animals has ever dreamed of: life without hunters."

There was a small chattery wave of affirmation.

Anastasia nodded. "*La belle vie.*[8] It is amazing. Beautiful. And it has never happened before in the history of the world." She looked at the array of furry faces around her, so hopeful. "In the old days, half of our children would be killed by hunters before they even grew up. And a terrible lie created by our enemies encouraged warren leaders to allow this."

Holly, who lived with the ferocity of predator attacks written on her body, spat and threw the rage sign at this mention of the false god, Dah. Several other rabbits followed her example.

"Now, every little animal born has a good chance of living a full life." Anastasia smiled. "Whatever gods you prayed to, thank them for me now."

There was a nervous laugh and some elbowing among the backbenchers.

"Elsie MacGowan willed it," growled Wendy.

Nicodemus let the chatter die down. "Hidden deep in this wonderful news is a terrible secret," he said. "It is a blessing that can also become a curse. And the most beautiful thing in the world can become the ugliest." He looked at Anastasia. "Our Loving Auntie is going to show you how."

Anastasia nodded. Her eyes swept the group. "This is our future." She reached into the bag and took out a smooth river stone and placed it on the earth in front of her. It was a stippled brown with quartzite flecks that caught the light from above. "Year one," she said.

---

[8] The good life

Most of the animals looked confused. Nicodemus closed his eyes.

Anastasia looked around the group. "Every year, the number of little animals in the Million Acre Wood will double." She took two pebbles out of the bag and dropped them on the first stone. "Year two."

The stones clicked together. The animals in the back rows craned their necks to see what was happening. Anastasia used both paws to bring out four stones, and she dropped them on the small pile. "Year three."

A ripple of murmuring was slowly growing. Death Rage polished her needle with the fur of her foreleg. Anastasia reached into the bag and counted out eight stones, adding them to the pile. "Year four."

The murmuring was louder. Love Bug quickly scanned the room, making eye contact with members of the Loving Auntie's Guard.

Anastasia scooped out several pawfuls of stones, then slowly counted out sixteen, adding them to the pile. Her golden eyes tracked slowly around the room. "Year five."

All the animals stared at the growing pile of stones, each new addition obliterating the last.

Then the Loving Auntie picked up the bag and upended it, dumping thirty-two stones onto the pile. Her eyes swept the crowd. "Year six."

The murmur became a general groan. Everyone could see what this meant, could understand that their brief moment in paradise was already slipping through their paws.

Anastasia tossed the bag away and stood. "Year seven: There will be sixty-four times as many animals as there are in the Million Acre Wood right now." She walked along the front of the seated creatures. "It is true that a doe may reabsorb her litter if she is pregnant in a hard time, but this growth will far outrun the ability of our does to respond." She dragged her foreclaws through the earth. "I don't know what year it will be when we strip every leaf from every plant and die in a wasteland of dust and bones, but it will happen in our lifetimes."

She stooped down and kissed the head of a three-month old kitten snuggled into her mother's flank. Then she raised her eyes to take in the group as a whole. "*In our lifetimes.*"

The animals were dead silent. Anastasia looked up at the wan light coming through the skylight. "We have much to learn. About them"—she gestured eastward towards City of Oom—"and us." She pressed her paw to her heart. "We have queried all the Readers in the Million Acre Wood and found no answers. Which is why we will be sending out small teams to travel to the uplands to find and learn what we need to know. The world is big, and there are creatures in it much wiser than we are and much stronger than we are. None are friends. Some are enemies." Her golden eyes slowly moved across the anxious faces looking at her. "You are in this gathering because you volunteered to serve your nation. Now you have been chosen to go and learn."

The Loving Auntie pressed both forepaws to her mouth and then spread them in a wide gesture of thanks. "I salute your courage." The pale shaft of light made the golden circlet on her brow shine. "Now, we will learn, or we will die."

Aliyah

The moment of birth was coming, but not yet here. Aliyah lay in her birthing den on a bed of soft moss and leaves. A dim light filtered down the long entrance ramp, and her body heat had warmed the space. Gaetan had long since been sent outside to guard the doorway to the den, but Grammy Kark was with Aliyah, enacting her traditional role as the welcomer of new souls into the pack.

Aliyah was panting, her eyes heavy-lidded. Grammy Kark fluttered to one side of the den and picked up a sprig of winter berries that Gaetan had found while roaming, and offered them to her. Aliyah bit down on a few, and let the juice run down her throat.

She would not have chosen to be having pups just at the moment when her world had been destroyed. She had once dreamed of creating a Summerfrost Clan with her silver-furred lover, and she would have if Tennyson had survived. But now, if there was anything to cling to, it was the power and ancient lineage of the Summerdays.

Grammy Kark seemed to read her thoughts, and came to her, dark eyes warm and kind. "Beloved golden child," she said. "I chanted the birthing rites for so many of your strong, fierce, loving ancestors."

Aliyah laid her chin on the earth. Inside her, new and tiny lives were waiting to make the journey toward light and life.

Grammy Kark tucked herself in close to Aliyah's muzzle. "Hear now the gifts from your mothers who came before." The old crow's eye drifted toward the dim glow of the doorway. "I remember a time when a dark cloud came from the ground in the Southern Marshes. And it spread over all. Many creatures in the Million Acre Wood died. Hunting became very thin. And yet the Summerdays survived." She began to sing the blessing rites in the ancient patois of the crows, dating from the times when they had first begun to learn the languages of the Dead Gods, more than a thousand years earlier.

> *"Your grandmother's mother was ane swift one*
> *Vasty hunter she*
> *She birth her children in the dark noon*
> *Her fast blood come to thee"*

The old crow's voice became something entirely different when singing, a warm and smoky contralto creating a haunting melody in the ancient Phrygian mode that carried the certainty of many things seen and known. Aliyah rolled up onto her feet and paced restlessly in the small space, her body swollen with her children.

"There was a time when the golden wolves had split into two packs and were at war. It was a dangerous moment," said Grammy Kark. She walked alongside Aliyah as the wolf moved.

> *"Your grandmother was ane fierce one*
> *Alway fightest she*
> *She birth her children in the war time*
> *Her wild blood come to thee"*

Aliyah lay down on her moss bed. She could not get comfortable. Grammy Kark brought her some persimmon fragments and Aliyah took them in her mouth and chewed them roughly. The old crow patted her fur with her dark wing. "There was a time when all was easy. The children came, everyone was glad." Her warm and loving voice came forth from her once more.

> *"Your mother was ane kind one*
> *Ever loving she*
> *She birth her children in the fat day*
> *Her sweet blood come to thee"*

Aliyah turned to face the wall. She tried to speak, but found herself weeping. Grammy Kark fluttered over her body and then stood on the earth, rubbing the side of her head against Aliyah's muzzle. "Children come. Their story begins. And the golden fire lives on in them," murmured the ancient crow. "The world will be a better place because you are in it." When she sang again, her voice was soft and soothing, like a lullaby.

> *"You yourself are ane new one*
> *Speak ye what for thee?*
> *You birth your children in the harsh time*
> *Yet wolves will ever be"*

WARREN SANS GLOIRE

Anastasia nuzzled Mabel as the mice swarmed around them, laying out the large net required for rabbits to travel by Free Nation's newly created travel service, Songbird Air. More than a hundred songbirds were required to lift a full-grown rabbit, so the netting was arranged with cables of different lengths, allowing the songbirds to fly in tiers. Everyone was still new at this, so the wrangle took up most of the open space in front of Warren *Sans Gloire*, where there was still several inches of snow on the ground. There would be more days of dress rehearsals and tinkering before they were ready.

"Sorry we haven't had more time to talk about this," said Anastasia. "So many teams are being sent out." She looked distracted.

"It's all good, Loving Auntie," said Mabel. The Remembering acolyte and sometime party girl washed her face, smoothing the place where her black and white fur met in a swirl in the middle of her forehead.

"Is it?" asked Anastasia, looking away for a moment as a rabbit messenger ran up, gave her a piece of paperbark with figures on it, and ran off. Anastasia blinked as she looked down at the paperbark. "All good, I mean?"

Mabel stepped into her sight line. "We will make it good."

Anastasia focused her attention on Mabel, finally. She took a breath and smiled. "You were the first one to come and offer an alliance with *Sans Gloire*," she said, nuzzling the other rabbit's ears. "That changed everything. I remember when you sang a victory song as six hundred terrified souls marched out onto the field at the Battle of the Narrows. I could hear you from two hundred yards away, surrounded by hunters." She touched noses with the black-and-white bunny, and kissed her witchy eyes. "And I know you're doing your best to somehow make the false god Dah into something good." She chuckled. "If anyone knows how to make things good, it's you."

Mabel bowed her head as the songbirds descended around them, filling the rabbits' long ears with music. "Thank you, Loving Auntie."

The brown bunny chewed a foreclaw. "I have to say," said Anastasia. "I'm not sure why you chose Sunbeam as your companion. But I know she wanted to go."

"I think … there is more power in her than we realize," said Mabel. "And there's not too many people left in the Million Acre Wood who are willing to listen to me muse about the Dah reboot."

Anastasia chuckled. "You're right. And I know she's not my kid sister anymore. She's almost a yearling now."

"I'll do my best to take care of her," said Mabel.

"Okay," said Anastasia, shifting into business mode. "Now, I don't know exactly what I'm sending you into, but the tribe that everyone calls *Les Enchantés*[9] are said to have great wisdom. No rabbit we know of has ever seen one of these creatures. But we're pretty sure of this: if anyone can help with our population problem, they can." She didn't say the other thing that both of them knew about this mysterious group. *When people go there, they don't come back.*

Anastasia walked Mabel away from the storm of songbird chatter. "You're a good talker and you sound smart. I know you'll represent us well."

"I'll do my best, Loving Auntie," said Mabel, and jumped as a squad of bickering craftmice suddenly ran under her, dragging heavy cords and arguing about a bowline on a bight.

---

[9] The Enchanted Ones

City of Oom

"Here's the thing," said Anastasia. "This wonderful magic spell or tool or something that we get from them, it's not going to be free."

Mabel chewed her lip. "Nope."

"You know we don't have much in the way of moneystones. But any wood, any food, any valuable item in the Million Acre Wood, we will pay." The Loving Auntie chewed some ice out from between her paw pads. "We have those special stone outcroppings we use for *Terre Soleil* game pieces. Maybe rocks from there are worth something."

"Understood," said Mabel, fidgeting a little.

"And we have expertise that we can trade," said Anastasia. "Wood mice making tools, stone mice making blades, raccoons making trouble." She smiled ruefully and scratched her shoulder with a hind leg. "Don't give away crossbows. It's the one thing that makes us powerful."

"But if we all starve to death, it won't matter how powerful we are," said Mabel.

Anastasia looked at her for a moment. "If we get new Landlords, it won't matter how alive we are," she said. She looked up for a moment as a squadron of songbirds flew overhead, testing the strength of the cords and hollering across three octaves. "Our freedom is really the only thing we have. Let's hang on to it."

Mabel nodded.

"Last thing," said Anastasia. She turned and swept her paw across the crowded field, which was teeming with kits running, tumbling, playing, and getting in the way. "Our population is already exploding. We may not have several years before we hit the disaster point. We may not even have one."

Mabel's already serious face took on a worried look. "We'll be quick as we can," she murmured.

Out of the corner of her eye, Anastasia saw Death Rage scampering towards her over the snow. She looked angry.

"If I had any gods left, I'd wave my paws over you and pronounce a blessing," said Anastasia. "As it is, all I can offer is a kiss from a skinny brown bunny." She licked Mabel's forehead. "Come home safe, holy girl. And bring Sunbeam home, too."

Mabel looked a little damp-eyed. "I will."

Then Anastasia turned to meet Death Rage, who was already talking at her. Mabel cast a last glance over her shoulder as she lolloped away.

"Loving Auntie, you know my respect for you is great—" began the mouse.

"Sorry I didn't have time to explain everything first," said Anastasia, as she walked Death Rage away from the hurly-burly of the Songbird Air assembly grounds. "But we need you to get into City of Oom, learn something useful, and then bring that information back."

"—well, I'm not happy with the decision you've made about my mission," said Death Rage. "I'm going into the heart of enemy territory. I need to travel light."

"I know, I know," said Anastasia, turning to face the fierce mouse. "Here's the thing, honored warrior. The mice of Musmuski Grove have been such a strong part of making Free Nation happen—"

"You're telling me?" snapped Death Rage. "I was *there*."

"So now the mice leadership wants more representation as we develop." Anastasia started walking again.

"Of course they do." Death Rage scampered alongside her, her evershine rapier dragging through the snow.

"They know we're sending scouting teams into City of Oom, and they want to be part of it—"

"*I'm* from Musmuski Grove," broke in Death Rage. "They *are* part of it."

"But they... well..." Anastasia looked up at the leaden clouds for inspiration and found nothing but a new flurry of snowflakes falling.

"What?"

"They want one of their own to go," said the Loving Auntie, apologetically.

"You mean they want to barge in and take over." The warmouse's tone was suddenly very icy.

"Not exactly," said Anastasia.

"When I put out the call for help last summer, it was the mice from Old Turnip Row and Scraggle Bottom who answered. Not the fine families on Sunflower Hill."

"I know. And they loved you and fought hard for us, "said Anastasia. "But these powerful mice are here now. And they control most of Musmuski Grove. So we need to hear them."

Death Rage stopped walking and folded her arms. "So no matter what I do, it's not enough."

Anastasia seized her tiny hands and kissed them. "You know you are woven into the warp and woof of this community. *And* my heart," she said. "This is not about you. This is about playing nice with an influential mouse tribe. For the good of the nation."

Death Rage put her hands on her tiny hips. "Why does it have to be me?'

"You're the most famous mouse in the Million Acre Wood. It's *because* of your reputation that they want to send someone to accompany you." Anastasia smiled and tried to put some polish on it. "It's the winner of this year's Young Fiercemaker award. She's probably *good*."

Death Rage drew the Kiss of Death and speared a falling snowflake. "You know who wins that award? Mice who live in big houses and have seed piles that last all winter long." She ate the snowflake from her sword tip. "Little schlumps like me from families that are just barely hanging on? We win the Crappy Radish award." She sat down on a nearby twig. "Loving Auntie, I *earned* my place. And I'm not taking some spoiled kid with me on the most dangerous journey of my life."

Anastasia looked at Death Rage for a long time. Then she laid down in the snow so that their eyes were on the same level. She spoke softly. "My love, the first victory is just keeping Free Nation together," she said. "I can't do it all by myself." She rolled on her side, still looking at the mouse as she curled her body around her. "Some tasks are big and glorious. Others feel small and petty. But we will need to hit *every* target if we're going to make Free Nation survive." Anastasia opened her mouth and caught a snowflake. "You are in charge of you." She turned her head and looked up at the pearly gray sky. "Will you refuse the honor of this critically important mission to City of Oom because your feelings are hurt?" Her golden eyes were warm in the cool air. "Your nation awaits your decision."

Death Rage spread her forepaws and leaned against Anastasia, pressing her tiny tummy against the rabbit's warm belly.

"Loving Auntie, you fight dirty," she said, and blew out a long, slow breath. "When do I leave?"

Chapter 3

You say wolves can't read
Yet we read tracks in snow to
Their beautiful end

—2nd Prize Winner
37th Annual PredPoetry Slam

Anastasia

In Anastasia's dream, she was flying over the Million Acre Wood. Now swooping down close to the tree tops, now zooming up hundreds of feet in the air. She was at the southern end, soaring over the marshes fed by many small streams pouring out of deep channels in the Boreal Cliffs, which loomed more than two hundred feet high at that point. The water fell in fine silvery arcs, then pooled into a wide wetlands and flowed past islands of red spruce, great rhododendron, and chokeberry as it slowly made its way toward the sea.

It was summertime, and the air was warm and sweet. She flew without effort, directed by her desires. After a few minutes over the lush greenery of the Southern Marshes, she turned toward the Boreal Cliffs.

She had never seen any part of the uplands during her short life, but now she gazed upon a wide tableau spread out before her. An elegant carpet of green meadowlands dotted with wildflowers grew along the edge of the cliffs. Two hundred yards from the edge, an ancient forest began. Hard maples and lodgepole pines reached for the skies. And the Douglas firs soared upward over a hundred and seventy feet, their deep memory reaching back to times when the Dead Gods walked the earth.

And all this came to her easily on the warm breeze.

As she passed over the cliffs and looked down, she could see a place in the midst of the trees where it looked like a great claw had repeatedly raked the earth. The surface of the ground was torn into many deep channels, intersecting and dividing, each carrying a rushing stream at the bottom.

She had heard of this place. The upland rabbits called it the Braided Gorges, where the Delf River exchanged one course for many as it approached the soft limestone of the cliffs. And they avoided it, because if an unwary rabbit fell or slid down into one of these narrow gulches, there was no way to climb out. The next big rain would likely wash you downstream until you were thrown out into the air a hundred feet above a splash pool.

It was a wild country, fierce and uncaring. And as she flew high above it, a sudden warmth ran over her back and pooled in her belly. *Something amazing will happen here.*

Musmuski Grove

The grand old mouse families of Musmuski Grove traced their lineages to a time three centuries earlier when a Dead God had decided to build a home on the hill overlooking the Shandy River. Partway through the project, Porcine Recombinant Virus reached this area and everything stopped.

Gradually, weather and entropy began to bury the construction debris. So when the mice of Musmuski Grove came creeping back, they found a treasure trove of building materials and other useful items among the leaf litter. Soon, fierce battles were raging and the most ruthless mouse gangs were rewarded richly.

Over time, their descendants waxed wealthy and powerful and forgot their grimy beginnings. As the years passed, the semi-fictional tales they told of ancestral derring-do were codified into a culture and a new identity: the noble warmouse.

And the very finest families lived on Sunflower Hill. Here the old construction site, long since subsumed by the earth, still provided the bones for marvelous domiciles. These centuries-old family seats housed families numbering in the hundreds, presided over by mouse patriarchs with numerous wives and almost uncountable children.

And so it was that Death Rage came to be trudging up the snowy path toward the main entrance to Hammerkill Hall, a grand old pile incorporating a jumbled stack of ventilation ducts and concrete blocks, long since buried by centuries of autumn leaves.

A group of children saw her first, and to her surprise they recognized her immediately and ran up to her, admiring her rapier and nuzzling her paws. And soon more were coming. The crowd of mouse pups escorted her up to the grand entrance, which was half a cinderblock tastefully adorned with carved pine cone furnishings and an intricate design of sunflower petals framing a dried rose. Soon, she was in an audience chamber featuring an elegant curved ceiling made from a lovely ventilation duct U-joint.

Despite the friendliness, Death Rage felt overwhelmed by all the pomp. It made the tiny earthen burrow she had grown up in feel plain and shabby.

A few moments later, a young mouse doe entered. Her fur was a rich ombre, starting with a dense vermilion on her paws and fading upward to a deep rose on her ears and along her back. Her eyes were a bright gold, and in the fashion of the young does of Sunflower Hill, her ears were twined about with dandelion floaties. It looked as though she were wearing a crown of stars.

Death Rage frowned. The mouse came toward her. "You must be Death Rage." She curtsied, holding her tail in one hand. "Throat Punch Hammerkill. I'm so honored to meet you."

Death Rage awkwardly touched noses with her. "Greetings from Free Nation," she said, stiffly.

Throat Punch touched her chest and leaned forward in a slight bow. "Proud to answer the call of my country," she said. "And how glorious to meet a real live hero of the revolution! I want to go see beautiful things. And *cities*. And *bears*."

"Well, I—" began Death Rage.

"We can't stay here," said Throat Punch. "Mumsy and her Spring Tournament Committee are meeting today. Let's walk

City of Oom

and talk." She seized Death Rage's forepaw in her own and led her down an earthen passageway, keeping up a stream of cheerful chat.

As they went, Death Rage noticed a magnificent greatsword strapped to her back. Along the scabbard, fine lettering read "Metropolitan Museum of Art." Death Rage had no idea that it was a tiny replica of a twelfth-century greatsword, once given away as a high-end tchotchke, but she could tell by the handle that it was evershine, the same kind of sharpstone that her rapier was made from.

In Musmuski Grove, metal was rare, and most weapons were made of wood, except for those borne by the scions of Sunflower Hill. Death Rage had practiced—and dueled—with wooden weapons her whole life, until she got her needle from Bricabrac back in the spring. And here was this fluffy creature packing the kind of weapon an experienced hero would be overjoyed to carry. She found herself gritting her teeth.

"Nice bugsticker," she said.

"This old thing?" said Throat Punch. She turned and threw a smile back at Death Rage. "Just kidding, I know I'm lucky to have it."

"Yes, you are."

They arrived in a large earthen chamber almost filled by three plants with spiky leaves, bathed in pale light from above. "This is our pineapple room," said Throat Punch. "Our chewy diamond ceiling lets in light so they can stay warm and grow year round." She settled down by one of the plants. "It's usually quiet here, so we can chat."

Death Rage nodded and sat down facing her, breathing in

the thick sweet scent of the plants. "This will be a dangerous trip. I know you won the Young Fiercemaker award—"

"Oh, that's nothing," said Throat Punch.

"But have you fought animals besides mice?"

Throat Punch sat up straight. "I sparred with a squirrel using a thorn for a rapier. He had studied at your school."

Death Rage's ears perked up. "How was it?"

Throat Punch shrugged. "A little scary. A squirrel is a large animal—"

"Ish," said Death Rage.

"So the big thorn point coming at me backed me up. Fast." She hopped up and began to act out her story. "But then I cut the tip of his thorn off on *riposte*.[10] I thought the referee might throw a red card, but no." She drew her blade, and it shone in the winter sunlight. "I keep it sharp."

There were tiny letters incised into the blade. Death Rage, like most mice, could read well enough to understand a few simple words and sound out longer ones. She slowly read aloud the inset lettering. *"Thank you ... for your ... donation."* She looked up at Throat Punch. "What does that mean?"

"It's a curse on my enemies," said Throat Punch proudly.

Death Rage looked at her for a long moment. It was time to be clear. She blew out a long breath. "Throat Punch," she said, probably a little more brusquely than she intended. "Where we're going, there are *no* referees. *No* red cards. *No* rules at all." She drew her rapier and flexed it. "I once wiped this bloody rapier on a coyote's muzzle. *That's* a large animal."

---

[10] Counter attack.

Throat Punch looked at her with big eyes.

"We're going to City of Oom, where no one from the Million Acre Wood has ever been," said Death Rage. "We need to find out something—*anything*—useful that will help Free Nation, and then get that information back to the Loving Auntie." Death Rage dropped into a deep lunge and whipped the Kiss of Death through the air. "I can't babysit you out there. It's going to take everything I have just to keep myself alive. Are you sure you want to do this? You might not come back."

Throat Punch sat down and hugged her knees. When she spoke, her voice was small but clear. "I want to serve my nation."

Death Rage thrust her rapier into her scabbard and turned away. "Then you will see bears. And you better hope they don't see you."

Anastasia

The traveling teams were leaving, two by two. The goal was for them to blend in and move through the landscape without being noticed. Some were searching for answers to the overpopulation crisis, seeking out reputed centers of wisdom. Others were scouting the activities of the bears and the Municipal Wolves. Several teams were being sent into City of Oom itself, but traveling separately, with no information about the other teams. That way, their whole effort would not be compromised if one team was discovered.

Gregoire, the elderly Healer, stood on the snowy meadow in front of Sans Gloire, dispensing last-minute medical advice and tips. "Remember, if you're injured, always apply spiderweb to the wound first. It kills the bad magic. *Then* matte the area with fur."

There were plenty of quiet and grim nods, followed by tense embraces. Juniper, the young Healing intern, ran among the travelers, stuffing wads of willow bark into backpacks. "Chew and chew, then swallow your spit," she reminded them. "Don't eat the bark itself. You'll get a bellyache."

Anastasia kissed them all goodbye. She felt bad about sending people into danger while she remained safe. She had started talking about going on an investigative trip herself, but Wendy had told her in a friendly way that the idea of allowing their leader to go on a long trip into unknown territory with a single companion was *stupid stupid stupid.*

Anastasia acquiesced, and so found herself late at night in her bramble garden, doing her ritual dances by the chill light of the winter moon while she quietly sang protective spells for each of the brave travelers.

Of course, there *was* a burning question on the home front. So Anastasia gathered her privy council in the new map room at *Sans Gloire*. This was a chamber they had just created a few weeks before, when a team of diggers extending a passage had run into a bank of almost pure clay. Initially, they had just backed out. But Nicodemus had looked at it and immediately seen its potential. So the rabbits had hollowed out a large chamber with a flat surface of clay on two sides. On one surface, they drew a map of the Million Acre Wood. And the other, they left blank and smooth for use in making sketches or diagrams during council meetings.

Now Anastasia stood next to the map, looking at the small

group of her oldest friends at *Sans Gloire*. "Should we try and build defenses at the top of the Stone Stair?"

"The hard truth is, if we *don't* do anything, the forces from City of Oom will likely build fortifications there," said Nicodemus. He groomed his silver fur. "If it's valuable, they *have* to seize it."

"We saw what just a few falling boulders can do," said Freddie, his black-and-white face anxious. "Imagine ten times that many."

"If build at top, we have defend it," rumbled Wendy. "All day. Every day." She took a few steps closer to the map, which made her necklace of raptor claws jangle. "Or we just *giving* it them."

"The problem is, we don't really know what's up there," said Anastasia. "Except for what the songbirds have told us about the grass and trees growing along the edge." She nibbled a foreclaw. "If I'm going to make a decision about this, I want to see it." She tapped on the stair drawn on the clay map. "For myself." She didn't mention her dream.

"Bah," said Wendy, frowning.

Love Bug stood, looking thoughtful. He threw a *respect* sign in Wendy's direction. "I hear you, Commander," he said. "But as Captain of the Loving Auntie's Guard, let me offer this." He spiffed his white fur. "We could take several units of the *Armée Libre* for basic area control. Our tactics could handle anything up to a few wolves. We learned that at the Narrows. But our concern, of course, is the safety of *Tante Aimante*.[11] That trumps everything."

---

[11] Loving Auntie

Freddie tossed a *thank you* paw sign at him.

Love Bug nodded. "We could use our new capability, Songbird Air, as our emergency fallback. Bring a complete air squad with netting ready to go. Have them travel near the main group but stay in the downlands, away from the upland songbirds. Keep them on alert."

"So if we run into a City of Oom force—" said Anastasia.

"The *Armée Libre* units drop into defense," said Love Bug, moving toward the map and drawing on it with his foreclaw. "Songbirds fly up, scoop up Anastasia, and they're over the cliff edge and down into the safety of the Million Acre Wood in a minute or two."

"Great idea," said Nicodemus. "She's the indispensable one. Just pull her out."

"I want to do it," said Anastasia. "Leaders need to lead from the front, not the back."

Wendy nodded judiciously. "Might work," she rumbled. "Let's run drill."

Summerday Clan

The new Summerday pups were born with the agouti gene set, so while their fur was golden like their mother, the tip of each hair was silver like their father, Tennyson. This made them look as though they were wreathed in an incandescent silver sheen that swirled over their bodies when they moved.

They were gorgeous, playful, and loving. Were it not for the fact that their births had occurred during the utter destruction of her world, Aliyah would have said these last two weeks were the happiest days of her life. As it was, even though so

City of Oom

much darkness and uncertainty hovered around her, she found herself wrapped in a blanket of golden cozy that felt sturdier and more real than any other part of her life since the battle. Her children were now here. Her Summerday Clan was waking. She was doing as Sephora had asked in that dark moment when mother, father, and daughter lay pressed against the earth behind a pile of dead bodies, the dark magic of farkiller blades flying over their heads. *Run back. Start again. Make us proud.*

After two weeks of life, the new family had arrived at Naming Day, and Aliyah was ready. She had been observing her children closely and had their names all ready for them.

This would be their first time outside the birthing den. So today she had gone out and pulled down juniper boughs and spread them just outside the entry to make a carpet of fresh green, lush and aromatic on this clear and cloudless winter day. Grammy Kark had gathered winter flowers—hellebore, jasmine, snowdrop, and cyclamen—and strewn them upon the juniper. Even Gaetan had allowed himself to be caught up in the occasion, grateful to be included for once, and had gathered winterberries, pears, and persimmons to complete the baronial welcome.

Now the three were sprawled on their party spread, and Aliyah bowed her head. "I thank you, friends," she said. "Our family is small now, but one day it will be great and powerful, just like the golden warriors of old. And the Summerday wolves will sing songs commemorating those who were here this day."

Gaetan was startled, but did his best not to show it. Was *he* a member of this new clan? A small tickle of warmth flowed across his shoulders. Then the bitter voice of experience began to murmur in his ear. But he batted it away and decided to enter into the moment.

Aliyah turned and looked down the ramp into the den. She locked eyes with her oldest pup. "Come, my daughter."

The puppy walked unsteadily up the ramp toward the light.

"This one thinks and listens to her mummy," murmured Aliyah to her companions. As the baby wolf reached the end of the ramp, her forest-green eyes cautiously swept the area outside before she stepped into the sunlight for the first time in her life. "You are so smart to look first," said Aliyah. She took a few steps forward and nuzzled her daughter's head. "I name you after your grandmother, the wise and kind mother of a nation. You will bear the name, *Sephora*."

"Sephora," said the wolf pup in a tiny voice, looking about unsteadily.

"Welcome, Sephora," said Grammy Kark. "*May your crows always lead you to a full belly.*"

Gaetan realized he should also offer a blessing, so he intoned the classic coyote benediction. "*La Mère de la Faim ne te connaîtra jamais.*"[12]

The new, tiny Sephora tottered over to explore a hellebore blossom that Grammy Kark had brought, her silver fur tips sparkling.

Aliyah looked down the ramp at her second born. "Come, my son." As the pup approached, Aliyah glanced at the others. "Snuggly and makes me laugh," she murmured. He reached the top of the ramp and tottered toward his mother, maple-green

---

[12] Hunger Mother will never know you.

eyes bright. She nuzzled his back and said, "I name you after your father, who will be with you always, and his laughing spirit will guide you. You will be bear the name, *Tennyson*."

Grammy Kark and Gaetan echoed the name and the offered their blessings. Tennyson walked unsteadily over to Sephora and nose-bumped her flank.

Aliyah looked down the ramp and saw her youngest child looking up at her. "Come, my youngest son." As the small puppy climbed the ramp, Aliyah murmured her aside. "Gets into everything and will run right into trouble. This one could use some looking after." He reached the top of the ramp, sat for a moment squinting his aquamarine eyes in the bright sunlight, then wobbled cheerfully toward the edge of the juniper flooring. Aliyah laughed and intercepted him. She pushed him back towards safety. "I name you after your grandfather. Just like you, he loved life and embraced it fiercely. You will bear the name, *Micah*."

After the old crow and the crippled coyote repeated the name and spoke their words of blessing, Micah ran to his littermates and was soon tumbling with them. Aliyah lay down on her side and watched them, smiling. "They don't know it yet, but these little wolves are going to change the world."

Gaetan felt an ugly prickle run across his neck. As a coyote, he knew that it was never a good time to tempt the gods.

Anastasia

Wendy and the *Armée Libre* units were leading the way up the Stone Stair. The squirrels flickered quickly and quietly upward, and the songbirds rose to hover at the edge of the clifftop, scanning for danger. Then came the rabbits, bite blades bright and ready. The warmice began quietly humming a marching tune as they climbed, until Wendy glared down at them and threw the *hush* paw sign.

Anastasia paused for a moment before climbing onto the first step, her Claw cold and heavy on her forepaw. This straightstone wonder built by the Dead Gods clung to the face of the Boreal Cliffs, rising up in a series of switchbacks. Over the centuries, some places had cracked and crumbled, leaving sections leaning outward, with railings long gone to join the rickrack at the base of the cliffs. A thin blanket of snow carpeted the stair treads, but the risers were mostly bare. Anastasia noticed a faint inscription cut into the lowest riser, and she was a good enough reader to make out some of it.

> *"Now entering a restricted area*
> *Have you had your pig pox booster?*
> *—CanAmerican Park Service"*

Of course, she had no idea what a 'booster' was—nor, for that matter, a 'pig'—but as so often with these communiqués from a vanished past, she sensed the fear in the words.

Love Bug hopped up on the first stair and looked back at her. "*Dangereuse?*" [13]

She nodded and climbed up. Soon she was marching up the switchbacks with the rest of the squads. It was a curious sensation to be slowly rising up through the bare tree branches overhanging the stairs, and then to find herself passing the

---

[13] Dangerous One?

tendrils at the tops of the trees and looking out over the woodland from above. It reminded her of her dream.

A few more steps brought her to the top of the stair, and she stepped out onto the uplands for the first time in her life. She was standing on a flat strip of land, covered with several inches of snow over dead meadow grass and flowers. It had not snowed since the skirmish two weeks earlier, and she could see many tracks in the crisp white surface. Wolf. Crow. Raccoon. Seeing the raccoon tracks among the enemy reminded her that the relationships between the animals of Free Nation could not be taken for granted.

The edge of the cliff was rocky and crumbling. In the distance, she could see the beginning of an ancient wood, tall and dense. Love Bug threw out a perimeter of the Loving Auntie's Guard. Wendy was already sending squads of rabbits and squirrels out to map the area, her broad paws flying as she issued complex instructions. "Not good build," Anastasia heard her muttering. "Flat. Bare."

Freddie came up next to her. She noticed him squinting as he looked around, trying to understand the landscape that his farblindness turned into a colorful smear. He lolloped toward the cliff edge to get a better look. "Lots of boulders here, just barely hanging on," he said. "No big roots to hold them in place. Didn't take much for the raccoons to push them out of position. A few straight branches would have been enough."

Anastasia nodded. "If we're going to protect our Wood, we need to understand the uplands a lot better." She could feel the beginning of a *thrum* pulling her southward toward the Braided Gorges.

Wendy galloped up. "*Och!*" She turned and swept her forepaw across the flat grassland. "Good field of fire. We see all." She sucked her teeth. "But no cover. *They* see *us*. Need build earth bank and deadfall. Then we have protect." Her dark eyes locked onto the Loving Auntie. "And if kill us and take farkillers…"

The sentence was too awful to be completed. The crossbows were a kind of functional magic, performing a trick almost unheard of in the animal world: doing serious damage at a distance. With them, Free Nation was a strange and frightening upstart, an *enfant terrible*,[14] blessed by unknown powers, a world changer. But if their enemies got hold of even one crossbow and could study it and learn to make more, the playing field would once again be very, *very* level. And their season in paradise in a land without predators would come to a quick and nasty end.

Anastasia looked at her without blinking. "I hear you, Commander," she said, and touched noses with Wendy. "It's critical we don't do anything rash and lose our advantage." She lolloped a few paces south. "I want to see more."

Love Bug sucked in his breath. "Do we want to leave the Stair? That's our way down."

Wendy scanned the area. "We need learn more. Maybe find place fight besides here." Love Bug nodded. Wendy rapped out a series of orders to her messengers, sending the squirrels into the woodland to form a widespread picket line to provide advance warning of trouble. Their songbird quick escape team would travel south with them, hugging the cliff edge without impinging on the territory of the upland songbirds.

---

[14] Terrible child

City of Oom

The *Armée Libre* moved south. They found some areas along the cliff that had low hills with some scrub, and other areas were fissured by ravines that cut deeply into the white limestone below. These required extensive detours that took them near the forest edge. After they had gone a couple of miles, they came to a deep gorge. Eighty feet below, they could see a stream of whitewater swirling past a few miniature trees that grew in the private world at the base of the gorge. It was a strange, dramatic landscape, cut off from the world above.

This must be the first of the Braided Gorges. Anastasia's pulse quickened. *Something amazing will happen here.*

She wanted to see more. About a mile inland, there was a high hill that would allow a better view. From there she could look out over the whole Braided Gorges landscape. The *thrum* was calling her strongly now. It was like the pull of shiny boulders of quartzite or chalcedony. She needed to go there. The call was like an itch. Like an ache.

Her leadership team was standing clustered around her. She felt crowded and pushed her way out of the group. "I want to go to that hill," she said abruptly. "I want to see more."

"If we leave the edge of the cliffs, we can't bring the songbirds," said Love Bug. "They're your emergency escape."

The *thrum* was pulling hard. "I'll be fine," she said, trying not sound snappish. "If we run into trouble, I'll hightail it back to the cliff and everyone else can take off for the Stair. I'm fast. You know that."

Wendy groomed her long droopy left ear. At last she spoke. "Only to hill. Then we go home."

Anastasia touched noses with her. "Then we go home."

Chapter 4

At the beginning of the world, the Goddesss made weasel. Then some other god made the civilians.
　　　　　　　　　　　　　　　　　　—Book of Woozel

DEATH RAGE

Death Rage and Throat Punch stood looking up at the mighty Shandy Falls, where the river fell eighty feet from the uplands and landed in a great churning basin of water below.

The most direct route to City of Oom was to follow the Shandy east to where the City sat at the confluence of the Shandy and Rime rivers. And they needed to move quickly, so here they were, two mice kitted out with freshly sharpened weapons and heavy backpacks.

Throat Punch had changed the dandelion floaties around her ears for braided lantana camara blossoms. She had colorful dried spider lily strips twined about her tail and the scabbard of

City of Oom

her greatsword. Death Rage had her bottlecap helmet strapped firmly to her head, and the cold spray from the falls made the Canada Dry logo on it look moist and refreshing.

Since both mice had grown up in Musmuski Grove, a few miles downstream from the falls, they knew there was a way that peddlers from City of Oom raised and lowered their boats here, but they didn't know exactly how it worked.

Now, with all the power of a hundred-yard-wide waterfall thundering down from above, Death Rage was second-guessing her decision. As she watched the hurtling mass of white water, she shouted over noise of the falls, "I don't know about you, but I don't want to go anywhere *near* that."

"I'm not afraid," shouted Throat Punch, with a determined scowl.

Death Rage looked at her for a long moment. *This one's too dumb to know when to be scared.* "Well, I *am*," she said.

Looking around, she noticed a small inlet on one side of the river, some distance below the tumbling waters of the basin. They walked down to it and followed along the edge, trudging through the muddy snow. After they had gone a ways, they came to a place where a narrow channel had been dug, just a dozen feet wide, that led towards the base of the cliffs.

"Maybe the boats come down here?" said Death Rage, as they walked.

"The rat peddlers I've seen are all about money," said Throat Punch. "There must be some kind of easy way, or they wouldn't be doing it."

When they reached the foot of the cliffs, they saw a long braided cord hanging down from the top of the cliff. It was worn and frayed. Scratched into the rock face were some crude letters:

"RNG BEL"

They looked at each other. "Bingo," said Death Rage. She took hold of the rope and pulled it. She ended up lifting her body weight but the rope did not move. So Throat Punch joined her, and they both tugged but nothing happened.

"Not made for mice," said Throat Punch. "That's not very inclusive."

Death Rage scoffed. "Get used to it, fiercerina," she said. "Where we're going, mice don't count for much."

They fiddled some more, and eventually they both seized the rope, braced their legs against protrusions on the cliff, and pulled downward with all their might. Far above them on the cliff, they could faintly hear a bell ring.

They waited for half a minute, and nothing happened, so they braced themselves against the cliff and tugged again. A few seconds after the bell sounded, a raccoon appeared above them, looking down.

"Wazzup, bruh?" called the raccoon. He looked around. "Where's your boat?"

"Don't have a boat," called Death Rage. "Two mice that want to come up."

The raccoon shook his head. "Don't waste my time," he said, and then disappeared.

"We've got two dimes!" shouted Throat Punch.

Death Rage glared at her. "Don't yell out our opening offer," she whispered fiercely. "Make them offer first."

City of Oom

"But he's leaving," whispered Throat Punch.

"We could ring the bell until he comes back," whispered Death Rage. "For free."

The raccoon head popped over the edge again. "Two dimes, you said?"

"Actually, I was thinking two nickels," said Death Rage.

"What?" said the raccoon.

"We heard that's the going rate," called Throat Punch.

"Got some gnarly info there, mousie," said the raccoon. Then he smiled and rubbed his forepaws together. "Two dimes is good."

"What about seven cents each?" asked Death Rage.

The raccoon held out his paws. "Don't have change, sorry," he said, although he did not look very sorry. He left the side for a moment and then a log swung out over the edge. The racoon leaned out again. "We use a counterweight for the boats, but I'll just pull you up by hand." He looked at the sky to the west and said. "Storm's blowing in. You want up or not? Two dimes is a good price. Boats are fifty cents."

The mice glanced behind them and saw dark clouds were scudding in from the sea. "We'll come up," said Death Rage.

"Show me your dimes," said the raccoon.

Throat Punch dug them out of Death Rage's pack and held them up.

The raccoon squinted down at them, then nodded. He tied a small basket to the end of a light cord and tossed it over the log. Then he let it fall quickly, the cord sliding through his fingers. When the basket plopped on the earth next to the two mice, they climbed in.

"Welcome to the Shandy Lift," said the raccoon, as he

pulled them up. "Name's Vicodin. Me and my bros run this biz."

Soon they were above the tree tops, marveling at the new view of their familiar wood. Below them, the wide Shandy flowed away peacefully to the sea.

"There's Musmuski Grove!" cried Throat Punch.

"Looks so small," murmured Death Rage. And it did look small. And vulnerable. She imagined squads of Municipal Wolves coming down the Lift, then loping along the Shandy, laying waste to the many riverbank communities. The setting sun painted the snowy meadowlands along the water a deep red. She shuddered.

A few moments later, the basket reached the log and Vicodin was swinging them in and tipping out the basket on its side.

"Welcome to Land of Oom," he said.

Gingerly, they took their first steps on the uplands. "Is that what you call it?" asked Death Rage.

"The bears like it when we call it that," said the raccoon. "And I like happy bears." He put out his paw, and Throat Punch dropped the coins onto his long-fingered hand. He smiled. "Thanks," he said. "Remember to tell your friends you got high on the Shandy Lift." He grinned and snapped his fingers. "Eh? Eh?"

Death Rage smiled politely. She noticed that Vicodin had wide smears of blue clay on the sides of his face. And his ears were tipped with the same substance. Behind him was a small market stall with a few wares arranged on stones, mostly cordage, pegs, blades, and other items of a nautical bent, along with a few tubs of fermented apples. And nearby, several dead fish were hanging from a tree branch by their tails. Death Rage wrinkled her nose at the dense smell of carrion and alcohol that hung over the area, even with the breeze blowing.

Everything was dwarfed by a tall forest of elm and maple that grew close to the edge of the cliffs, bare limbs intersecting to make gothic arches. Scattered stands of holly bushes peppered the gray landscape with bright red berries. A narrow channel of water snaked upriver towards the Shandy.

Vicodin hovered nearby. "Where ya heading, meeses? If you don't mind my asking," he said. "No boat and all, so the great goddess Shandy won't be taking you anywhere."

"Uh ... erm," said Death Rage. She had practiced her cover story, but she still had a hard time saying it. Her unbending devotion to honor meant she found it hard to squeeze out even little white lies, unless she was under great duress. This had not always served her well.

The raccoon chewed a claw waiting for her response.

"Just going upriver to see some family," said Throat Punch casually. "Any boat traffic heading up?"

Vicodin nodded. "Ya, had two come up yesterday morning. Catamaran and a trading scow. So they'll be a day ahead of you. But they'll be stopping and dealing, so you might catch them up."

A few drops of cold rain spattered around them.

"Going to be a cold one tonight," said Vicodin, his scent oily and helpful. "We got rooms for mice in our squat. Want to bunk overnight? Since you're good customers, just a nickel each."

Throat Punch looked interested. It was definitely coming

on rain, and her lantana camara blossoms were starting to look a little soggy. Death Rage was divided. A warm berth would be nice, but they were already spending money faster than she had planned. And the three dollars in change issued by the Free Nations treasurer had to last them all the way to City of Oom.

"Just one thing," said Vicodin. "Once the bros get into the dirty apples, it's best if you stay in your holes. I mean, it's totally safe, but"—he grinned, and his long teeth were gray and yellow against his dark fur—"that's what a *smart* mouse would do."

Death Rage felt Throat Punch's eyes on her. "Thanks," she said. "I think … we're going to head out."

The raccoon shrugged and pointed at her with both index fingers. "Catch you later, gator."

Mabel

Mabel was holding a strand of netting between her teeth as a hundred songbirds whizzed her along just a few dozen feet above the tops of the trees. She blinked as occasional raindrops spattered against her face. She was learning a lot of things on this flight, with the first one being she had a terrible fear of falling. Most rabbits spend their lives on the ground or under it. They like low, cluttered, quiet spaces filled with belly hair, old grass, chewed-on twigs, and other rabbits. Flying through a wash of cold air all by herself, looking *down* at the tops of trees, while an entire company of quarrelsome songbirds argued about aeronautics and dead reckoning just overhead left her feeling breathless and heart-poundy.

Mabel had never been farther from the ground than she could jump, so now she was clinging to her net hammock with everything she had. She soothed herself by making up new verses for the *Book of Secrets*.

And Dah spake unto Newly Beloved saying, 'Surely, you shall fly this day, my daughter.' And Newly Beloved felt the good earth under her paws and shook her head. 'Nay, Lord,' quoth she. 'Flying is for rabbits who open their big mouths and volunteer for—'

Mabel's scriptural meditation was interrupted by the sound of Sunbeam on a neighboring flight. She cast a hasty glance at her companion. Sunbeam was lying on her back, looking up at the sky and singing a dreamy song about bones.

Just then, the songbirds above began calling out, "The Spires! The Spires!"

Mabel looked up ahead and saw the tall pillars of gray stone rising out of the dense and spiky stands of beech, elm, and basswood. She knew this area, up at the far northern end of the Million Acre Wood, was where the golden wolves of the Summerday Clan had lived. And she felt a moment of awe that a scrappy band of rabbits had bested the lordly animals who once ruled from this grand palace.

"Over there," called the flight team captain, a large goldfinch, now wearing his faded winter plumage. "By the Midsummer Path."

A moment later the songbirds were banking, and her hammock swung wide as they leaned into the turn. Mabel grunted and dug her claws into the cabling a little tighter. "No hurry!" she called in as a pleasant a voice as she could manage.

Below, she could see a group of rabbits working on

finishing the crossbow emplacements, struggling with a mess of wet snow and hard earth. These were the defenses being built to guard the Midsummer Path, the other main point of entry from the uplands. Nearby, a crossbow squad with raccoons and Ascending Squirrels was practicing shooting at pine cones. And she could see the entrances to the underground warren where all the animals lived together. *That must be Summer Base.*

A few moments later, the songbirds were dropping down through the trees, and the white snowy ground crisscrossed with dark branches was racing up to meet her. Then her feet were in firm contact with the snow and the netting was laying flat on the ground around her. *'Well flown, my Lord,' murmured Newly Beloved.*

As Mabel stepped out onto the land that had once been the territory of the wolves, she checked that her bite blade was still in place, hanging from its tough braided agave fiber necklace. Since she was going on a dangerous journey, she and Sunbeam each had been granted a bite blade made of real sharpstone, created long ago by the Dead Gods and cut into shape by the craftmice. It was snug in its scabbard and ready.

The goldfinch dropped down next to her and perched on a cluster of mistletoe. The other birds from the flight landed and began stretching a bit, bathing their hot wing muscles in the cool snow and chatting about bugs.

"That's the bottom of the Midsummer Path over there," said the goldfinch, gesturing with his wing. "Don't know how long this will take you. Loving Auntie asked us to stay here so we can bring you back at a moment's notice." He groomed the feathers under his wing. "We'll keep sentries by the top of the path. If you come running, we'll see you."

Mabel nodded, feeling suddenly alone now that she was about to leave the Million Acre Wood that she had always called home. "Thank you, captain." She touched her forehead in the *respect* sign. Fifty yards away, she could see Sunbeam pretending to sneak up on an old sumac stump.

The goldfinch fluttered near to her and touched her shoulders with his wing in the ancient songbird gesture of blessing. "*May all your keys be major.*"

Mabel bowed and it took her a moment to come up with the correct response. "*And your melodies resolve with joy.*"

The goldfinch nodded gravely, then took to wing. Mabel looked west and noted the dark storm clouds pushing in from the sea. She took a moment to dig into her backpack and find the last bit of dirty apple she had brought with her. As it melted in her mouth, she felt the warm burn soothe her jangled nerves from the flight. She had been hoping to bring a whole one, but had forgotten to arrange it in the rush to get going.

Then she went looking for Sunbeam, who was practicing slipping along silently through the snow. "We need to stay together," she said. "It could be dangerous to get separated."

"Yes, Auntie Mabel," said Sunbeam, using the term of affectionate respect for older friends, common among the rabbits of the Million Acre Wood.

They set off toward the Midsummer Path. Their route brought them right past the embankment. The rabbits and mice working there were very, very focused. Mabel stopped a honey-colored rabbit covered with slush and earth and asked him how it was going. He wiped a smear of clay off his face.

"We're working triple-shifts to get these fortifications done. After what happened at the Stone Stair, it's only a matter of time before the Municipal Wolves are at *our* door."

Mabel introduced herself and related their mission. He seemed surprised. "Oh, you're going up?"

She nodded. Out of the corner of her eye, she saw Sunbeam fidgeting.

"Take care," he said. "It's a different world up there." He went back to his digging, but then turned back to her suddenly. "Different rules," he said. Then he picked up some twigs in his mouth and bounded off.

Mabel lolloped toward the long path that twisted and turned on its way up the cliff face. *What have I gotten myself into?* She felt suddenly tired. Sunbeam seemed excited and chatted about mythical creatures she was hoping they might meet. "Maybe we'll see a unicorn. Or a unabomber. Or even a woolly yarmouth."

"Mm hmm," said Mabel.

The cliff here was partly a stone face, and partly a very steep earthen wall. The path itself passed along ledges of stone in some places, then turned and climbed steeply in narrow gullies worn into the earth. A thick network of dense switchgrass and little bluestem held the soil in place, but it was a slow, slippery climb in the snow, and the cliff here was more than a hundred feet high.

The cold rain spatter picked up. Mabel bit her lip, plunging her claws into the earth for purchase as the snow got even more slippery. *Best to get up this path now.* She hurried Sunbeam along, and soon they were standing at the top of the cliff, looking at a wild and cantankerous mixture of

City of Oom

chaparral, juniper, and scrubby pine that spread before them like a prickly blanket.

Unlike other parts of the western uplands, this area was not bare trunks and limbs, but instead a dense cloud of evergreen foliage which reduced visibility to a few feet. And the understory was thick with dead branches and leaves, which would make it hard to walk without making a racket. It was the last kind of place a rabbit wanted to venture into.

The rain was thickening into a drizzle. Mabel cast about for the best way forward. Sunbeam lolloped along the edge, quietly humming.

"Hush, now," said Mabel, wiping rain out of her eyes. "Let's not attract any attention."

Sunbeam continued in silence, the rain damping down her golden fur and showing the same lean, ropy muscles that powered her older sister, Anastasia. After a few more feet, she turned and gestured to Mabel. "Look."

Mabel, came up to her, and stood shivering as they both gazed at a narrow track entering the wood. With this weather, she had half a mind to go back down and spend the night in the warm coziness of Summer Base. But the rain would have made the path even more slippery. And a hundred-foot fall would certainly claim their lives. So she batted away thoughts of warm burrows and nudged Sunbeam ahead.

Soon they were following a narrow path which led with many twists and turns away from the edge of the wood. The evergreen branches above them sagged lower as they collected water, and soon the path began to feel like a tunnel. They went quietly, listening hard.

After a few minutes, Mabel said softly, "Let's keep an

eye out for a hollow log where we can bunk for the night. Otherwise we'll need to stop before sundown and dig a scrape." Sunbeam nodded.

They had been going for about an hour, and the cold rain was getting denser. Then, through the gray curtain of falling water, Mabel saw a strange creature on the trail in front of them, forty yards distant, half-hidden by a curve in the path. It was tall and slender, with a large head, and it was swaying gently from side to side. Mabel halted as soon as she saw it, and held out her paw to stop Sunbeam, who had a tendency to daydream as she walked.

"Have you ever seen anything like that?" she murmured to her companion.

"No." Sunbeam shook her head. "But it's not an animal," she whispered. "It's the wrong shape."

"We don't know what shapes animals have in this country," whispered Mabel. She considered leaving the path, but the thought of all those leaves crunching underfoot seemed like a bad idea. "We can't stay here, so let's go up a bit," she whispered. "If something bad happens, bolt for the cliff. If your life is in danger, take the Midsummer Path."

Sunbeam looked at her with big eyes. "Yes, Auntie Mabel."

They crept forward, moving along the side of the path to take advantage of the cover. Mabel drew her bite blade and held it clamped between her teeth. Sunbeam did the same. Mabel glanced at her and nodded. For all her moony ways, she had a reputation as a fierce fighter.

They closed on the strange creature, swaying gently in the rain. The head was narrow, with long jaws and fearsome teeth,

City of Oom

and the body was impossibly lean. It was hard to see clearly in the rain and fading light. A gust of wind set a branch above bobbing, and Mabel could see that the creature bobbed along with it. Then a bolt of lightning flashed through the clouds, and in the brief moment of hot white light, she saw that the creature was hanging from the branch. As the growl of thunder rumbled, she realized the head was a skull, and the body was made of bones strung together on a long cord.

Spooked by the vision, she stood staring. *Who would make a thing like this?* As the obvious answer came to her—*no one you want to meet*—she slowly started to step backward down the path.

Sunbeam sat, unmoving.

"Sunbeam!" hissed Mabel, her scent bright with fear. "Let's *go*!"

"What kind of animal is that?" murmured Sunbeam.

Mabel forced herself to move back toward Sunbeam and the skull thing. "Come *on*." She nipped the golden bunny, which made her jump and squeal. Then she tried to push her down the path. Sunbeam, surprisingly strong, resisted, staring upward at the hanging tower of bones.

As Mabel scrambled, raking her claws through the mud and pushing against Sunbeam, she did not notice another creature coming down the path behind her. Then she was startled to hear claws moving through slush and whipped around to see a bulky, black-and-gray shape covered with sharp points looming over her, white teeth flickering in the twilight.

Her heart banged like a drum, and for a fleeting moment she thought of leaving Sunbeam and dashing back down the path, but instead she thrust her bite blade forward, dropping into fighting stance. A moment later, Sunbeam did the same. In the next second, she realized she was looking at a raccoon wearing a cactus skin vest studded with thorns.

The raccoon grinned and Mabel saw red leaking through the lower teeth. The voice came out, low and throaty. "Like my bones?"

In Mabel's world, raccoons were not dangerous, but the rules were different here. And those red teeth. Ouch. Still, this animal didn't seem on the edge of attack. *Maybe we can learn something.* "What are they for?" she said, around her bite blade.

"This is my Local Truce marker." The raccoon took a step toward the hanging bone tower and slapped it with a heavy paw. "Pretty gnarly, eh?" The bones rattled and swung crazily. "We call Truce a hundred yards out. And we *do* enforce."

"Out from what?" asked Mabel. Her jaws were beginning to ache from gripping the bite blade so tightly.

"Our apple snuggery," said the raccoon. Then she smirked. "Those mouth swords are hella fierce. Glad to know I'm a threat."

Mabel, suddenly feeling ridiculous, said, "Everyone's a threat."

"Ya, sure, I'm dangerous," said the raccoon. "Gonna kill you with good vibes." Then she bowed slightly. "I'm Lunesta. Dirty apples my game."

"Well," said Mabel, as she dropped her bite blade. "Can't be too careful."

"You want to come to our place?" said the raccoon. "I just ran out to get some more winterberries. Rainy nights like this really packs them in." She wiped her mouth with the back of

City of Oom

her paw, and Mabel noticed that she was carrying a handful of red berries in her other hand.

Mabel and Sunbeam shared a glance and carried on a quick conversation with paw signs. "Lead on," said Mabel.

Armée Libre

Fifty-five miles south, the rain was still light. Anastasia stood on the crown of the high hill, looking out over the Braided Gorges. She found the many intersecting courses mesmerizing in their austere beauty. Each one enfolded a tiny world, all on its own, below ground level. And up above, the narrow strips of flat land were in some places bare and rocky and in others grown up with enormous Douglas firs and other boreal giants, their roots snaking out through the gorge walls. What stories had happened there, in those miniature river valleys?

The rain drizzle began to thicken. Wendy came up to her, her long ears droopier than ever now that they were wet, and double-bumped her side. "You see what you want. I see what I want. Now we go."

Anastasia was startled out of her reverie. How long had she been standing there? She looked around and saw Love Bug and the rabbits of her Guard standing in a wide perimeter, looking small and cold. Freddie, already farblind, could probably see nothing in this rain. He was sitting under the broad leaf of an elephant ear. Other rabbits and mice were milling around. Some huddled together, shivering. Feeling suddenly embarrassed that she had brought everyone out on this cold wet mess of a journey, Anastasia nodded. "Yes, let's go."

Wendy barked orders repositioning the squirrel scouts,

and the *Armée Libre* units began to move down the side of the hill. Soon, it was raining hard. It was a long trudge through trackless woods, but spirits were high. They had boldly ventured far into uncharted territory, and now it did not seem so scary. Plus, they were heading back. In a few hours they would be warm and dry in the snug underground chambers of Stone Base, telling travelers' tales and biting into dried winterberries.

Freddie fell into place beside Anastasia as she walked. "My next snugglebuddy will be one who has strange yearnings to nibble kale in a warm burrow," he said, smiling.

She shot him a glance. "I had to go. I felt the pull." She touched her chest with her forepaw. "It was hurting me."

"I know, my love," said Freddie, kissing her. "And I was just kidding. Where you go, I go." She leaned into him as they walked, and he rested his chin on her head.

Then came a sudden wave of excited chatter rippling back toward them from the *Armée* units up ahead. They saw Wendy go galloping up toward the leading edge of the formation. Soon there was confused shouting.

Anastasia grimaced and ran forward, with Freddie following. Half a minute later, Anastasia pushed through a stand of holly bushes under the cottonwood trees and could see what the talk was about. A tiny rivulet flowing down a gully that they had easily crossed on their way to the hill had been turned into a raging torrent by the rain.

Wendy stood staring at the wild water, amazed. As an animal who had grown up on a small island, she had no experience with the impact of rain on large watersheds, which can create a massive flood in just a few minutes.

She looked at Anastasia with frightened incomprehension in her eyes. The look chilled Anastasia and caused a spiky prickle to run over her. To see her rock-ribbed war leader thrown off balance and at a loss for words made her feel suddenly very scared.

Love Bug ran to Wendy and nuzzled under her long droopy ear, whispering. Freddie stepped up on a small rise and shouted out. "Flash flood! We'll be here for awhile. Let's dig some scrapes for shelter."

Love Bug stepped away from Wendy and called, "Probably just a few hours. Or maybe a day. Let's get settled and safe. Mouse pickets at fifty yards. Squirrels at two hundred." The animals turned to their tasks.

Anastasia stared. *I led us out here, and now we're trapped.* Freddie started digging a scrape. And after a few moments, she joined him. *Why am I always so stupid?*

Chapter 5

Who killed the world? Is it not right that they should pay?
—*Clavis Aurea, Seer*
Star Sanctum

MABEL

"So what is 'Local Truce?'" asked Mabel as Lunesta led them down the path.

Lunesta chuckled. "You're from the downlands, right?"

Sunbeam started to speak, but Mabel casually laid her paw on her shoulder and she stopped. "What makes you think that?" asked Mabel.

Suddenly Sunbeam was squirming. Mabel looked at her and she gestured toward the deep woods. Mabel looked in the direction the younger rabbit was pointing. She thought she saw a flash of white in motion for a moment, something different from the snow, but then it was gone.

"We've had a rush of hunters up the Midsummer Path in the last two months," said Lunesta. "Your mouth swords are famous." She turned and came close to them, looking them over carefully, lingering on the bite blades hanging around their necks. "Radical," she pronounced. Then she stepped back and sized them up. "Your folks got real aggro with the big teeth set. I don't mind that." She turned and pushed up her cactus skin vest and showed the rabbits a large and jagged scar running down her back on one side. It was the kind of injury inflicted on a running animal. "Couple of coyotes on a moonless night. Got my thorn vest after that."

"I like it," said Sunbeam, touching a thorn with her paw pad.

Lunesta started walking again. "Word to the wise, hoppies," she said. "I wouldn't wear those mouth swords in the snuggery. A little *too* interesting, you know?"

Both bunnies nodded. As Mabel was pulling her braided necklace cord over her head, she heard her mother's voice playing in her head. *This stranger's taking you to some mystery hole, and you've just disarmed yourself. Are you a smart girl?* She hesitated, but went forward anyway. *We need a way to learn the lay of the land*, she told the voice. Then she took a deep breath and asked, "So how does the Local Truce work?"

"In our space, it's all about hanging loose," said Lunesta over her shoulder, waggling her right paw with thumb and pinky extended. "First time you touch someone, you're out. Those bones mark the edge of our territory."

It took a moment for Mabel to gather the implications of this. "You're serving Blessed—I mean hunters—and little animals *together*?"

"It's a big world, dude," said Lunesta. "We got dirty apples to sell." They came around a bend in the path, and saw through the rain a warm golden light shining through small windows in a wall of logs, stones, and earth, tucked under a large overhanging rock. Above a low doorway was an agave leather banner with an image of two raccoons embracing as they held a wrinkled brown apple. Lunesta half-turned to face them and gestured toward the door. "Welcome to Hella Cozy."

Armée Libre

The rain was coming down in waves that were astonishing in their ferocity. And the cold sucked the strength from the rabbits of the *Armée Libre* as they dug. Still, they tore the earth from the bank as fast as they could, pushing it out with their back feet where it instantly added to the mud. At least two dozen holes were being driven into the hill, each by teams of rabbits, with Anastasia and Freddie at the end of a ragged line. Nearby, the mice and squirrels remained on watch.

Wendy was still stunned by the sudden flash flood, so different from her home island. Which meant Love Bug was trying to cover for her. But he really had his hands full as Captain of the Loving Auntie's Guard, so it ended up that no one was in charge and orderliness of the *Armée Libre* units began to fray.

Small streams of water were running down the hill now, splashing over the gnarled cottonwood tree roots and gathering into larger flows as they went. Some were becoming large enough to move the rocks they flowed around.

Anastasia was no longer wasting energy on recriminations.

Instead, she and Freddie and several other nearby rabbits focused all their energy on clawing their way into the hillside.

Freddie was closest to the entryway. Anastasia kicked back a load of earth with her rear feet, and Freddie pushed it the rest of the way out. As he was standing there, hurriedly shoving the mud away from the hole, a bolt of lightning came down less than fifty yards away. The sound was fantastically loud, and it sounded like the fabric of the world being torn in two.

Startled, he leaped sideways and came down with his back paw in one of the rivulets flowing down the hill. Automatically, he took a step, but he slipped on the saturated soil and went backward down the hill instead. Another step, and another, and now he was running in place as the water pulled him downhill. A moment later, he was drawn into one of the larger streams.

"Hey, can someone…" he said, calling uncertainly, but everyone was still dazed from the nearby lightning strike just seconds earlier, and they could not hear. He didn't yet realize the danger he was in, and just kept half-running and half-swimming toward the edge of the stream.

Anastasia noticed he was gone, and looked out of the hole. She saw him being carried backwards toward the rolling tumble of water that now filled the gully. Her heart leaped into her throat, and she dashed toward him, yelling, "Help Freddie!"

Her bodyguard, half-blinded by the rain and chilled to the bone, was slow to respond, but Love Bug shook the water from his eyes and floundered forward. "Coming!"

Freddie was now just a few feet from the gully, and the

current swirled behind him like the body of an enormous serpent, muddy green and dangerous. He could now see the peril he was in, and he tore at the slimy bank in a frenzy, but the more he moved, the faster he slid over the water-logged ground.

Anastasia, clambering quickly down a gravelly part of the bank, saw a gnarled cottonwood tree root not far from Freddie's path down the muddy flow, and she fought her way clumsily toward it. Then she hooked her back feet in the root, and as Freddie's slippery, mud-coated body came near her, she sank her teeth into the scruff of his neck. Love Bug was slipping toward her, shouting, his voice torn away by the wind.

Freddie's body continued its slide, and Anastasia tensed for the moment of truth. Then she groaned as her ankles hanging on the root felt the shock of his weight and her body was stretched out. She clenched her teeth and would not let go of Freddie's wet, heavy body. For a moment, it seemed as though his momentum might tear him from her grasp, but she bit into his fur and skin as hard as she could, tasting salty blood pooling around her teeth.

Then he passed the bottom of his arc and began to slide upwards, swinging on Anastasia's long body like a pendulum. For a moment, the pain in Anastasia's legs and back lessened, and she closed her eyes in relief.

A few seconds later, Freddie was coming to rest on the gravelly bank a safe distance from the water and Love Bug was shouldering him toward safety. Anastasia could not hold her jaws shut any longer, and loosened her grasp while she was still in motion. The changing angle unhooked her ankles from the root, and suddenly her lower body was swinging down toward the gully.

Her slide was shockingly fast, as all her momentum was used against her. She was spinning, unable to grasp anything solid with her teeth. In just a few seconds, she felt the cold fist of the water close around her. The icy shock forced the breath from her lungs, and she struggled to keep her head above water.

As she was swept downstream, the last thing she saw was two rabbits fighting. Freddie was trying to leap into the water, and Love Bug was braced against a cottonwood tree root, shoving him back towards safety. And just before her head was pulled under, she heard Freddie's anguished voice arcing across the water. "*Anastasia!*"

Mabel

Mabel felt like she had walked into another world as she was hit with the hateful stink of killer mixed with the warm comfy smell of rabbit.

Hella Cozy was crammed with creatures of all kinds, lounging on soft moss as they lazily sampled a fine spread of comestibles. Mice, rats, and songbirds chatted over small mushrooms doing duty as bistro tables. Coyotes and raptors were sharing dirty apples and other snackage spread out on flat-topped boulders. And most amazing of all, rabbits, raccoons, foxes, and weasels were gathered together around elegant tables made of succulent leather and twigs, gabbing and noshing. And there was no killing. Not even a hint of it. Just tipsy-loud talk while a squirrel and mouse duo played upbeat tunes on a small corner stage. And the body heat of all the animals inside made it warm and snug.

"I gotta get to work," said Lunesta. "I'll leave you guys at the bar." She walked them to a packed earthen berm along one side of the room. At one end, it was very low, and several boisterous mice were standing with elbows on the bar as they nibbled fermented berries and sesame seeds. The other end of the bar was two feet high, and a group of serious coyotes were taking occasional bites of a handsome spread of dirty apples and dried mushrooms as they carried on an intense but quiet conversation.

Snatches of their discussions drifted through the close air.

"It's been weeks since *les Loups Municipaux*[15] made a sweep, eh?" said one coyote.

"Ursine Law, pffft," said another. "Big talk, no teeth."

"The only law here is *la Loi de la Pomme*,"[16] said a third, which brought on a general chuckle, followed by some boisterous munching of fermented apples.

Mabel and Sunbeam found themselves at a section of middling height and stood gawping at the panoply of mixed animality around them. Mabel found that the scent of all the predators in the enclosed space was triggering her body's chemical alarms bells to the nth degree. Just being near all these teeth and claws made her breath come fast and her heart race, and she struggled with the urge to flee.

She tried to distract herself by examining the large bioluminescent mushroom growing out of the bar. She had heard of

---

[15] The Municipal Wolves
[16] The Law of the Apple

mushrooms that glowed a faint blue-green, but had never seen one that provided a warm golden glow that lit up the space around it. She noticed some letters running up the stem and turned her head to read them.

"EverSun™
The Living Lamp
IkeaGreenpeace®"

She could not make heads or tails of this, but a moment later, a curvy raccoon approached the bar and offered them a winning smile. "I'm Sonata. Gnarly one tonight, eh?" she said, indicating the rainstorm outside. "The Womb of Ocean is coming for us." Mabel noticed that she was wearing short thorns in her ears as stud earrings. She leaned her elbows on the bar. "Show me your moneystones, ladies."

"Oh, right," murmured Mabel. Embarrassed, she shrugged off her backpack and pawed through it.

While she was doing this, Sonata started listing their offerings. "Hokutos, Freckled Tawnies, Red Bellies, Black Gaias, Tingletongues, Scallywags, aaaand we got a few of our Mangrove Jacks left. Got some yummalicious snackery for bunnies: oat hay with a garnish of seedheads or some nice dried plums with a splash of winterberries."

Mabel put a dime on the counter. "How much is it?"

"Apples are seven cents and one is plenty for two bunnies," said Sonata, her scent warm and relaxed. "Or you could split a half apple for five. Sides are three."

Sunbeam leaned against the bar and looked out at the crowd of animals. She didn't look jittery, but her nose was wiggling quickly. Mabel, unsure whether she was frightened or excited, patted her. "We'll take a half Scallywag. Can we get south side of the tree, late harvest?"

Sonata gave her a look of surprised respect. "Bunny knows her apples," she said. "You come here a lot? I haven't seen you."

"No," said Mabel. "Actually, I've never been to a"—she groped for the word—"snuggery like this, but I … live near an orchard."

"Really?" Sonata leaned toward her. "We're the only orchard around here. Where you from?" She clapped her paws together. "No, let me guess. I know *all* the orchards in this part of the uplands."

Mabel felt a little prickle of this-is-going-in-the-wrong-direction. "Oh, just along the cliff a ways," she said, waving her paw in what she hoped was a convincing gesture. Sonata looked like she was about to start naming orchards, but Mabel pushed the dime toward her across the packed top of the earthen bar, polished to a smooth sheen by a thousand furry elbows. "Could we get that order soon? Been a long day." She half-shrugged an apology and slumped down to show how tired she was.

"Fer sure," said Sonata, and she swished away.

Mabel was just looking down at the bar, thinking, *And Newly Beloved yakked everyone's ear off and called a lot of attention to herself*—when suddenly a white weasel was at her elbow, giving her a friendly half-smile.

"The *appeliers*[17] in here are so pushy, aren't they?" said

---

[17] Apple stewards

City of Oom

the weasel, as she was patting her damp fur dry with a handful of dried ryegrass tied in a bundle. "A girl can't get a minute to herssself."

The hot reek of weasel surrounding her at short range made Mabel's heart pound. "Oh, I don't know," began Mabel, pulling down her ear and cleaning it as she edged away from the slinky creature. "Just friendly, I guess."

"Oh, it's a friendly area," said the weasel. "I love it. Been here all my life." She smiled. "I couldn't help but overhear you're traveling. Can I help you find anything? I'm kind of the community welcome wagon." She turned and leaned against the bar, then noticed the flower-shaped scar on Sunbeam's forehead. "Fancy scarwork. Where'd you get that?"

Sunbeam slid away without answering, and then began drifting through the crowd.

Mabel did her best to lean casually on the bar, but she jumped when Sonata came up behind her and plonked down her half-Scallywag. *Don't blurt out everything that's on your mind*, came her mother's voice. *That's what people down in the mud runs do.* She turned and took a big bite, savoring the burn of the fermented juices as they ran down her throat. The warm feeling was the best way to soothe her spiky anxiety and take the edge off her mother's flinty voice.

The friendly weasel was still talking, to no one on particular. "Just something about me. Love to help. Touched by the Goddesss." She munched a piece of her apple. "And now I guess we're part of Land of Oom. That's what the bears say, anyway. Even though Oom is like, oh, fifty miles from here." She noticed Mabel's apple. "Hey, we're both having Scallywags!"

"Mm hmm." Mabel was having a hard time getting a read on this effusive stranger. Her demeanor was relaxed, but her scent was spiky, shading toward aggression. But maybe that was just a weasel thing? Mabel had never been near a weasel for more than a few seconds during attacks and had no idea what *off-duty weasel* would smell like.

"Well, there are so many people living around here," said Mabel, deciding the role of wide-eyed newcomer might help her gather information. "Who even are they all?" She chewed a bite of apple and felt the warmth of the alcohol run into her belly, then noticed that Sunbeam was over by the musical duo, quietly stamping along to the beat.

The weasel launched into a long ramble about tribes of squirrels poaching each others' nuts and fox families competing for the most beautiful tail award. Mabel, remembering the Oga For Young Goats breath training from Dingus, quietly breathed *in, two, three, hold, out, two, three, four* as the weasel blathered, trying to help the dirty Scallywag quiet her nerves, still jangling from the proximity of so many killers.

At last, the topic she was waiting for came up. "And *Les Enchantés*," said the weasel, deep into her apple. "Now that's a different story. They're up in the hills by the Rime River. Some people say they're ghosts, these beautiful ssspirit animals, and you can't see them coming. Other stories say they have *huge* tusks, bigger than my head, and ya, they know how to use them." She mimed her head as a tusk attacking the bar. "Even the *bears* think twice about tangling with them. Maybe that's why people who go there don't come back."

Mabel felt her stomach dropping as these rumors washed over her, but she did her best to reveal nothing. Then she

City of Oom

noticed that Sunbeam was now sitting on the other side of the room, near the coyotes who were having such an intent conversation. She seemed to be inching nearer to them. Mabel raised her paw and threw the sign for *come*. Sunbeam seemed not to notice.

"How do you know all this if nobody sees them?" asked Mabel, trying not to sound too interested.

The white weasel giggled and leaned in close. "You wanna see the *Enchy*?" she asked, clearly tipsy from the dirty apple she was putting away. "Me too."

Sunbeam was definitely too close to the coyotes now. Mabel clicked her tongue in annoyance. Without really knowing the rules, she couldn't tell when the line would be crossed, but any fracas would be bad and call attention to them. "Pardon," she said to the weasel, and dashed across the room, threading her way through the crowd of animals. She came near to Sunbeam and nipped her lightly, causing her to yelp. As she escorted the younger rabbit back to their place at the bar, she realized she had left her backpack sitting on the ground. When Mabel approached, the white weasel turned from chatting with the bartender and said, "Welp, getting late. I'm gonna turn in." Then she stretched, and as her fur riffled, Mabel could see the scars of many puncture wounds across one side of her face and down her neck and shoulder.

She noticed Mabel and turned to her. "Nice to meetcha," she said, and offered a friendly nose touch. "What was your name?"

"Mabel," said Mabel.

"Sssweet," said the white weasel, her scent coiling around Mabel like a snake. "I'm Saskatoon."

Gaetan

Gaetan, in his guard den, could already hear that the pups were terrified by the storm. And he could hear Aliyah's voice as she attempted to soothe them. Suddenly, he heard Grammy Kark's creaky voice. "Golden child," she said. "Stow your armor in your backpack."

"Why?" Aliyah sounded irritable.

"This much rain can make the earth move," said Grammy Kark. "you don't want to be wearing your armor in the water."

"We're safe among these boulders," said Aliyah.

There was another flash of lighting, and the pups whimpered as the thunder rolled. Grammy Kark spoke again, her raspy voice cutting through the noise. "Granddaughter of my daughter, *do it now*."

There was some grumbling, then he heard the shimmer of the chain mail being moved. A few moments after, Aliyah's soothing murmur began again, calming the babies. He laid his muzzle on his forepaws.

A few minutes later, Gaetan felt something strange under his body. He growled and leapt upright, glaring at the wet earth where he had been laying. There was nothing there. Then he felt it again, vibrations coming into his paws.

"Get out *now*," rasped Grammy Kark. The pups began to raise their anxious clamor.

"Listen to Grammy," said Aliyah. It sounded like she was still trying to calm them. "Let's go outside."

And then the earth beneath him started to become liquid. There was a loud, startled bark.

"*Run!*" shouted Aliyah. Gaetan ran the few feet to the

City of Oom

mouth of the birthing den in time to see Aliyah pushing the tiny golden wolves out through the doorway as the boulders above them began to groan and shift. Grammy Kark was the last out, just as the massive stones crushed into the space below where the little refugee family had sheltered. He thought her heard her shriek.

Then they were out on a hillside that was turning into a wave. There was no plan for this. There could be no plan for when the earth becomes ocean. All these creatures were simply swept down by the mudslide.

Aliyah only had time to cry one thing, "*Stay together!*" before they all hit the water at the bottom of the ravine.

The racing current jerked them to the side, saving them from certain suffocation by the tons of earth slipping down from above. As they all hurtled down the flume together, Gaetan caught sight of Aliyah and did his best to swim towards her. The current whirled her around. And as another lightning strike splintered across the sky, her maple-green eyes were for a moment locked onto his, terrible fluorescent pools of panic and despair. It was the last thing he remembered.

FREDDIE

Freddie was racing along the streambank, trying to follow Anastasia as the roiling water pulled her away from him. Love Bug was a few steps behind him. With his farblindness and the dimming twilight, she was rapidly vanishing into the turbulent water. Freddie felt a cold claw seize his guts.

He began calling out her name as he rushed forward. Behind him, he could hear Wendy shouting orders to the

Armée Libre units as she ran, marshalling them into some kind of order. She was throwing her squirrel scouts out into a long line on her left, so they were not running blind through hostile territory. Out of the corner of his eye, he saw them as blobs flickering through the trees, moving from branch to branch faster than the rabbits and mice could move on the ground.

Freddie came to a thick stand of cattails growing along the side of the stream, and had to veer wide around them. Then a dense stand of cottonwoods demanded an even wider detour. They were losing valuable time. Freddie sobbed as he ran. Love Bug was silent and fierce.

By the time they got back to the stream, it was dropping into the earth, and was now fifteen feet below the surface. Freddie could hear a roar coming from some distance ahead and winced as he ran. That was the sound of big water. In another half minute, he was there, standing on a high bank and looking down twenty-five feet into a wide flow of water in a deep gully that crossed his path. Below and to his right was the stream they had followed, pouring itself into the froth.

Anastasia was in there somewhere. He felt sick as he stood looking at the maelstrom of forces swirling through the confined space. Anastasia, who he had always loved, who was building a better world, was now in the grip of terrible danger, and he could not save her. He could still feel the burn from the bite she had left in the scruff of his neck when she saved him from the stream. It was like an endless, anguished cry, rising from her lips.

He stared at the arctic tumble of water. They could not even follow her likely path toward the cliff because they couldn't cross the smaller stream. What to do? Freddie found himself slipping and stumbling along the sodden, crumbling edge of the cliff, feeling a strong urge to do *something*. He was just starting to steel himself for a plunge into the icy water when Love Bug ran up to him. "No!" he shouted, and shoved Freddie back away from the edge.

Wendy arrived with her squads racing alongside. She growled as she stood looking down at the wild water flowing between high banks, stamping in rage. "*Stupid stupid stupid!*" she shouted.

A few seconds later, a wave of squirrel scouts came whipping toward them through the willows growing on the banks of the larger stream. They looked like they had seen something. Moments later, they were on the ground, surrounding Wendy, their eyes wide. "Coyotes coming! Big pack!" their voices were shrill but compressed by the need to be quiet.

A wide groan rose up from the little animals. Freddie felt as though he might throw up.

Wendy was still as a stone. "How many?"

"About twenty," returned the squirrel captain, breathing hard.

"Know we here?" asked Wendy.

The squirrel shook his head. The other squirrels were twitching with anxiety.

"How long?" she asked.

"Five minutes," said the squirrel, wringing his hands.

The army-wide groan rose in pitch.

"Let's hide," burst out Freddie. "Wait til they go past, then figure out a way to get down to the water."

"Brother," said Love Bug. "We have to *go*."

"We can't leave," shouted Freddie. "We can't leave *her*."

"No," said Wendy. "We go now."

"*I'm* not leaving," said Freddie "You go without me."

Wendy turned to him, and her dark eyes drank what was left of the fading light. She came near to him and put her mouth close to his ear. The voice that flowed into him was as deep and comforting as the rumble of his mother's blood when he was in the womb. "*Must live to help.*" Wendy pulled back and looked at him and he stared at her in anguish. She came close to his ear again. "*She want us live.*"

Freddie found himself nodding. "Yes. Yes." Thinking about what Anastasia would want steadied him.

Wendy nuzzled the side of his face for a moment. An instant later she turned and shouted, "*Run!*" As the army took flight, she rapped out a series of orders, organizing the squads so that it was a retreat, not a rout, and no one was left behind.

Except Anastasia.

Chapter 6

There is nothing without the murder.
—Corvid proverb

ANASTASIA

Anastasia was fighting to keep her head above water as the currents swarmed around her, spinning her this way and that. Her lean body was heavy as a stone, with no float in it, and she was forced to keep kicking her way to the surface. Her muscles burned with the effort, and she began to sink.

For a moment, she was looking through a gray-green gloom where boulders and weeds came rushing toward her. She struck a rock and groaned as she rolled off it, air bubbles trailing behind her. The swaying plants clung to her as she whipped past. Now she had been underwater for many tens of seconds. The air hunger was overwhelming everything else. She fought to keep her mouth closed, but instead breathed in some cold muddy liquid. Instantly, the pain of it caused her to spasm and cough underwater, losing the last of her precious air.

Panicked, she put everything she had into a frenzy of strong kicks that pushed her to the surface. Just as she broke through and gratefully gulped a hard breath of air, she was smacked in the face by a leafy twig. As she turned away from it, she realized it was attached to a small branch from a fir tree sluicing down the channel with her, floating high in the water. She immediately seized the twig in her jaws, and just floated there for a few moments, thankful for the chance to rest, lips pulled back to she could breathe through clenched teeth.

Then she heaved herself onto the branch, and managed to wrap her legs around it, bracing herself in a fork where two smaller limbs grew out. She closed her eyes and rested as the branch was swept downstream.

Soon, the sides of the gully were rising and getting steeper. Now there were plants growing overhead, long tendrils hanging down. Then there were trees growing up above, branches arching over. The stream began to feel like it was flowing through a tunnel.

Then she was washed into a larger stream, and her branch was suddenly whipped to the right as the current seized it. The walls on each side were very high now. Up above was a thin strip of sky. Ahead, the gully split into two courses. The larger stream veered left, and the current swept her along with it. She noticed that all the floating debris in the water followed her as she found herself in a new gulch, now fifty feet below ground level, with streaks of red iron oxide on the cliffs on each side.

She clung resolutely to her branch. At last she was

beginning to have a moment to think. *This must be the Braided Gorges.* She lifted her head and tried to look downstream. Up ahead, the course split again. The larger stream went left, and the other ran under an overhanging rock and disappeared. She shuddered as the current whipped her away from the ravenous maw drinking an entire gullyful of water and sent her down a new stream, along the rest of the flotsam traveling with her.

Half a minute later, she was dumped into a larger stream. The gully was wider, maybe thirty feet. The water slowed down a little in the larger space. She struggled to think. *All these streams are going to*—The image from her dream came sharply to mind: torrents of water spouting out from the Boreal Cliffs and falling more than a hundred feet down to the Southern Marshes.

A new panic struck her. *Have to get out of the water. Now.* She once again lifted her head to try and look downstream. Ahead, the water seemed to be dividing into two, but then she realized it must be a narrow island. The current was pulling her toward the right, a stream only four feet wide. On one side was the wall of the canyon, the other bank was the island of sand and earth, with a few small trees. As the branch entered the confined space, its wide spray of limbs started to scrape the sides of the narrow channel. At the last moment, she realized what might happen and clamped her teeth on the nearest small limb while bracing her legs against the fork.

Then the branch got jammed against the rough sides, and suddenly the water was gripping her like an ice-cold hand, doing its best to rip her off the branch and pull her down the chute toward the waterfall awaiting her.

Heart pounding, she managed to hang on, brace her legs,

and quickly shift her teeth a few inches along the branch towards the island. Then she readjusted her legs to a new spot and did this again. And again. Little by little, she crept along the branch until she was standing in just a few inches of water by the shore of the island.

She dug in her back feet and lunged over the last foot of water. She landed and rolled on the sandy soil. Nearby, a large elephant ear was growing, its canopy of wide leaves sheltering a nook between two boulders from the heavy rain. She crawled there, every muscle exhausted, and fell into the deepest sleep of her life.

Gaetan

When Gaetan woke, surrounded by a terrible cold and the blackness of deep night, his first thought was, *now I am dead.*

He lay on his side, motionless, pressed against giant teeth, and he was so weary he could not move. *I am in the mouth of Hunger Mother. Soon she will eat me. And I will be forgotten.*

A heavy weight was pressed against him, holding him against the teeth. As his eyes adjusted to the dark, and his mind slowly began to rise from the depths, he slowly realized that the teeth next to him were actually large stones with spaces in between, and he was held against them by the flow of icy water. He turned to look at the weight behind him, and saw, even in the dark, the dim shine of golden fur.

Instantly, the events of the preceding hours rushed in at him. A deep groan rolled up slowly from his innermost self. Then he dragged himself upright and found he was standing in shallow water. The current had cast them into a shallow basin near the bank, and the water was only a foot deep. A loose line of boulders had held them, and prevented them from being swept back into the main current. *Thank you for your teeth of mercy, Hunger Mother.*

Gaetan struggled to stand upright in the current, even in the shallows. When he rose, the limp body of Aliyah was pushed forward against the teeth stones. Was she alive or dead? There was no way to know.

He closed his teeth around her thick scruff and pulled. She moved easily, half-floating in the water. He dragged her toward the shore. As the water got shallower, it was harder to pull. Finally, he had all four legs braced, sinking deep into the gravelly mud as he walked backwards, pulling her up onto the bank in small jerks. The slipperiness of the mud helped her slide.

The rain seemed to be slackening. In the pitch dark, exhausted as he was, he did not even try to find cover. He just dropped down on the mud next her and fell into a dreamless sleep.

Mabel

Mabel awoke with her head pounding, snug in the lovely bunny nook Hella Cozy had provided for the very reasonable price of nine cents. She turned over on the soft bed of moss to find that Sunbeam was already stirring.

"Ugh," said Mabel, sitting up and rubbing her head. "I nose-bumped a *weasel*."

"That's okay, auntie," said Sunbeam in her girlish voice. "You were trying to learn about our journey."

"That was one friendly little killer," said Mabel. "Don't mind if I don't ever see that creepypants again."

Sunbeam started fiddling with her backpack, and that made it start jangling, as usual. Mabel pressed her paws against her head. "Honey, can you not right now?" She blew out a compressed breath. "What is all that noise?"

"That's my wire," said Sunbeam, as she gently finished rearranging her backpack and closed the top with her teeth.

Mabel frowned. Three hundred years after the last Dead God had set the last snare in the last hedgerow, rabbits still remembered and loathed *wire*. It was a demon character in many of their songs and folk tales. "Dare I ask why you're carrying that?" asked the older bunny as she dragged herself to her feet.

"Wire is truth," said Sunbeam.

Mabel shot her a glance. With her brilliant green eyes and golden fur, she looked angelic in the early morning light. *Kids these days.* "Okay," sighed Mabel as she shrugged into her pack. "If you can keep it damped down today, Auntie would appreciate it."

And when the people cried out to Dah for something to ease their hangovers, he created willow bark for them to chew. 'Truly, your love is without end,' saith Newly Beloved.

They lollopped several feet down a rabbit-sized passage and found themselves emerging from the earthen rear wall of Hella Cozy. The raccoon sisters who ran the snuggery were up and doing their morning chores. A few other overnight guests were stretching and yawning. Some raccoon kits ran by, chittering.

As Lunesta was scurrying around, tidying up and straightening the tables, Mabel approached her, trying not to move her head too much. "Wow, your Local Truce really works," she said. "That's kind of amazing."

Lunesta chuckled and brushed a stray wisp of fur out of her eyes. "Just animal nature," she said as she fluffed up a moss couch. "People love dirty apples and a place to yak more than they love grabbing a free meal. And if you go gnarly and we cut you off, it's a looong way to the next cozy."

Mabel nodded. "Do you know this area pretty well? I need to find *Les Enchantés*. Could you point me in the right direction?"

"Hmmm." Lunesta thought for a moment, then led her outside and gestured with her dark paw. "Follow that path eastward along the ridge," said Lunesta. "You'll come out on a grassland. On the far side is a tall forest by a river. People say they're around there. Haven't been myself."

Mabel thanked her and ordered a strip of willow bark and a dirty apple for the road, wrapped in broadleaf.

"Scallywag?" smiled Lunesta.

"No, no," said Mabel. "Anything but that."

ANASTASIA

A cold dawn was breaking. Something woke her. Anastasia slowly opened her eyes in her spot between the two boulders. The broad leaves above had held most of the rain off, but she was still deeply chilled. Her Dragon Claw was icy cold against her foreleg. She shivered as she tried to piece together what had happened.

Images of Freddie slipping down the bank, her reaching out to him, and then sliding into the water herself started to play in her mind. She closed her eyes and grimaced. As usual, she had done it to herself. Over and over. Her dream had drawn her to the uplands, and her head sickness had pulled her further and further along. Then her love for Freddie had driven her into the stream.

She could see, far above, the narrow strip of sky between the cliff walls that rose on either side, with long rusty streaks running down over the pale limestone. Overhead were some small trees, dwarfed by the depth of the gully she was in. The sound of the rushing water was loud and close.

She felt a terrible wave of loneliness sweep over her, but she pushed it aside as she struggled upright and looked around at her dismal surroundings. *What now, crazy girl?*

Finally, she realized what had woken her: the sound of whining. It was an electric jolt. *Someone is here.* That could be dangerous. She crept forward very slowly, and gradually realized it was the noise of several animals.

When she reached the end of the crevice between the boulders, she carefully peeped out and saw another tree branch jammed in the narrow channel between the island and the cliff wall, just as hers had been. And clinging to the branches with their teeth were several—she squinted in disbelief—wolf puppies. And soaked and dirty as they were, they were *golden*.

They were shivering, whining, moving feebly. Anastasia stared. Where did they come from? Was there no end to this plague of golden wolves? Must they follow her even here, into the bowels of the earth?

Her heart did not go out to them just because they were crying puppies. They were killers.

She shrugged, remembering what she had learned of wolf

lore. *Let Hunger Mother take care of them.* And if they were swept downstream, problem solved.

Then she lolloped through the gray dawn to the other end of the tiny island, some sixty feet away, and began to dig herself a warm, dry burrow.

Death Rage

The sky was blue and cloudless, and the sun felt strong, even though it was not far above the horizon. Death Rage and Throat Punch were traveling down the river trail, scampering around puddles left from last night's rain.

They had tried traveling off the trail in order to be under more cover as they moved, but in just a couple of hours had gotten hopelessly lost since the leaf litter of a forest floor is usually deeper than a mouse is tall. Also, it was slow, and Death Rage was determined to move quickly so she could find and deliver the precious intelligence to Anastasia as fast as possible.

So after they finally found their way back to the trail, they decided to stick to it. Death Rage's solution was to run along the edge, so she was usually under overhanging leaves of grass and bits of twiggery, poised to plunge into the clutter if needed.

Throat Punch asked Death Rage to stop while she changed outfits. And as she was digging through her backpack, Death Rage sat down and adjusted her bottlecap helmet, thinking, *let me guess, a winter jasmine tiara with a purple crocus thingy?*

But then Throat Punch pulled on a hood and cloak made of leather from the ghost plant, a succulent with naturally gray leaves. With splotches of lichen of different colors sewn on, she looked like an old piece of bark bumping along in a stiff breeze when she was walking. And when she stopped moving and huddled down, she looked exactly like a stone.

"Huh," said Death Rage, after a quick demonstration. "That looks pretty ... useful. Who made that for you?"

"I did," said Throat Punch. "It's my scouting outfit. I studied plantcrafting before I started my warmouse training."

Death Rage rubbed the ghost leather between her fingers and ran her hands lightly over the lichen. *Hmph. Nice.* "Well," she said, finally. "Maybe you'll make it there alive."

Then they took off down the trail, keeping eyes peeled for predators, but still moving briskly. To their left was the Shandy River, a hundred yards wide, bloated and muddy brown after last night's rainstorm. It was filled with floating branches and small pieces of ice that had broken free from the banks.

Across the river, they could see that the tall forest they were standing in continued. The lofty bare elms and maples stood like columns, their gray and brown trunks holding up a mezzanine of spiky shapes.

As they walked, Death Rage found that she had a continuous stream of tips rising to her lips, and she shared them freely. "You know, if you apply a light coating of oil to your sword, you'll always be able to draw it quickly. It won't get stuck."

Throat Punch considered this as she hopped through a small stony area. "But if I oil it, dust and leaf bits stick to it, so it won't be shiny."

"Why does it have to be shiny?" asked Death Rage as she skirted another puddle.

"Because, as an acolyte of *La Belle Mêlée*,[18] it's my responsibility to make every fight as beautiful as possible," said Throat Punch.

Death Rage stopped and gave her a serious look. "Fights are not always beautiful," she said. "But if you're lucky, they can be honorable."

Throat Punch shrugged as she breezed past her. "Why not both?"

Freddie

The sun was shining, but the three rabbits sitting under a loblolly pine near the foot of the Stone Stair looked very grim. Freddie had clearly been crying, and Love Bug probably had, too. Wendy looked even more fierce and lumpish than usual.

Stan, Air Captain of the *Armée Libre,* had just been read in on what had happened to Anastasia, and he sat silently on a low hanging twig, plucking savagely at his feathers as the rabbits sank into their own dark thoughts.

Up above, they could hear the coyotes that had followed them back to the Stone Stair the night before, yipping and playfighting.

"What will happen to Free Nation without the Godmother?" asked Stan, finally.

"That's not the question," said Freddie fiercely, unwilling to even countenance such talk. "The question is *how do we find her?*" His scent was cold and brittle.

---

[18] The Beautiful Affray

The other animals looked at him in uncomfortable silence. Finally, Love Bug said, "After the coyotes leave, we can send a squad to run along the edge of the first gully in the Braided Gorges. So we can see if she's washed up anywhere in there. But we can't cross the gorges to search any of the others."

"That's a start," said Freddie.

"Since those upland songbird putzes won't allow us to fly freely up there, we can't scout the whole gorge system from the air," said Stan. "But we can send flying teams to look at the mouths of gullies that are emptying into the Southern Marshes. So we can see the last few hundred feet of all of them."

"Good," said Freddie. "What about the rest of the gorges?" There was a long silence. "We said we were going to help," he said sharply, looking at Wendy.

She did not look away. "Tell me how, smart boy," she said. "You say it, we do it."

Freddie felt a cold weight descending on him like a heavy blanket of snow. "I'll think about that," he said, finally, his voice going high and breathy. "I'll … come up with something." Love Bug offered him a friendly shoulder nuzzle and Freddie shook him off. Then he forced his way into an upright position and looked at the others. "I know what you're thinking," he said. "But Anastasia is smart. And she is strong. If any rabbit could survive this, it would be her. That means there's a good chance she's somewhere in the Braided Gorges right now, waiting for us."

Love Bug and Stan nodded.

Wendy breathed out a long rumble. "Who know about this?"

"Just the *Armée Libre* units that were with us," said Love Bug.

"I sent a messenger songbird to Nicodemus this morning," said Freddie.

"*No one else*," growled Wendy.

"What if we need more help with the search?" asked Freddie.

"More animals know, weaker we are," said Wendy.

"But what if we—"

"Weakness bring attack," rumbled the *Armée Libre* Commander. "From outside. Inside. *Every* side." She shambled over to Freddie, her dark eyes locked on his. "You love this bunny? You want break her Nation?"

Freddie did not blink. They stood for a moment, breathing each other's breath. "I love this bunny," he said. "*No one else*."

Mabel

Not far from Hella Cozy, they found the path running along the low ridge, and Mabel took the lead. The dense, scrubby woodland was still heavy with water after the rains of the night before, and most of the snow had been beaten into the leafy mud. The sun was out now, but the wan white wafer, low in the sky, did not have the energy to dry anything out. It was a wet slog.

'Your journey is long,' saith Dah unto Newly Beloved. 'But if your foot is light, it will surely bring you home again.'

At first they were very quiet, concerned about running into predators, so they went with their ears pricked for noise.

But after a couple of hours of hearing nothing but their own squelching feet, they started to chat.

"Weird being in that place last night, huh?" said Mabel. "All those hunters creeped me out."

"We're surrounded by death always," said Sunbeam. "It's just that last night we could see it."

"I already *know* it. I don't have to *see* it," said Mabel. "My goal is focus on something *good*, for Dah's sake." Then she felt a little embarrassed that had slipped out, but at least she was with probably the only other person in the Known World who still thought about Dah at all.

Mabel cast a glance back at Sunbeam, who had once been a young zealot. She was humming a little song as she jumped over puddles. The older bunny frowned. Her plan to reimagine Dah as a kind and loving god was not going very well. And would anyone even care?

They came around a turn in the trail and found clusters of winterberries hanging on the branch. Both rabbits immediately stopped for a quick bite, and in the sudden silence, their ears picked up the *squelch squelch squelch* of someone walking behind them on the trail. After a few steps, it stopped.

They locked eyes, and instantly they were bolting down the trail, flinging up slush and mud behind them. After a minute's sprint, they were a quarter of a mile down the path. At a signal from Mabel, they both stopped and listened intently, ears cupped backward. All was silent.

"What was that?" gasped Mabel, breathing hard.

"Don't you know?" said Sunbeam, as the breath raced in and out of her. "It's the Loved One, coming to take us home."

Gaetan

The sun's rays on Gaetan's eyelids woke him. He opened his eyes and saw the muddy bank. Up above was the dark tracery of the branches of the willows and cottonwood trees, cast into high relief by the sun.

He rolled over and saw the sodden, muddy mass that he had once known as Aliyah Summerday. He could not tell if she was breathing, so he put his nose next to hers. At first he felt nothing, then he realized that he could feel a very faint touch on his nostrils, like a light feather borne on a breeze.

He put his muzzle alongside Aliyah's and nudged her gently. She did not respond. He pushed her again, a little harder. And again she did not move.

He whispered, "Aliyah," and there was no answer. So he whispered again. "Aliyah, *pouvez-vous m'entendre?*"[19]

There was no answer. So he whispered again. And again. Finally he heard her draw a breath. Then words came out in a slow breath that was close on to silence.

"Let … me … die."

The sadness and finality of this was breathtaking. It was the last act in the death of an idea that had lived in him for most of his life. He realized, as he lay in the cold mud under a wan sun, that he no longer saw her as a princess, a goal, a love object, a protector. Not a goddess, a boss, an aristocrat, a client. It was the end of the murderous Golden Lady, who must above all be obeyed.

---

[19] Can you hear me?

Instead, he saw a tiny spark of life that was flickering on a cold night. A tiny flame that was guttering before an icy wind. And he was seized with a desire to keep this flame from going out.

Chapter 7

The best bear is way over there.

—Fox proverb

Death Rage

The two mice came to a small rise in the land that allowed them to see several miles along the riverbank. Up ahead, the river curved in a large loop that surrounded a vast freshwater marsh that was thickly grown with reeds. These were all a golden brown, as it was winter.

Up ahead, the path forked. "Maybe we can cut across here and make up some time," said Death Rage. "That'll help us catch up to the trading scow."

Throat Punch agreed, so they took a course that led around the edge of the marsh.

As they got closer, they slowly realized that there were piles of reeds lying down along the edge. And a few minutes later, they could see there was much activity around these piles.

As they drew close to the first pile, they saw many golden-brown mice working with the reeds, nibbling the ends to trim them into similar lengths, then binding them together with strips of braided cord. Some of the collections of reeds appeared to be rising into structures.

The path seemed to be petering out as they entered the boggy ground, and it was hard to see amidst the tall standing reeds mixed with the piles. After losing their way, they decided to ask for directions. So they approached a nearby mouse who was wearing a curiously long and narrow bag over his shoulder. He had it pushed up onto his back as he stood weaving cord through several reeds stacked together.

"Hi," said Death Rage, offering the usual Musmuski Grove gesture of greeting, rubbing the forepaws together and then displaying the palms to show they were empty of weapons.

"Good morrow," said the tawny mouse as he stopped working and turned to them. He made a curious gesture of fluttering his fingers as he blew on them. Death Rage had never seen this before.

"Um, we're travelers," said Death Rage.

"Yea, I make you wood mice," said the other mouse. He did not seem particularly friendly. "What is your business in Wicker Flats?"

Death Rage started to answer, and ended up stumbling.

"Just going upriver to visit family," broke in Throat Punch.

"Then you may move yourselves along," said the mouse and turned back to his work. "We are busy folk." Death Rage and Throat Punch shared a glance. This was not heading toward getting directions.

After a moment, the mouse looked over his shoulder. "Still here?"

Just then a group of golden-brown mice headed past at a brisk pace, carrying a bundle of reeds on their shoulders and singing a marching song to keep in step.

"We are reed mice and we make
All that bends and does not break
Every day we take the gift
Of the Shandy and we lift
Golden stalks and raise them high
For the mighty sun to dry
Then our clever fingers build
Further glories for our guild
We are reed mice, see us make
We will bend but do not break"

"Oh, you're the *reed* mice," said Throat Punch, looking surprised and pleased. Her scent was suddenly bright and sparkly. "Folks back home talk about you guys all the time. Like that amazing thing you made..." She snapped her tiny mouse fingers. "The um..." She turned to Death Rage. "What was it called?"

Death Rage was startled but gamely tried to look thoughtful. "Erm ..."

"Are you speaking of the faithful heartweave?" said the reed mouse. "Yea, we invented that. It's the strongest binding there is."

"The heartweave thing, *yes*," said Throat Punch. "Mumsy mentioned it in prayer circle." She leaned forward and clasped her hands. "The whole community is very grateful for your work, sir."

"Well," said the reed mouse, making a little dismissive gesture. "Just doing our best to serve the Land of Oom." He patted the reed stack to him. "Ken ye that we are suppliers to the Civil Raccoons in the City? And we just opened a shop there."

"Really? No," said Death Rage, happy to pipe up with a true statement.

"Yea," said the reed mouse proudly. "I go there myself sometimes. It's early times yet. But we are bringing the glory of reed to the wide world."

Throat Punch and Death Rage *oohhed* and *ahhed* appropriately.

The mouse, seeming a little embarrassed about his earlier stiffness, wiped his hands and stepped toward them. "I'm Poison Wind," he said.

The Musmuski mice introduced themselves and they all nose bumped. There was a brief, more-friendly silence, and Throat Punch seized the moment.

"Master Poison Wind," she said, "We're trying to find a route around the marshes so we can join with the Shandy going east. Ken ye how we may best do this?"

"Yea, surely. There's a path that starts about a hundred yards from here," said Poison Wind, and started giving them directions using multiple reeds as landmarks. They hung on his words anxiously, brows furrowed, until he finally said, "I'll take a moment and walk with you."

Soon they were threading their way through the towering forests of reeds and clambering on fallen reeds over boggy patches.

Throat Punch kept up a stream of chat as they went, tickling more information out of Poison Wind.

"The bears are changing everything," he was saying. "The *Pax Ursorum*[20] keeps the wolves out of our demesne now. Not that they ever cared much for mice. Coyotes are still a problem when they've a mind to be, strewth." He paused as they all climbed up a long rickety leaf over a stinky puddle. "It's really the foxes and weasels that hunt us day by day now. But yea, we've recently concluded negotiations with the bears that will allow us to defend ourselves, inside our fiefdom." He blew out a short breath. "Within limits. It's a sign of our value as craftmice." He turned and looked back at them. "That's why the faithful heartweave is so important. It bought us the ability to save lives."

Death Rage nodded as she gazed at him. Fighting for your life was something she understood. "What are you defending with?" she asked.

Poison Wind reached into his long shoulder bag and withdrew a piece of reed about three inches long. "Ken ye what this is?" he asked.

They shook their heads.

"The greatest gift of the Shandy," he said. "Our newest invention. The dreamstick." He raised the reed up and held one end to his lips. He sighted along it for a moment, then blew

---

[20] Peace of the Bears

out a sudden, strong puff of air. A flicker of white and gray leaped from the other end of the reed, and a moment later, a small dart came to rest in the stalk of a nearby reed.

Poison Wind stepped forward and plucked the dart from its target, then held it out for them to admire. "My practice dart," he said. Death Rage peered at it. She could see that it was made from the tip of a thorn, with fletching made of dried reed leaf. And most curiously, around the center of the thorn was a pussy willow puff.

"Well done," she said.

Throat Punch reached out and touched the dart gingerly. Death Rage slapped her paw away. "Don't touch other people's weapons," she said. "It's rude."

Throat Punch glared at her.

Poison Wind rubbed the point of the thorn with his forepaw. "In the field, the darts will be tipped with dreamjuice. A small amount makes you sleep like the dead for a day. A larger amount means you never wake up."

Death Rage stared at him. "What a wonderful weapon," she said, her eyes intent, and her mind starting to race. "Might one of these be available for ... purchase?"

Poison Wind smiled and shook his head as he tucked his practice dart back into his dreamstick. "These are for the protection of the Wicker Flats homeland."

. "So ... are there *any* conditions under which a ... mouse from away ... might have access to this marvelous machine?"

Poison Wind chuckled as he closed the fastener on his long bag and shouldered it. "Friends of the Flats only, I'm afraid."

Death Rage nodded reluctantly. "Understood."

City of Oom

Poison Wind took a few steps. "Come," he said. "I'll walk you to the path."

A few minutes later, they came out of the marshy area into a yellow grassland dotted with small trees and a few patches of dirty snow. In the distance, they saw the Shandy.

Death Rage reached into her backpack and pulled out a penny with a bobcat and an armadillo on it. "For your trouble," she said.

Poison Wind bowed. "Many thanks," he said, and blew on his fingers. "Please visit our shop in the City."

ANASTASIA

The next day, Anastasia woke in the snug burrow she had dug for herself under a grove of tiny winter pear trees. She had slept for most of the last twenty-four hours and now dragged herself to the mouth of her burrow, hungry and thirsty. There was an immediate din in her mind. *What now? What now? What now?* But she did her best to ignore it. She could feel that panic was just a few bad thoughts away. And if she entered into full panic mode in this hole—she glanced up at the narrow sky—then she would likely beat herself bloody on the rocks. And she could not afford that if she wanted to live.

So she practiced the breathing from Oga For Young Goats. *In, two, three, hold, out, two three, four.* And very deliberately, she began to examine her surroundings. Several small brown winter pears lay on the ground, having fallen from the trees above. She bit into one. And as a winter fruit, it was fresh and juicy. She chewed through the rind and swallowed the pulp. Then she stood on her back legs and pulled down a leaf and ate it.

Soon she felt better. She took a few steps to the stream and drank from it. Then she allowed herself to look at where she was.

Her island was about sixty feet long, mostly flat, and twenty feet wide at its widest point. She was sitting in front of a small group of trees. In the middle of the island was a small glade of coconut palms, finding a toehold in Canada's newly warming climate. And at the far end were several boulders with a large elephant ear plant, a winterberry bush and several agave plants growing among them. There was a smattering of grass sprouting from the mix of gravel, sand and earth that made up most of the island.

On one side was the narrow channel where her branch had gotten stuck. On the other, a roaring stream filled with tumbling whitewater some fifteen feet wide. The gully as a whole was about forty feet across, and the walls were sheer, with a ledge partway up with some carrion bushes growing on it. The sides looked to be very high, beyond her estimating skills. Even the trees on the island reached only halfway to the top. It was a miniature world. Just her … and … and… Finally, she allowed them to enter her awareness: the golden wolf pups.

Still breathing deeply, she lolloped down the length of the island, passing a number of coconuts scattered on the sand among the wild columbine, marram grass and scrubby witch hazel. Soon she could hear the pups' whines and small yelps over the constant roar of the water. As she drew near the far end, she could see them.

They were gathered around the winterberry bush, standing on their back legs, reaching upward for the tiny fruits. They were clumsy and seemed half-blind, even though their

City of Oom

eyes were open. Their vocalizations were a mixture of talking and whining. They looked very young. She guessed them to be just two or three weeks old.

Two of them were very unsteady on their feet, but the third seemed stronger. Judging by the voices, it was a female. She was helping the others, nudging them toward the best fruit with her short muzzle. After a struggle to reach a berry, one of the pups sat down to cry. Anastasia could hear many repetitions of the words, "Mummy" and "milk." The stronger one went to offer comfort, providing licks and nuzzles.

She gazed at them unblinking, mostly hidden among the spiky witch hazel. They seemed helpless now, as they cried for milk, but she knew that in just a few weeks they would be crying for meat. And she was the only meat on the island.

She could not really get a sense of what might happen in the coming months. Maybe the water levels would drop enough over time that she could walk upstream and eventually come to a place where she could escape the Braided Gorges by following side channels? But the long summer with its low rainfall was half a year away. Maybe there would be some kind of amazing rescue from Free Nation? Her heart leaped at the idea, but she quickly pushed it down. *They must think I'm dead.* She raked her claws through the sandy soil. *And even if they looked, how could they find me? I'm a little brown smudge at the bottom of a ditch deeper than a tree is tall.*

Now the pups were trying to work as a team. One was standing on the backs of the other two and trying to reach up to a cluster of winterberries. It flailed and then fell off. Anastasia sucked her teeth as she watched them. At ten pounds each, they were already double her weight. In just a few weeks, when they grew into their bodies, they would easily be able to overwhelm her. And she would be dead.

She gnawed on the casing of her Claw. Even taking a moment to consider using it on the pups made her shudder. Attacking with it in battle was one thing. Using it on helpless creatures was... Her mind shied away from it.

Should she try to kick them into the water? Her powerful back legs could probably push an animal twice her size. In which case, the time to act was *now*, while they were still helpless lumps. Even two weeks from now might be too late.

She imagined herself waylaying these puppies one by one, back feet lashing out in surprise attacks as these half-blind creatures bumbled past. Then she heard their panicked voices as the white water took them and sucked them downstream to their deaths. Again, something within her rebelled at this. She remembered her argument with Wendy about the pointed stakes at the bottom of the deadfall, just before the Battle of the Narrows. *We don't kill helpless animals.*

She scoffed at herself. *Then what? They'll be getting stronger every day.* A thought occurred to her. *If they're eating. What they really want is milk, which they're not getting. And the only thing they can eat on the island are these winter fruits.* She imagined herself going around to all the winterberry bushes and pear trees, eating all the low hanging fruit she could, and biting off the rest and throwing it into the water. She could live on leaves and grass. They could not. She could starve them.

It was a very workable idea. Then images of starving babies and their pitiful cries began to play out in her mind. She blew out a long slow breath and looked up at the weak sun, framed for a moment in the narrow slice of sky above her head. She just didn't want to do that.

She had hated the identity of 'killer' that she had acquired when she struck down the coyote to save Nicodemus's life. Maybe she was finding out something about herself now. It felt good, in a way. *Maybe I'm not a killer.*

Another part of her spoke very, very clearly. *If you are not a killer rabbit, you are a dead rabbit.*

She tried to push the whole conversation away. *What I really want to do is get out. I have a Nation to look after.* She looked up at the ledge with its carrion bushes. It ran along the cliff, climbing as it went, and turned out of sight at a bend in the stream.

Her eye traveled along its length, and then flicked across her island. Among the grove of coconut palms was a slender dead tree, ravaged by termites. It was already leaning, and like the others, high enough to reach the ledge. She lollopped toward it, and very tentatively dragged her incisors across the fibrous surface.

Mabel

As the two rabbits reached the end of the forest and came out into the wide grassland that Lunesta the raccoon had told them about, they noticed that the trail wandered a bit and then just vanished among the clumps of dormant meadow flowers. An ocean of yellowed grass pocked with occasional splotches of dirty snow reached to the horizon in gently undulating waves. And here and there were natural stone columns, similar to the Spires in the northern Million Acre Wood, carved into fantastical shapes by the wind and rain. Some of them reached more than a hundred feet into the air.

Looking back over the wood they had just passed through, they could see some columns jutting above the tree tops here and there. They had not seen them earlier because of the thickness of the evergreen forest.

So they stood for a moment at the edge of the grasslands, watching their kindly companion, the path, disappearing before their eyes.

"Dah's teeth," murmured Mabel, as she felt her anxiety buzz climbing. "That's not good."

"Are we lost?" asked Sunbeam, her green eyes large.

"Ermmm ... no?" said Mabel. "Just might have to wander a bit here, which isn't great since Loving Auntie needs us to come back with an answer as soon as we can."

Sunbeam squinted into the distance. After a moment, she said, "What's that?"

About a hundred yards out into the grass, they saw a flash of white in motion behind a flower clump. Then there was a little jiggle, and the white shape moved more fully into view. They could see then that it was a white weasel, wearing a green backpack. It looked to be digging in the earth.

Mabel cocked her head. It was very strange to see a weasel doing this in the open under the sun, instead of the usual weasel activities like sneaking, stalking or attacking in dim light.

"Let's make a big circle around, and keep downwind," said Mabel quietly. Sunbeam nodded. "Bite blades up, just in case," whispered the older bunny.

Just then, the weasel turned around and saw them. She

bounced up with an expression of delight. "Mabel!" she cried, scampering across the dead grass toward them, and doing a little undulating happy dance that made her backpack jiggle. "What a sssurprise! Fancy meeting you here." In a few moments, she was within a dozen yards, and slowed to a walk. She patted her chest. "Saskatoon! From Hella Cozy."

'Again with this creepy little monster?' thought Newly Beloved. 'Truly, some of thy creatures make the skin of thy daughter crawleth, my Lord.'

"Oh, hi," said Mabel, around her bite blade. She bumped into Sunbeam as she backed up. Her anxiety got even spikier.

"Cool weapons," said Saskatoon as she drew near. Mabel noticed a strange expression pass over her face, then it was gone. The weasel looked around apprehensively. "Is there someone dangerous nearby?"

Mabel felt awkward. "No Local Truce here," she said, finally. And then, "That's close enough."

"Oh, right, *right*," said Saskatoon, smiling. She waved her paw back and forth in the space between them. "The whole … prey … thing." She stood up and put her forepaws on her slender hips. "But I don't think of you like that." Her scent was bright and fruity. "We're buds now. We got appled together. We're members of the Sssisters of the Scallywag Hangover. Am I right?"

Only tramps take up with strangers, dear, came her mother's voice. *It's the first step to getting eaten.*

"It's all good," said Mabel blandly, still holding her bite blade. "Nice running into you. We're just going to be on our way."

"Actually, I'm on a pilgrimage," said Saskatoon. "It's

because some kind of blight has struck my family." She sat down by a dead thistle and looked mournful. "So I'm on a journey to visit *Les Enchantés,* because they are supposed to be great healers." Her scent was now small and scattered. "And when weasels go on pilgrimages, we only eat bugs. It's a gesture of our faith in the Goddesss." She examined her paws. "I was digging for ants just now." She noticed an errant ant on her left forepaw and licked it off. Then she sighed deeply.

"I'm sorry to hear that," murmured Mabel, and immediately felt foolish. *Stop chatting with this loon.*

"Ya, it's tricky out there," said Saskatoon, indicating the meadowlands with a wave of her paw. "Good thing I have my map." She patted her backpack.

Mabel and Sunbeam exchanged a glance. "What kind of map?" asked Sunbeam.

"Map for crossing the Sea of Grass," said Saskatoon. "Otherwise, you go out there and start walking in circles." She walked two of her claws around and around in the air. "And after a while ... well ... you know." She turned her paw over and made a sad little descending sound. "Wah, wah, wah, wah."

"Where did you get that?" asked Mabel.

"Peddler who comes through here on the reg," said Saskatoon with a cheerful smile. "Known him for years." She slipped off a backpack strap, reached in, and pulled out a piece of folded paperbark. "It shows the stone columns, so you don't get lost."

The two bunnies squinted at the paperbark from a distance. All they could see were dots and lines.

Saskatoon got up and stretched. Once again, Mabel could see the scattering of small scars down one side of her face and neck. *Is that the blight?* "Fifty cents this cost my family," said the weasel, tapping on the paperbark. "But we're desperate for healing." She bowed to the rabbits. "Welp, guess I'll be on my way." She smiled. "Don't want to take up any more of your valuable time." She slipped her paperbark map into her backpack and turned to go.

Mabel frowned as she wrestled with her thoughts. At last, she surprised herself by opening her mouth and saying, "Would you mind if we … followed you … at a distance?"

The weasel looked surprised. Then she smiled, and for a moment her white teeth shone. "You know a people pleaser like me can't say 'no.'"

Chapter 8

The Allshroom feels not only all that happens, but all that is about to happen. Open your nose and listen.
—Clytemnestra, Queen of Sorrows

DEATH RAGE

It was morning and Death Rage woke in the snug sleeping spot they had found the night before, tucked among the gnarled roots of an ancient sprawling thorn bush that would deter curious hunters. Wicker Flats was behind them and the two mice were back on the path between forest and river, heading toward City of Oom.

A little ways away, she heard Throat Punch murmuring her daily prayers. Death Rage got up and started packing. She was hoping to catch up with a boat soon. Every day they spent just getting to Oom was a day wasted. They had much to do.

With her sharp ears, she could hear Throat Punch's simple,

cheerful melody as she recited the familiar words Death Rage remembered from her childhood.

*"Gramsy and Grampsy
I love you
So I sing my
Song for you*

*I know you are
Safe and free
Won't you please
Watch over me?*

And Mumsy and Dadsy and..."

Throat Punch went on to name a long list of family and friends. Death Rage remembered that as a mouse pup, she would complete her list, then fearful that she had left someone off, would start over and do the whole list again. That was long ago. She jerked the strap to tighten her helmet.

A few minutes later, having made a quick breakfast of windfall walnuts, they were hastening along the path to try and catch a rat trading vessel. After a few minutes of silent scampering, Death Rage started offering soldiering tips again, even though she knew it irked the younger mouse. There was really no way around it. She owed it to Anastasia and Free Nation to make her team as strong and effective as it could be.

Soon the trail veered closer to the river and began to wind among the boulders scattered along the gravelly shoreline. Death Rage noticed there was an eddy along the river bank, flowing upstream toward a large boulder near the shore, a few tens of yards away.

After an hour of helpful information from Death Rage, Throat Punch suddenly asked, "Why do you have such a hard time saying things that aren't true?" The tone of her voice indicated that she thought this was mildly provocative banter, probably aimed at gaining some breathing room from the elder mouse's relentless pedagogy.

But Death Rage heard it as accusatory and invasive. "Our honor is the only thing we have," she said shortly. "If we lose it, we may be breathing, but we're not really alive."

Throat Punch, who was in the lead, cocked her head and said, "Seems like a tough code to live by."

"It's not hard," said Death Rage. "If it's the only thing that makes it possible to live with yourself."

"Sorry, didn't mean to pry," said the younger mouse, glancing back over her shoulder as she spoke. In the next moment, she carelessly stepped past the edge of a large boulder and almost walked on a brown-and-yellow cottonmouth warming itself on a large flat stone under the pale winter sun.

Instantly, she shrieked and darted away from the snake, dashing off the path to her left.

The cottonmouth's lidless eyes swept the space as it came out of its doze, its vertical pupils engaging like alien targeting reticles. Death Rage stared in horror as it followed Throat Punch off the path, the terrible smoothness of its glide eating up the space between them.

There had been no snakes in the Million Acre Wood for time out of mind, but mouse lore was filled with information about this ancient enemy. So she remembered that snakes were heat seekers, which meant the scrubby grass and brush that grew along the river's edge would be no cover. It looked to be about four feet long, and the head was thick and blocky. It continued its sinuous roil, and a moment later was lost to sight among the jumble of large stones.

Death Rage snatched the Kiss of Death out of its holster and clambered up a nearby boulder, hoping to get a better view. Within a few seconds, she reached the top and scurried forward through a jumble of stone fragments, twigs, and dead leaves. Then she reached the far edge and looked down to see Throat Punch backed into a nook formed by two boulders lying close together, half-filled with dead stalks and leaf litter. She was struggling to draw her greatsword, and the snake was swaying its head back and forth slightly as it created a heat map of the area, drawing in a picture of Throat Punch with the heat-seeking pits between its eyes and nostrils. The thin cover would not help.

"Aren't you so warm and lovely," said the snake, in a throaty, intimate voice. "Let's have a snuggle."

Death Rage was unsure what to do. The cottonmouth was easily big enough to devour them both. She considered leaping down and driving her rapier into the tail, which was near her boulder. That should pull its attention off of Throat Punch. What she would do with that attention exactly, she wasn't sure. She had already been in one predator's mouth and had no desire to be in another one. The other problem was that the snake's tail was twitching back and forth. It would be hard to time her leap so that she hit it. If she missed, she would just be throwing away her brief advantage of surprise.

The snake began to draw its head back to strike, but then

it hesitated and started scanning again. It seemed to be having trouble locking in on Throat Punch, standing with her back to a sun-warmed boulder. She had her greatsword out now, and she was slashing the air in front of her as she yelled threats in a quaking voice.

"This thing is razor sharp! It's killed better snakes than you!"

"You're quite a firebrand," murmured the snake. "Do work up a sweat."

Death Rage racked her brain as she ran along the top of the boulder. At least all this chat was putting off the moment of truth. She noticed a large stone laying atop the boulder, partly overhanging the edge. It was too big for her to push by herself, but she remembered what Freddie had taught her about the principle of the lever, so she sheathed her rapier and seized a nearby twig. A moment later, she rolled a pebble near the stone, jammed her twig under the edge, and started pushing down as hard as she could. The stone lifted up and tilted forward slowly. Seconds were passing. Death Rage felt desperate, but she could still hear Throat Punch doing her best to squeak out threats below.

"Snakes are my specialty! I'll cut my way right out through your belly!"

"We both like thinking about you in my belly," chuckled the snake. "Let's be friends."

Then Death Rage bounced up and down on the farthest point of her twig, and the stone tilted forward and disappeared over the edge. Almost immediately, there was a storm of angry hissing from below. Death Rage ran up to the edge of the boulder and looked down. The snake's body was whipping around as it fought its way out from under the stone. Out of the corner of her eye, Death Rage glimpsed Throat Punch disappearing around a clump of grass as she escaped from the niche she had been trapped in.

Then Death Rage saw the snake notice her on her boulder, hot and sweaty against the cool winter sky. The alien eyes with their unearthly vertical pupils locked onto her just as it finished pulling free. An instant later, the mouth was yawning open as the head rocketed toward her, almost too fast to see. Death Rage yelped and flung herself backward away from the edge. A frantic scramble took her across the boulder as the open mouth of the snake crashed into the spot where she had just been standing.

Then she was looking down at the water below. She was afraid of the icy turbulence, but just below her was the upstream eddy. A glance over her shoulder revealed that the snake had fallen back, but the thrashing sounds below showed that it was trying to climb the boulder. This was her chance to disappear.

She pulled her sword belt tight, gripped her backpack straps, and threw herself off the edge, plummeting down to the water below. The coldness of it made her gasp and choke, but as soon as she bobbed to the surface, she started swimming upriver, helped by the eddy.

After a minute of strong swimming, she saw Throat Punch peeping out from behind a dead branch. Then the vermilion mouse was running across the stones toward her, reaching out her hands, and helping to pull her out of the water. They were both too breathless to speak. Just as they saw the first flash of the brown-and-yellow banded skin several yards away through the jumble of debris, they turned and a moment later were hightailing it up the river trail as fast as their legs could carry them.

GAETAN

The sun was drying out the muddy riverbank. Aliyah lay as before, the mud around her hardening into a crust.

Gaetan talked to her, but she would not respond. He brought her kills, but she would not eat. If he tried to drag her, she did not resist.

When he lay next to her, he could feel—just barely—the heat of her body. When he pressed his ear against her, he could faintly hear her beating heart.

She was sinking toward the big dark, and if she went, she would take with her everything about the world he had once known. His love for his sister Lilou, his warm affection for every friend he had ever had, his relationship with every creature he had ever known in the Million Acre Wood. All these had been stripped away, and his connection with them was now a single thread. And if that thread broke, it would be as though his whole life had never existed. The panic he had been fighting down for days rose in him again. He felt breathless, his lungs were somehow too small, his ribs could not expand enough to let him breathe.

His ochre eyes swept the skies for Grammy Kark, again. He had seen no sign of the old crow since the storm. Although he had often felt envious of their intimate relationship, he knew that if she were there now, she could reach Aliyah in a way that he could not.

City of Oom

So what would she say? He tried to focus on this and not the tightness in his chest. He raked over what he had heard during his time with the Summerday Clan, then he lay down with his muzzle alongside Aliyah's muzzle and began to speak.

"Golden child, those who loved you once, love you still."

There was no answer, but he had expected none.

"Your mother and father are at this very moment roaming the Forever Forest, and their hunting is very, very fine."

There was a slight quickening of her breath.

"You are the Summerday to come. Blood Father and Hunger Mother have allowed you to enter the harsh time. It is hard, golden one, but it is not more than you can bear. *Car les loups le seront toujours.*"[21]

He thought he saw an eyelid twitch.

"Your beloved children are safe with your mother and father. Sephora, Micah, and Tennyson are even now running free and—"

Suddenly, Aliyah's powerful body was in motion. She rose like a golden wave and crashed into him, bowling him over, her long teeth around his throat. "*Don't you talk about my children.*"

Gaetan was shocked, but he forced himself to lay without fighting back. This was good. It was life. "Your children are wonderful. And always will be."

Her words hissed out as her teeth were closing around his windpipe. "*Don't you—*"

---

[21] For wolves will ever be.

"*Yes*, Aliyah. Fight," wheezed Gaetan. "Fight for your life. Fight for your family."

She stood over him, her powerful jaws locked on his exposed throat, her growl grinding like a chainsaw.

Gaetan lay still, his vision going red. "*You* decide. Will Clan Summerday live or die?"

Just as his vision dipped towards black, she threw him aside and walked away along the muddy shore, her scent whirling out of her like a storm of knives. He seized a deep breath. Then another. And another. *Thank you, Blood Father.*

Free Nation

Everyone was in full scramble mode. Love Bug was leading the small group of sworn-to-secrecy *Armée Libre* units in a search of the areas around the icy pools where the streams from the Braided Gorges fell from the Boreal Cliffs and landed in the Southern Marshes. Stan and his flying teams were daily searching the mouths of the gullies.

And Nicodemus was carrying on the day-to-day leadership of Free Nation, as he often did, standing in for Anastasia when she was away. Yasmin, the Home Guard Captain, and Holly, the Home Steward, were accustomed to Anastasia disappearing for long periods on her own schedule, so they took it in stride.

But there was also an increasing murmur, fueled by Anastasia's recent speech about the dangers they faced, that was slowly growing. A string of visitors from all over the Million Acre Wood, unfamiliar with Anastasia's remote and prickly ways, were beginning to arrive at Warren *Sans Gloire*.

City of Oom

They wanted to see the Loving Auntie. And when Nicodemus blandly put them off, they tended to hang around in the common areas, already overrun with kittens, their anxious eyes large and scanning. And every day, the murmur grew. *Where is she?*

Down at the Stone Stair, the pack of coyotes that had chased Freddie and the others from the Braided Gorges were now milling around the top of the cliffs, yipping, laughing, and occasionally howling. Freddie had figured out a way to modify the crossbows so they could fire upward at a steeper angle, and Wendy was using them now to harass the coyotes.

Every once in a while, one would show itself at the top of the stair, and a quarrel would go flying. Most were misses, but the occasional yelp would signal that one had found its target. Unless they were right at the cliff edge, they were protected by the earth.

The sun was low and wan when Freddie came out of the main gate at Stone Base, where he had been talking to some craftmice in a desperate search for new ideas for finding Anastasia. A cloud of anxiety surrounded him like a whirl of epinephrine gnats. As he stomped along, he ran into a rat peddler. "Finest fantastical mushrooms," said the peddler. "Left by a boogle of artisanal weasels after the regime change. Show you things you've never seen—"

Freddie brushed by him. "No thanks." A few moments later, he was striding up to Wendy, as she stood engaged in an intense conversation with Dingus, looking up at the coyotes. "How much longer do you think they'll be there?" he asked.

Wendy shrugged and grunted noncommittally as she squinted down the firing track of a crossbow.

Freddie could not stop himself. "Because you know we can't send a team to search the edge of the Braided Gorges until—"

"I know," rumbled the other rabbit.

"And Anastasia could be starving to death on a sandbank somewhere—"

"I *know*," barked Wendy. She glared at him out of the side of her eye. "You think you only one that care?"

"I'm sorry," said Freddie. "I just want to be doing *more*."

"You want do more?" said Wendy. "Find me way throw rocks up there. Not quarrels. Rocks. Throw high. Fall down. Need get past cliff edge." She shouldered into Freddie and pushed him off the crossbow embankment. "Come back when done."

Freddie slipped down the muddy side of the embankment, muttering. He had been doing his dreamtime meditations, but had been unable to make any headway. As he pulled himself upright and kicked off the mud he ran across the rat peddler making the same mushroom pitch to a pair of tired mice just coming off sentry duty. *Show you things you've never seen.*

He got a little tickle and found himself marching up to the peddler. "I'll take 'em all."

Mabel

After a day out in the Sea of Grass, Mabel was glad they had a guide, even though the guide was a *very* chummy weasel. The rabbits had walked for many miles, and although she could tell by the sun they were headed generally west, she had no idea where they were other than that. The one thing she made

City of Oom

sure of was to stay at least fifty feet behind the weasel, bite blades at the ready.

The gently rolling hills of yellow grass, dotted with clumps of brown meadow flowers and leftover snow islands, seemed to reach the horizon on all sides. Only the tall stone columns, carved by the wind, bore witness to the unchanging landscape.

But always there was a relentless stream of chat from Saskatoon, thrown over her shoulder as she walked. They learned about her beloved home, the terrible blight, her adored siblings, her fractious cousins, and her favorite stories, buttressed by her endless supply of songs. There were even, during the long afternoon hours, occasional forays into long strings of knock-knock jokes. The bunnies, who had only seen two doors in their lives, found these mystifying.

And always, there was a running inquiry: *So what do you want from Les Enchantés?*

Mabel provided vague answers and kept Sunbeam from accidentally volunteering anything. Broadcasting the problems of Free Nation, and their efforts to solve them, did not seem wise.

At the end of the first day, Mabel quietly decided that she and Sunbeam would take turns keeping watch during the night, and she assigned the first watch to herself. She took a few bites of the fermented Red Belly apple she had in her pack, to take the edge off the anxiety spikes traveling up and down her spine. *Getting stewed on a sleepover?* came her mother's pointed voice. *That's a little trashy, don't you think?*

The second day was more of the same, although now Mabel noticed Saskatoon was acquiring a tendency to close the gap between them. It was easy enough. If she just walked a little slower, the rabbits would catch up. So they in turn walked more slowly, and this kept up until the tiny group of three was marching at a snail's pace while Mabel gnawed at her cuticles in frustration.

It was actually a relief when a large gyrfalcon sailed by high overhead, and then turned back for a second look. They all had to sprint for several hundred yards to find cover near some stone columns. Of course, Mabel made sure she and Sunbeam huddled at the foot of a different column than Saskatoon.

In the end, inevitably, Mabel started to get worn down. After the third day, she started to lose count of what day it was. She was still maintaining a distance of thirty feet from Saskatoon. That was right, wasn't it? It was hard to focus. And the weasel, with all her jolly chat and general helpfulness, was coming to seem, if not completely credible, then at least non-threatening.

One afternoon, several days later, Saskatoon was dawdling along, well into her dozenth song.

> "*I like bugs,*
> *Cuz bugs are crunchy,*
> *They're good for brekkie,*
> *And twice as good for lunchie*"

Mabel was plodding ahead, mostly day dreaming, and just as they crested a hill, she heard Saskatoon stop singing and say, "And the Goddess gives us treesss!"

She looked up and was astonished to see the first redwoods

City of Oom

she had ever seen, soaring upward from the foot of the long descending slope and reaching over three hundred feet in the air, dwarfing the stone columns they had been passing. After days of the flat horizon wearing a stripe across the middle of her eyes, the verticality of the redwoods was exhilarating.

Saskatoon yelped in delight and ran forward, with the two rabbits dashing after her. In a few minutes, they had reached the edge of the redwood grove and were walking among trees that were fifteen feet in diameter, with an understory of light bushes and ferns. For the rabbits, it was very soothing to have something overhead again after being in the open for so many days. It was quiet and peaceful, and they heard, not far off, the sound of water. A few minutes walking brought them to the banks of a cold, fast-flowing river, heading southwards.

Saskatoon consulted her paperbark map. "This must be the Rime," she announced. "If we turn left and follow this river upstream, it will bring us to the land of *Les Enchantés*."

For the first time since she had climbed the Midsummer Path, Mabel felt herself begin to relax. They were on the right track. They were near to their goal. She was accomplishing the task Loving Auntie had set for her. And she felt grateful to Saskatoon for helping them.

So that night as they were preparing a place to sleep, she impulsively decided to share the last of her fermented Red Belly with the others. *The Great God Dah said, 'Let there be a place for everyone at your table.' And Newly Beloved spread her forepaws wide.* Saskatoon was more than willing, and even Sunbeam, who rarely had dirty apples, wanted to join in.

So they were soon sitting in a small glade by the river, under the pleasantly bright light of a gibbous moon, tippling and talking. The alcohol warmth felt good in Mabel's belly. Her anxiety cavalcade seemed to be taking the night off. She didn't even think of chewing her cuticles. And the distance between them had shrunk to fifteen feet.

Saskatoon shared a cluster of winterberries she had found. The quiet night, the fermented apple, and the shared journey seemed to put the white weasel in a thoughtful mood.

"You know, it's not always great being a hunter," she said. "Lotsss of people avoid you. Unless I'm in some place where there's a Local Truce, the hard truth is that nine out of ten people who see me will run from me. And that's not easy for a people person."

"I've never thought of it like that," said Mabel. "No one runs from a rabbit."

"Sssometimes they do," said Saskatoon.

Mabel's eyes flicked toward her.

Saskatoon settled back in a posture of great repose. "I know you're from the Million Acre Wood," she said sweetly. "Goddesss knows, as soon as you pull those mouth swords, anyone who sees you is going to know that."

Mabel gathered her feet under her. "What do you think of that?"

"Your people are trying a great ... experiment," said the weasel slowly, her scent smooth and serene. "I'm sure the huntersss in the Million Acre Wood weren't happy about it, but ... I understand you wanting to live free."

"Mm hmm," said Mabel.

"What I'm curious about ... from a distance ... is how it's going?" said Saskatoon. "First time ever, and all that?"

"Honestly, the strangest thing about it for me is having

our scripture shredded," said Mabel. "I was a priest ... *am* a priest." She took a bite of Red Belly. "But finding out your religion was built on a lie just breaks your world into tiny pieces. I'm trying to salvage what I can. Not sure if anyone will be interested."

Saskatoon scoffed. "Trying to fix up a lie that was designed to control you? Maybe it's the Red Belly talking, but if a friend of mine told me that, I'd say, '*snap out of it, girl! You're too good for him!*'"

Mabel looked at her toes and then shot a glance at Sunbeam. Was her attempt at rehabilitating Dah some kind of pathetic foolishness? Sunbeam's green eyes were opaque in the semi-darkness.

"You already *know* what's good," said Saskatoon. "Fresh food. Warm den. Dance by the light of the moon. Make yourself high priestess of *that*. Who cares about some crap made up by crowsss?" She smiled. "To tell you the truth, I don't mind a world with a few less wolves." She leaned back and patted her belly. "More for me." She waved her paw in an intimate gesture. "Present company excepted, of course." She jabbed her paw at Mabel and Sunbeam. "We're buds now. You're off my lunch list."

Mabel swallowed a bite of Red Belly and nodded slowly. It had never really crossed her mind to consider what hunters might think about ... well, anything. They were just *enemy* and that was that. "Food for thought," she murmured.

Saskatoon smiled and raised her bit of dirty apple. "A toast to your successs," she said, and ate the fragment. Then she lay down on her side and propped her head up on her elbow. "So tell me more about ... what're you calling it? Free Nation?" She licked her paws. "Cute."

"We're fine," murmured Mabel, still lost in thought about the Word of Dah.

"Any problems with raccoons? They're really hunters, you know. Distant cousins of the bears." She sucked apple juice off her fingers. "It's hard to imagine them actually becoming *tame*."

Mabel shrugged and lay down on her side. "A few issues. Nothing big. Things are good."

Saskatoon nodded and trailed her claws through the earth. "Afflictions of the comfortable? Diseases? Boredom? Bratty kits?"

Mabel scoffed. "Why are you so anxious to find a way that it's bad?"

Saskatoon chuckled and rolled onto her back. "You're doing a totally new thing. I'm just interested in everything, including the underbelly. Having problems doesn't mean you're bad. It just means you're alive." Her scent was warm and sweet.

"Okay," said Mabel slowly, starting to chew her nails.

Saskatoon lifted her back legs and began to play an invisible upside-down marimba with her toes. With one arm she hugged her chest, and with her free forepaw she stroked her chin. "Problems between the tribes?" she murmured solicitously. "Everybody happy with rabbitsss lording it over everyone else?"

"We're not lording it over other tribes," said Sunbeam, sounding a little slurred. "We work hard to make it fair for everyone."

"Oh, sure, sure," purred Saskatoon. "Of course, that's what any group in charge is going to say." She smiled. "What was it the Summerdays used to call themselves? *Wise and kind stewards of the Million Acre Wood.*" She snickered.

Mabel felt herself getting a little hot. "Actually, they're lucky to have us," she said. "I mean, what would they prefer, a government of weasels?"

"If it was a fun government, maybe," said Saskatoon. "You know weasels bring the party." She put her paws above her head and twinkled her claws while she executed a supine bump and grind.

"Fun for you," said Mabel. She tried to tamp down her bubbling annoyance, since she was fascinated by this peek into the weasel worldview. And it seemed like it could be useful at some point.

Saskatoon rolled up into the lotus position and steepled her forepaws under her chin like a tiny psychoanalyst. "Or what about the bear in the room?" she said gravely. "Popular founder. Adoring followers. No oversight. What does that spell?" She adopted a singsong tone as she answered herself. "*Tyranneeee.*"

Sunbeam stood up, swaying from the Red Belly. "Anastasia is *not* a tyrant! Things are *good*. The only issue we're having is that our numbers will double every year. *That's* the problem we have to solve."

Mabel glared at the younger rabbit.

"Ah," said Saskatoon kindly. "You said a mouthful."

Chapter 9

Raptorfall is the cleansing finger of life.
—Songs of the Eyrie

Anastasia

Anastasia gnawed fiercely on the dead palm tree, visions of her potential escape driving her on. Though it had seemed close to impossible at first, the dead and brittle wood, already half-eaten by termites, was giving way. So it looked like she might indeed be able to cut through enough of the remaining wood to make it fall against the ledge. She was anxious to get up there and explore. If the ledge led up to the surface on the far side of the bend, it would be her first step to getting out of this hole and back to the fight that mattered: the preservation of Free Nation.

As she ripped at the wood with her incisors, she thought about the variation in water flow that she had seen in the streams of water pouring out of gullies in the face of the Boreal Cliffs. In the winter, it was often a fierce current, with the streams arcing far out into the air as they fell. In the summer, the flow was much less, sometimes just a dribble. So she was feeling mostly confident that in the summer, the water in the stream would drop enough that she could walk out of the Braided Gorges and return to Free Nation. But that was the backup plan. In six months, there might be no Free Nation to return to.

So she redoubled her efforts at the tree trunk. Her mouth was full of splinters, and she could taste her own blood. She tried to distract herself with thoughts of who was waiting for her. She yearned for the touch of Freddie's soft black-and-gray fur and the love in his kind eyes. She closed her eyes and gave herself the gift of imagining a snuggle on their soft moss bed, drifting off to sleep with his tender kisses on her cheek.

The sound of the golden wolf pups whimpering broke through her consciousness again. She frowned. The crying of these little ones never stopped. No matter where she was, her sharp ears picked up the sound. So the question of what to do about them was often before her mind. She found herself continuing the conversation she was having with the voice in her head.

Those pups are killers.

It was the voice of experience. The voice of wisdom. The voice of the world.

"Those pups haven't killed anyone," she said aloud, pausing for a moment to pull a splinter out of her mouth.

They are wolves. They will be killers.

"But the actual puppies on this island have killed no one."

She wiped some wood fragments off her paw onto the tree root.

Yet.

"And they haven't tried to harm me."

You know they will.

"So what should I do?"

Kill them now before they kill you.

"If I was comfortable killing, I wouldn't be a rabbit."

You would be a wolf.

"Exactly."

So kill them.

"I just don't want to kill innocent people."

How are they innocent? They are born of wolves who fed themselves on the bodies of people just like you.

"These babies didn't choose that."

It doesn't matter. Your people have already paid the blood price. If it's guilt you need, their bodies are made of it.

"Is there any other choice?"

Yes, you can do nothing and then die.

You can let Free Nation flounder without you.

You can let it fall victim to infighting and gradually weaken and break apart.

You can let the thing you built on fantastic strokes of luck that can never be repeated fall into nothing, and condemn infinite generations of your own people to die terrible deaths because you were too much of a coward to act now, when it matters most.

And so it went on, hour after hour, as she gradually wore through the base of the palm tree.

After two days of this, Anastasia finally said, "You're right. I'm already a killer. I will do it."

Today.

"I'm doing it right now," she snapped.

A moment later, she was marching down the length of the island. A light snow was falling. She followed the sound of the pups' miserable voices and found them huddled in a space between a boulder, a small tree trunk, and a fallen coconut.

She went directly toward them, not hiding, and suddenly they saw her for the first time. In their half-blind state, there was no telling what they actually saw, but the shape of an animal as large as themselves suddenly appearing and moving nearby must have been terrifying. They whimpered and tried to crawl away from her.

She eyed them, trying to pick out which one she should kick toward the water first. The smallest and weakest one would be easiest. Her heart resisted. She felt frozen.

They are nothing. They are just lumps. They are victims of bad luck. They are already dead. You are just delivering the news.

Then she saw the oldest one rallying the others to defend themselves. In a few moments, they were standing on unsteady feet, attempting to growl in her direction. Just as when she had seen them trying to harvest the fruit, something about watching them take action made them seem less like nameless blobs and more like little people. People who wanted to live. People who had a spark of life and were doing their best to keep it lit.

A lump of nothing that was already dead could easily be cast into the icy water. A tiny person fighting for their own survival was very different, and somehow demanded respect.

She stood up, with her front paws leaning on the coconut,

and looked down at them. Then the eldest spoke, her voice soft and lisping over the tiny stumps of teeth just beginning to appear in their mouths. "Please don't hurt us."

Kill them, commanded the voice of her ancestors.

She closed her eyes, and suddenly unleashed her long shiny incisors. She felt them tearing through a hairy surface that was firmer than she expected, and then her mouth was wet. When she opened her eyes, she found she had ripped a hole through the coconut. Shaking, she rolled the coconut toward the pups, and they felt and tasted the rich milk pouring out on their faces. In the space of a few seconds, they began drinking it, eagerly, joyfully.

She was trembling as she turned away and stumbled back toward the tree. The voice in her head was loud.

Stupid rabbit.

Death Rage

The next morning, Throat Punch was sitting under a broken maple branch where they had spent the night. A new light dusting of snow coated the bushes and stones by the river's edge. She was oiling her greatsword with a piece of oleaginous cotton boll that Death Rage carried in her backpack. Death Rage, as she was packing up, noticed her sniffling as she did it.

She came and sat down next to the younger mouse. After a few moments, she said, "Are you crying?"

"No," scowled Throat Punch, as she vigorously rubbed her weapon.

Death Rage nodded and rested her elbows on her knees. "You had your first big fight. You stood your ground when it counted. You didn't get killed. You didn't get anyone else killed." She sucked her teeth. "Congratulations. You're no longer a punk."

Throat Punch sighted along her finely crafted blade and flicked off a few stray fibers. "Thanks," she said, guardedly.

"Oiling your weapon, smart choice," said Death Rage. "Next time you'll be able to get it out faster."

"Yep." Throat Punch thrust her greatsword into her sheath and began to gather her things and stuff them into her pack.

Death Rage noticed her surreptitiously wiping her nose as she packed. The older mouse stood up and pulled on her backpack. Then she stood looking at Throat Punch for a moment. At last, she said, "No shame in crying."

Throat Punch shot a glance at her from the side of her eye.

Death Rage strapped on her helmet. "Crying after battles is what warriors *do*." She buckled on her rapier. "If you're not crying, you're not fighting hard. And where's the honor in that?"

Throat Punch looked away and wiped her eyes with the back of her hand. "Crying is for weaklings," she said. "I never cry."

"Okay," said Death Rage, and she turned toward the river.

A few minutes later, they were scampering down the river path. After they had gone as fast as they could for two hours, they came around a bend in the river and saw a wide-bottomed trading scow tied up to a sharp rock jutting out of the water about ten feet from shore.

It was much bigger than the small peddler watercraft they had seen on the Lower Shandy. Bricabrac's catamaran was only thirty inches long, since he traded in small high-value items like Dead Gods artifacts and finely wrought wooden tools and instruments made in Musmuski Wood.

The trading scow they were looking at now was a two-master, fully seven feet long, and three feet abeam at the waist. The wide deck was piled high with woven baskets, cups, mats, and other large reed items, probably from Wicker Flats. The prow was high, with a large oaken figurehead carved in the form of a rat, rampant, holding aloft a wooden loonie, the most valuable moneystone in the Known World. Death Rage had never seen such a thing before.

In the morning mist, the rat crew looked as though they were just finishing some repairs. And some were climbing the masts and unfurling the sails, which were a handsome cream color, much faded by time, and patched here and there. As they bellied out in the steady wind coming from the west, they looked strong and flexible, despite their great age. Each sail bore a curious set of runes in the center. As the mice hotfooted it toward the ship, Death Rage, not a great reader, tried to puzzle out the mysterious name, doubtless the sigil of a great trading house. After sounding it out in her head, she realized that it read, "SPANX."

As they reached the shore near the ship, Death Rage called out, "Hey, cousins! May we buy passage to City of Oom?"

At first the rats ignored her. So she pulled off her backpack and shook it, so they could hear the moneystones jingling.

A rat that seemed to be in charge stepped to the side of the ship and looked them over. "Twenty-five cents each. And you have to take a turn in the galley."

"Agreed," said Death Rage.

"Show your stones," said the rat captain.

City of Oom

Throat Punch dug in to Death Rage's pack, pulled out two quarters, and held them up.

The captain gestured to the rat standing at the wooden wheel on the poop deck at the back of the ship. So as soon as the rats cast off from the stone where they were moored and the ship began to move upstream, it glided into a path that would take it along the shore.

The two mice stood expectantly on the marshy turf, and as the vessel angled toward them, they only belatedly realized it was not going to stop.

"Look alive, shorelubbers," called the captain, "we're not losing speed for a couple o' mice."

Death Rage and Throat Punch cast about, and finally saw an old milkweed stalk leaning out from the shore at an angle. As the ship sailed past, they ran out on the milkweed and leaped toward the deck. After a bit of a scrabble at the edge, they pulled themselves onto the flat planking, where baskets were piled high overhead.

The rat captain approached, amid a general chuckle from the crew, who looked to be crusty old mariners with river water in their veins.

"I'm Captain Hodgepodge," he said, and pointed toward the back of the ship. "You can stay under one of the baskets aft. Your shift in the galley will be this afternoon. And don't get underfoot, or we'll toss ya."

"Yes, sir," said Death Rage. She handed over their coins.

"No refunds," he barked as they scampered toward the back of the ship.

"These Spanx people seem kind of jerky," whispered

Throat Punch as they threaded their way through the towering piles of reed goods.

"I'm just glad we don't have to walk the rest of the way," said Death Rage. "I think it's at least fifteen miles."

"How far is that anyway?" asked Throat Punch.

Death Rage shrugged. "I think if we kept walking from here, our grandchildren would get there one day."

Soon they were near the stern. She touched one of the overturned baskets. "This looks like a good place to camp."

Up above them on the high poop deck, an old rat with his hands on the ship's wheel adjusted his faded petunia petal bandana and murmured an ancient river shanty.

> *"Fifteen rats on a dead rat's chest*
> *Yo-ho-ho and an apple of fun*
> *RatBGone had done for the rest*
> *Yo-ho-ho when the day is done"*

Mabel

Mabel was shocked awake by a sudden unearthly screaming. And the first thing she saw as her eyes flicked open was Saskatoon pawing through her backpack, less than two feet away.

Saskatoon immediately jumped back and took her head in her hands. "Oooh, where am I?" she murmured, sounding dazed.

Mabel scrambled backward away from the weasel, her mind racing in many directions at once. The shrieking sounded like no animal she had ever heard. It was many different sounds mixed together into a piercing onslaught. She could feel Sunbeam fumbling around nearby, trying to get her bearings.

Mabel darted toward Saskatoon and pushed a forepaw under her backpack strap and half-pulled it onto one shoulder, jerking the closure cord with her teeth as she backed away.

"Bite blades!" she hissed. Both rabbits seized the bite blades from the holsters around their necks.

And the shrieking went on and on. Now there was a storm of white-hot snarls and deep-bellied grunts coming at them, along with frenzied breathing and the sound of clumsy, struggling blows. Judging by the sound, the creatures involved must be fantastically large. Much bigger than any animals Mabel had even seen.

As she woke up enough to start pinpointing the location of the sound, she realized it was coming from a densely wooded area of small trees and brush about a hundred yards away. It was too dark to see what was happening, but large forces were shaking whole *trees* of the understory.

She shared a glance with Sunbeam and they both started backing in the opposite direction. After a few yards, she realized Saskatoon was following them.

"Can I come with you?" she was asking, her voice high and breathy. "I'm scared."

Mabel did not answer, but she was determined to keep her distance. The only thing that kept her from bolting at full speed was that she just might need more help finding *Les Enchantés*. And Saskatoon had the only map.

As she blundered backwards through the underbrush in the dark, getting slapped on the side of her face with the dead underlayer twigs and other detritus near the forest floor, she heard Sunbeam whispering in her ear.

"You know who that is, Auntie?"

Mabel shouldered into Sunbeam and pushed her back, trying to open up more space between herself and the weasel, whose white form kept appearing and disappearing in the harsh chiaroscuro of dappled moonlight and black shadows.

"Don't leave me," called Saskatoon. *Was she weeping?* Mabel could see nothing.

"It's the Loved One," whispered Sunbeam fiercely. "He's here."

"No," said Mabel, around the bite blade clenched in her teeth. "Just keep walking."

"Please," whispered the younger rabbit, her mouth close to Mabel's ear. "We have to go back." Her voice was urgent. The wire jangling in her backpack was loud as they stumbled along together.

Mabel's eyes swept the shadows, looking for any sign of the weasel. Saskatoon's pleading face flicked into being for an instant and then disappeared into shadow. Mabel could spare only half an ear for Sunbeam's crazy zealotry. "Dah's teeth," she snapped. "We're not going over there." She tripped over a small branch, and went sprawling, dropping her bite blade. "Just shut up and keep walking," she rasped as she spat out a mouthful of dried leaves. She tried to draw a deep calming breath. As soon as she stopped talking, the unearthly cries rushed in on her again, although now they were at least two hundred yards away. The noise seemed to be heading in the direction of the river. She seized her bite blade once again.

"There is so much love," said Sunbeam, her voice high and joyful.

Where is that weasel? It was a few seconds since Mabel had seen the white face, the huge eyes.

"He's coming for us," said Sunbeam. She dropped her bite blade and started to sing a snatch of an ancient hymn.

"Coming for who?" barked Mabel.

"All the sad killers," murmured Sunbeam. "He forgives us." And then she was gone.

Mabel felt the cool space at her back where Sunbeam had been just a few moments earlier. She turned and cast a hasty look over her shoulder. Darkness. A jolt of panic punched through her chest. "Sunbeam," she called. There was no answer. "*Sunbeam!*"

She stepped on something hard and cold. She reached down to scoop it up with a forepaw and found that it was Sunbeam's bite blade. *She's thrown off her weapon? Is she crazy?* Her panic multiplied exponentially. *You can't lose Anastasia's little sister.* "Come here, honey," she called, trying to sound calm and authoritative instead of terrified and furious. As she spoke, she hurriedly looped Sunbeam's bite blade over her own head. "We'll get through this. Just come to me."

"Thanks for waiting," came Saskatoon's voice, right behind her. She turned and saw Saskatoon standing in a patch of moonlight. Twin images of the gibbous moon were reflected in her dark eyes. The reek of weasel was strong about her.

"What's happening?" asked Mabel around her bite blade as she took a step back.

The weasel chewed her foreclaws. "If you anger *Les Enchantés,* they will come for you," she whispered. "That's what everyone says." She pressed forward. "I would not have believed it until this night."

"They're monsters who murder people?" asked Mabel, backing away from the weasel as she spoke. *Why are we even here then?*

Saskatoon looked shocked. "Ah, *wisht wisht*," she said, scrubbing the air in front of her with her paws. "Don't let them *hear* you." She leaned toward Mabel. "*Les Enchantés* are very *good* and *wise.* But you must be *respectful.*"

The screaming ended suddenly, and the distant thrashing and growling seemed to be far away, by the river's edge. It was a relief to be able to think again, and she needed to go look for Sunbeam. There was no telling where that moony doe-child had gotten to. She looked around and realized Saskatoon had backed her into a deep crevice between two redwood tree roots.

"Let me by," she said.

Saskatoon was standing in a stippled patch of moonlight. She wrung her hands and said, "I wish I could."

A chill ran over Mabel's shoulders. *Here it is,* she thought. She wanted to take a step back, but the damp clot of the root tangle was right behind her. Trying not to reveal her fear, she asked, "Why were you looking in my pack?"

Saskatoon smiled and a curious transformation ran over her body. The round-shouldered forward-leaning community helper of the last few days disappeared and was replaced by a cool and erect hunter, with her long neck undulating from side to side like a cobra.

She smiled, and the long spikes of her teeth gleamed white in the moonlight. She spoke slowly. "I'm curiousss … about the criminal rabbitsss … in the Million Acre Wood."

Mabel felt her heart sink into her toes. She clenched her teeth onto her bite blade. Yes, she had marched out onto the field at the Battle of the Narrows. She had sung the battle song, she had bink-bladed with the others, and she had, amazingly, been part of a force that changed the balance of power for the first time in the history of the world. But she was no killer. And even her sharpstone bite blade shining in the moonlight felt trivial compared to the teeth and claws of the born-to-it killing machine in front of her. *Weasels are killers. And if you for a moment thought otherwise, you are a fool.*

"What are your needsss?" asked Saskatoon as she swayed back and forth. She started to hum a killing song in time with her movements. "What is your weaknesss?" The music and motion was strangely hypnotic. "You've told me some. I want to know more." Her scent was hot and spiky, and it was wrapping around Mabel like a thousand points of darkness.

The terror buzz at the base of Mabel's skull was now so loud that she could hardly hear or think or even assemble a sentence. To buy some time, she managed to whisper the only words that came to her, "I thought we were friends."

These words had an electric effect on Saskatoon. She stopped swaying and her long neck curved like a gothic arch. She ran both her forepaws over her face and down her neck. As she riffled her fur, the scars of the dozens of puncture wounds that trailed across her cheek and down her neck and shoulder reflected the cool white light of the moon and shone like stars.

"*You hurt me!*" Her voice ripped out of her like a bandsaw. "*Look what your warmice did with their nasty spears!*" She took a step toward Mabel, her forepaws reaching out, razor sharp claws clacking together. A long breath flowed out of her. "Now you will tell me *everything*."

Time slowed to a crawl. Mabel's heart banged like timpani, but the space between beats seemed to take forever. Was this the Giving? She wanted to fight. *Use your weapon*, she raged at herself. But she felt frozen.

Then, over Saskatoon's shoulder, she saw another shape appear out of the shadows. The ears were long. The golden fur shone in the moonlight. Mabel hardly had time to register what that meant before her next thought crept into consciousness. *But she doesn't have her—*

Then she saw Sunbeam lifting her two front paws up to her face, up over her head. And in between them, a length of braided wire, attached to her wrists with fabric cuffs. The wire gleamed in the moonlight, and a highlight flicked along its length as it moved, higher and higher.

Saskatoon was taking another step forward, claws still clicking. Mabel stared, unable to move. Time was crawling. Sunbeam brought her wrists together. The line of wire bowed into an arc above her head. For a moment, it framed her face like a halo, the flower-shaped scar on her forehead shining. Now the wire was coming down, dropping past Saskatoon's ears, eyes, mouth. The weasel blinked and started to turn her head. Now Sunbeam was pulling the wire back, crossing her wrists. The loop drew tight around the weasel's neck.

In an instant, Saskatoon's eyes became huge. Her forepaws flew to her neck. The garotte was already disappearing into her fur. Her body was twisting, claws reaching, eyes pushing to the side as she tried to see her attacker. And a shrieky snarl ripped out of her.

Now her long body was curling into a circle as her rear claws flailed furiously. One claw ripped down Sunbeam's flank and Mabel saw her stagger and almost fall. She suddenly realized she was already several seconds late to this fight, so she shoved herself out of her freeze and lunged ahead with her bite blade. She landed some solid slashes, but she was afraid of cutting Sunbeam in the whirling ball of fur that was now before her, so she couldn't strike as hard as she wanted. One of the weasel's claws ripped her across the face and a moment later her left eye was filled with bloody tears.

Now the weasel's snarl was fading as her breathing was choked off, and Mabel could hear Sunbeam's grunts as she struggled to get her feet solidly on the ground. She lunged ahead with her bite blade and the weasel's rear claw raked down her belly, tearing a shriek of pain from her.

Mabel staggered back, then forced herself back into the fight, lunging at Saskatoon several more times, slashing wildly. Then she hit Sunbeam's leg by mistake. The jolt of pain caused Sunbeam to lose her focus on the wire, and she loosened her grip. This enabled the weasel to turn toward her, so Sunbeam was suddenly confronted with a full set of whirling teeth and claws at very close range.

Instantly, the two animals were surrounded by a penumbra of floating fur, gleaming in the moonlight. Saskatoon closed her teeth on Sunbeam's right ear. The rabbit groaned as the weasel's teeth met through the cartilage, and her hold on the garrote loosened. Saskatoon thrashed her head wildly from side to side as she wriggled out of the wire's embrace, a piercing shriek of pain and rage rending the air.

In another moment, she was free and disappearing into the

shadows, and there was a long flurry of leaves as she dashed away into the night.

The rabbits, desperate to leave this terrifying place, raced through the dark woods for a long time, they knew not where, while the blood from their injuries soaked their fur. Then as their adrenaline burn faded, they found a hollow log and crawled inside and slept like the dead.

Chapter 10

In the raccoons' great love of water, we see their collective memory of what most animals have forgotten: the Womb of Ocean.

—*Thimble Thimbalian*
History of the Known World

Freddie

Freddie could not rest. The need to find Anastasia was a constant goad. If he was eating, he felt guilty because she was hungry. If he was resting in a warm burrow, he felt sad because she was cold and alone. He had come to treasure the pain from the bite injury she had left in the scruff of his neck, because it was a sign of their connection, written in his flesh.

She was alive. She was waiting to be rescued. He refused to even consider any other possibilities. And he wanted to be doing more. So he made the trek to Warren *Sans Gloire* to get the tools to make that happen.

First, he went by the healing hall, which was a new set of chambers that had been dug a few dozen yards downstream from *Sans Gloire* to prevent contagion.

He found Gregoire the Healer and his young intern Juniper sorting medical herbs.

Freddie slipped into the chamber. "Hey, um…" he started, then came to a sudden stop. He couldn't say anything about the Loving Auntie. "This thing with the bears has got me spooked," he said, groping for a story that didn't reveal anything. "I can't sleep. I can't stop working. But everything's so hard. I feel like I'm running in quicksand."

Gregoire, who was almost blind, came near and moved his sensitive nose along Freddie's side, inhaling deeply. "I don't smell any infection," he said, at last.

Juniper ran her soft paws over his body. "Nothing here … all normal," she murmured. Freddie jumped when she came near his mouth. "Sore jaw muscles. Tender gums," she said. Then she peered into his mouth. "I see extra wear. Have you been grinding your teeth?"

Considering that no one's doing anything to save Anastasia? Of course. Freddie fidgeted. "I don't know," he mumbled. "Maybe."

"Sounds like you have a case of the darks," said Gregoire. "There's a lot of it happening now. War fear. Totally understandable."

Juniper ran out of the room and came back holding some dried herbs. "Saint-John's-wort will lift your mood and help you sleep," she said, tucking the sprigs into his backpack. "It's good for the terrors. Just a daily nibble."

Gregoire nuzzled his shoulder. "And remember, no matter what it feels like, everything's *not* depending on you."

Freddie gave him a long look and fought down a grimace. *Really?* "Thank you so much," he murmured, and then hurried away.

Next he went to see Nicodemus. As he approached the main gates of Warren *Sans Gloire*, he was surprised to see several dozen small creatures gathered on the greensward. They stood in a circle, surrounded by playing kittens, chanting, *Where is she? Where is she?*

Freddie looked around, squinting, and noticed a Nicodemus-colored blob off to one side, in his favorite spot under the azaleas. He liked to sit there and think. Freddie ran to him, then turned and gestured at the demonstrators with a questioning look.

Nicodemus leaned in and spoke into his ear. "Anastasia did almost too good of a job scaring everyone about what Free Nation is facing. She wanted to get their attention and drive them to action, but now there's fear spreading through the Wood. And they want to *see* her."

Freddie nodded. He himself felt besieged by fear. "Is anyone suspicious?"

The elder bunny chewed a foreclaw. "Right now, it's just about demanding her presence. They love her and want to be comforted by her." His dark eyes flicked across the chanting animals. "No one has any inkling she's missing. I shudder to think what will happen if *that* idea gets out."

"We need to move fast," said Freddie. "I'm cudgeling my brain for some way to find her."

"Me, too," said Nicodemus. "But so far I haven't come up with anything workable. I'm better at understanding the world than creating new ideas. I don't have your gift, Freddie."

Freddie nose-bumped his shoulder. "I think I have some things to try, but I'm going to need help making them happen."

"Anything that can be done for her, I will do," said the old Reader.

"I need more raccoons," said Freddie. "At least a hundred. I know the raccoons rotate in for weekly stints of service. Can you arrange an extra group to come down to the Stone Stair?"

Nicodemus sucked in his breath. "Another hundred? The raccoons are already complaining about having to do all the work."

Freddie brushed this aside. "They're always complaining."

"Well, there's some truth to it," said Nicodemus. "And they're allies, not subjects."

Freddie looked out over the animals on the crowded greensward. "They don't know it," he said. "But they're waiting for *me* to solve their problems and bring Anastasia back. If we want to hold off a panic, I need every available pair of hands."

Nicodemus chewed his lip. "Can't argue with that." He nose-bumped Freddie's flank. "I'll do everything I can." Then he turned and hurried through the big gates.

Freddie stood for a moment, blinking, as a group of kittens and mouse pups ran past him. It was time to think. He needed another meditation entry point. Where to go?

He remembered the day, nine months ago now, when he

and Love Bug had run down to the stream to gather spider web for Anastasia to use in healing the foxes. The orb weavers had been busy among the cattails, and the rabbits had collected as much of their webbing as they could.

He recalled the geometric precision and complexity of their webs. That sounded like a good way into the dreamtime. And also the connection of the place with Anastasia and the history of Free Nation seemed like a good omen. So he ran down to the stream and found that the warm weather had brought the spiders out in full force. Their webs were everywhere, and their black-and-yellow bodies gleamed in the sunlight.

He found a spot near a large stone where he could sit in the sun and not be bothered. Then he shrugged off his backpack and looked into it. At the bottom were the ordinary-looking brown mushroom fragments he had bought from the rat peddler. *Show you things you've never seen.* He took a deep breath and scooped up some pieces and ate them. Then he settled into a comfortable position and let his mind come to rest on the webs and their beautiful and precise geometry.

Soon, his perception of the webs was flickering, and he was slipping around the edges of dissociation, sliding into full inattentional blindness as his mind's eye opened.

He began to consider the elasticity of wood. The crossbows were a marvel, but they were tiny. How could that be made bigger? Could a whole plant be brought into service? A whole tree? The goal was to throw many small stones to a great height. A rope of agave cord could be attached to the top of a sapling, with a net tied to the other end. Pull down the tree, fill the net with stones, release the rope. He played this out in his mind. The tree would fling the net upward, but the forces involved would just keep the stones in the net as it flew over the top of the tree and then reached the far side. It would end up just swinging back and forth, then coming to rest.

Freddie frowned. The netting must be *open*. The stones must be free to fly. How to do that with one point of contact? He ruminated but could not come up with a way. Two trees then. Agave rope tied to a pair of trees, netting in the center of the rope.

He played it out. Pull down netting, fill with stones, and release. Stones fly out. Can it be repeated? Yes. Pull netting to same point every time. Downside: direction can't change much. Trees must be well chosen.

He ran through experiments in his mind for awhile, looking at it from different angles, working through details. The idea seemed doable. Then he paused and slipped back toward the surface to take a break before tackling the hard problem: finding Anastasia.

His eyes rejoined with his consciousness and he became aware that he was looking at an orb weaver web. He had been in the dreamtime for at least an hour. It didn't seem like the mushrooms were having any effect. He felt a flash of irritation. Ripped off by a rat peddler. Once again, the world was a crappy place.

He tried to brush the feeling aside as he rested his eyes on the marvelous structure of the web, shining in the sun. He crept closer so he could see it clearly. It was more than three feet in diameter, an enormous construct made of fibers thinner than a hair. The main supporting lines radiated out from the center, functioning as the spokes of a gossamer wheel, creating an almost perfect circle. Uncountable finer threads connected the spokes, defining a flexible plane.

He posed the question: how to find Anastasia, lost somewhere in dozens of square miles of rugged terrain? He strove to descend again into the dreamtime as he usually did, an effortful movement through layers of consciousness.

Then the world began to look different. The fibers of the web were not simply there, they were *vibrating* with life. Every kiss of the breeze caused waves to flow through it. When a butterfly flew within a few inches of the web's surface, each beat of the wings caused ripples to form in the web and radiate outward. The waves moving along the web affected the cattails the support lines were connected to. And when the cattails moved in the wind, their motion was finely echoed in new waves created in the web. All this had always been there, but now he could *see* it, as the psilocybin made itself manifest.

As he studied the web from a few inches away, he noticed the orb weaver start to move across the tensile structure. It was clear she was picking up information at each touch. Each leg was feeling and responding to the motions of the threads. And the spider herself was creating ripples which flowed to the edge of the web, then caromed off the cattail stalks and came back across.

The tinkling music of the stream flowed outward, struck the rock behind him, and echoed back into his sensitive ears. The buzzing of the bees sounded near, then far, then near again. Up above, songbird calls sounded, repeated, transmogrified, multiplied.

The interconnectivity of everything was astonishing.

He was rapidly falling toward a fugue state. His sense of self was fading like an irrelevant memory as all his attention was caught up in simply seeing and knowing and *enjoying* the muchness and manyness of life. He could hardly even remember his goal, but his urgent love for Anastasia punched through his euphoria with a final articulation of his question.

How can you speak to someone who is lost in the *anywhere*? And the universe answered in its vast benevolence. Send your voice *everywhere*.

Death Rage

Death Rage finished cleaning her gear and slipped out under the rim of their basket house to look around the ship for a bit. She noticed they were gliding through a stretch of very placid water, so she decided to take this opportunity to sing her daily liturgy.

Tucking herself between two large reed cups, she laid herself on her belly, gazing down at the smooth and serene surface of the river. Then she sang quietly:

> "*I see you*
> *You see I*
> *On this journey*
> *You and I*
>
> *Now we will do*
> *I and you*
> *The things that*
> *Make the world*"

City of Oom

After a few minutes of contemplation, she got up and went back to the basket house. Throat Punch was carefully sharpening her greatsword. She looked up as Death Rage slipped under the rim.

"Doing your daily thing?"

"Yup," said Death Rage.

Throat Punch cocked her head. "Why don't you pray to your Gramsy and Grampsy, like most mice do?"

Death Rage always dreaded this question. She sat down and started oiling her rapier. "Because they've gone over the Very Seedy Bridge and can't help me," she said carefully.

Throat Punch looked shocked. "Don't you love them?" she asked.

"Of course I do," said Death Rage. "They were kind and loving people, but they can't hear me if I ask them anything. So I don't ask."

Throat Punch thought about this as she plucked stray cotton fibers off her greatsword. "Then who do you sing your daily hymn to?"

"I'm singing in communion with The One Who Makes The World," said Death Rage.

Throat Punch looked confused. "Who is that?"

Death Rage wiped her rapier down with her cotton boll. She turned and looked at Throat Punch, finally. "If you have to ask, you're not ready to know."

Just then, there was a loud rapping on the basket. They rolled out under the rim to find Captain Hodgepodge standing over them. "Time for your galley shift," he said. He seized the two mice by their scruffs and began to march them across the deck.

"What even is a galley?" asked Throat Punch, as she was half-dragged along.

"The kitchen," said the captain, as he chewed a dark wad of leafage. He opened a hatch and they looked down to see a thick rat surrounded by an array of fruit, carrion, insect eggs, and other ratty foodstuffs. "Cookie," he said. "Here're your assistants for the day."

The rat, looked up and smiled, showing long brown teeth. "Lovely," he said. "We've got a big batch of fresh maggots that need to be whisked with a rosemary-lemon mélange."

Anastasia

Anastasia was gnawing fiercely at the dead palm tree when the pups started whining again. Another day had passed. She was almost through. She could hear the wood crack when the wind blew. The laboring calmed her. And it also helped keep the crushing loneliness from devouring her. The snug passages of *Sans Gloire* were ever on her mind, filled with small warm furry bodies and oceans of love.

The cries of the pups grated on her nerves. She turned and looked toward the other side of the grove. She could see the puppies, wobbling on their squat legs, their golden fur smeared with mud. One of them was licking the rough hole she had torn in the coconut, even though she could see even from a distance that it was dry. The other two were feebly gnawing at a larger coconut. Of course, it was defeating their soft, tiny teeth. All of them were quietly making miserable noises, calling for a mother who would never come.

She lolloped forward and stood, half-hidden behind a

City of Oom

coconut, unsure of what she should do. Or even wanted to do. The eldest pup noticed her moving shape and came toward her, zigzagging down the beach on shaky legs. The other two trailed after.

As the baby wolf came near to Anastasia, she tried to touch noses with her. Anastasia pulled back. Then the pup said, "Thank you for milk," in her soft baby voice. A moment later, on the cold riverbank, she lay down next to Anastasia, snuggling into the rabbit's lean body. A few seconds after, the other two pups arrived and curled around her, hungry for warmth.

Their wolfy scent surrounded her. It was a smaller, fainter version of the predator scent her ancestors' bodies had taught her to fear. And as she breathed in the smell of their shivering bodies, she could see their future selves, who were coming, bounding toward her. They would *be here* in a matter of weeks. And small and helpless as they were now, the day would come when they could choose to kill her and her life would be in their hands.

The voice did not speak. It did not need to. The atavistic fear of the murdering wolf pack was tearing at her, the chemicals in her body roaring at her to run run *run*. She took a deep, gulping breath, then got jerkily to her feet and bounded away from the crying puppies.

In a few steps, she was back at the dead palm, and she attacked it fiercely. She just wanted to *get out*. Her teeth ripped through the brittle wood. A gust of wind came down the gully, and the tree leaned, swinging back and forth several times. Then there was a loud crack and it fell, toppling over and coming to rest against the stone ledge far above her head.

Death Rage

Death Rage was sleeping soundly under their overturned basket when she was startled awake by Captain Hodgepodge whacking the outside of the basket with a stick.

"Look alive, shorelubbers! We'll be at City of Oom in a few minutes." Death Rage leaped up, wiping her eyes and tripping over Throat Punch's still sleeping form. She rolled out under the lip of the basket to find the sun was bright in a cloudless sky. And the day was surprisingly warm.

"We're going to the docks in Dirty Town," said the rat captain. "You need to go in through the main gate of the City, or they'll run you out later when they find you."

Her mind awhirl, Death Rage, managed to get out. "Where's the main gate?"

"We'll drop you on the riverbank on this side of the Rime," said Captain Hodgepodge. "Go west til you find the old road, then turn right and look for the city gate." He stumped away. "Shake a leg, mouses! You're going over the gunwale in ten minutes, ready or no."

Death Rage dashed back under the basket and began to grab her things. Throat Punch sat up and yawned.

"Sorry to interrupt your beauty sleep, princess," said Death Rage as she buckled on her bottlecap helmet. "Pack up. They're throwing us off the boat in two shakes of a mouse tail."

"Don't 'princess' me," said Throat Punch. "Last night you were snoring like a dragonfly in heat. A girl couldn't catch a wink in here." She scooped up her gear and started stuffing it into her backpack.

A few minutes later, they were standing on the port side of the ship, as the gentle curves of the SPANX sails billowed above them. The ship was angling in close to the shore, which was reedy marsh interspersed with cottonwood trees and willows. They were surprised to see that the rat crew had come to see them off. Throat Punch looked around for a gangplank. Then, as they came within two feet of the marshy ground, the rats picked them both up, did a couple of rhythmical swings, and with a "heave-heave-ho," tossed them toward the land.

Death Rage almost made it, but still got her feet wet. Throat Punch, with her heavier greatsword weighing her down, fell short and was completely dunked in the icy water. A few moments later, they both stood spluttering and shivering on the wet ground.

"Pretty casual attitude toward service," said Throat Punch, shaking out her wet fur. "I'm going to have to say 'three stars.'"

"At least this helps wash off the smell of the maggot mélange," said Death Rage, wiping off her rapier.

They set out across the marshy woodland, clambering up fallen dead reed stalks to cross numerous creeks and inlets, and in a few hundred yards came out on a sturdy floodplain grown up with broad elm trees. They soon found themselves trekking through a dense understory of wild grape and Virginia creeper, clotted with the remnants of dirty snow. After a few minutes of this, they found a long trail of dark, crumbly stone, leading through the center of the wood. Many plants were growing up thorough it, including whole trees, but the long thirty-foot-wide gray streak continued in both directions as far as the eye could travel. It was like nothing else they had ever seen.

"This must be the 'road,'" said Death Rage. "Some kind of Dead Gods thing." She led them to the right, and they scampered along the ancient highway. In spite of the hurried awakening, Throat Punch was in good spirits and began to sing a song about her favorite nut.

"A walnut on a winter's day
A nibble in a storm
It takes away the cold
And it makes your belly warm."

In a few minutes, they came to the edge of the wood and had their first sight of City of Oom. Looking down the road, they could see a hill rising out of the flat floodplains. And it was swarming with astonishing shapes. It seemed so alien, they instinctively crouched down behind a creeper leaf as they stared, open mouthed.

In her short life, the closest Death Rage had come to seeing any building was the bunker created by Magdalenium's survivalist family. It was filled with straightstone, which she knew to be a favorite of the Dead Gods, but it was also underground, which suited her understanding of living spaces. Even the fine families of Sunflower Hill lived in luxurious palaces dug in and around wonderful construction detritus that had been buried by leaf litter and time. Underground was where you lived, loved, raised families, and conducted business. Which meant underground was where you built.

So when the two mice looked at the hill covered with the buildings of the Dead Gods, they had no idea what they were seeing. It was made more confusing by the fact that this

City of Oom

walled compound had been built by the Dead Gods in the early twenty-second century, when two architectural schools were colliding and melding. One was *Neo Futurism*, beloved of airport designers. And the other was *Nouveau Revival,* in which the Dead Gods, already terrified by the changes that climate change was wreaking, sought to propitiate the nature gods by building with organic shapes and covering their buildings with oversized leaves and gigantic butterflies.

So the physical plant of City of Oom was the apotheosis of *Futurist Nouveau*. And to country mice seeing the city for the first time, it looked like a dream. Or a hallucination.

They stood side by side, staring at the wild whirl of shapes.

"I don't want to go in there," whispered Throat Punch.

Death Rage bit her lip and whispered, "Neither do I."

She adjusted her helmet chinstrap, and Throat Punch snugged her scabbard. Then their little fingers touched, accidentally, and curled around each other.

Looking straight ahead, Throat Punch said, "We're going to see beautiful things."

Death Rage turned and looked at her. "And bears."

Mabel

Mabel awoke in the bright morning to find that last night had not been some kind of nightmare. The fear was still strong in her and lay like a heavy stone in her gut. She noticed Sunbeam's right ear was still bleeding where the weasel had bitten a notch out of it, and she now lay groaning quietly in her sleep.

Mabel slowly crept out of their hollow log sleeping chamber and into a bright sunshiney day. There was a hint of sulfur in the air. She sniffed anxiously as the strange smell, then went to find some spider web to press on Sunbeam's wound to help it heal. She also pulled some strips of bark off a white willow she found down by the river.

The touch of Newly Beloved is the touch of a healer. 'Whithersoever there is pain,' saith she, 'that is where I go.'

When she returned, Sunbeam lay rubbing her paw over the scars on her forehead, a gesture of self-soothing that Mabel had noticed her doing before. Mabel gave her the willow bark to chew for its painkilling effect. Then she pulled the wad of spiderweb off her chest and pressed it against the torn flesh. Once it was well stuck on, she took some tufts of soft fur from her flanks and gently patted them on the injury to soak up the fresh blood and stop the bleeding. Sunbeam winced and caught her breath a few times as Mabel did this, but she did not cry out. Then the younger bunny pressed some spiderweb against the lacerations on Mabel's face and belly.

Having finished the care that they were able to render, the two bunnies lay in the sun outside their hollow log, soaking up the small amount of warmth shining down. Mabel was still trying to push down the panic that had seized her last night and refused to let her go. After they lay quietly for awhile, she took a deep breath and said, "Thank you for saving my life."

After a long while, Sunbeam said, "That's what I was born to do."

Mabel, surprised by this answer, turned to look at Sunbeam. "What?"

Sunbeam lay without moving. "Mommy explained it all to me when I was a kit. When a warren needs a destroying

City of Oom

angel, they choose a young one and train them up in the ways of killing. It's a great honor."

Mabel turned on her side and looked at her. She laid her paw on the younger bunny's forehead and stroked it. "And who were you sent to kill?"

Sunbeam opened her eyes and looked directly at the sun. "Anastasia."

Even after what they had just been through, Mabel felt a wave of horror sweep over her. *Was there anything that monster Olympia would not do?* "Oh, baby girl, no," she murmured, as she rubbed Sunbeam's cheek. "Your mother was wrong to do that. She was *wrong*."

"In the end, I didn't have to," said Sunbeam. "Which was good, because it made me sick, thinking about..." She stopped talking, and drew a long shuddering breath. "But Mommy said I was helping Dah, so if I had to do it, I should be glad."

Mabel rolled toward the younger bunny and snuggled against her. "Dah doesn't need your help," she said fiercely. "Not then. Not now. Not *ever*."

Sunbeam turned on her side, away from Mabel. "I don't want to talk about it anymore."

Mabel kissed her, and then sat up. Her gaze swept the redwood forest around them. "The question for us is: should we go on? We don't have the map anymore, but if we follow the river upstream, we're probably going in the right direction." Sunbeam seemed disinclined to talk, so Mabel just continued on. Talking about plans seemed to help manage her fear. "Was that thing last night some kind of attack by *Les Enchantés?* Or maybe they were being attacked. Or maybe it has nothing to do with them."

She stood up and started to pace. Movement also made her feel less afraid. "Anastasia would not have sent us to a tribe of known killers. But they might kill—probably *do* kill—as needed." She stopped and looked down. "Just like us." She chewed her lip. "It seems dangerous, but if we turn back now, we're failing Loving Auntie and Free Nation. And they'll just have to send someone else, because we're desperate, and—"

"Auntie Mabel?" said Sunbeam, with her eyes closed. "The world is full of monsters. That's not a reason to let down our friends." She turned over and looked at the older bunny.

"Let's go on."

Chapter 11

I'm not just hiding nuts, I'm planting trees.
—The Squirrel Affirmations

Freddie

The woods around the foot of the Stone Stair were abuzz with activity. Based on his dreamtime vision, Freddie had scouted out eleven pairs of young trees that could be turned into stone throwers. And now the hundred raccoons sent by Nicodemus were swarming over the site and the surrounding area.

Some were gathering agave fiber and braiding it into rope and netting. Others were climbing the trees with saws from the straightstone burrow and the bunker, lopping off limbs to clear a path so the ropes and netting could move freely. Others were gathering stones about the dimensions of an apple, which Freddie had determined to be the best size, dragging them to the site in their many travois.

At the top of the Stone Stair, the coyotes could still be seen lounging around, indulging in microhowls and calling out insults to the *"viande à dîner"*[22] below. Wendy had long since stopped wasting quarrels on them, so they were getting bolder.

"I'll take the big hairy one," called one coyote. "With plenty of mustard."

"I'll have two skinnies," called another one. "I like 'em crunchy."

Freddie was standing by a stump, supervising, chewing on his daily Saint-John's-wort as he referred to a sketch he had drawn on a clay tablet the raccoons had made for him. It was a slab of clay on a flat piece of slate. He could draw on it with a claw, and it was fitted with two shoulder straps so he could carry it like a backpack. He rubbed his paw over Anastasia's bite mark on his neck as he made notes. It was healing, and there was almost no pain now. But touching it was almost like touching her. It soothed him to do it.

Stan fluttered in over his shoulder, landing on the stump. "You rang?"

Freddie nodded. "Yes, thank you." He leaned close to him. "I think I have an idea that will help find Loving Auntie."

Stan looked surprised. "Your mouth to the Big Bird's ear."

"Now this may sound crazy, but tell me if you think it's possible," said Freddie.

Stan groomed his feathers and settled in to listen. "Gimme the deets."

---

[22] Lunchmeat

City of Oom

"You've talked about how much songbirds like to learn and share new songs," said Freddie. "What if we seed the upland songbirds with a song we make up? I know they won't let you fly up there, but your people could fly along the edge of the cliffs within earshot and sing the new song over and over. If they learn it and start repeating it, it could travel from bird to bird, like an infection. And spread over the whole uplands."

"Huh." Stan squinted and ran a wingtip over his balding head. "Maybe ... it ... could work?" he said slowly. "If it's short and bouncy. Easy for these mooks to pick up." He scratched under his wing. "You know, an earworm."

Freddie nodded. "Great to hear. And hopefully, it will spread to where Anastasia is, and she'll hear it."

"Is she gonna understand it?" asked Stan.

"Well, it has to be simple," said Freddie. "And she has to recognize it's meant for her, but it can't have her name in it. We're not sure how organized the bears are getting about songbirds, but we don't want to take any chances."

"Yeah, yeah," said Stan.

"And it has to tell her to make up her own song, so it can travel back to us."

Stan nodded, stroking his chin with wingtip. "So what are you thinking?"

"Something like this," said Freddie. Then he sang:

"Freddie loves you, that's a fact
If you hear this, please sing back"

Stan frowned and hummed it. "Jeez, I dunno..." He murmured it through a few times, tweaking the melody to make it bouncier and more earwormy. "Hmm, maybe..." Then he opened his throat and brightly sang the revised version in a classic songbird musical style.

A few seconds later, a nearby songbird repeated it back. It was a little slurred and not exactly what Stan had sung, but it was understandable.

The rabbit and the bluebird looked at each other. "This ... could ... be a thing," said Stan slowly. He took to the air suddenly and belted it out. A moment later, they heard it echoed back to them from farther out in the wood. Stan dropped onto the stump. "This could be a frickin' *thing*, brother."

DEATH RAGE

City of Oom was a brilliant swirl of shapes under the bright winter sun. The elegant *Futurist Nouveau* buildings of the Dead Gods were bleached a brilliant white, covered with a tracery of deep green vines that had been growing over them for centuries. And the spaces between were grown up with trees and other plants.

Slowly and carefully, Death Rage and Throat Punch walked up the road leading to the main gate. As the mice got closer to the city, they could see that the road led onto a bridge that spanned a fast flowing river, which Captain Hodgepodge had called the Rime. The bridge was flanked with parapets of what looked like stone, with oak leaves and large butterflies swarming over the surface in bas-relief. As they drew close, Death Rage noticed a plaque set into the surface, reading "*Everstone*™ by Additive Artisans®." She sounded out the words, but found she could make little sense of them.

City of Oom

There were some raccoons on the bridge, pulling loads of fruit, handicrafts, and dried fish in travois. Two rats were carrying on an earnest conversation about a thumbtack as they scampered along the parapet. And a group of foxes were lollygagging along one side, talking and laughing. The two mice gave them a wide berth.

Suddenly, Death Rage noticed that all the creatures on the bridge were wearing simple hoop earrings in their ears. She nudged Throat Punch. "Look," she said. "They all look like rat traders."

Throat Punch, who had grown up in a household that regularly bought and sold from these traveling peddlers, nodded. "Ya, that City thing. Don't know why they do it."

"Helps keep you from getting eaten," said Death Rage.

As they approached the far side of the bridge, the wall loomed over them. It looked to be about twenty feet high, and its ornate surface was pocked with holes and scars. There was a large gateway set into the wall, and an elegant arch spanned the roadway, with images of apples, oranges, nuts, wheat, corn, and other foodstuffs scattered across it.

There were a few metal letters set into the arch, in a tall graceful typeface that Death Rage had never seen before. It looked as though there had once been many more letters, but the ones that remained spelled out, "CITY OF OOM." The area around the name was covered with many small indentations that the Dead Gods would have recognized as being caused by machine gun fire. Of course, that meant nothing to the mice.

Below the arch was an elegant guardhouse. Leaning on a small counter by a window was a raccoon, sharpening a collection of quill pens with a tiny blade. He looked up as the mice approached.

"Whuzzup?" he asked. "Visitor or resident pass?"

The mice looked at each other. "Visitor?" said Death Rage, uncertainly.

The raccoon looked around. "Who's vouching for you?"

"What?" said Death Rage.

"You need one resident to vouch for you to get a visitor pass, dude," said the raccoon. "Did you yak your homies?"

Death Rage looked sideways at Throat Punch. "Oh, totally," piped up the younger mouse. "We yakked ... a *bunch* of homies."

"But they're not here," said the raccoon.

"No," said Throat Punch. "And boy, I'm going to give them a piece of my mind."

"Mmmm." The raccoon turned to a large collection of paperbark sheets next to him, loosely bound with metal rings. "Resident name?"

"Bricabrac," said Death Rage.

The raccoon flipped through the thick pages, then stopped and ran his claw down a page. "Right, here he is. Aaaand he's in town." The raccoon looked up at them. "You have three days to find him and bring him to the Pass Board." He looked at them seriously for a moment. "Do not fail to do this. No pass. No protection."

"Got it," said Death Rage, as she adjusted her helmet.

The raccoon chose a very fine quill from his collection and dipped it in a small bottle of ink. "Come around to the side door please."

The mice did so. The raccoon stepped out and knelt

down. He gestured. "Take your helmet off. Hold your right ear steady." Death Rage took hold of her ear tip with her tiny hands. Squinting, the raccoon wrote a number on the inside of her ear.

"What is that?" asked Death Rage.

"That's the number of days since winter solstice," said the raccoon. "That's how we know how long you've been here. If a Municipal Wolf checks your date and finds you've been here three days without a pass, you're in violation of City law." He yawned. "That will be a major bummer. For you."

"So he'll kick us out?" asked Throat Punch.

The raccoon scoffed. "I guess that could happen," he said. "More likely he'll just eat ya."

Anastasia

Anastasia was doing test climbs on the dead palm tree now leaning against the stone ledge far above her head. As a rabbit, she found climbing to be totally alien. She would much rather be below the earth than above it. But this was her way out, so she forced herself to try, again and again.

After awhile, the wolf puppies came and watched, sitting in a small clump a few feet from the tree, and murmuring quietly to themselves.

She took a deep breath and made another foray. The trunk was rough and fibrous, with many leaf stubs sticking out. She could climb it almost like a ladder. She fumbled her way up. The worst part was the fear. The farther she got from the ground, the more she tended to tremble, and that was what made it hard to climb.

So she decided she would only look up. She started up the trunk again, digging in her claws. Up above was the ledge, crowded with carrion bushes. Their big leaves were wide and green, even in winter. And their long purple fruits were heavy, pulling the branches down.

It seemed like she was a third of the way up now. So she must be at least ten feet from the ground. When she had the urge to look down, she stopped and rested her face against the dry leaf stubs. She could feel herself trembling, so she took a few deep breaths, then started up again. Down below, she could hear the pups whining anxiously.

Anastasia crept upward. She was getting close to the top now, and her trembling was getting worse. She tried not to imagine how high she was, and just focused on the ledge. There was the edge. There was the bank of muddy earth. There were the gnarled roots of the bushes.

She knew it was foolish, but she started to hurry. She just wanted this moment to be over. Her paws were shaking violently. One of her back claws slid out of position. She tried to hug the trunk with her forepaws, but the sudden movement loosened her grip and she started to slide. The fear burn rushed over her, and her back feet started to rake the trunk, the same way she would rake the earth in a sudden moment of danger on the ground. But that was the wrong thing to do.

Now loosed from the tree, she was slipping down, and her frantic motions only pushed her farther away. A moment later, she realized she was falling backward through the air, looking up as the ledge and freedom receded and raced skyward.

Then there was an instant of white light and everything went dark.

City of Oom

She opened her eyes to find herself on a beach by a wine-dark sea. A vast spinning roil of eyes, teeth, fur, snouts, and claws was rising out of the water. She knew immediately what it was. She had been here before.

"Anima Mundi," she said, as the chill wind blew in off the sea and made her shiver.

The voice that was made of a thousand voices spoke in its whispering, roaring, cawing unison. "What you think is a burden is really a gift."

"How is it a gift?" asked Anastasia.

"Life calls to life," said Anima Mundi, the multitude of eyes shining. "Love creates love."

Anastasia was shaking with cold. She felt chilled to the bone. "I don't understand."

"When you do what no one else will, it changes everything," said the tumbling spirit.

Anastasia spread her forepaws. "But I don't *know* what to do."

The swirl of paws and clawed feet reached toward her. "I am *you*," came the answer. "*We* know."

A warm breeze blew out from the whirling tumult of life and caressed her cheek. Anastasia leaned into it, hungry for it. A dreadfully hard ache of cold was growing in her innermost core.

"And remember, beloved," said the spinning ball of life energy.

"What?" whispered Anastasia.

The thousand voices spoke. "Breathe."

Anastasia opened her eyes and gasped. High above, the winter sun was shining. She lay in the shallow water just off the gravelly beach, and the cold hand of the rushing stream gripped her like an icy fist.

She managed to turn on her side and drag herself up out of the water. Then she lay, too exhausted to move, with black speckles in front of her eyes, while her body shivered violently. She closed her eyes, too weary to fight on, and sank back toward the big dark.

And then suddenly, there was warmth, all around her. The puppies were kissing her face, her ears. They lay down next to her. The sun broke through the clouds, and made their silver-tipped agouti fur shine.

Anastasia was enveloped in a snug afternoon of cozy. It was warm. It was golden. And it was good.

Freddie

Wendy had insisted they do everything they could to keep the coyotes at the top of the Stone Stair in the dark about the new stone throwers. So Freddie had done his firing tests at another location. And both the trees being trimmed and the stones being gathered were arranged to look as though the *Armée Libre* was building fortifications at the foot of the Stair.

Then, when everything was ready, the raccoons spent a single night quietly getting the ropes and netting in place, pulling the trees back to cock them, and filling the nets with stones. And Love Bug marshaled several squads of rabbits and squirrels, ready to rush up the stairs if there was an opportunity to slip by, with a platoon of songbirds attached for scouting.

In the very early morning, before dawn, the songbirds quietly rose to the top of the cliffs and confirmed that the two dozen coyotes were snoozing, sprawled out over the grassy area around the top landing of the Stone Stair.

Freddie held his breath as he watched Wendy find a place in the moonlight so she could address the troops via paw signs. Most of the *Armée Libre* was at least conversant in this sign language now, and even the raccoon militia members had learned enough to get by.

After covering some basics, and thanking the troops for their hard work, Wendy paused, then thumped her chest twice. *Hooah*.

The several hundred *Armée Libre* members double-thumped their chests in return. *Hooah!*

Wendy touched the right side of her head and extended her paw upward. *Get ready*. The fighters touched their heads twice and lifted their paws. *Ready*.

Then Wendy extended her right paw, pads down, and jabbed the air three times. *Attack*.

A moment later, the raccoons cut the trigger ropes holding the nets back, and the first three stone throwers lofted hundreds of stones into the air. Several seconds later, there was a storm of yelps and whines from the top of the Stone Stair, followed by much angry shouting. Then, at a signal from Wendy, the next three fired. The yelps and the shouting began to disperse as the coyotes raced away from the falling stones.

Freddie had anticipated that the coyotes might run along the cliff edge, so he had built flanking stone throwers on each side that would cover the areas fifty yards away on each side.

Wendy fired those now, and the coyote yells fell back away from the edge. The other three were held in reserve. The raccoons immediately started filling the stone thrower nets with more rubble. The songbirds rose to scout the area, and came back singing that the area around the top of the stair was empty, with the coyotes running around in a panicked and enraged swarm several hundred yards away from the cliff edge.

Love Bug and his hand-picked squads dashed up the Stone Stair and raced along the cliff edge toward the Braided Gorges to look for the Loving Auntie.

Mabel

As the rabbits walked upstream along the Rime River, the land got hillier, and the redwoods grew closer together. A white mist clung to them. Soon, even though they knew the sun was shining somewhere up above, they were walking through a white fog.

They could see no more than thirty feet in any direction. There was no path, so they steered by keeping the sound of the Rime River on their right. And they kept their ears cocked for any sound that could be a warning. In addition to the river noise, there was a continual *plip, plip, plip* of water dripping from far above. Other than that, silence.

Walking was painful with the injuries they had sustained in the fight with Saskatoon. They were each carrying willow bark with them in their packs, and they chewed it all through the day for its painkilling effects. Mabel had changed the spiderweb dressing on Sunbeam's ear that morning, but the wound looked as though it might be getting infected. Sunbeam did not complain, but Mabel could tell by the way she winced when it brushed against a leaf or twig that it was getting more painful.

The sulfur smell was gradually growing stronger. It was like nothing Mabel had ever experienced before, with the exception of the time a clutch of songbird eggs in a tree near Tumble Stone Warren had gone rotten.

"What do you think that is?" Mabel asked Sunbeam.

The golden bunny stared at her. "The smell of power?"

"I thought it would smell better," said Mabel, and then lapsed into silence.

And as Newly Beloved walked through the ghostly air, her thoughts were dark thoughts. The smell of monsters was everywhere, but she durst not turn back, because her captain had entrusted her with this quest. Worst of all, there was no more dirty apple, so she must face her nights alone, and—

"Did you hear that?" whispered Sunbeam, nose bumping her shoulder.

"What?" asked Mabel.

Sunbeam put her right paw up, pads forward, in the *stop and hush* sign. Mabel stopped moving and cocked her ears. Far in the distance came the sound of laughter. But it was a kind of laughing that Mabel had never heard before. A mixture of bass and soprano, floating through the air as a grinding rumble mixed with interjections of soprano squeaks and yelps. "Sounds like at least a couple of ... people?" she hazarded.

"Maybe those are *Les Enchantés*," said Sunbeam.

"Maybe," said Mabel. "Or maybe the things from the other night." She chewed her lip. "I'd say bite blades up, just in case." The two rabbits armed themselves and then went forward cautiously. Mabel started to rehearse her greeting speech again in her head. *We are peaceful travelers from a distant land, and a great problem has been laid upon us. We seek your wisdom because—*

There was the laugh again. Closer. It died away and the silence rushed in. *Plip, plip, plip.* Then there was another laugh, from a different quarter. And then a third. So there were several of them. Mabel felt the hairs on the back of her neck stand up. The sound of the voices suggested small bodies.

Mabel stopped walking. "They sound young," she whispered to Sunbeam.

"Or maybe they're just small, like weasels," said the other bunny.

Mabel shuddered. Another laugh came from surprisingly nearby. It was maddening not to be able to see in the mist.

Is there a whole pack of them? thought Mabel, feeling a fear burn creep up her legs. They could hear movement in the understory now, and it sounded close. Mabel took a step closer to Sunbeam. There were at least several creatures moving.

Mabel's nerve broke, and she let herself be swept up by a rabbit's first instinct and ran. Sunbeam was hot on her heels. They tore through the misty, cathedral-like forest as the laughs echoed on every side. Eventually, the laughter receded into the distance and they were racing through their bubble of white space all alone, in silence except for the sound of their harsh breathing and the leaves crackling under their feet.

After a few minutes, they stopped near a tinkling brook and stood, panting and squinting into the uncaring fog. When Mabel's breathing had slowed enough, she leaned down and took a drink from the stream. When she lifted her head, she saw Sunbeam staring at something, eyes huge.

She turned and saw a large white shape looming forward

out of the mist. It was much bigger than any animal she had ever seen. The smell of sulfur was strong, and so was the smell of their own fear.

ALIYAH

Aliyah felt as though she had been forced through a tiny space, struggling and thrashing, while her fur and even her skin had been scraped off, leaving her naked and cold, with every touch a burning hot fire. Everything had been stripped away, her world, her life, all those whom she had loved.

Then she had spent eons swimming upward through a murky gloom. She had been lost for days, but she had a memory of a voice calling her. Slowly, she had gotten her bearings, and swum toward the light, powered by a tumble of invigorating rage against death and a fierce yearning for life. Now she felt leaner, more compact, more agile. So many encumbrances were now stripped away. Dark forces had taken her clan. The storm had taken her children and Grammy Kark. But the memory of her family felt small and orderly, like a box of precious gems she could choose to look at when she wished, and choose to put away when she wished.

She was reborn. Everything was new. Everything had to be decided. So everything *could* be decided. She felt strong and alive, and she wanted to act. After her long visit to death, the ability to *do* seemed unutterably precious.

Now she was standing on a high hill, blinking under the winter sun. The touch of the wind on her face was electric in its intensity. The colors around her looked bright as fire. Possibilities came rushing at her. "Maybe I will roam the wide world. I will be the last golden wolf. My life will be simple and pure." She pawed the earth. "Maybe I will go to the City," she said. "I will join the wolves. I will be a soldier in the greatest army in the Known World. I will fight. That is how I will honor the memory of my loves." She looked up at the sun. "Maybe I will—"

She suddenly realized she was speaking to someone, and turned to see who it was. Her gaze fell on a coyote she knew. It was Gaetan. But he looked different. He no longer had the hangdog look she remembered. His ochre eyes were bright, his mien relaxed. He was gazing at her intently.

A question arose in her. "Someone helped me," she said. "Someone called me out of the darkness." She took a few steps toward him, her green eyes brilliant. "Who did that?"

He looked down for a moment. Then his eyes flicked up and held hers. "Me."

Chapter 12

Are you kwee-kwee-koo this morning?
Come and chirr-chirr in my tree
We can ko-ah-kway together
When you lee-loo next to me
    —*Traditional love call of the red-crested warbler*

DEATH RAGE

As Death Rage and Throat Punch passed under the arch into City of Oom, they immediately found themselves on a wide boulevard. Buildings with ornate facades featuring nature motifs lined both sides of the street, and trees and other plants were growing up through the everstone pavement in many places. Vines were hanging off the buildings, with the bleached white surfaces showing through in high contrast under the bright sun.

And everywhere were animals in the midst of city life.

"Walleye! Getcher walleye here!" shouted a raccoon with a basket of fresh fish for sale. "Don't fill up on junkfish. Get the good stuff!" A middle-aged coyote stopped to haggle over the price.

"Weaselpalooza!" called a brown-and-black weasel, handing out small pieces of paperbark. "At the Big Bowl tonight! Who's gonna get voted off? Come get yer shimmy on!" A red-tailed hawk coasting low and fast over the crowd dropped down to heckle the weasel, and ended up leaving with a piece of paperbark in its beak.

The two mice stared about themselves in wonder as they gingerly made their way down the street. They had never heard so much racket in one place.

A pleasant-faced young mouse approached them. "Are you happy with your claws?" she asked, conspiratorially.

"What?" said Throat Punch, startled.

The mouse clucked sympathetically. "Just in from out of town?" she asked, shepherding them toward a small shop. "Treat yourself to a spiff." They arrived at an area where several raccoons, foxes, and squirrels were lying on moss beds while teams of energetic young mice busily attended to their feet. Some were rubbing a light oil perfumed with sage on tired paw pads. Others were sharpening claws with pieces of sandstone and then buffing them to a high shine with pussy willow puffs.

"Ten cents for first timers." The mouse wrinkled her nose in an engaging grin. "I think you deserve it, don't you?"

Throat Punch looked hopefully at Death Rage. "Ermmm, thanks," said Death Rage, taking Throat Punch by the elbow and steering her away from the salon area. "We'll think about it."

They continued down the street, passing a building with

City of Oom

many open balconies, all decorated with giant bas-relief caterpillars. On one balcony they could hear a group of young crows chanting in unison under the direction of an older crow with graying feathers.

> "*A is for Apple*
> *They're dirty and sweet*
> *B is for Bear*
> *They fill up the street*
> *C is for Crow*
> *Just like my teacher*
> *D is for Duck*
> *A mythical creature.*"

Her mind awhirl, Death Rage whispered to Throat Punch, "Let's try to find where rats go. Bricabrac can help us get passes. Then we can plan our next step." Throat Punch nodded, and they crept down the edge of the boulevard together, trying to stay out of the way of the many large animals who were in constant motion around them.

As they went, Death Rage slowly became aware that a raccoon with a scar on the side of his muzzle was looking at them as he walked. Then he adjusted his course so that instead of walking past them, he was angling toward them. Since they had already been buttonholed by several street vendors, this didn't seem dangerous. Still, attention was always potential bad news, so she nudged Throat Punch with her elbow to make sure she noticed.

Just as they came abreast, the raccoon suddenly sidestepped and made a grab at them. The mice yelped and dodged away, taking shelter under a large mass of roots growing out of a nearby tree that had pushed up through the pavement.

The raccoon knelt down to look under the roots. He grinned, and his yellow teeth shone. His breath was hot and rank. "Ya, I was right. No passes, lil dudes. Thanks for joining my personal ecosystem."

He reached under the root and started groping for them, his wide black palm feeling around. "Country meeses. Gotta love 'em," he chuckled to himself.

Death Rage retreated to the shadows. Throat Punch drew her greatsword and nervously slashed the air in front of her.

"Thank you for your donation!" she shouted.

The raccoon saw the tiny metal blade flashing and frowned. "Ooo, that looks hurty." He withdrew his big gray-and-black paw, and started stirring through the tree litter nearby. But he stayed kneeling in front of the roots, so they could not run out.

"What are you doing with that thing, mowing hay?" barked Death Rage. "Can't you put the point of your weapon someplace useful?"

"It's a greatsword," snapped Throat Punch. "I'm a slasher, not a dancer."

"With bigs, you have to surprise them," hissed Death Rage. "As soon as they see your weapon, they will take other measures. Once it's straight head to head, you will always lose."

"Well, that's not fair," said Throat Punch.

"Nothing is fair!" shouted Death Rage.

The raccoon sounded like he had found something helpful. They saw the lower body shift as he reached out and picked something up. Then a big stick came sliding under the roots. The raccoon leaned down and squinted into the shaded area as he swept the stick across the space, trying to catch them and push them out.

Once he seized them, it would be over quickly. Death Rage could see the hubbub of the boulevard just a few feet away. They had just arrived here: what a pointless way to die. Randomly killed. Nothing accomplished. She raked through her memory for anything that might help.

Suddenly, she remembered the night she had freed Bricabrac from the jar where the rabbits had imprisoned him. He had embraced her and whispered in her ear: *"If you are ever in dire need and a rat can help, say these words."*

She was in dire need. Maybe a rat on the boulevard would hear. Still dodging the stick that the raccoon was sweeping around, she got as close as she could to the street and yelled out:

"O Camembert, O muffin crumbs, O ripe food service slurry.
I bear the name of Rat Friend, and I need help in a hurry!"

Nothing happened. The stick came through the shadows again. This time, since she was distracted, it caught her across the leg. She groaned as she limped away from it. Throat Punch was now trying to rush forward and stab the raccoon's hands, but he was too canny to allow that.

It was just a matter of seconds now. Death Rage stumbled toward the street and shouted again:

"O Camembert—"

"I got you," came a voice. A young rat materialized out of the crowd. The crown of her head was cropped close, leaving just a strip of long fur as a tiny mohawk. And there were tears tattooed under each eye, with her light tan fur shaved over the tears so they were visible.

"Amoxicillin," she called. "Sorry, you're gonna have to find another snack. I'm vouching for these two."

"What?" Amoxicillin the raccoon looked very disappointed. "But I was just jonesing for country mousie."

The rat walked up to the raccoon and stood with her hands on her hips, looking up at him. "Rat Friends," she said. "Call for help must be honored. Rattus Rattus, *High Code of Craft & Ethics.*"

"Awww, Crapola!" said Amoxicillin, throwing down his stick in disgust. "That is gnarly, man. You're harshing my mellow."

Crapola reached up and patted his leg. "Thanks, Mox."

"Get your dirty little hands off me," said the raccoon.

Crapola pulled her hand back. "Right, right." Then she looked at Death Rage and Throat Punch and jerked her head toward the street. "Let's get your passes."

A few moments later, they were threading their way down the boulevard toward the Pass Board while the two mice offered profuse thanks.

Crapola brushed off their heartfelt words. "Don't thank me, just being a rat." She adjusted her black echeveria leather vest which had a single large clothespin across the back. "Who gave you the call sign?"

"Bricabrac," said Death Rage.

"Oh ya, I know that little toad," said Crapola. "Typical rat bro. Not quite the crafting genius he thinks he is."

"Well, he's been very helpful to... to... us ...." Death Rage stuttered and stopped as she realized she was about to start blabbing about Bricabrac and the history of Free Nation and blowing their cover.

Crapola didn't seem to notice. They arrived at a building covered with carved oak leaves and acorns with a large metal loop over the door. They went inside and found a sleepy raccoon behind a counter.

"Two for Visitor Passes," said Crapola. "I'm vouching."

"Gotcha," said the raccoon. He gestured at a tiny stairway that would bring the mice onto his countertop. They ran up. "Lay your head here. Just relax."

He got out a nail and small hammer, and positioned the tip of the nail against the inside of Death Rage's left ear.

Throat Punch, watching, rubbed her own ears nervously. "Does it hurt?" she asked.

The raccoon gave her some side eye. "No," he said, and then banged his hammer.

Death Rage had never yelled so loud.

Anastasia

Anastasia was sitting under the agave plants, ripping fibers out of the long leaves with her teeth. She wanted to try climbing the tree by the ledge again, but she was afraid to. So she was harvesting and braiding fibers to make a safety rope. Her plan was to throw a stone with her rope attached over the limb of a sturdy carrion bush on the ledge, and use that to belay herself as she climbed, holding the free end of the rope in her strong jaws.

The pups were at the far end of the island, under the winter pear trees. She gazed at them as she worked. Her loneliness was rushing in at her. She longed to see Wendy's broad scowling face and hear her cryptic grunts. To cringe at Love Bug's awful jokes. To feel Freddie's warm kisses.

She tried to push off the bleakness by thinking about her conversation with Anima Mundi. What was the thing that no one else will do? Did she want to change everything? She had already changed a lot. Sometimes she felt elated by the changes she had been able to make. Other times she felt exhausted by them.

The puppies wanted to be near her. Of course they did. They were likely orphans, cast by happenstance on a deserted isle. Every instinct they had cried out for their mother. And since she was not there, a replacement mother. A source of food, warmth, kisses, wisdom.

Anastasia finally let herself consider things she had been avoiding. These were golden pups. They must be part of the Summerday Clan. Who had survived the Battle of the Narrows? The rabbits didn't know every Summerday Clan member, but they knew enough to realize that the famous Aliyah Summerday was not among the dead.

So she must have escaped, found a mate, created these children. Where was she now? Since the pups had been in the water, close to drowning, Aliyah likely had been, too. She would have been near her children and tried to save them. So she had likely been pulled in. She might have drowned. Or she might have been swept to the end and thrown out into the air, a hundred feet above a waterfall splash basin. Or she might be in the one of the narrow canyons, marooned somewhere, just like Anastasia was.

City of Oom

The brown bunny shivered at the thought of a big hungry golden killer stalking through the Braided Gorges. Surely, a grown wolf could not survive until summer, when Anastasia might be trying to walk out.

Of course, the survival of these pups was also uncertain. Even if they devoured her, that would be a single meal, not enough for months.

Could they get fish from the stream? Did wolves do that? Anastasia realized she knew so little about the ordinary lives of wolves. She saw them as enemies and did her best to fight them. What it would be like to simply live with them, she had no idea.

Something was nagging at her. What was the gift? Where was the opportunity? What was the undone thing? The idea slipped into her mind so quietly that she hardly noticed it, until it suddenly ran across the forefront of her consciousness.

What was the thing that no one else would do?

Love these children.

She immediately scoffed. What an absurd notion. Love the ones who would be driven to kill her in a matter of weeks? Insanity. Or at best, a strange fable best told in a snug burrow on long winter nights. And how could you just love someone anyway? That couldn't be done on demand. Love was elusive, not biddable. It followed its own unknowable course.

Then a vision of what that might mean for Free Nation came to her.

Could a killer be ... tamed? Could a killer live among the Free Animals without killing them? It was perhaps not as absurd as it seemed on its face. Ordinary raccoons killed mice. Free Nation raccoons agreed not to, because it was in their interest to do that. They—mostly—abided by that agreement.

The pups came running toward her, surrounding her, nuzzling her. She opened another coconut for them, and they gathered around it, drinking the rich milk, tumbling over each other, playfighting in their clumsy way. Anastasia rested her golden eyes on them as they fed and rough-housed. They were getting stronger.

She had not thought much about the endgame of her struggle with predators. The immediate goal had been survival. For herself, then a few, then many, then a nation. They were defending themselves now. Dug in, built out, hunkered down. They could probably do this for a long time. But what lay beyond that? The endless years of war stretched out. For centuries. Forever.

It was wearying to think about. She was no warrior queen. What she really wanted was a quiet burrow by a little waterfall, with baby creatures growing up around her.

So what was the gift? Could these wolflings be a way out of the forever war? Maybe a window onto the peaceable kingdom. An experiment. An example. That was the crux. If it could be done once, it could be done a thousand times. A million times. Every time.

Their feeding done, the little wolves came and gathered around her. Their warm bodies felt good. She felt less lonely. As their scent enveloped her, the voice of her ancestors awoke and joined the conversation in her head.

Talk, talk, talk, clever one. You have another week to figure out how you will feed these murderers-to-be. Then you will have your last chance to kill them.

Mabel

Mabel stood, frozen, gazing at the white shape emerging from the mist. Her heart pounded. She could feel Sunbeam pressed against her. She had seized her bite blade out of habit, and her teeth chattered against the grip.

Then she caught her breath. The animal that stood before her was a kind totally unknown to her, and it was the most striking creature she had ever seen. Sapphire-blue eyes gleamed in the midst of a coat of thick white hair, which flowed over a massive head of noble proportions and down onto powerful shoulders. The snout was long and elegant, tipped with a large sensitive nose that was even now scenting her. Two gleaming white lower tusks jutted outward, and two more tusks grew down from the upper jaw, then curled upward to create a ripping armament of fearsome power. It was terrifying and beautiful at the same time.

The animal regarded her with a cool and fierce intelligence, but made no move toward her. The scent coming toward her was brisk and bright. The brilliant blue eyes rested on her, unblinking. They seemed to look through her, as though she were insubstantial and they were gazing at something real.

Then she noticed that the sides of the face and shoulders were covered with a filagree of old scars. And there was a new scar that dragged across one shoulder and down the back. It must have been a terrible wound. She trembled a little.

Then it spoke in a language that Mabel had never heard before. The voice was the same curious mixture of bass and treble that she had heard earlier, but much deeper, with a rumble that made her head vibrate. It sounded male.

Another white-haired giant stepped forward out of the mist behind them. Mabel felt her heart rate kick up a notch. Were these *Les Enchantés*? Her mind clicked through the descriptions. *Big. White. Tusks. Scary.* Seemed right. Though it was hard to imagine them as helpful healers.

The urge to run was burning along her back legs, but she stayed still. She had learned early that the act of running is itself enough to create a chase, and she did not want this behemoth chasing her. She glanced at Sunbeam and saw her eyes tracking quickly around the space, even though her body did not move.

Mabel dropped her bite blade—it seemed pointless in the face of this massive killing machine—and struggled to find her voice. "We are from … a distant land and … and…" she was having trouble marshaling her prepared speech. Sunbeam was squirming next to her. "We have a problem … and are hoping…"

Two more of the white giants appeared, so they were now flanked on each side. As her eyes anxiously swept around the group, Mabel noticed that they all had blue eyes, but the shade was different for each one. And they all bore deep scars on their necks and shoulders, some old, some new.

Mable tried to continue her speech as the great ghostly beings stared at her. "With your great wisdom … perhaps you could…" Sunbeam took off running suddenly.

The one with the sapphire eyes rumbled a few words in the unknown language. Two of the creatures leaped away, surprisingly nimble for animals of their size. Through her footpads, she could feel the deep vibrations of their heavy hooves striking the earth, which faded as they disappeared into the distance.

Mabel's nervous system was hot like fire, and the urge to run was almost overpowering. The animal before her raised his hoof, and she saw that it was cloven, like a deer's. He swept it down toward the ground and the message was clear. *Stay*.

A few moments later, the other two appeared. One was carrying Sunbeam by the scruff of her neck. She struggled and grunted, trying to scratch him. He dropped Sunbeam next to Mabel, and the two rabbits huddled together.

The first one came near to them, and Mabel again had the curious sensation that the sapphire eyes were looking through her, that she was, in some way, a distraction. Then he rumbled out the first word she had been able to understand.

"*Come.*"

Death Rage

"If I know Bric, he's at the Speakeasy," said Crapola, as they stood on the boulevard. She pointed down the street.

"Thank you," said Death Rage, touching her bloody ear with its new earring carefully. The mouthful of willow bark she was chewing helped some for the pain, but she wished it was more. Throat Punch wasn't complaining, although she was chewing her wad of willow bark like there was no tomorrow.

"It's in Dirty Town," said the rat. "Look for the sign that says, 'Hygienic Containment District' next to a big 'X'." She paused. "Can you read?"

"Ish," said Death Rage, around her bark wad.

"Lucky you," she said. "Most people can't. If big words are hard, just look for the X. That's what it's for."

The mice nodded.

"The Speakeasy is a little door near the sign," said Crapola as she fluffed her mohawk. "Knock on the window and say the password."

"What is it?" asked Death Rage.

The rat looked at them and leaned into an annoyed eye roll. "*Moneystones are the best revenge.*"

The mice looked serious and repeated the words carefully.

"We're not supposed to leave Dirty Town after dark, so if he's not there now, he def will be later," said Crapola. She started to turn away. "Now get outta here."

"Thank you so much," said Throat Punch. She leaned forward to touch noses with Crapola in a gesture of affectionate farewell.

The rat took a step back. "You don't wanna do that," she said. "You're a city mouse now. Act like it." Then she disappeared into the crowd.

The two mice looked after her, then continued down the street, scurrying along the edge of the buildings so they didn't get stepped on. Soon they were passing through a large square. On the hillside above, a large amphitheater was nestled, overlooking a large round stage. On the top of the hill, raptors swirled lazily, taking off and landing from large perches. And at the highest point of the peak were five redwood trees, planted in a circle.

As they moved through the square, they came across animals doing things they had never seen before. A female fox, her face smeared with white clay and black daubs above and below her eyes, was acting out some kind of battle scene, all by herself, in front of an audience of rapt foxes. She was utterly silent.

As she came to the end of her story, a male fox stepped forward. "That was *My Journey Through Rabbit Rage*," he called. "Please make some noise for Juliette, dogs and vixens." As the audience members beat their paws on the ground and yelped approvingly, three half-grown foxes ran forward with baskets in their mouths, and started collecting moneystones. "Thank you!" called the male fox over the clink of the coins. "Juliette and Isadore. We'll be here all week."

The mice stared in wonder, and then moved on. They soon found themselves on a street, still moving in the direction Crapola had pointed them in. As they walked along, Death Rage nudged Throat Punch and said, "Sorry I yelled at you about your sword, back there with the raccoon." She chewed her paw. "The thing is, you need to learn how to fight big animals, or you're going to get us both killed."

"You're right," said Throat Punch. "And I'm sorry I keep muffing it. I promise I'll listen better from now on."

"Good," said Death Rage.

Then she noticed a wave traveling up the street through the bodies of the animals she could see. All together, quickly, fluidly, the animals were shrinking to the side of the street. They threw themselves on their bellies and covered their eyes. Coyotes, foxes, raccoons, weasels, rats, and mice were all hiding their faces. Even the raptors and crows were laying down and burying their heads under their wings. A low groan arose from the carpet of living creatures. *Why are they doing that?* thought Death Rage.

Suddenly, a large dark shape came around a bend and moved down the street toward them. It was rounded and massive, like a building that had stepped forward and was filling the street with its bulk. Even on a sunny day, it seemed to shade the street with its presence. The movement was like water loosely held in thick fur. Legs like tree trunks lifted, moved forward, and then fell heavily to the ground on thick paws.

The lumbering shape drew closer. Vast currents of power swirled under a tsunami of bronze fur. Deep-set eyes of startling violet swept the area. And then an inundating wave of musk as profound and ancient as the earth itself flowed down the street toward her. Now she knew why the animals were falling on their faces. It was because they could not *not* do it. She was seized by an atavistic terror, and her overriding goal was to avoid being seen. She must not be *noticed*. She could not have this storm cloud thing see her or want to know about her, because just the attention could be *fatal*. This is what her body was telling her, and there was no gainsaying it.

Death Rage pressed herself into a crack where the wall met the pavement, and never had she been so glad to be a small animal. The crack yawned open like a friend and she forced herself into the welcoming darkness of the space. At her toes, she could feel Throat Punch doing the same thing.

Her eyes were closed. She could not risk seeing it.

As the musk rolled over and through her, she felt the slow measured thud of the paws coming down the street, the great bulk blotting out the sun. And she heard the deep and magisterial breath of the living mountain, the earthen god, the owner of all things which she now knew to be the one they called *bear*.

Chapter 13

Leaping bunnies bring diving raptors.
—Rabbit proverb

Gaetan

At first the coyote and the wolf ate winter fruits as Aliyah revived from her long fast in the darkness. Then they hunted a bit and regained their strength. After a few days, they made their way east out of the Braided Gorges area, finding at last the place where the Delf River was single and whole. Then they loped along its banks, moving joyfully over the floodplains, now meadowland dusted with snow, dotted with black willow and silver maple.

After their long sojourn in the land of death over the last hundred days, they felt the freedom to move as a marvelous gift. So they ran. They feasted. Then they lay down under a white oak and gazed out on a world that looked fresh and new.

Gaetan talked about the beauty of the earth. And his love for the knowledge that deepened his understanding of the beauty.

Aliyah spoke of her family. Her love for them. How she would continue to find joy in them, even though she could no longer nuzzle them or smother them in tiny kisses.

"But I've talked enough," she said finally. Her large green eyes fastened on his. "Tell me about your family, Gaetan."

He held her gaze. "*Ma mère*[23] was kind and strong, and her love for me and my sister Lilou had no end. The best memories I have are the many happy nights snuggled in the family den, just the three of us." His smile turned sorrowful. "Then one day she was attacked by a coyote with the chaos plague." He looked out over the river, dark and gray under the iron sky. "His eyes were wild, his mouth thick with drool, and he attacked us without reason. My mother fought like a hellion to protect us. It was then, running from this diseased killer, that I fell from a high place and broke my leg. It never healed right."

Aliyah nuzzled his shoulder as he spoke.

"She saved us from him," he said. "But then the chaos plague took hold in her as well. In time, I watched her change before my eyes. She became a stranger. Just before the killing time came, she drove us away, to save our lives. We didn't know what was happening. We begged to stay with her." His eyes were very dark as he remembered the moment his life was upended by this disease that had terrified even the Dead Gods. "In the end, she leaped from a high cliff before she could hurt anyone else."

---

[23] My mother

Aliyah's large eyes were filled with tears. "I'm so sorry, friend," she whispered. "Your mother was a noble animal." She laid her muzzle next to his. "Shall we raise a totem call to honor her memory?"

Gaetan was surprised and warmed that this mighty creature was moved in this way by his ancient tragedy. "*Je serais très reconnaissant*,"[24] he said.

Aliyah lifted her head and started a slow climb of a howl, phrases rising by sevenths and falling by thirds, the classic canid bereavement motif. Her powerful voice flowed upward with a gentle, aching kind of beauty.

"*Where are you?*
I miss you
I need you
I love you."

Gaetan added his own rougher voice in a splintery harmony, and their voices rose together, soaring over the river valley in a sweet *pas de deux* of the mourning cry.

Anastasia

Anastasia had just finished making her safety rope and attaching the stone to the end. Her shoulders burned from the concentrated effort of braiding the agave fiber using her claws. She stood up and decided to run around her island a few times to loosen up before trying another climb up the tree.

---

[24] I would be very grateful.

Round and round she went, thinking about her plans. Her laps were much more orderly than the high-spirited zoomies that some animals engage in. So the pups were mystified.

"Why you running?" called the biggest wolfling in her soft voice.

Anastasia did not answer. She did not want to start chatting with people she might be murdering in a few days' time.

Then the pup who seemed the youngest started to chase her, trundling after her on his wobbly legs. Of course, she easily outran him, but on her next lap around, he tottered forward and made a playful lunge at her, mouth open.

Anastasia felt an adrenaline burn rush down her back. This was exactly the path she did not want to go down. She spun and faced him. "Stop it!" she said fiercely.

The pup looked abashed and lay down on his belly. He whined anxiously, looking up at her with big eyes. The bigger one ran up. "He's sorry," she said, as she nuzzled him. "Aren't you, Micah?"

Anastasia felt her stomach flipflop at the mention of this name. She stared at the tiny green-eyed killer, and then her eyes slowly tracked up to the other pup's face. "What's your name?" she asked.

"Sephora," said the pup proudly.

A rush of sounds and images whipped through Anastasia's mind. Her time in the pit at the north end of the Narrows, surrounded by the snarls of the killer army, with Micah Summerday's massive golden form looming over her. Sephora Summerday cooing insults at her while she was in the wood and wire cage. Then the two wolves being cut down by her crossbows while Dingus's silver voice rang in her ears. *Let us lay down these golden angels so their blessings may run free.*

The third pup ran up. "I'm Tennyson," he said, with a small tail wag.

That name, at least, rang no alarm bells. They all looked at her expectantly. This might be a moment to say something. What could she say that no one else would, that would change everything? She groped for some wisdom and found that no amazing words were forthcoming, so she said simply, "If you want to be near me, be nice to me."

She lay down on the cool gravel, and Micah bellied down next to her, leaning against her muscular flank. He licked her shoulder and then settled in, tucking his head under her chin. A moment later, Sephora and Tennyson were pressing around her, nuzzling her sides and making soft contented sounds.

It felt so warm and secure. She was hungry for snuggles, and with her own friends far away, she was surprised to find how good it felt. Of course, the killing problem did not vanish, but she did her best to hold it at bay for a moment.

To take her mind off the horde of dark fears, she started listening to the birdsong she could hear faintly from the birds in the trees seventy feet above, at the surface. Birds rarely came down into her narrow gulch, even though there were trees and bushes on her island, and even some fruit. They stayed up at the level of the rest of the world, participating in the ongoing birdsong conversation, in which many singers, many songs, and many ideas jostled for attention.

Her keen ears picked up snatches and fragments flickering across her sky, a kaleidoscope of noise. Then a word pinged against her ear. Familiar, unexpected, and then surprisingly, repeated. Her ears rotated in sync to find the sound. Would it repeat? And she heard it again. Yes. *Freddie.*

Her heart beat faster. *What?* She frowned in concentration, then rose up suddenly, standing up on her back legs to gain the extra inches closer to the singer. The puppies stayed near her, letting out small inquisitive arfs.

Blind to the world, she stood, her total focus on the tiny flickering sounds, broken and garbled, up by the narrow sky. There it was again. *Freddie.*

Why would a songbird sing that name? How would a songbird *know* that name? Or was she dreaming? Was this just some fantasy, her mind playing tricks on her while she went mad, locked in a ditch with dangerous children? It came again. There was more of it now.

Freddie loves you.

Suddenly her heart hurt. She wanted to hear it again. And again. She ran to get her safety rope, then dragged it over to the leaning palm tree. She seized the rope in her mouth, a few feet from the end. Then she whirled the stone around and threw it toward the carrion bushes.

It took more than a dozen tries, but she finally got the stone over a branch. Then she jiggled the other end until the stone worked its way to the edge of the ledge and fell off. Soon she had one end of the rope tied around her middle, and was holding the other end taut in her jaws as she stood at the foot of the palm.

The fall had scared her pretty badly, so she felt her heart start to race as she put her paws on the trunk. Then she heard it again, from far above.

Freddie loves you.

She took a deep breath and began to climb. Quickly, methodically, she climbed the leaf stems like a ladder, moving her grip on the rope to keep it tight. She tried not to think too much about what she was doing. The rope gave her a feeling of safety, so she did not start trembling this time.

Soon she was on the ledge, thirty feet above the island, almost halfway to the sky. The ledge was cluttered with carrion bushes, and the purple fruit reeked of death, as usual, but she ignored them.

She stared up at the narrow ribbon of the world above, focusing all her attention on what was up there. She noticed vines hanging down, the wide, jagged canopy of an oak tree, and a cluster of red-leaved palms growing on one side, their scarlet fronds bright against the silver sky.

She could hear more songs, more competition. Then there was a moment of pause, and in that instant, clear and bright in the air, she heard this song:

"Freddie loves you, that's a fact
If you hear this, please sing back"

She was stunned. She had heard birds sing many things, but always about the lives of birds or big doings in the Million Acre Wood. She remembered them singing about the coyote she had killed. But a personal message? From someone else? Never.

Could it be real? What would that even mean? Could it be Freddie speaking to her? How would he do that? How would he send a bird to her? Downland birds couldn't come up here.

She ran along the ledge, trying to hear it again. As she ran, her back feet were kicking off dead leaves and twigs, and she jostled some windfall carrion fruit and sent it falling to the rocky beach on the island below.

She followed the ledge around the bend and found that it dead-ended suddenly. So it was never going to be a way out. In the excitement of the moment, she hardly registered it.

She cocked her ears and heard the song again. And now a different bird was singing it. Then a third. How was this happening? The melody was bouncy and bright, like songbirds liked. Could they all be singing it? She knew songbirds were constantly picking up new songs, then discarding them. Had Freddie created this and turned it loose in birdworld via the downland songbirds? Or was it some clever snare, created by the many enemies who wanted her dead? A trick to get her to reveal her location?

What should she do?

Death Rage

Death Rage and Throat Punch had lain in their crack for many minutes after the bear had passed. It was unnerving to know that they shared the world with such creatures. Death Rage had heard of bears, of course, but she had been imagining something like a fierce lumpy wolf, not the world-shaker that had just passed.

So, long after the other animals on the street had gotten up and continued about their business, the two downland mice had slowly crept out and shaken themselves off. Then they continued down the street in search of Dirty Town and Bricabrac.

After a few minutes, they began to chat again, to try and regain a sense of normalcy. Throat Punch was talking about the special words that Death Rage had learned which had summoned Crapola so effectively. They were so mysterious and beautiful. After some effusive musing, she said, "What even is 'slurry'?"

"I don't know," said Death Rage. "But it sounds delicious, doesn't it?"

"Mmmm," said Throat Punch. "I could go for some ripe slurry right now."

Death Rage smacked her lips. "Me, too."

Momentarily distracted by fantasies of chunky edible liquids and other aspirational delights, they took a wrong turn without realizing it, and then spent some time wandering the streets of the City. They saw many things they had never seen before, including a shop with a large basket hanging above the door, and a sign saying, "Wicker Flats Reedcraft." They looked inside but saw no sign of Poison Wind.

It was getting toward sunset when they at last saw a sign that said, "Hygienic Containment District" with a big 'X' next to it. The buildings along the street frontage looked like the others in the city, meaning they were crawling with bas-reliefs of plants and animals, but they had also been painted with many iterations of a curious design made of four interlocking circles. It looked as though it had once been red, although now it was faded to a sepia stipple.

And along with the circles, there were words, repeated over and over:

"DANGER BIOLOGIQUE – BIOHAZARD
MIS EN QUARANTAINE JUSQU'À NOUVEL ORDRE
QUARANTINED UNTIL FURTHER NOTICE
RÉPUBLIQUE DU QUÉBEC"

Death Rage's light reading skills were overwhelmed by this strange text, so the mice paid no attention to the sign at all. They did find a small door set into a wall and approached it.

A tiny window in the door slid open as they approached and a dark-faced rat looked out. Death Rage could feel his eyes taking in their bloody ears, new earrings, and generally messy appearance from days of travel. He sucked his teeth.

"Jingle?" he growled.

Death Rage rattled the coins in her backpack.

"Password?"

"Moneystones are the best revenge," piped up Throat Punch.

The rat closed the window without saying anything, and the two mice looked at each other. Then the door opened, and the rat invited them in with a jerk of his paw. As they entered, he said, "Slumming tonight?"

Death Rage had no idea what this meant, so she just nodded noncommittally as she scooted by and headed down a ramp.

"You can freshen up in there," he said, pointing them toward a side chamber.

They followed his gesture and entered a small space where an ancient water tap was dripping over a broken porcelain bowl.

"Let's try not to look like such country bumpkins," said Death Rage.

"I've got a thing or two with me," said Throat Punch.

They took turns washing, and Throat Punch spiffed herself up as best she could, twining the last few dandelion floaties in her backpack around her ears. Then she put on a soft golden shrug woven of autumn yucca fiber with hibiscus accents, which very nicely set off her vermillion-rose fur and contrasted smartly with the ancient metal of her greatsword scabbard. She looked cute as a bug. A very fierce bug.

Death Rage, feeling distinctly underdressed, washed and polished her bottlecap helmet, then buckled it on loosely, pulling it down low over one ear, like a beret. And she borrowed a couple of floaties from Throat Punch to twine about her rapier.

Then they headed down the ramp and found themselves in the main room of the Speakeasy. It was a vast space. On one side of the room was a bar, and the rest of the floor area was filled with an attractive scattering of low plastic tables filched from ancient Barbie Dreamhouses. The tables were surrounded by comfortable beds of moss for easy lounging, and a few rats were already getting their evenings started. Some were munching on fermented berries, others were sharing large communal chunks of dirty apple. Some were snacking on sunflower seeds, others on spiced insect eggs. Busy servers scurried through the space, taking orders and delivering delightful treats.

A host-rat showed them to a table, and a server with the fur on her head tied into little topknots appeared to take their order. As they sat, they gazed around themselves in wonder.

The walls and ceiling were covered with tiny bits of metal,

gleaming in the soft golden glow of countless bioluminescent mushrooms. Screws, earrings, bolts, pendants, nuts, clips, rings, keys, washers, charms, thumbtacks, key fobs, hinges, clothes pins, rivets, and more crawled across these wide surfaces in mosaics of astonishing complexity. And there were parts of countless machines made by the Dead Gods, now unrecognizable, which added to the precious hoard and provided every possible shape needed to create the perfect art.

And what art it was. The centerpiece was the image of an enormous rat, sensitive, strong, and beautiful. One paw supported a large book and the other was raised, with the palm outward, and in the center of the palm was an eye. Festooned around the rat were scenes from a life. There was an image of the rat peering closely at the label of one of the bottles so beloved of the Dead Gods, while a light shone down from above to create a tableaux of epiphany. Another image showed the rat being chased and attacked by all the animals in the world, while the same design of the four interlocking circles they had seen outside hovered in the background. And, another, most poignantly, showed the rat bringing the gift of reading to all animalkind.

The mice stared, agape. Metal was rare in the Million Acre Wood. And even the wealthy families of Sunflower Hill in Musmuski Grove considered metal items to be precious heirlooms, appropriate for hoarding, fighting over, and occasionally sharing on ceremonial occasions. So to see this wealth so nakedly on display, so abundant in its richness, so beautiful in its presentation, left them feeling that they had stumbled into a cathedral.

Their server brought them each a fermented blueberry and

some grass seeds tossed with dried mushroom buttons. The warm buzz soon had them lounging on their moss couches and chatting while they waited for Bricabrac to show up. And their conversation turned, as it often did, to honor and beauty.

"You know," said Throat Punch. "When you saved my life from the snake, that was kinda beautiful."

Death Rage took a big bite of her blueberry. She was starting to feel tipsy. "If you had gotten killed … would that have been beautiful?"

"Mmm," mused Throat Punch. "Young mouse, so many dreams, killed on my first big fight." She munched some grass seeds. "Ya, it would have been beautiful in a sad way."

"That is nuts," said Death Rage. "It would have been a tragedy and a waste."

"But I would be with Gramsy and Grampsy on Trail Mix Mountain," said Throat Punch. "So there would have been a happy ending."

"Ah," said Death Rage, and she looked through the grass seeds in front of her.

Throat Punch gazed at her. "Don't you want to go to Trail Mix Mountain?"

"Of course I do," said Death Rage, as she bit off the end of a handsome fescue seed. "But I don't know how to get there." She spat out the husk and chewed the germ. "The only world I've seen is the one in front of me. And I'm going to leave a mark on it." She patted her rapier handle.

Throat Punch smiled. "So chasing glory … is that honorable?"

Death Rage looked at her without blinking. "It is if you do it right," she said.

Throat Punch rested her chin in her paws. "And how do you do that?"

The older mouse leaned forward. "Keep your sword sharp. Fight on the side of right. And don't run out on the ones who love you." She sat back. "If you do that, you'll always…" She looked down. The alcohol was loosening emotions she usually kept under wraps. "You'll always be…" She trailed off.

"Something happen?" asked Throat Punch gently.

Death Rage looked at her for a long moment. "My father was a warmouse," she said. "But always a little fearful, because of an attack on his family when he was young." She rolled a mushroom back and forth between her paws. "One day my sisters and I were out gathering seeds with him, and we were surprised by a weasel. He drew his weapon, then his nerve broke and he ran." She took a bite of blueberry. "I was the only one of the children to survive."

Throat Punch touched her shoulder. "I'm so sorry."

Death Rage drummed her paw pads on the table. "The Warmouse League shamed him. They took his title. They took his sword. That's why my family had no hardstone weapon to give me." Her eyes drifted around the table and came to rest on Throat Punch's greatsword. "So I got my own."

There was a sudden commotion from the bar. They looked up to see that a very important rat had just entered. He was standing with his back to them and Death Rage could see that he was wearing a gold necklace, shiny bracelets, and a vest of braided silver echeveria leather. The back of the vest featured an ornamental armor plate of delicate and complex beauty which the Dead Gods would have called an *integrated circuit*.

The rat was surrounded by a cluster of friends, and servers

and barkeeps hovered at the edge of the group, delivering an array of top-shelf comestibles. The rat raised a rare fermented lychee in a toast, and all of his fellows quaffed with him. As he bit into his high-end libation, he turned, and they could see that it was Bricabrac.

Aliyah

She had been making her way through the City's demesne for some days with Gaetan by her side. If she thought about it, she could recall that another Aliyah had known another Gaetan in a previous life. But so little about that life mattered now. They each had jewel-like memories of those they had loved, and the rest they were content to leave in the darkness they had escaped from.

So she and the coyote ran lightly over the grass and through the woods. She was bold and free. And so was he. She often wore her golden armor just for the sheer joy of its beauty. On those days, Gaetan would wear garlands of winter jasmine and hellebore twined about his ears. And he would tug blossoms though the rings of her chain mail with his teeth. They hunted together in the early evenings and then slept casually in whatever nook presented itself.

And so one day they came into a lovely glade not far from the City. It was green with cool bowers of eastern pine and white spruce, and a small stream flowed through it, dancing with light under the cool rays of the winter sun. After a moment, they noticed five gray and white wolves drinking from the stream, with a small murder of crows near them.

Four of the wolves had amber eyes and copper hoops

through their left ears, and one of them had three hoops and eyes of arctic blue. They all gazed intently at Aliyah.

Those must be City wolves, she thought. Now that she was looking at them, she felt suddenly divided in mind about what she wanted. These last few days with Gaetan had been so free and unfettered. She was not sure she wanted to enter the dreary world of wolves again, with its endless hierarchies and posturing. But if she was going to honor the bright memories of the ones she loved, she would need to seize the attention of a killer army.

As a full-blooded golden Summerday, she was larger and heavier than these gray wolves. But she was also outnumbered. She and Gaetan shared a glance, and then she approached the wolves with her head high, maintaining a carefully neutral stance.

"You are from City of Oom," she said.

The wolf with three hoops stepped forward and said, "You are the golden warrior roaming our land." His icy blue eyes shone with a keen intelligence, and they slowly scanned her golden armor, bedecked with flowers. When he spoke, his voice was smooth and cool. "Atticus Peacemaker," he said. "Commander, Municipal Wolves."

The other four wolves casually spread out their line and then moved to stand in a wide circle around Aliyah and Gaetan.

Aliyah felt the hairs on the back of her neck rise. His manner was easy but his encirclement tactic was aggressive. Just the sort of thing high-ranking wolves do. A memory of her father Micah greeting a smaller pack of interlopers in another life rushed at her, and she batted it away.

City of Oom

If she was going to step into this hierarchy, the time to negotiate her position was now. She could do more for her cherished ones from a position of greater power.

Atticus and the other wolves were looking at her in silence. She realized they were waiting for her to respond and decided to take an oblique position.

So she did not expose her neck in submission. Instead, she raised her head and inhaled deeply. "I love this country," she said. "It is wild and fine."

Atticus nodded. "Yes," he said. "It is fine. And closely patrolled." His blue eyes held hers. "Land of Oom is a garden, not a wilderness."

She came close to him and breathed in his scent. "So you drive out lones?" As she came near to their leader, the other wolves tightened their circle. She could hear Gaetan's breathing speed up.

"The City is a wonderful place for wolves," said Atticus. "We are the muscle and bone of the *Pax Ursorum*." He smiled. "And we would have much to offer Aliyah Summerday."

She carefully held his gaze. "You know me?"

He did not blink. "How many golden wolves are there?"

Only one now. But there was no rush of sadness. It was just a fact. "State your offer," she said.

"Why don't you come to the City?" said Atticus, his tone light and reasonable. "See what we have. Then we can talk about the insurgents and discuss how we might work together. I'm sure you have much special knowledge that would benefit us." His gaze took in the other wolves in a collegial way. "If not to your liking, you're free to go."

Aliyah stared at him. It sounded perfectly pleasant, but of

course, saying, *you're free to go*, meant that he was asserting the right to determine whether or not she would be free to go. Aliyah tossed her head and glanced at Gaetan. "What say you, coyboy?"

Gaetan's yellow eyes swept across the faces of the wolves. The jasmine blossoms about his ears were bright white in the sunlight. At last, he said, "*J'irais*."[25]

Atticus shared a look with the other wolves. Up to that moment, they had ignored this limping coyote wearing flowers on his ears. "Our coyotes reside in auxiliary militias," Atticus said smoothly. "Near at hand, but not underfoot." He gave Aliyah the special *wolf speaking to wolf* look. "He can join one of those."

The sun flickered as a feathery cirrus cloud passed in front of it, and Aliyah's golden armor, adorned with flowers, sparkled with warm fire. She said, "I would have my friend stay with me."

Atticus gazed at her, unmoving. There was just the suggestion of an irritated growl rolling up out of his throat. She could see that behind his cool blue eyes, he was rapidly going through a series of calculations. She recognized this look because she had often worn it herself, back in her old life. *What is this resource worth to me?* Now that she was no longer a lord of her realm, she no longer had to make such calculations. It was very freeing.

Finally, he said, "Come to the City. We can talk more later."

Aliyah glanced at Gaetan, then stepped forward and touched noses with Atticus quickly and casually, as an equal. "I will come," she said. "Thank you, brother."

---

[25] I would go

Chapter 14

What do you call a crow school dropout? A falcon.
—Corvid joke

Anastasia

Anastasia could not rest. She paced. She ran. She listened. And still the song came from the sky.

Please sing back.

She wanted to. She ached to believe that it was a message from Freddie. That she could speak to him. That she might be near him again. Soon.

But everything about her experience in the world told her that danger was everywhere. Seen and unseen. She had been thrown out to hunters by her own mother. She had been poisoned by someone who lived with her at *Sans Gloire*. She had been seized from above when she thought she was safe at the Narrows, then imprisoned and threatened by a thousand killers. She had come close to drowning while trying to help someone she loved.

And she knew that large forces were arrayed against her. The masters of City of Oom could not allow her to live in peace, as her very life was a threat to them. And they had already shown themselves capable of bending songbirds and other creatures to their will.

Her own uncertainty drove her to ceaseless motion, whipsawed across the point of a blade by fear and longing.

On yet another time around her tiny prison, she passed by the carrion fruit she had knocked off from the ledge above. The long purple fruits lay scattered, their wrinkled skins cast into high relief by the winter sun. She turned her head as she passed, but then a thought struck her.

Days were passing. The pups would need more than milk soon. Their instinct to attack was already beginning to emerge, which meant the day of their execution was coming fast. The voice of her ancestors was already a continuous background shriek. *Save yourself. Kill them now.*

Maybe there was something useful here? She knew sometimes hunters ate dead animals they found.

No one knew what was inside a piece of carrion fruit since most creatures avoided them. The terrible odor and the strong reminder of death made them taboo among the prey animals. But maybe there was something in there that these little killers could eat. That might buy her some time while she figured out what to do about the birdsong.

She took a deep breath and then held it as she began to gnaw a piece of carrion fruit. The purple skin stripped away quickly. Underneath was a hard shell, like a coconut. She took

City of Oom

a few steps away, snatched another breath, then dashed back and attacked the shell. It was tough and fibrous, but her sharp incisors were tearing through it. After a couple of minutes of determined gnawing, she broke through.

The intensity of the smell that was released made her retch, and she had to run to the streambank to clear her head. She dunked her face in the cold, fast-flowing water and went back to the fruit. In a few more minutes, she had ripped open a tear in the husk, exposing a dark and slimy mess within.

The pups, ever-curious, came to investigate what she was doing. She found the innards of this fruit disgusting, but maybe these carnivores would like it? They ate disgusting things all the time. They gloried in filth. They *rolled* in it.

As the pups approached, Anastasia gestured towards the open fruit and did her best to make a *yum!* sound to let the pups know this was food. They came forward, mesmerized, and looked at it carefully, sniffing it, breathing it in, and gazing at each other.

Then, as one, they rendered their verdict. "*Yuck!*"

MABEL

For some hours, Mabel and Sunbeam had been marching through the tall redwood trees, climbing steadily uphill through the mist and an understory that came to be composed mostly of ferns and cycads. The white behemoths around them walked mostly in silence, moving surprisingly gracefully for creatures of their size. It seemed as though the ancient wood opened to let them though, and then closed after they passed. The rabbits had to scurry along to keep up. The trailing *Enchanté* followed closely behind them. They could hear his great breath, always just a few steps away. It was unnerving.

Mabel was quiet, but her mind raced. It wasn't clear whether they were visitors or prisoners. And she couldn't tell if the creatures around them were guards or escorts. Her injuries were sore, and the deep scratches on the side of her face burned. She glanced at Sunbeam. The ear where Saskatoon had torn a bite was a dirty mess of dried blood, spider web, and matted fur, and it looked like the exertion of the steady uphill climbing was making it bleed afresh. Sunbeam was whimpering softly as she lollopped along, taking great pains to avoid any foliage touching her ear. Mabel offered tiny kisses as they went. She had little else to give.

After awhile, they were walking on a path. At first it was narrow, but then it broadened out. The sulfur smell was stronger, and it seemed wet. She became aware that there were more animals around them. In the distance, she saw a raccoon walking, carrying some kind of load. It was limping as it moved. It was only visible for a few seconds before it was lost in the mist.

A little later, she saw a fox off the trail on one side, standing on its back legs, pulling clusters of winterberries off a bush. When it heard them, it turned briefly and glanced in their direction. For a moment, she could see that one eye was covered in the milky whiteness that caused blindness. The fox seemed uninterested in them and turned back to the berries.

Not long after, the path they were on passed under a broken arch. Mabel had never seen an arch, but its alien form suggested to her that it was some remnant of the Dead Gods.

City of Oom

The center of the arch had long ago collapsed, leaving just the curved uprights on either side, ending in jagged stumps. As they came near, she could see that the surface of the arch was covered with carvings of water plants: duckweed, hyacinth, water lilies, and lotus.

Up ahead on the trail, she saw a deer coming toward them. It had a great wound on its neck that looked to be partially healed. Five deep tears ran in parallel from the ear down onto the back. As it came near, Mabel had the same sensation she did when *Les Enchantés* looked at her. The deer saw her, but the deep brown eyes seemed to look through her.

As they walked on, they saw more and more injured animals. On one side of the path, a crow with one wing was cracking seeds on a stone table. And gathered around the table were a group of mice, some with terrible, ancient wounds, sorting the broken seed fragments and singing quietly. Up ahead, a coyote came toward them, pulling a travois of winter gourds. It was missing a foreleg, so the travois had been modified with a strap that fitted around the coyote's chest. As the coyote drew near, she saw again the dreamy, distracted eyes.

Mabel's mind buzzed with questions that hammered at her with ever-growing intensity, even though she tried not to show it. *Who is harming these animals? Are we going to be attacked? What is this place?*

Freddie

Freddie had been busy up north at the Midsummer Path, setting up stone throwers to support the crossbows there. It was vital that Free Nation prevent the top of the Path from being seized by a hostile group, as the top of the Stone Stair had been.

Since it was forty-five miles from the Shandy River to the Path, Freddie had flown there via Songbird Air. Of course, there was no way the songbirds could airlift a hundred raccoons, so Freddie was working with the local raccoon tribes as his labor force. He found it very challenging. The northern folk thought of Free Nation as an invention of the South Shandy rabbits. For them, *Sans Gloire* was very far away, and they were quick to see them as overlords making demands. Still, the work was getting done. And there was one good thing about the frontier mentality. They weren't demanding to know where Anastasia was because most of them had never seen her.

But Freddie was anxious to know. And it gnawed at him daily that Stan's air corps had heard nothing back from her.

One night, while bunked at Midsummer Base, he had a nightmare. He was reaching toward Anastasia, and his forelegs stretched out until he could hardly see the end of them. But she was sinking farther and farther away from him, her golden eyes dimming, falling into a great gash cut deep into the earth. And the farther he reached, the faster she sank. He was trying to call out to her, but his voice was garbled. He was making sounds that were not words. And the more he tried to form clearer words, the more his lips and tongue were melting into sludge.

He woke up with his heart pounding. *I need to send another message.* And this time, it had to be clearer that it was to her. But he still could not include her name. What could he say that would do this? He racked his brain, combing over everything he knew about Anastasia, rubbing the scar on his neck from her bite to feel closer to her. At last, he come up with a sweet memory, their casual snuggle in Stone Base before the first wolf attack.

He had sung a little rhyme for her, picking up on a name that he sometimes called her. His heart felt a little lighter at the thought of it. Maybe this could be the flag that said, *this is for you, only for you, and not a trick.*

He got up and paced, walking round and round the central area. He murmured and gestured, sliding halfway toward dissociation, and finally put together a new rhyming couplet.

*"Pookie, this is to remind you
Please sing back, help Freddie find you"*

Death Rage

"Death Rage! What up? What up?" Bricabrac spread his arms wide, framed by the shiny metal mosaic on the wall behind him. "It's the mousie angel who freed me from the rabbits who were going to do me in!"

Death Rage jumped up and ran to him, with Throat Punch trailing after. "Your magic words saved our lives!"

Bricabrac enfolded her in his forepaws, his collection of ratty bling jingling softly. And unlike their previous awkward hug, the night she had freed him from a glass prison chamber and Anastasia's wrath, Death Rage was glad to have this embrace. After the long journey to City of Oom, with the many strange creatures and places to wrangle, it felt so homey and comfortable to see a face she knew well.

Then she remembered what Crapola had said and stepped away from him. "Oops, I'm hugging a rat," she said. "That's bad, isn't it?"

Bricabrac shrugged. "Whatever busts your walnut," he said, turning on an automatic smile. "I've had all my shots."

After introductions had been made all around and the mice had told of their rescue by Crapola, Bricabrac took a few steps away from his posse, leaned an elbow on the bar and ordered the three of them a round of fermented pineapple morsels. Soon they were all enjoying cleverly crafted little cups of pineapple skin, with the fermented pulp still attached.

"Sure, Anastasia wanted to kill me," Bricabrac said, chuckling expansively. "But she also made me a *very* comfortable rat. All the *materiel* that I got as barter payments for making the weapons for *Sans Gloire* turned into a sweet stack of moneystones once I got back to the City." He kissed his paw tips. "Life is good," he said. "I'm a high roller now. Throwing the molars with the *crème de la crème* of rat society."

"Wow," said Death Rage, and even Throat Punch looked suitably impressed.

"For a poor boy like me," said Bricabrac, "Born in a pile of diseased animal carcasses, it's pretty sweet. I just wish my dear old mam was here to see it."

Throat Punch looked astonished and deeply moved. "You poor thing," she murmured as she laid one paw on her heart and with the other touched Bricabrac's forearm.

Death Rage had by now heard so many different origin stories from Bricabric that she was inclined to take the latest installment with a pawful of salt. "Well, allrighty then," she said briskly. "Glad things are going so great for you. I'd like to ask if you could see your way clear to helping us out on—"

"Not gonna choose sides again," said Bricabrac quickly, picking some invisible lint off his fine braided vest. "That's what almost got me whacked last time, remember?"

Death Rage steepled her fingers. This was going to require some tricky jibber-jabber with a good friend, convincing them to do something that was perhaps not in their best interest. It did not seem that the coming conversation really had the smell of *honor* on it. She looked sideways at her companion. "Throat Punch?" she murmured.

Throat Punch, startled to find herself on deck, jumped and sloshed a bit of her pineapple highball. "Erm, yes. Good Master Brac," she said. "Ahhh … we wouldn't dream of asking you to … do anything that doesn't crack your pecan … but we would love to offer you this opportunity to…" She paused, raking through her memories of conversations between her wealthy parents over lavish piles of seeds on long winter evenings. Then she fell easily into the plummy tones she had heard so often. "To … to more fully backstop your portfolio by launching a mutually beneficial relationship with a startup nation that is looking for a well-placed partner and brings nontrivial resources to the table." She leaned forward, eyes sparkling. "Because even a rat of wealth and taste could always use a bit … *more*. Am I right, sir?"

Death Rage gave her a tiny thumbs up.

Bricabrac chewed meditatively on the rim of his pineapple leather tumbler. "Mmm, I would not raise even a finger on behalf of your project, of which I have no knowledge. But if some ruffian were to loiter and hear me speaking, I would be, regrettably, unable to stop it."

"Tragically, that is true, Master Brac," said Throat Punch.

"I occasionally find moneystones in my vicinity," said Bricabrac. "Which sometimes causes me to pray aloud."

Throat Punch leaned toward Death Rage and had a whispered consultation. Then she said, "Mouse hooligans are looking for places to live while in the City." She took a moneystone out of Death Rage's backpack and leaned it against the bar.

Bricabrac raised his paws and looked up at the big mosaic of the kind and beautiful rat. "Thanks be to Rattus Rattus for creating Mousenook. Which a minor criminal might find if they went out the side door, turned left, and scampered down the alley."

Throat Punch nodded and tapped her pineapple cup against Bricabrac's. "Let's hope there are no microthugs nearby."

Aliyah

"The bears have been in wintersleep for the last three months," said Atticus to Aliyah as they paced down a wide boulevard in City of Oom, with thick flakes of late winter snow drifting down. "We have to wait for them on big decisions." His honor guard of six wolves strode behind them in echelon formation. "Clavis Aurea awoke first this year. And now Force Majeure has been seen on the streets nearby."

"Mmmm," said Aliyah, distracted by the jumbled sights and sounds of the City street.

Atticus saluted as several injured wolves passed, some

City of Oom

limping from great tears across their shoulders and down their flanks. "Well fought, captain," he said to a wolf with two earrings through her left ear. "Land of Oom thanks you. You'll be up for a commendation."

Aliyah listened with half an ear as Atticus continued to tell her about the fights consuming their time, with the rabbit skirmishes as a late addition to a long list. Most of the names meant nothing to her. Her eyes swept across the panoply of color and the riotous profusion of scents that swam around her. She could hardly believe she was here, in the capitol that had dominated her world for time out of mind. After spending her life in the quiet of a dense wood, in deep relationships with a few people, she found the tumble of activity, the swirling shapes of the buildings, and the raucous calls of the animals hawking wares to be overwhelming.

She could see that the City was a world unto itself, filled with lives, goods, struggles, ambitions. Uncounted dramas were played out here every day. And all of her life that had happened so far was so small that it didn't even matter. The destruction of Clan Summerday and the rise of the downland rabbits was just another piece of news, one out of many stories to be chatted about, then dealt with. And tomorrow there would be a new story. She had never felt so small.

She saw Gaetan running in and out of the shops and round about the stalls of the street vendors, poking his nose into everything, his eyes wide, his nostrils flaring. And of course, as the only golden wolf in the world, animals stared at her everywhere she went. She was surrounded by a circle of curious eyes, not all of them friendly.

"Have you ever seen a bear?" asked Atticus.

"No," said Aliyah, distracted by a raccoon offering spiced apricot halves. She did not notice Atticus share a glance with the other wolves.

"We'll see how you like it," he said.

Aliyah sniffed at the apricots, and then walked on. Her mind was whirling, but she strove to make the most of this moment. *You are in the belly of this beast. Look closely.* "How many Municipal Wolves are there?" she asked.

"Over a hundred now," said the commander. "The bears want to expand the territory under *Pax Ursorum.* And as Land of Oom grows, we need to grow also." He looked at her. "That means we'll have a need for more experienced officers." It was clear from his voice that he considered this implied offer very valuable.

Some fox pups ran up to her, entranced by her golden armor. She touched noses with them and allowed them to crowd around her for a few moments. She felt a warmth rise in her as she gazed into their tiny, excited faces, speckled with snowflakes. Then she pushed it down.

"Is there much hunting?" she asked.

Atticus shooed the pups away. "The bears only hunt for sport now. Some don't hunt at all. There are rules about wolves hunting within the *Pax* area, but we're free to hunt as we please outside."

Aliyah nuzzled the last little fox, and then sent her on her way.

"Most of our time is spent keeping the peace and fighting expansion battles. Some of the bears take the lead in pacifying new territories," said Atticus. "The Civil Raccoons keep the City fed with fish from the Shandy."

A small crew of mice ran up to her and began to polish her foreclaws. "Would the lady care for a buff 'n sharpy?" asked the mouse crew leader, smiling up at her. A large snowflake landed on the mouse's head and she brushed it off.

"Thank you, no," said Aliyah. It was strange to see prey animals approaching her so boldly. She gently stepped past them.

Suddenly, she noticed a strange phenomenon. The animals farther down the street were parting like a wave, running to the sides of the street and casting themselves on their bellies with their paws over their eyes. Then she saw a mountain of dark mahogany fur and muscle enter the boulevard from a side street. A massive head and shoulders loomed over the nearby animals, and the eyes were a bright violet. Thick muscles lifted legs the size of trees and let them fall carelessly to the ground as the creature moved forward in a rolling shamble.

This must be a bear. It was larger than she had expected. It was somehow built on the wrong scale, as though a piece of earth had come to life. She had always known herself and her family to be the largest animals in their world, so it was shocking to suddenly feel like one of the littles. To see so much careless power. This creature could kill her without even noticing it.

She wanted to back away from this monster. Just being near it felt dangerous. A thought flashed through her mind. *This must be how a rabbit feels.* It was a new idea.

She could feel Gaetan pressing against her, his breathing fast. She heard a quiet groan rising from the animals lying on their bellies, hiding their faces. Out of the side of her eye, she could see Atticus and his wolf pack moving to the side of the street. So this was truly a dangerous moment then. These tyrants might strike even their own retainers.

Aliyah felt a strong urge to follow the Municipal Wolves, to make the safe choice. But something held her fast in the middle of the street. Earlier, she had not known what she wanted to do. But now, in this moment, she did. She was a Summerday. She was here to honor the memories of her loved ones, and she would not fail. *I have visited death and come back.*

She did not want to be an officer in some wolf army. She was the messenger of world-changing chaos. She wanted to wake these wealthy navel-gazers and hurl them at the rabbits that had stolen her life, her loves, her future.

The bear came near, paws thudding onto the ancient pavement. She did not move. The general groan of the animals watching raised in pitch, acquired a questioning element. Atticus was calling to her but she could not spare a moment to hear it. The desire to leap to the side and disappear into the crowd burned along her nerves. Her legs twitched. Gaetan was trembling. She pressed her claws into the cracked pavement. *I am the speaker of what is real. I stand fast for those I love.* The deep, earthy scent struck her like a wave. She breathed it in and felt the profound and ancient power flow into her and around her. Her heart pounded.

The violet eyes of the bear were locked on hers now. She lost herself in the pool of unearthly color as the snowflakes tumbled past. The massive jaws opened, and a voice rumbled out. It carried the weight of the heavy orthogneiss and migmatite that underlay the ground where they stood. "*Ain' tu, aureus ille minutulus?*"[26]

---

[26] Are you lost, tiny golden one?

City of Oom

She had no idea what the bear had said. Was it a threat? A command? The broad face was unreadable. Gaetan was whispering to her now. Her ears were closed to everything but the bear, so she placed her forepaw on his.

The bear breathed in a great rush of air, and then blew out a long exhalation. It stank of a thousand dead fish. Should she start speaking now? She felt suddenly very foolish. She was taking a life-ending risk for nothing.

The mighty jaws opened again, and the rumble came out. "You come near bear, and you know not the language of power?"

Aliyah shook her head, but she did not look down. "I know the language of truth," she said, and shivered as she spoke.

The violet eyes blinked. It almost seemed as though they might be amused. The Eocene-deep rumble poured out and surrounded her like an irresistible hug. "Speak, puppy."

Aliyah turned her head and looked down at Gaetan. He whined and licked his lips. Then he nodded, his yellow eyes hot. *Do it.*

"The end of your world is coming," said Aliyah, as the *bear-geist* washed over her. "Unless you make all your power manifest now." Hundreds of animals were staring from the sides of the wide boulevard.

The bright eyes of the great grizzly tracked away from Aliyah and came to rest on Atticus Peacemaker. "Who is this?" he rumbled.

"A refugee from the new downland war," said Atticus.

Aliyah bristled at this description. "I stood to inherit the Million Acre Wood as my own fiefdom," she said. She recalled some words the downland crows of long ago had found on a Dead Gods page and written into the Word of Dah. "Look on my works, ye mighty, and despair."

Atticus took a few steps closer to the bear and exposed his neck in submission. "Counselor, we just heard of this war while you were in wintersleep," he said. "Some rabbits and mice had a grievance and refused arbitration. We have been taking proportionate action."

A deep groan welled out of the great belly of the bear. The dark bottomless eyes came to rest on Aliyah again. "I have just returned from the dream country of Ursa Major," he rumbled. "I ran with the Sky Bear across the spheres of heaven." The claws on one of his forepaws flexed, perhaps unconsciously.

She knew this was an inauspicious time to be making her case—even as a pup, she had learned not to bother Micah Summerday when he was rising from sleep—but she reckoned her chances for an audience with one of these monsters would be few.

Gaetan was whispering to her again. Grasping for ideas, she opened her ears to him. "Farkillers," he was murmuring. "*La mort de loin.*"[27]

"My Lord—" she began. A snicker ran through the animals watching.

"Objection, I am not your *Lord*," said the grizzly, a hint of irritation manifesting in his bottomless rumble. "I am a simple drudge, slave of the people."

---

[27] Death from away.

Aliyah felt her ears starting to lay back. *That's why everyone's terrified of you.* But she adjusted her mien and pushed her ears up so they were high and gracious. What was it Atticus had called him?

"Counselor," she said, bowing deeply. "Farkillers have returned once again to our world. They make a mockery of the power and strength of—" she glanced at Gaetan. What she was about to say sounded so absurd. He nodded fiercely. "—*slaves* such as yourself."

The bear didn't smack her for saying this. *It must be how they talk here.* She pressed on. "Only chain mail armor will turn the killing blades, and I see but little of it here. Though I know you have the skills. Perhaps that is why the City's response has so far been ... measured." She glanced at Atticus. His glare was cool as arctic ice. "No shade on the courage of the Municipal Wolves," she said hastily. *This is all coming out wrong.*

Gaetan was whispering again. "Just say what is true."

"My family was attacked by rabbits," she said. "We thought it was nothing. And now they're all in the Forever Forest."

The bear dragged a foreclaw across the ancient pavement. The sound of the sharp keratin points scraping across the everstone was loud in the sudden stillness. Then his eyes swept the crowd and came to rest on Atticus Peacemaker where he stood in the forefront of the animals. A single word thrummed out of the earth-deep chest. "Bailiff?"

A moment later, the commander and his guard were leaping forward, surrounding Aliyah and Gaetan, pressing against them and ushering them off the street in a way that could not be resisted. Behind them, the great bear continued his shamble down the boulevard, huffing and groaning.

"Fine stunt you pulled," Atticus was saying in her ear. "I guess you never heard of *going through channels* down in the Million Acre Wood, did you, Your Highness?"

Chapter 15

Seize the jumble, seize the ruckus
Shape and form the needful thing
Bringing beauty from disorder
This is why my fingers sing
　　　　　　　—Hymn of the Craftmouse

Anastasia

Big fluffy snowflakes were drifting down on Anastasia's prison island, and the temperature had dropped. While she was foraging, she saw the pups in their accustomed nook between the boulders, trying to keep warm. The snow was falling down on them, then melting on their bodies. This left them wet and shivering, and they were too young to know how to help themselves.

Anastasia's burrow was warm and dry. She could venture out when she pleased, then retreat to her warm space whenever she felt chilled. Now that the weather was turning cold again, the contrast between her life and the pups' was thrust into the forefront of her mind.

As usual, she tried to ignore it. But as her search for food brought her nearer to the pups, their cold and miserable whining slowly penetrated her mental armor.

Finally, on impulse, she dashed over to them. They crowded around her, hungry for warmth.

"Look," she said. "Dig under here"—she started pulling the sandy earth out from under one of the boulders—"and you can make yourselves a little burrow." The dirt she was digging out formed into a mound, and she kicked it down toward the beach. "See? Like this." She clawed out some more soil and began to create a protected space with the boulder as a ceiling. Soon, the pups were clumsily helping, pushing the excavated earth toward the streambank. Then she dug a catchment basement by the entrance to collect rain and meltwater, with the burrow rising toward the back to create a dry area that also preserved body heat.

When the rude shelter was done, they crowded in with her, kissing her and thanking her. She had gotten used to their scent now, so being in a confined space with them no longer set off her chemical alarm bells. It was cozy and snug and actually much warmer than her own burrow, since there were so many bodies.

"Our old mummy made us a den under some rocks like this," said Sephora. She no longer lisped, but her voice was still soft.

"We loved our old mummy a *lot*," said Micah.

"Then the big rain came and broke everything," said

City of Oom

Tennyson glumly. "I saw our mummy in the water. She was … she was… " His voice faded into quiet sniffles.

Anastasia chewed her lip. Her love for baby animals of all kinds was not coexisting comfortably with her memory of Aliyah Summerday, who had been one of the uber-predators of her world.

Sephora snuggled into her, pushing her short puppyish muzzle under the warm ruff of fur around Anastasia's throat. When she spoke, her voice was so quiet, it was almost a whisper. "Will you be our—?"

"No," said Anastasia softly. "But we're having a nice snuggle now. Let's just enjoy that." It was all getting too complicated. She batted away the storm of voices in her head, reaching for the *be here now* she had learned from Dingus.

As she lay, quietly drinking in the warmth rising from the bodies of her people's ancient enemies, she heard the faintest snatch of birdsong come drifting down from high above.

"*Pookie, this is to remind you*
Please sing back, help Freddie find you"

The effect on her was electric. *Pookie* was a name for her known by no one but Freddie. It was the audible signature, the proof, that this communiqué was real and true and good. And this was her way out of this confusing mess.

In that instant, all her questions were stilled. Her sweet boy, the anxious nerd with a big mind and a strong heart and nerves of not-quite-steel was speaking to *her*. Had found *her*. Had loved hard enough to find a way to reach *her*.

And he was waiting … for *her* … to speak.

She bounded out into the snow, with the pups running

close behind. She had been thinking about this and had a song ready. So she ran to the leaning palm and tied herself into her safety rope that was still hanging over the branch.

Sephora, who had watched Anastasia belay herself the last time she climbed, took charge of the free end of the rope. And she organized the other pups to help her keep it taut as Anastasia climbed the tree trunk.

Soon Anastasia was on the ledge with the carrion bushes, peering upward. She could see the oak tree and the cluster of red-leaved palms that grew on the surface, just above her island. Where were the songbirds?

As she scrabbled along the ledge, trying to find a way to get close to the singers, she irritably nipped off twigs that were in her way and bit through the stems of the hanging purple fruits, letting them fall to the beach below.

Finally, she had gotten as close as she could. She could see the flickers of color as birds flew overhead, often pausing on the wide branches of the oak tree. She took a deep breath and sang her couplet.

> *"Freddie dear, I love you so*
> *Five red palms, I am below"*

She knew it would take many times to be heard and noticed. So she sang it again. And again. And again.

Mabel

It was late in the afternoon when the two rabbits and their guards arrived at a high hill bedecked with a stately series of terraces rising in graceful succession, each featuring pools of steaming water. The rabbits were led upward on a winding path, lined with lotus plants and glowing golden mushrooms, flecked with new snow. The smell of sulfur was very strong here, and when they passed close to the warm pools, Mabel realized it came from the water itself.

And Newly Beloved gazed at the strange land and thought, 'Surely, this is the home of powerful magic. Perhaps we may yet find the succor we seek...'

Partway up the hill, there was a building with tall and graceful lines, ribbed with high, pointed arches, in the style the Dead Gods knew as *Elvish Liminal*. It was covered with everstone inlays of lotus leaves and the thousand faces of Gaia, whose cult had grown very large in the late 21st century. And it was surrounded by a grove of CRISPR-generated mallorn trees, tall and lovely with their silver-gray bark and golden leaves on upward-sweeping branches.

As their guard escorted them through the enormous main doorway, they stepped over an ancient mosaic that read:

"Welcome to Le Tabernacle de la Déesse d'Eau[28]
Canada's largest natural hot springs
Please check phones and firearms"

Mabel scanned this hastily and managed to glean a few words. Inside the main chamber was a large pool shaped in a sinuous curve. Warm water appeared to be bubbling up in the center

---

[28] Temple of the Water Goddess

of it, and the overflow of the pool was carried by cunningly designed channels to the smaller pools lower down the hill. The plentiful steam inside the stone building made the space as warm as a tropical jungle, even in the midst of winter. The everstone floor itself felt heated. It had long since been broken into shards by relentless plant growth, so cannas and calla lilies grew thickly around the pool, interspersed with hibiscus and bromeliads. The upper reaches of the chamber were filled with the wide leaves of tree ferns that were nourished by shafts of sunlight shining down through cracks in the ceiling.

On one side of the pool was a dais, and upon it they saw a group of *Les Enchantés,* engaged in fierce and quiet conversation.

The white warrior who had accompanied them stepped forward. He began to speak in another language, then glanced at the rabbits and started over. "As the Queen of Sorrows commanded, I have brought the rabbits."

Mabel and Sunbeam looked at each other, unsure what to do. A little nudge from behind sent them lolloping forward, accompanied by a muttered "Stop touching me" from Sunbeam.

The Queen of Sorrows turned to glance back at them, and Mabel saw her first in profile. Her thick hair was snowy white, and Mabel could see that her eye was a brilliant cerulean blue. "Thank you, Aeschylus," she said. Her voice was a richer, warmer version of the mixture of rumble and treble they heard from others of her kind.

Then she turned to walk toward the rabbits, and Mabel caught her breath as she realized that a terrible scar raked down the right side of her face. Five identical deep slashes had left her face and neck deeply scored and taken her right eye, leaving the bright lines of proudflesh where no hair grew. As she came toward them, filled with grace and power, in the full flower of midlife, her cloven hooves clacking on the everstone, she was a striking presence.

"I am Clytemnestra," she said in her mellifluous voice. "Welcome to *Le Sanctuaire*."[29]

Mabel felt a warmth spread over her body. This powerful lady surely had the ability to help them, if only she would. Perhaps she was kind. Mabel noticed that like the others, she seemed to be looking through her. The black-and-white bunny bowed deeply, and she elbowed Sunbeam to cue her to bow as well.

"Our time is short," said Clytemnestra. "Why came you?"

Mabel rapped out a series of commands to herself in her head. *Be quick. Be likeable. Make a clear ask.* Then she launched into her story. But she was not able to stick to the speech she had rehearsed and felt herself rambling. There was so much to say. The wolves. The bears. Too many babies. Sunbeam left her side and started to prowl among the calla lilies at the water's edge. Mabel bumbled around their overpopulation problem, suddenly unsure of how to present it.

After a minute or so, Clytemnestra stopped her. "We have problems of our own, and are not desirous of more."

Mable felt her heart sink. "Why did you send for us?"

Clytemnestra's cerulean eye rested on her for a long

---

[29] The Sanctuary

moment. "After you entered our land, you were seen doing something ... different."

Aeschylus raised a hoof and pointed it at Sunbeam. "That one." He drew his hoof across his throat. "Weasel." There was a murmur from the other *Enchantés*.

Mabel bowed. Any interest from this powerful lady was good. "We have made many weapons," she said. "As we seek to create space for ourselves in the world."

Clytemnestra came near to Mabel, and her bright cool scent surrounded her. "No other rabbits have done this," she said. "How do you know how to do it?"

"Pages," said Mabel.

Clytemnestra looked away. And both the counselors and the white warriors shifted uneasily. Aeschylus stepped forward and murmured a few words to his queen.

"That's how we learned how to make farkillers," said Mabel. "That's why we need your help now. We've driven the hunters out. There will soon be too many of us."

"Say you so?" Clytemnestra took a few steps away and stood looking into the steaming lake. She inhaled deeply and blew out a long slow breath. "Will there be too many of you when the bears and their wolf army overrun your defenses and lay waste to your people?"

Mabel felt a pit open up under her stomach. "We think we can defend ourselves." She swallowed hard. "We have to plan for victory, or it will turn into defeat."

Clytemnestra looked at her and nodded slowly. "Mating without children. What you ask is serious magic." She paused, and her gaze swept the other *Enchantés*. "We do not know the answer, but it may lie in our library."

Mabel took a step, leaning forward on her toes. *Ask. Ask. Ask.* "Would you ... would the great queen's people ... be willing to look? We would offer much for this wisdom."

The Queen of Sorrows walked through the lilies and took a few steps into the warm pool. "The Dead Gods were powerful, but we do not yearn to release more of their magic into the world." She dipped her muzzle into the misty water and drank. "Unwanted things may happen, and they cannot be undone."

Mabel felt as though she were sliding backward down a hill, away from the solution her people desperately needed. *Just keep talking.* "You must have known the Dead Gods well."

Clytemnestra barked out a short, bitter laugh, startling Mabel with its ugliness. "All too well," she said.

Mabel felt a slight adrenaline fizz run across her neck. *Something important here.* "What were they like?" She tried to say more, but was so uncertain of her ground that anything further seemed clumsy.

The Queen of Sorrows stepped out of the water and came towards her. "This is deep history," she said, a dark undertone rising into her warm rumble. "The Dead Gods *hated* my people." Her blue eye was piercing. "They imprisoned us on an island, in a lake of blood and tears."

A low growl rolled out of the throat of the great warrior Aeschylus.

Mabel took a step back. "I'm so sorry," she said.

Clytemnestra's scent was a storm of bitter spikes. "They came for our children. And killed them. And devoured them." The cerulean blue of her eye drifted toward deep midnight. "It was our great tribulation. And it went on for *centuries*."

Mabel felt overwhelmed as the darkness of this vision swept over her. There was no adequate response. She made a murmuring noise as she retreated from the queen's words.

"They called us *pigs*," said Clytemnestra. "And the name of our prison was *Iowa*."

Suddenly a bleeding messenger burst into the temple. "Bears! At the river!"

A moment later, the *Enchanté* were racing to battle, and the rabbits were left alone.

DEATH RAGE

Death Rage and Throat Punch found Bricabrac in his workshop in Dirty Town. The cluttered space was on a ground floor off the main alley. There was a fitting area for clients that was several feet high and could accommodate animals as large as wolves. A rat-sized workbench bristled with many tiny tools, and there were also some large tools that Bricabrac had adapted to his use with counterweights and other clever tricks. Behind them were shelves that were densely packed with materials that Bricabrac had foraged, like nails, cans, wire, and machine parts. Death Rage thought she recognized some items that had been in the tumbledown cabin near Warren *Sans Gloire* that the rabbits called the straightstone burrow.

"What up?" said Bricabrac distractedly, as he ground a rusty nail against a large metal file attached to the wall. "Got a big order here, not too much time to chat." He looked at them for a moment, and then grinned. "Unless it's time for prayers."

Death Rage looked at Throat Punch. The younger mouse

City of Oom

pulled a nickel out of Death Rage's backpack and leaned it against a broken socket wrench handle. "Ah, Master Brac," she said. "The news of the world is finding its way to you." She adopted the concerned tones of a low-level city official speaking at departmental meeting. "Mousie riffraff are seeking to find out what the newly awakened bears will do about the war with the Million Acre Wood. How can this tragedy be averted?"

Bricabrac folded his arms and gazed at the icon of Rattus Rattus that was set up above his workbench. It was a beautiful mosaic made entirely of zippers and rivets. He made a mystical gesture with his forepaws and said, "May the monosodium glutamate be with us."

Then he paused. Throat Punch looked uncertain. Death Rage, who had by now spent a lot of time around both rats and rabbits, guessed at the correct rejoinder. "And our expiration dates be many years off."

This seemed close enough, because Bricabrac continued on, "Loving Hero of the Rat Tribe, I pray that no mice would head south along the main street, turn right at the City Guard building, then turn left at the third door once they reach Precedent Park. For if they do, they will be in the study of Ex Cathedra, leader of the Nation of Oom."

Then he kissed his forepaw and touched the image of Rattus Rattus. That done, he returned to his work grinding the nail, whistling tunelessly as though the mice were not there.

Death Rage and Throat Punch took the hint and were soon scampering along the main boulevard, threading their way through the throng of animals and thick stands of plants growing up through the everstone pavement. After a few minutes, they were passing though the central square.

They saw many of the small stalls and performers they had seen before, including the fox with white clay on her face, accented with black clay triangles above and below the eyes.

On another small stage nearby, Death Rage saw a rabbit standing before an audience pulled from animals passing by. He had thick cream-colored fur and black feet and ears, and his voice alternately soared and wheedled as he stood smacking his paw and gesturing widely. It sounded like he had a downland accent, and she thought she might have seen him before. On his forehead was a heart stained into his fur with henna.

> *"And then the one known as Newly Beloved said,*
> *'I remember when the sea was fresh water*
> *I remember when the moon was nearby.'"*

Death Rage had already noticed that there were not very many rabbits in the City, so it was unusual that there were so many rabbits in the audience watching this evangelizer. And many of them also had the henna hearts.

Death Rage had heard vaguely about Newly Beloved from the circle of clerics around Anastasia. But she had paid little attention, so she had no real notion of the source of this idea. She and Throat Punch looked at each other for a moment, then continued on their way to Precedent Park.

A few minutes later, they were standing outside the third doorway. An ancient sign on the wall nearby was barely legible:

*"Terrains de Pickleball Olympiques
Membres Seulement*

*Olympic Pickleball Courts
Members only"*

Inside, they could see that, as with most buildings in City of Oom, there were plants and even whole trees growing through the floor, so the room was filled with leaf litter and fallen branches. This made it easy for them to creep in unseen.

It was a single large chamber, several hundred feet across, and the walls were covered with carvings of animals with strangely elongated bodies leaping gracefully through the air. Death Rage had no idea what the Dead Gods looked like, so she couldn't know that these images of international-caliber pickleball players were the first Dead Gods she had ever seen.

In the center of the chamber was a large, flat stone about three feet high and five feet long. A great grizzly, with dark bronze fur going gray about the muzzle, stood with his forepaws resting on the stone looking down. A ray of light shone down from a crack in the ceiling and bathed the stone in pale light.

At another, smaller flat stone by the edge of the space, a Civil Raccoon was standing. His stone was covered with pieces of paperbark. There were bound volumes of paperbark pages spread across other flat stones scattered near the walls. Death Rage thought she saw some collections of pages from the Dead Gods as well, as she had seen in the straightstone burrow.

The two mice found a comfy spot under a dead branch near the door and settled in to watch. For a long time, the old grizzly looked down at the pages on his stone. They could hear the slow rumble of his breath, and the ancient earthy scent of bear washed over them. Even from a distance, the bear had the power to terrify, so they snuggled into the leaf litter until only their eyes showed, and made as little noise as possible.

After a few minutes, there was a rumbling growl at the doorway, and the sound of huge paws crushing the dead leaves moved past them into the room. The bear's gaze swept the room briefly, and they saw violet eyes bright against mahogany fur. Death Rage and Throat Punch froze, moving only their eyes to track the movement of the bear near them. Death Rage squeezed her eyes down to tiny slits. The new bear began huffing rapidly, forcing out rapid short exhalations, punctuated by groans.

The old grizzly stood upright, his huge bulk filling the center of the room and glowing under the pale light. A deep growl rolled from his chest, and he huffed as his claws raked the surface of the stone, scattering the pages. The raccoon ran over from his reading stone and started gathering the paperbark pieces, staying low to the ground and keeping as far away from the bear as possible. When the bear's claws came near the raccoon as he raked the stone, the raccoon lay down on his belly and covered his eyes for a few moments. Then when the bear moved a step or two away, the raccoon dragged himself up into a crouch and continued gathering the bits of paper and bark.

At last, the bear near Death Rage stopped huffing. With his right forepaw, he reached across and touched his left shoulder, and then struck the ground in front of him, sending

City of Oom

leaf and twig fragments flying. A deep rumble flowed out of him, making the mice's heads vibrate. "*Salve*,[30] Ex Cathedra."

Then Ex Cathedra touched his own shoulder and struck the stone desk in front of him. His ancient rumble recalled the Paleoproterozoic rock of the allochthon, which lay deep beneath the City. "*Salve*, Force Majeure." After a final huff, he said, "You may approach."

Force Majeure shambled toward the older bear and came to a stop about thirty feet away from him. Ex Cathedra stood behind his reading stone, dark eyes fathomless. Both bears looked at each other for a long moment.

"A new war started while we were in wintersleep," rumbled Force Majeure. "Clavis Aurea took a defensive action with the songbirds of the realm. And the Municipal Wolves have made a probe." He huffed. "Inconclusive."

Ex Cathedra nodded his massive head. "Loyal cadres." He scraped his copper-colored claws across the everstone floor. "Not the deepest thinkers."

Force Majeure sat very still. "It's in the downlands."

The elder bear rested his paws on his reading stone. His wide shoulder hump rose above his head as he leaned forward, framing his face with a muscle-and-fat mantle of power. "Why do we care?"

A long rumbling breath rolled out of Force Majeure's chest. "Wolves say farkillers have been seen. Refugees say they changed the balance of power in the downlands."

A low growl came pouring out of Ex Cathedra's vast

---

[30] Greetings

mouth, and his claws raked gently over his reading stone. The mice could feel the vibrations a hundred feet away.

Force Majeure leaned forward. "I spoke with our flying eyes. It's true."

Ex Cathedra coughed out a sudden bark. "Farkillers are dead."

The younger bear shook his head gravely. "Objection, *Servus Populi*.[31] They live again."

Ex Cathedra rose and stood looking up. The shaft of light shining down through the ceiling made the gray fur in his muzzle shine. A low growl escaped him. "The farkiller is an abomination."

Force Majeure nodded. "Yes."

Ex Cathedra began to pace around his reading stone, heavy paws crunching the dead leaves. "The farkiller undoes the order created by bear."

"Yes," said Force Majeure, moving backward to maintain a safe distance, huffing quietly.

The Civil Raccoon picked up his reed pen and began making notes on a piece of paperbark.

"So even though our docket groans, we must assign a lead counsel to this case," said Ex Cathedra.

"I concur," rumbled Force Majeure. Then he knelt down and lifted his forepaws. "General Counsel," he said. "I have completed my penance. And I have been training for a larger role." He huffed quietly. "I submit to the realm that I am ready to prosecute this effort."

The Civil Raccoon scribbled furiously.

---

[31] Slave of the people

The elder bear looked at him appraisingly for a long moment. "Would the Sky Bear agree?"

Force Majeure cast himself at full length on the broken leaves and covered his eyes with his paws. A long moan escaped him, making the mice shiver. "I have proven my value and loyalty to Land of Oom. Shall I be punished forever for past transgressions?"

Ex Cathedra stepped away from his reading stone and paced around the back of the hall. Dead branches snapped under his paws as he walked. After a long moment, he said, "There is talent in your family." He stopped and looked at the younger bear, his dark eyes cool. "And trouble."

Force Majeure did not move. "What must I do?"

Ex Cathedra strode back to his reading stone as the raccoon raced forward and placed a piece of paperbark in the center. He glanced at the paperbark and nodded. "We need an *amicus curiae*."[32] He looked up at Force Majeure. "Throw the bones."

---

[32] Opinion from a friend of the court

Chapter 16

Sky is my nation. Ground is another country.
—Raptor proverb

Gaetan

After the awkward scene with the Municipal Wolves on the high street of City of Oom, Atticus Peacemaker had rather pointedly not offered Aliyah a bunk at the City Guardhouse where all the wolves lived. And anyway, Gaetan's position there would have been iffy at the best of times.

So after some wandering about the City, they ended up at the neighborhood for Gaetan's people, *Place du Coyote*. It was a block of partly collapsed buildings, thickly overgrown with gnarled trees. Gaetan was amused to find out that the common nickname for the area was "Thieves & Whiners." Aliyah was prepared to be angry on his behalf, but he just nuzzled her shoulder softly. "I *am* a thief," he said. "I stole you from death." Then he grinned. "And *Mère de la Faim*[33] knows I've whined enough in my life."

Of course, the other coyotes were amazed to see a limping coyote show up looking for accommodation with a gorgeous golden wolf wearing shining armor at his side. To have any wolf show an interest in staying with these unloved children of the city was surprising enough, but to have this huge and splendid vision of queenly power sauntering through their streets was astonishing.

So the two of them nosed around and picked out a comfy nook where three oaks were growing near a jagged wall with a juniper nearby, creating a leafy bower with a thick bed of fallen leaves to snuggle into. As they did this, Gaetan could see the coyotes' brains spinning into high gear. *So, you two are ... what now? Friends or, uh ... special ... friends?* The coyotes showing them around couldn't stop looking back and forth between them, but no one wanted to ask right out. Gaetan chuckled and let it go at that.

Aliyah shook off her backpack and arranged her mementos from the Spires and a few other items under the dense foliage of the evergreen, so they would be protected in case it rained or snowed. Gaetan pulled off some juniper berries and scattered them over the fallen leaves of the bedding area. Then he added some purple and white blossoms he nipped off a stand of hellebore that was growing nearby.

After they were settled, they decided to go out and explore the City. He could tell that Aliyah was excited from her

---

[33] Hunger Mother

chat with the bear. And for the sad little coyote from the hinterlands that he had always been, just to be alive and here in the capitol of his world was amazing. He was grateful for that.

So they wandered the streets. They saw freelance raccoons from outside the City selling apples and other foodstuffs in market stalls. There were tiny storefronts with rats selling small, clever items made of metal, with custom fabrications on offer. They walked past a hospital, and saw an injured wolf being carried inside on a stretcher travois pulled by raccoon orderlies, while a tawny bear hovered and rapped out a series of urgent commands.

And they ran into occasional patrols by the Municipal Wolves, who ostentatiously gave them the cold shoulder. They shared a quiet little eyeroll and smirk when this happened.

Finally, right next to a sprawling establishment where animals of many kinds were lounging and enjoying snacks as henna patterns were applied to their fur by teams of industrious mice, they saw a small store with a large basket hanging above the door. There were sample woven reed wares of all kinds in a display near the street. There were also words on a wall, which they could not read. Gaetan could see that something about these items attracted Aliyah's eye. She nudged him and then went inside.

A mouse wearing a vest of fine reed fibers woven into an attractive pattern scampered forward along a display shelf to greet them. He bowed. "Good morrow. Welcome to Wicker Flats Reedcraft. I'm Poison Wind."

Gaetan smiled as he saw Aliyah touch noses with the mouse. He had never seen a wolf do that with any small creature.

Poison Wind gestured toward the interior of the shop, which was stuffed with everything from small wicker bowls and boxes up to large wicker tables and settees. There were containers, shelters, platters, decorative animal shapes, and more.

He proudly sang their jingle:

*"We are reed mice and we make
All that bends and does not break"*

Aliyah was already nosing around some large boxes.

"How may wicker make your life better today?" asked Poison Wind.

Aliyah was peering closely at the construction of one of the wicker items. Gaetan joined her. "This grassy stuff..." she murmured.

"Wicker," said Poison Wind, crisply.

Aliyah glanced at him. "This *wicker* seems very sturdy." Her scent was bright and curious.

"Yea, that is the faithful heartweave," said Poison Wind. He scampered over to the canids and ran his tiny hands over the complex surface of the box. "It's the strongest weave in the Known World, strewth." He leaned against the box and folded his arms in the classic sales power move. "We invented it," he said, letting his arrogance show just a little bit. Then he gave Gaetan a friendly bro-to-bro smile. "Think you can rip it apart, Master Coy?'"

Gaetan scoffed and took a half-hearted chew at the box, coming away with nothing. Then Aliyah pushed past him and brought her teeth into play, hard. Her shiny canines clattered over the ribbed surface, but she could find no purchase. At last, she said, "I can't get a grip on it."

Poison Wind simply smiled and nodded slowly. "Exactly."

Aliyah's maple-green eyes came to rest on him. "Could this stop a blade?"

Poison Wind pursed his lips and stroked his chin judiciously. "It would not stop a blade wielded by a bear," he said. "Any other creature, it would withstand. And more than stop the blade, it would *eat* the blade." He pushed the flattened fingers of his left hand through the open fingers of his right. "A piercing weapon would partly penetrate and then be held fast."

Gaetan blew out a long appreciative breath. He could see where this was going, and it was giving him chills. The good kind.

Aliyah paced quickly around the box, making a few playful lunges at it with her teeth. "Could you make something ... new?"

"Oh, yes, Golden One," said Poison Wind, rubbing his hands together, eyes smiling. "Wicker can make all our dreams come true."

Force Majeure

Force Majeure was shambling up the Great Hill in the center of Oom, reminding himself not to plod. *This is our chance. Seize it, my brother.*

So the huge grizzly lifted his head and marched up the ancient road that circled around the large amphitheater built into the side of the hill. At the top, he could see the five redwood trees planted in a circle. Over a hundred feet tall, they stood like columns supporting the wide northern sky.

As he came out onto the flat top of the hill, he saw many raptors clustered on the wide branches of the airy spruces and lodgepole pines that grew there. The area under their roosts was carpeted with small bones and a scattering of skulls. And the late winter season was calling forth the first few attempts at building nests.

A few hundred steps brought him near the redwoods, and he could see the wide plaza of hard-packed clay in their midst. The nineteen stars of the constellation of Ursa Major were set into the clay as disks of mother-of-pearl as wide as his paw. A large circle surrounded the constellation, with fifty-two large milky moonstones set along the rim, one for each week. A sudden shaft of sunlight broke through the cloud cover and made all these iridescent surfaces gleam.

Clavis Aurea, a female grizzly with chestnut fur and gray streaking her muzzle, appeared from the small tumbledown chapel, thickly overgrown with trees. Her golden eyes became thoughtful as she caught sight of him.

As he approached, a Civil Raccoon roused herself from a den built into the side of the chapel and came forward, holding a ledger of bound paperbark sheets, a pen, and a small gourd of ink. She took up a position by a flat reading stone near the star plaza and spread out her tools.

Immediately, both grizzlies began to huff and groan, circling each other at a distance of fifty feet. It was all pro forma. He knew that Clavis Aurea had little interest in projecting physical threat. That was not the source of her power.

In less than a minute, she rumbled, "You may approach."

Force Majeure came forward and knelt down in the leaves about thirty feet away from her. "*Salve*, Seer and *Servus Populi*."

She looked at him keenly, with the mixture of pity and wariness he was used to seeing in the eyes of older females. "*Salve*, Counselor."

"Your *writ ursorum avis*[34] to the songbirds was ... prescient. It has slowed the penetration of the downland forces into our realm."

She inclined her head in the slightest of nods. "The rabbit revolution is an infection. The goal of infection is always to spread." Her claws raked over the reading stone. "I was the first to wake from wintersleep this year, so I took the needed action."

Force Majeure made a gesture of respect. "Brilliant. As always." Then he huffed. "I have a question for the Sky Bear."

She nodded. "Do you wish to reveal?" A bright moment of sun picked out the geometric lines of scar tissue across her broad forehead.

Force Majeure stirred the leaves near him. "Yes."

Clavis Aurea glanced at the raccoon, who picked up her reed pen and dipped it in the ink. Then she looked back to Force Majeure.

He took a deep breath and rolled out a long rumbly exhale. "*If I am granted what I desire, what is my near future?*"

The raccoon wrote. The older bear nodded. "Very well." She went into the green tangle of the chapel and came out

---

[34] Command of the bears to the birds

holding a small bag in her mouth. With a flick of her head, she tossed the bag across the space separating them. Then she sang the ceremonial words in a growly contralto.

> *"A gift for the one who needs wisdom*
> *The bones of the mighty will speak*
> *Arise to the high place and cast them*
> *And then you will find what you seek*
>
> *The Founders will give of their knowledge*
> *The seer shall make their words clear*
> *And so shall the answers be written*
> *Ask what you will, and then hear."*

Force Majeure took the bag in his mouth and began to climb one of the redwoods. The trunk was many feet in diameter, but the bark was soft and the channels in it were deep. It was easy to sink his long claws into this welcoming surface and pull his great bulk skyward. In less than a minute, he was more than fifty feet above the clay plaza, with all the stars of Ursa Major spread out beneath him.

He shifted his teeth on the bag, so he could dip into it with a huge forepaw. Then he scooped up several faded carpal bones of revered forebears and tossed them toward the star plaza. They dropped away from him, spreading as they fell, and then struck the hard surface and bounced, finally coming to rest scattered across the stars. Then he threw another pawful, and another, until he had thrown nineteen in all.

When he was done, he climbed down and stood respectfully at the side of the star plaza as Clavis Aurea came forward and carefully nosed over the bones, noting where they lay on the body of the Sky Bear. She spent many minutes padding back and forth over the smooth surface, murmuring. The Civil Raccoon held her reed pen ready.

At last she spoke. "Note the preponderance of bones gathered on the forepaw," she said. "The forepaw is the organ of doing. The bones are saying there will be action."

The raccoon wrote quickly and neatly in the paperbark ledger as the seer talked.

The bear walked to another part of the plaza. "Note the pattern of bones near the forehead," she continued. "They are close to the front of the head, signifying command." She paused and looked again at the head. "These bones near the canine teeth suggest that the action is a forceful attack."

Force Majeure chewed his lip. It looked as though the bones were leading in the direction he was hoping for. He felt his heart rate accelerate a little.

Clavis Aurea walked to the edge of the circle of moonstones measuring the weeks. "See the pattern of bones indicating the moonstone at the coming equinox, the balance point when all is in harmony. The Founders are telling us this date for the coming action will have great consequence." She looked up at Force Majeure, and then at the raccoon, who was writing busily.

Then the graying grizzly returned to her station near the tumbledown chapel. She stood and folded her forepaws over her chest. "Action. Command. Attack. Consequence. This is your conditional future." She blinked slowly. "The wise ones have spoken. The scrying is adjourned."

Force Majeure knelt down at the edge of the circle facing

the elderly seer. He knew he was being given the chance he craved. A warm rush swept through him, and he trembled a little. Perhaps he could finally throw off his ancient guilt. He touched his forehead to the ground. "*Gratias tibi ago.*"[35]

Clavis Aurea gazed at him as the sun came from behind a cloud and shone on her forehead, making the constellation of Ursa Major writ in scar tissue gleam. Finally she spoke. "I knew your mother," she said. "Don't shame me, little bear."

Anastasia

Every day, she sang her couplet for several hours up on the ledge. She had no idea if the birds were even hearing it, let alone learning it. She didn't hear anyone repeating it. But she kept on. It was her only chance to be found.

As she sang, she watched the wolflings playing down on the island. From above, it was easy to see what attracted them. Movement. A pear falling from a branch called forth a pounce.

A leaf blowing in the wind generated a chase, culminating in their tiny jaws seizing the leaf and shaking it to bits. She shivered as she thought about how easily this behavior would be transferred to her.

She needed something for them to do that would soak up this energy. So she mulled it over as she sang, until she came up with a plan. Then when she finished her singing shift, she went and found the pups. She was still being wary with them, so they were always glad to see her approach.

---

[35] I give you thanks.

They were roughhousing together by the boulders. Sephora noticed her approaching first. She nudged her siblings. "Look," she said. "It's ... it's ... " There was a pause, and Anastasia could see on the puppy's face that she was running through a list of possible words, already grown enough to realize that some would be suitable and some would not, but unsure which was which. "It's ... *her*," she said finally.

The others turned. "Her! Yay!" cried Micah, running toward her and pushing his nose under her warm ruff.

Anastasia allowed them to gather around her, wriggling and pressing against her. After a few moments, they settled in, and she felt them breathe out a comfy exhalation together.

"Running is fun, isn't it?" she said.

The pups all yelped in agreement.

"And chasing someone is fun," said Anastasia.

The young wolves growled in happy assent.

"Do you want to know how to have the most fun chasing someone?" asked Anastasia.

Her pupils let out small inquisitive arfs.

"When you catch up with them," she said carefully. "Touch them with your nose to show that you *won*. Then *you* get to run and they have to chase *you*."

The pups seemed confused by this. She knew that a million years of ancestors were already whispering in their ears. *Run. Chase. Kill.*

"But—" began Micah, softly.

"You win by *touching* them," said Anastasia in a firmly cheerful voice. "Then when you're a winner, you get to run wherever *you* want, and everyone has to follow you. *You're the leader.*" She nuzzled them. "It's good to be winner."

Micah squirmed uncomfortably. Tennyson turned and looked at her with his maple-green eyes. The pale winter sun came out from behind a cloud and made his silver-tipped golden fur gleam for a moment. "I want to be a winner," he said.

Anastasia kissed his forehead. "And so you shall be."

This kiss set off a storm of wriggling in the tiny pack. "Me, me, me! I want to be a winner!" shouted Micah.

Anastasia kissed him. "Now you know how," she said.

Sephora gazed at her, her evergreen eyes taking in everything. "I want to be ... like *her*," she said.

Anastasia felt a special tug at her heart. This one wanted to be the good daughter. The daughter Anastasia had always wanted to be. She nuzzled the pup's head and then kissed her. "You will be whatever you desire."

The pups snuggled around her. Anastasia was pleased that her idea seemed to be gaining traction, but she also felt torn. For all this happy moment made her body feel good, she knew she was just using their need for affection. It was working because she knew things that they didn't. And she had very good reasons for what she was doing. It all seemed uncomfortably close to the behavior of Olympia, her own mother, who had honed expedience to an art form and cast Anastasia out when needed.

Anastasia shook herself and sat up suddenly. "This kind of fun is called a *game*," she said, adopting a storybook voice. "And this is the oldest game in the world. Animals have been playing it since before the dawn of time. It's called *tag*."

Aliyah

After asking many passersby for directions, Aliyah and Gaetan finally found their way to Force Majeure's study in the repurposed athletic complex that the bears had named Precedent Park. They stopped just outside the entry to a crumbling curling court, and they could hear Force Majeure speaking within.

Aliyah looked at Gaetan. "Are we really going to do this?"

"He listened to you before," said Gaetan. His scent was hot and shiny. "And now he's in charge of the war effort." He put his muzzle close to her ear. "You talked and bears *listened*."

"I mean going over Atticus' head? He's not going to like that." She scraped her forepaw over the cracked everstone pavement, feeling suddenly uneasy. This had all seemed like such a great idea a few hours ago when they first heard of Force Majeure's appointment as lead counsel on the downland war. Now the repercussions of approaching the bears again were looming larger in her mind. And as a wolf, she knew wolves had long memories concerning hierarchical slights.

"He wants you to be his subordinate," said Gaetan. "Is that what *you* want?"

"No," said Aliyah.

Gaetan nuzzled her. "I'm just your excitable friend," he murmured. "Don't let me talk you into anything you don't want to do."

Aliyah stretched and shook, making her armor rattle. Then she glanced at Gaetan and jerked her head toward the doorway. As they entered, she saw the grizzly bear standing by a reading stone in the center of the chamber, which was almost a hundred feet wide. His left ear was bleeding around new rings that had been added. Now there were four. He was speaking aloud and a Civil Raccoon at a smaller reading stone near the wall was writing quickly in a paperbark ledger.

A sugar maple was growing up through the middle of the floor and a stand of balsam fir was clustered along one side. The floor was carpeted with dead leaves and pine needles.

Atticus Peacemaker was lying against the wall on the other side of the chamber, flanked by a guard of four other Municipal Wolves. He got up quickly as she entered.

Force Majeure looked up and saw her. She felt the same atavistic fear wash over her as the violet eyes came to rest on her, but it was not so fierce as the first time. She was getting used to it. Gaetan lay down against the wall behind her.

"Counselor," she said, and bowed to the grizzly bear.

He growled softly.

"Commander," she said, bowing to the wolf.

"This is a war council," said Atticus, standing stiffly. "There's no place here for freelancers. Please be on your way."

She began with a determinedly cheerful tone. "I have an idea that could be helpful to the war effort—"

"There's a procedure for that," broke in Atticus. "Go to the City Guardhouse and you will be interviewed." He made a dismissive gesture with his head.

Aliyah did not move, but she lowered her head into a conciliatory stance. "This will take some time to execute," she said quietly. "It would need to be acted on quickly—"

The Commander's eyes flicked to one of his subordinates, who immediately rose and began padding toward Aliyah.

"We'll escort you to the Guardhouse," he said. "Thank you for your assistance."

Force Majeure growled and blinked slowly, his violet eyes unreadable, drifting toward indigo. Just as the Municipal Wolf reached Aliyah, he said, "I will hear this refugee."

The Municipal Wolf coming toward her stopped. She immediately launched into the words she had prepared. "It's about farkillers. I know metal is scarce and chain mail cannot be universal, but there's a way—"

"We went. We observed. We adapted," interrupted Atticus. "That is what *professional* fighters do." His blue eyes were cool. "We entered their space and used trees and scrub for cover. They fired at us but our casualties were few."

"You played your surprise card," said Aliyah. "You won't have it to play again."

Atticus scoffed.

"Unless those rabbits are fools, they are cutting down those trees *right now*," said Aliyah. "They have the raccoons and tools to do it." She took up a more aggressive stance, head high. "And they are *not* fools. You won't get down the Stone Stair again without major bloodshed. And the same goes for the Midsummer Path."

Atticus started to speak, his tone rising, but Force Majeure cut him off with a wave of his massive paw. "What is your idea?" he rumbled.

Aliyah took a deep breath. "The Wicker Flats mice can make lightweight shields that will stop and catch the blades their farkillers throw. There can be a grip that a wolf seizes in her mouth to hold and carry it. It won't solve every problem, but it will severely blunt the power of farkillers on the battlefield."

Atticus and his cohort whispered among themselves. Force Majeure looked at her for a long time. Finally, with a gesture that took in both her and Gaetan, he rumbled, "Where are your Visitor passes?"

Aliyah glanced back at Gaetan. He scrambled to his feet. She looked down. "We have none. We have no friends here." She could not keep herself from glancing at Atticus' icy blue eyes. "Our three days are almost up."

The grizzly bear turned to his raccoon scribe. "Kindly escort these refugees to the Pass Board," he growled softly. "I will vouch."

FREDDIE

The meeting of conspirators at Warren *Sans Gloire* was getting tenser by the minute. "You see what's going on outside," said Nicodemus, as the sound of distant chanting and thumping came faintly into their meeting room. "People are afraid something has happened to Anastasia. Everyone from Holly and Yasmin down to the littlest craftmouse is quizzing me. I can't keep up this pretense forever."

Even deep underground, they could hear it. The three slow stamps, in time with the three-word chant. *Where is she? Where is she?*

"The thing is," said Freddie, "if they find out now, there are going to be riots." His gray-and-white fur looked bedraggled. He had been traveling up and down the Million Acre Wood for many days, working on fortifications at the Shandy Lift and other secondary targets, all while hoping desperately for some word from the songbirds.

"Especially when they find out youse been lying right to their faces," said Stan. "It's a frickin' miracle the story hasn't leaked already, considering how many people were there when she fell."

"*Armée Libre* discipline good," growled Wendy.

Love Bug stood, looking leaner after the many patrols he had led into the uplands over the last few weeks. A red bandana of woven agave fiber around his head gave him a very fierce aspect. "It isn't just discipline," he said. "The fighters love her. They risk their lives for her."

The vibrations from the hundreds of animals stamping in time outside were making little showers of loose earth fall from the ceiling of the chamber they were in. *Where is she? Where is she?*

Wendy let out a low rumbling growl. "Still have work need done. Anastasia or no." Freddie flinched at the *no*. Wendy ignored him. "Need two hundred more raccoon."

Nicodemus grimaced. "I can't keep this up. These heavy labor levees are exhausting our allies' goodwill," he said. "Even now that we're able to include some payment, they still don't like doing it." He spread his paws. "They're small businessfolk. They fought to be free, not to be our slaves."

Wendy scoffed. "Need more help cutting down trees at Stair and Path," she said. "Need clear for crossbow." She leaned forward. "Let wolf and bear come down, then you see *slaves*."

Freddie turned his eyes to Stan. "Have your people heard anything? From … ?"

The bluebird shook his head. "Nah, and everyone's totally wired for any sign of…" he trailed off. Just talking about their failures in searching for Anastasia was so painful that sometimes they just found themselves murmuring and gesturing. Because saying it outright made it feel so much more real.

They decided to take a break, and Freddie took the moment to slip outside and size up the throng. These people—*their* people—could become enemies if all did not go well. He went out through a side entry and stood at the edge of the greensward, watching the mass of animals steadily, relentlessly articulate their anxiety, with a nascent threat of violence bubbling just beneath the surface.

Even though he could not see them well, their movements and voices were all too clear. Rabbits slapped their powerful back feet on the earth. Mice and raccoons struck the ground with heavy tools. Squirrels stamped their branches so hard they made the trees shake. And the songbirds led the chant. Propelling it, underscoring it, elaborating on it.

Where is she? Where is she?

And everywhere, there were young animals running and playing. Baby raccoons, baby rabbits, baby mice, baby squirrels, and baby birds were dashing among the demonstrators. They were fearless and happy, engaging in a festival of zoomies, adding to the chaos. They were beautiful and terrible in their inexhaustible, unstoppable energy. The dark side of freedom from hunters was making itself manifest so much more quickly than anyone had expected.

Freddie felt sick to his stomach. Everything they had fought for seemed at risk. And once again, the threat was from themselves. He looked down, seeking comfort in a complex intaglio of termite trails exposed by bark peeling off a fallen log.

Then he heard something, just barely audible over the noise. Bits of it came through in the moments between the chanted words. It was a single meadowlark singing. And a word jumped out at him.

Freddie.

His heart leaped. He ran toward the sound, away from the all-consuming chant. He heard it again. A single voice. Clear. Pure.

Freddie dear.

He was racing through the trees now, raging at the noise roaring behind him like a tidal wave. He was so afraid that the voice would stop. That he would lose it. There it was again. More of it.

Freddie dear, I love you so.

It must be her. It had to be her. She was alive. She had heard. She had understood. She had answered. It was every good thing, all happening at once. The adrenaline burned so hard that it hurt him, but he did not care. He ran, and he loved her. He loved her for being *alive*. He loved her for being the one who could make everything all right again. Who *would* make it all right again.

He was racing, gasping for air. He came out into a clearing and saw the meadowlark on the branch of a mimosa tree. And she sang so beautifully. So simply. So understandably.

"*Freddie dear, I love you so
Five red palms, I am below*"

He knelt down in the snow at the foot of the mimosa and sobbed as though his heart would break.

Chapter 17

The strength of the bear is not in the claw, it is in the writ.

—*Praetor Peregrinus*
Founder, City of Oom

Force Majeure

The City Guardhouse was a classic *Futurist Nouveau* monstrosity, its surface covered with bas-reliefs of cycads and colorful dragonflies the size of eagles. Just inside the heavy gate was a large courtyard, and it was filled with more than a hundred Municipal Wolves and two hundred coyote auxiliaries. Several hundred City Crows perched atop the walls, fluttering and cawing.

Force Majeure shambled through the gate as the sun reached its zenith. He walked to the center of the space and the animals cleared a wide area around him. A few moments later, Aliyah and Gaetan slipped though the gate and took up positions by the wall. Atticus glared at them.

The great brown bear stood upright, looming over the crowd. "*Salvete, omnibus,*"[36] he rumbled. Then he leaned forward. "Members of the City Guard. You know me. You know my crime." He looked up at the sun and a long groan escaped him. "You may not know I took an oath abjuring all personal violence as part of the adjudication of my case." He blinked and looked intently at the animals before him. "And more than that, I have come to see violence on the part of bears as a step backward into the dark. Not a step forward into the bright future the Founders imagined for us." Force Majeure dropped onto all fours, then dragged his long foreclaws over the broken everstone pavement. "You have nothing to fear from me."

The canids squirmed and looked at each other. The crows cawed softly.

"You have heard of the downland insurgents," rumbled the grizzly. "Their farkillers threaten the fragile *Pax Ursorum* we are trying to build in Land of Oom. So even though we have other campaigns and you have been busy, we must take substantive action."

Atticus Peacemaker growled in assent. And many of the clan captains growled as well, their double earrings flashing in the pale sun.

"We have thrown the bones and the Founders have spoken. The auspicious date for our attack will be the coming

---

[36] Greetings to all

equinox. There is much to be worked out, but we will not miss this moment."

He looked back at Aliyah and Gaetan. "Refugees from the war are sharing their knowledge."

The two downland canids bowed to the group. The members of the City Guard looked at them curiously.

"This is a new challenge, and we will be doing new things," said Force Majeure. "We need to throw our enemy off balance. Make them uncertain where our attack will be coming from."

"*Yes*," said Aliyah.

Force Majeure moved forward and the animals flowed away from him like water. "We all know that bears are not the best at new things." A little self-deprecating half-smile passed over his face. There was a general chuckle from the assembled fighters. The grizzly turned and swept the crowd with his violet eyes. "But you will find that I am a different kind of bear."

Mabel

Mabel awoke to find herself inside another of the tumbledown buildings at *Le Sanctuaire*. The last thing she remembered was going outside the Temple of the Water Goddess after they had been left alone, and running into a young *Enchanté* with sparkling periwinkle eyes who had said, "I've been sent to help." Then she had given them small sips from a gourd that hung around her neck, and they had felt no more pain.

Now Mabel was sprawled on a soft bed of moss and dried leaves, and Sunbeam lay near her. They were in a nook near a wall. Just like in the water temple, the floor itself felt warm, so she felt snug and comfortable.

And Newly Beloved thought long in the dreamtime and said, 'The one who brings fear may also bring hope. And—'

Suddenly she heard a soft tapping of hooves crossing the floor, and looked up to see the same young *Enchanté* approaching. "Greetings, fellow travelers," she said. Her voice was similar to the others, but her tone was considerably friendlier.

She carried a wooden box with a braided agave twine handle looped over her tusks. As she set it down on the floor, two mice scampered down from her forehead, ran to the end of her long snout, and leaped nimbly onto the box. Mabel noticed that one of the mice was missing a foreleg, and the other had the scar of a terrible bite on one side.

"I'm Calliope," said the *Enchanté*. "I'm one of the healers. And these are my interns." The mice each bowed and introduced themselves.

"I'm Mabel," said Mabel, sitting up. She noticed Sunbeam waking and stretching near her.

Calliope gestured with her cloven hoof for Sunbeam to come closer, and Mabel heard her quietly *tsk tsk* as she peered at the injury to her ear.

Then she nudged open the box with her nose. Inside were many different compartments holding herbs, flowers, and other supplies and tools.

"First," said Calliope. "Take a sip of this for pain." One of the mice offered a dried bean pod containing a fragrant liquid. Sunbeam took a small drink.

"What is that?" asked Mabel.

"Poppy milk," said Calliope. "You had this yesterday."

Then the mouse interns approached Sunbeam's ear and carefully cleaned it, applying water from another pod and slowly peeling off the matted layers of dried blood and dirt and leaves. Sunbeam winced as they worked, but relaxed as the poppy milk took effect.

When the injury was clean, the mice ran back to the box and picked up a sheet of woven spider webbing and dexterously applied it to Sunbeam's ear.

"How do you weave spider web like this?" asked Mabel. "Whenever we take it, it just balls up into a sticky mess."

Calliope smiled. "We don't just *take* it from the spiders," she said. "We help them. And they repay us by weaving these squares."

Mabel was surprised. She had never heard of anyone negotiating deals with spiders. These were some seriously unusual animals. It gave her hope she might get what she came for.

After the mice finished with Sunbeam, they cleaned and treated the deep gouges on Mabel's face and belly. Then they began to repack their box.

Sunbeam, weaving a little, stepped forward and kissed the heads of the mice one by one, and then embraced and kissed Calliope's long snout. "Thank you," she said. "I feel so, *so* much better."

"Say you so?" chuckled Calliope. "That's the poppy milk talking. I'll leave you this small pod. When it wears off, have another sip." She gave them a serious look. "You both came in with a special kind of bad magic called *infection*. You need to rest now."

"How is the floor warm?" asked Sunbeam.

Calliope's eyes twinkled. "The blood of the earth runs close to the skin here. We feel her warmth."

"Will we see Clytemnestra again?" asked Mabel.

"That depends on her," said Calliope. "City of Oom is many miles from here, but in recent moons, our leaders have been busy fighting off their attacks. She may not have time for you." Then she put her face close to the ground so her mouse interns could scramble onto her snout and up her forehead. Mabel noticed now that they each rode in one of her ears.

"Here, eat these," said Calliope taking some triangular leaves out of the another pouch that hung by her side.

"What are they?" asked Sunbeam.

"Lotus leaves."

"Also for pain?" asked Mabel.

Calliope smiled gently. "Pain of the soul."

The *Enchanté* was about to leave. There was one more question, an awkward one. Mabel could not stop herself from blurting it out. "Are we prisoners?"

Calliope gazed at her. "Of course." Her periwinkle blue eyes were suddenly cool. "Aren't we all prisoners of our past actions?"

GAETAN

Poison Wind, the tiny master of wicker, looked delighted to see Aliyah and Gaetan again. Force Majeure's raccoon scribe entered the Wicker Flats Reedcraft shop after them, a heavy bag of paperbark, pens, and ink slung over his shoulder.

Aliyah went immediately to the boxes where she had first

seen the impregnable faithful heartweave, nosing along them and raking her teeth over the surface. Gaetan hung back, observing the raccoon. As a canid, he couldn't read, let alone write, and he found the power invested in these small and burly city officials fascinating.

"We're ordering three hundred of the shields we talked about," said Aliyah, without preamble. "With mouth grips. We need them as soon as possible."

Poison Wind looked shocked, then delighted, then concerned. He rubbed his tiny paws together and looked up at the golden wolf looming over him, "Yea, that shall be a marvelous work and a wonder." He rubbed his head. "And the remuneration arrangements shall be…?"

The raccoon scribe stepped forward, already scribbling on a piece of paperbark. "Downland War. 79817," he said briskly. "Approved by Force Majeure. Half up front. Half on delivery." He slapped the paperbark down on the floor by Poison Wind and grinned. "A bodacious day for the grass mousies, eh?"

"Reed mice," said Poison Wind automatically. Then he caught sight of the figure on the paperbark and staggered back, hand over his heart.

The raccoon tapped the paperbark chit. "Present to the City Bank and get the cashola flowing, lil dude."

Poison Wind leaped into action. "Sisters! Brothers! I bid you come to the floor! The very lords of the City have entered our humble shop, strewth!" He dashed behind a table and came back pushing a small step ladder on tiny wheels. "And bring the measuring strips!"

Seconds later, mice were streaming into the front of the

shop, still wearing aprons and carrying tools from the work they had been doing in the back. Soon they were swarming over Aliyah, carrying out measurements and calling out numbers to Poison Wind, who stood collecting information in a small logbook below.

"Measure him, too," said Aliyah, jerking her head toward Gaetan. "We need some sized for wolves, some for coyotes."

Gaetan giggled as the mice climbed over him. He was not used to being touched, and in getting measured by a swarm of mice, he found that he was ticklish. "Better size up my measurements," he said. "I'm small for a coyote. Plus the..." He held up his injured foreleg and made a rueful moue.

Aliyah glanced at him. "Nah," she said. "You're perfect."

FREDDIE

It was late at night and the animals chanting outside Warren *Sans Gloire* had gone home. The conspirators, electrified by the news that Anastasia was alive and communicating, were engaged in an intense brainstorm in a meadow a few hundred yards away.

The need was clear. *Find her. Find her. Find her.* But they weren't sure how to do it, and all the energy burning through their muscles kept causing the rabbits to race around the meadow engaging in exuberant *binks*. Stan kept soaring suddenly skyward, then augering in doing barrel rolls, only to pull up at the last moment. Even Wendy allowed herself the occasional good-natured "*Bah!*"

Nicodemus was doing his best to keep the discussion focused. "We know what we're looking for now," he said. "Five red palms. So the first question is: how can we get eyes in the sky long enough to find them?"

Stan alighted on a nearby twig. "Here's what happens when we try to bust into their space. One or two uplanders will notice immediately and begin to attack. Then that action draws attention, so more of them come." He shook all his feathers as though snow bathing. "Then more and more, then their whole network starts mobbing in." He looked at the others. "A couple minutes of that and you're going to get croaked. You gotta retreat."

The downland brain trust had always felt stymied at this point. It seemed hopeless. But the energy buzzing through them now helped them push through this blockade.

"What if you stay low, under the treeline, so you can't easily be seen?" asked Love Bug.

Stan shook his head. "We tried that. They're thinly spread, picking bugs off branches, eating junk off the ground. And as soon as one of them sees us, they start yelling and the others come."

"Give you weapons," rumbled Wendy.

"Can't carry much," said Stan. "And there's a jillion of them, one or two of us. Can't hold out."

"What if there were many of you?" asked Nicodemus.

Stan shrugged. "A big cloud of us attracts more of them. It turns into a giant flying brawl, which of course draws in more on their side."

Freddie felt a little tickle happening in the back of his head. "How about … as many songbirds as you can get … in the smallest space possible? It would be"—Freddie dipped into his designer brain for a moment—"a sphere of birds.

That's how you get the most birds in a shape with the least surface area."

"And then do what?" said Stan.

"Stay low, just above the trees, so you can't easily be seen from a distance. And when the other songbirds do come—"

"Kill them," said Wendy.

Stan squirmed and looked uncomfortable. "Ehhhh, songbirds will kick the crap out of crows and raptors all day long," he said. "Killing other songbirds ... I don't ... I don't think they'll go for that."

Nicodemus looked thoughtful. "Maybe two or three of your people could seize them one by one as they come. Grasp their beaks with your feet to keep them from calling alarms. Weigh them down. Fall to the ground with them and hold them."

Stan looked dubious. "Maybe."

"It would just be for as long as you're in the area," said Nicodemus. "Then release everyone when you retreat."

"So you'd have a dense ball of birds moving and scouting quietly," said Freddie, beginning to pace. "Silently sucking in uplanders and throwing them down. As long as you start with a big enough ball, you could cover a lot of territory. Seems like it could work."

Stan flapped his wings and spat a large gob of phlegm. "Easy for youse to say," he grumbled. "You don't gotta do it."

"Any better ideas?" demanded Wendy, looking around the group.

There were none.

"Okay, okay," said Stan. He inhaled deeply and touched his breastbone with his wingtip. "Let's build this frickin' birdball."

Dingus

It was a quiet moment at the underground barracks at the foot of the Stone Stair. Stan had arrived suddenly and taken most of the *Armée Libre* songbirds and gone off to who knows where. He'd been acting mysteriously for weeks now.

There were a few Ascending Squirrels on sentry duty outside, but with the late hour, most of the animals were sleeping. Dingus was taking advantage of the stillness to work on his underground nut garden. He was building it in a wide chamber the rabbits had dug for him, with a small hole in the ceiling that let in a fine sliver of moonlight.

So now, as the other animals slept, he carefully arranged a collection of acorns atop a bed of sand he had brought up from a nearby stream. When all was harmonious, he got out a little rake made with a bundle of twigs and carefully dragged it over the sand, creating patterns that were like waves lapping at the shores of islands.

"I am flow," he murmured.

Suddenly, two Ascending Squirrels came racing into the main space, shouting, "*Attack! Attack! Attack!*" They ran around the perimeter of the hall, whacking the sleeping animals in their bunks along the edge, calling, "*Stations! Stations! Stations!*"

As the crossbow crews scrambled out, bleary-eyed, Dingus ran in from his nut garden. "What? What is it?"

"Crows!" shouted one the squirrels. "Attacking the crossbows!"

A hard burn ran along Dingus's spine. *Attacking*

crossbows? That didn't even make sense. Crossbows were huge. What could crows do to them?

He ran up the ramp and out onto the embankment, and by the light of the moon saw what appeared to be living shadows swarming over the light wood of the crossbows. *Doing what?* He was a few steps ahead of the crossbow crews, so he just threw himself into the tumbling mass of darkness and started scratching and grabbing.

It was strange; the crows weren't fighting back. They were just dropping straight down from the sky, thrashing around a bit and then shooting back up. As they rose into the moonlight, he could see the circles of metal around their ankles that showed they were from the City. And something else. They were carrying sticks, with pointy ends, and—

"*Quarrels!*" shouted Dingus in his ringy command voice, just as the raccoons and other squirrels arrived. "*They're stealing quarrels!*" The quarrel boxes lay open, their simple latch mechanisms picked apart. The *Armée Libre* had never anticipated this kind of attack.

The raccoons waded in, smacking crows out of the air with heavy, open-handed slaps. And the squirrels flew among them, biting and scratching, seizing quarrels in their hands. Dingus wrapped his arms around three quarrels that were rising next to him, held fast in the talons of a large crow. He was carried aloft for a few feet, biting furiously, until his weight became too much and the crow dropped the quarrels and sped skyward.

Some of the raccoon teams were loading now, with the bow riders taking up their positions. "*Fire! Fire! Fire!*" shouted Dingus, his command voice crackling over the battlespace.

And then something else became apparent. The crossbows on their coconut mounts could not rock backward far enough to fire up at the crows that were racing straight up into the sky.

They were defenseless.

Anastasia

Today is the killing day.

Time was growing short. The pups were getting big. They were almost too big for her to kick into the fast-rushing water of the stream. The bigger they got, the more of a fight it would be. And there was a new development. Recently, the pups had started complaining about being hungry, even after drinking coconut milk. That meant they were growing into their next phase. She was playing with fire by waiting.

A soft heart is a dead heart. Her tribal rabbit voices were talking to her urgently. Demanding. Yelling. *Today. Today. Kill them today.*

She needed a backup plan, and it was all too clear what that was. With her heart as heavy as stone, she dragged herself to the planar boulder near her burrow and stood there, scraping the blade of her Dragon Claw across the flat surface. It had been dulled considerably when she was hacking at the dead palm. Now she made it as sharp as she could. If she had to use it, she wanted it to go as fast as possible.

Then she maundered along the sandy bank, on the opposite side of the island from the pups, planning her approach.

She came across the purple fruit that she had pulled off the carrion bushes on the ledge above when she had been trying to get as high as possible. So these weren't windfalls, as the other fruit had been. And she noticed something different about them.

They did not stink.

She nosed among them. There was a mildly spicy smell. And something else she could not name. It didn't appeal to her, but it was very different than the dead animal smell she usually associated with these fruits.

She began to gnaw on the tough skins, in a desultory way. Just putting off the moment of truth for a few more minutes. It was a last ditch effort. If this was not food for wolves, today was their last day on earth.

In a few minutes, she had ripped one open. Inside was not the rotting mess she had seen before, but rather a long brown tube of something soft. There was the mild spiciness, and now she could also smell fat, and a charred flavor. As a rabbit, she felt a mild disgust, but maybe the pups would like it.

Her heart began to beat faster. She tried not to get too invested. These fruits had failed before.

She called the pups over, trying to sound casual. Ever ready for anything new in their island prison, they came bounding over, with Sephora in the lead. They immediately ran to the open fruit and nosed across the dark spicy tube. There was an inquisitive arf. A lick. A tiny bite. A moment to consider. A swallow. Then another tiny bite. Then another. And suddenly all three sets of fangs were tearing at the tender belly of the fruit, competing to get this thing, bite it, eat it. Happy, excited yelps.

Anastasia felt a wave of relief sweep over her. They had food. In abundance. She would not have to be the angel of death, ending their short lives. She felt weak. Dizzy. She lay down among the fruit, surprised at how much lighter she felt suddenly. She hadn't realized how much of a burden this was.

As she lay on the cold beach with the side of her face pressed into the sand, just a few inches away from one of the long purple fruits, she noticed, for the first time, tiny lettering on the bottom:

"Sausage2Go™
BeyondMonsanto®"

FREDDIE

Freddie and Nicodemus were in the library at Warren *Sans Gloire*, trawling through the collection of pages.

"I hope Stan gets his birdball working soon," murmured Freddie.

"Me, too," said Nicodemus, from the other side of the chamber. "Now I need your focus, Freddie. We're reaching a dead end on our farkillers. The crossbows are hard to move, with limited firing arcs. And the big stonethrowers can't move at all."

"I know, I know," muttered Freddie. "We need something light." He was pulling out pages and scanning them at random, hoping for some inspiration.

"Ideally, something an animal can carry," said Nicodemus.

Freddie shot a glance at him. "Raccoons can't aim," he said wearily. "That leaves squirrels, rats, and mice." He chewed his lip. "And a crossbow small enough for them would be so tiny—"

"I think that's the wrong track," interrupted Nicodemus as he flipped through a stack of ancient pages. "We need a *new* idea."

Freddie was nosing through a section of the library with new pages, and he found a crumbled half-page with *'Weapons of the Holy Land 136'* written across the bottom edge. There was a colorful image, now faded, of a large Dead God laying sprawled on the sand with a smaller figure standing above, holding some kind of stringy thing.

There was also some text.

"Have you seen this?" he said.

Nicodemus looked over his shoulder and read the text aloud:

"And David put his hand in his bag and took out a stone and slung it and struck the Philistine on his forehead. The stone sank into his forehead, and he fell on his face to the ground. 1 Samuel 17.49"

Freddie frowned. This sounded vaguely like the Word of Dah, although he had never heard these words before. But the page also featured a sketch of something labelled a *sling*. It looked very simple. Just two short pieces of cord joined by some kind of pocket. There were also sketches of a Dead God whirling it and using it to throw stones.

"This is some kind of weapon," said Nicodemus.

"Hard to imagine you can hit anything with a rock you spin around," said Freddie doubtfully.

"Looks like they're claiming you can kill with it," said Nicodemus.

"You'd have to be a crazy good acrobat and a genius at trajectories," said Freddie.

The elder bunny smiled as the pale sun streamed down

through the skylight and made his silver fur shine. "I smell squirrel."

Force Majeure

Force Majeure eyed the birds of prey in their tall pines as he approached the neighborhood atop the Great Hill in Oom that was known as Raptor Heights. The raptors were entirely unlike the crows. The dark flyers were loyalists, wedded to their wolf clans, and willing to serve larger goals. These cool-eyed killers required significantly more management. Fortunately, he had been able to bring some management tools with him.

The eagles, hawks, ospreys, and falcons offered no acknowledgement as Force Majeure moved through their space, but that was typical. Then he arrived at a clearing in the midst of the tall trees and reached into a bag hanging around his neck. His forepaw came out with a stack of ordinary-looking green leaves, and he scattered these on the ground near him.

Immediately, a riffle flickered through the raptors overhead. They shifted on their branches, and some soft piping noises began, slowly building into louder peals. A white-and-gray goshawk lifted from his branch and glided downward. Then an osprey unfolded her long narrow wings and swept toward the young grizzly. A moment later, a dozen hawks, falcons, and shrikes were in the air, converging on Force Majeure and his scattered leaves. Even an eagle or two joined in.

The goshawk was the first to land, and he darted his head down, snatched a leaf and tucked it into his cheek with his claw. Moments later, others were landing, grabbing leaves, and doing the same. Force Majeure watched them silently, until half a hundred raptors were gathered around him.

Then he reached his right forepaw across, touched his left shoulder, and smacked the ground in front of him. Twigs and bits of old frozen snow scattered.

"*Salvete, omnibus,*" he rumbled.

"We welcome you, Counselor," called the goshawk and some of the shrikes. The others just stared with their large, yellow eyes.

"I bring you this *go leaf* as a goodwill gift," rumbled Force Majeure. "It is fresh from our diamond house."

There was some cawing of thanks. Then the complaints started.

"Why has the *go leaf* been short lately?" asked a kestrel with thrashed-looking plumage.

"We were told there'd be a lot more *go leaf* soon," said a cranky-looking buzzard. "That was weeks ago."

Force Majeure ignored them. As far as the raptors were concerned, *go leaf* was always in short supply. It suited the bears to keep it that way. These death-from-above loners were hard to wrangle. *An anxious raptor is a motivated raptor.*

The grizzly assumed his friendliest voice. "I would also like to offer each of you"—he swept the group with his bright, violet eyes—"some fine fat rabbits who have grown careless. I ask only that you seize them at a time and place of my choosing." He scraped the frozen soil with his long claws. "It's many miles from here. *Go leaf* will be provided for all." He put on a toothy smile, his long yellow fangs shining. "All billable to the new downland war."

"Bunnies and *go leaf* on the City dime?" rasped the goshawk. "Sign me up, Counselor."

Chapter 18

If you don't love the boogle, do you even weasel?
—Weasel proverb

Mabel

Last night there had been the sound of a lot of commotion coming from far off in the hospital. Mabel had done her best to ignore it. In the dawn light, Sunbeam was investigating a pile of bloody, used bandages in a nook a few feet away.

Mabel lay on her moss bed, eating lotus leaves. They had an extraordinary ability to blunt the needles of anxiety that ruled her interior landscape. But they did it without the tipsiness, emotional heat, and foolish behavior that often came along with fermented fruit. Not to mention the hangovers.

'I wouldn't mind having these lotus leaves every day,' murmured Newly Beloved, as she dug her toes in the sand.

'Heck, I probably wouldn't even need the Book of Secrets if I could just turn down the noise like this. On the daily.'

Mabel got up and poked around. "Seen any more lotus?"

"Nah," said Sunbeam, sniffing a lump of something with a bad smell that seemed to have been left out overnight. "You know, I don't like it when you have those *look-through-you* eyes," she said.

Mabel looked up. "What's wrong with it?"

"I don't like people looking through me," said Sunbeam. "Keep your eyes to yourself."

Suddenly, noiselessly, Aeschylus appeared, huge and ghostly in the gray light, just as when they had first seen him in the misty wood.

"The Queen will see you," he said "Hurry."

They followed him through the labyrinthine twists and turn of the hospital, and Mabel was amazed to see so many animals of all kinds being cared for by the *Enchanté* and their interns.

Then they came out on a wide meadow, spotted with old snow over dead grass. Many *Enchanté* were milling about, tusks gleaming in the golden dawn light. Some of the *Enchanté* were freshly injured, blood spatter bright against their white fur. Some lay close to death. The cries of the wounded overwhelmed all other sounds. Healers moved among them, engaged in careful triage.

Mabel saw teams of mice suturing injuries under the direction of *Enchanté* healers, their fine fingers flying. There were also rats, squirrels, songbirds, and even some hawks, all with ancient injuries, working as orderlies, bringing fresh bandages and taking away the bloody wound dressings. Sunbeam poked her nose into everything.

Aeschylus led them to the Queen of Sorrows, who was kneeling by a grand old tusker with fearsome lacerations down his side. She nuzzled his cheek, whispering quiet words into his ear. Then she rose to let the healers take over, and Mabel saw that her cerulean eye was wet with tears. She also had a freshly bleeding gash on her leg.

When she caught sight of Mabel, she said, "We killed the world, and we will always be punished for that." She came near the rabbit and her eye shone like a lake of tears. "And that is right and good."

Mabel, torn by the suffering around her, could not say what she wanted to: *How is this good?* Instead, she simply knelt and said. "Yes, my Queen."

"We have searched our library. We may have your answer," said Clytemnestra.

Mabel's heart leaped. *Get it, get it, get it.*

The Queen of Sorrows walked them toward the edge of the triage area. "We have sent our winged friends flying, asking many questions," she said. Her eye flicked to Sunbeam. "Your sister is leader of your people."

Sunbeam nodded.

The *Enchanté* regarded her at length. "She makes the hunters crazy with fear. The ones coming out of the downlands talk of nothing else."

Sunbeam nibbled her claw and nodded again.

Clytemnestra came near to her. "Is she a moony killer like you?"

Sunbeam looked at Mabel, green eyes huge against her golden fur. They almost had what they needed. What was the right answer? Mabel chewed her lip. She was not sure what words would produce the magic help her people craved, but it seemed wrong to equivocate in the face of these suffering healers. She raised her chin ever so slightly.

Sunbeam turned to the Queen of Sorrows and said, "Yes."

Clytemnestra nodded. "I like the sad killers," she murmured. "No surprises."

One of the many healers ran up to her, and there was a hasty conversation in quiet voices. Then Clytemnestra walked with them along the edge of the triage area. "We are the best healers in the Known World," she said. "But we have no gift for war."

Mabel stared at her bright shining tusks and said nothing. Sunbeam lollopped away and watched a mouse carefully stitching a femoral artery while two others applied pressure to stop the blood flow.

"Like the Allshroom," said Clytemnestra, "we nurture life."

"What is that?" asked Mabel.

Clytemnestra gazed up toward the sun for a moment. "The Allshroom underlays everything. Connects everyone. The mushrooms you see are the Allshroom speaking." Her gaze drifted down and came to rest on the distant mountains. "We will all be under the mushrooms in the end."

Mabel fidgeted uncomfortably.

The Queen turned to her. "This is what I will ask for our learned magic." She lay down on the ground so that her eye was on the same level as Mabel's. "Let your terrifying queen visit me, so I may learn from her. Will you accept this fee?"

Mabel was stunned. *No treasure. No weapons. Just a visit?* Maybe there was something she didn't understand about this offer. Still, if she walked out of this place with the magic solution and hadn't traded away any crossbows, that would be a major victory. "Yes," she said. "*Yes*."

Clytemnestra rose and nodded. "Do you know a plant that some call *rabbit's bane*?"

"Yes," said Mabel. "It's poisonous, isn't it?"

The Queen of Sorrows shook her head. "The Dead Gods made it to be a special kind of weapon against your kind," said Clytemnestra. "But you can use it for your own purposes now." The early morning sun made her blue eye look like a bright summer sea. "If you eat of it, it won't hurt you. But there will be no children."

Aliyah

Force Majeure stood facing the Municipal Wolves and their coyote auxiliaries on the meadowlands just south of the City. The first shipment of wicker shields had arrived from Wicker Flats and now lay on the snowy grass.

Some of the canids were picking them up and tossing them around. There was laughter and roughhousing. Some crude joking. And the general attitude of the troops toward novelty imposed from above was the same as it has always been, for all armies, of all species. *Bigwigs making us do this. Prolly the usual hare-brained crap. Just play along and it will go away.*

Atticus stepped forward. "New ways to keep our troops safe are always welcome," he said, walking across the front of the crowd. "We don't have a full set yet, so I want to see everyone get a chance to try these out today. Just bite the grip, lift them and—"

A throaty intrusive rumble rolled out of the grizzly's throat. Atticus turned and looked at him. Force Majeure leaned forward. "Thank you, commander." The massive head swung toward Aliyah. "I will call the one with experience to the address the troops."

Aliyah dipped her head for a quick nuzzle with Gaetan.

"Summerday rules," he whispered.

She faced the mass of canid soldiers. "Your first encounter with the farkillers was lucky," she said. "Good cover. Good commander." She bowed to Atticus. He nodded his head stiffly, blue eyes cold. "But when you're out in the open, it will seem like blades are falling on you like a murdering rain. They will come from *nowhere*. Then they will be *everywhere*. Fired not by warriors, but by *nobodies*." Her green eyes flashed. "On every side, your colleagues will be bleeding. Falling." She walked among them, looming over them. "They aim for your face. They'll blind you if they can." Her voice floated over an ocean of silence. "And there will be *no one* to tear apart with your teeth and claws."

She pushed into the thickest part of the gathering. "Your only hope will be keeping every part of your body behind your shield. If your shoulder leans out, it will be torn to shreds." She opened her massive jaws and slid them over the shoulder of a coyote near her. He shrank back.. "If your foot is exposed, it will be cut to ribbons." She snapped at the foot of a gray wolf near her, and he jumped away.

An image of Micah Summerday, pierced and bleeding from uncountable arrows, flickered before her eyes. "They kill the strong ones first," she whispered. A deep groan rolled out of her. "The alphas. The glory hounds." She stopped for a breath, and it came out almost like a sob. "Don't be one of those. Fear is your friend. Use your shield and *hide* as you creep forward. *Hide* as you run. *Hide* when you make your final lunge." She raised her head high and her maple-green eyes burned across three hundred intent faces. "And when you get close, *then* you may do all the fine killing you desire."

MABEL

As Mabel and Sunbeam were in their nook in the hospital, gathering their things and preparing to leave, Clytemnestra came to them in a rush, her wound only partly bandaged.

"Something is happening," she said. "I feel it in the Allshroom. The bears are gathering forces, but they're not arrayed against us. I fear they are preparing to march against your people."

Mabel was startled and felt the fear burn start. After many days of eating the lotus leaves every day and slowly sinking into the dreaminess of *Le Sanctuaire*, it felt like a stinging whiplash to be plunged back into existential terror. Sunbeam began muttering to herself as she squeezed items into her small backpack.

"I know your queen is powerful," said Clytemnestra. "But this is no pack of wolves with a few hangers-on that will be coming. Likely it will be a full onslaught from City of Oom. *Ten times* what you've seen before."

Mabel shuddered. "We have... We are..." she could hardly form a sentence.

The *Enchanté* came near to her. "We know this army ... intimately," she said. "So I would send this message to your queen. What these hunters fear is not force, which they understand well because it has always been theirs." Her cloven hoof beat a rapid tattoo on the everstone floor as she spoke. "They fear deep magic. The dark mystery. The one who wields powers that will change not just the world but the hunters *themselves*."

"I understand," said Mabel, although she felt that she didn't really, and the thought of being sucked into another battle was making her feel like the world was tilting.

The Queen of Sorrows spoke quickly, urgently. "We can put you onboard the vessel of a rat peddler going down the Rime River tonight. You'll be at City of Oom late tomorrow. Then you can buy passage from a trader going down the Shandy and be home soon." She looked out at the late afternoon sun. "You have some time. A few days traveling is fine. You may learn something in the City. Maybe you can do something helpful there. But you must start moving now."

Mabel felt faint. Sunbeam jerked her backpack closed with her teeth and said, "I'm ready."

Clytemnestra nuzzled Mabel's head and said, "These are my words for Anastasia: *Be the witch*."

Love Bug

Wendy ducked as a stone flew over her head. "*Focus!*" she barked.

Dingus threw down his sling and stamped on it. "This is not a weapon!" he shouted. Then he let loose a string of what were presumably curses in Sciurid, the ancestral language of the squirrels. On his back, a special slinger's pack with several stones in it rattled as he moved.

Everyone was testy. Love Bug was feeling a little sick of the squirrels himself. *These little showboats really suck up all the air.* He put on his best manager's voice. "New weapons are hard." He patted Dingus, who shrugged him off. Then Love Bug leaned in toward Wendy. "It's going to take a minute," he said. "Squirrels are talented. Not magical."

"I don't need you to make excuses for me," said Dingus sharply.

"I'm sorry," said Freddie, looking around the greensward in front of Warren *Sans Gloire,* where this scene was being repeated with many teams of Ascending Squirrels and rabbit coaches. "We just based this on a sketch. Maybe we didn't make them right." His harlequin face was anxious.

Yasmin, the Home Guard Captain, came out of the main gate of *Sans Gloire* and lolloped toward them. "I don't love you experimenting with new weapons here," she said. "It distracts from our defenses."

Dingus scoffed. "You think something's going to happen right here?"

"Maybe," said Yasmin evenly. "We've taken apart the crossbows, to try and increase the range of motion, and this just adds to the confusion."

Nicodemus came toward them, moving stiffly with age. "Patience, little ones," he said, looking around at his younger comrades. "All is well. We have time to work this out." He sat down near Wendy, pressing his silver fur against her lumpy brown frame. Behind him, the tall narrow poplar tree growing over *Sans Gloire* stood like an unlit grey-brown torch in its leafless state.

Wendy got up and stalked away. "Don't have time," she snapped.

A high screechy noise tickled at the edge of Love Bug's consciousness. He rotated his ears to pick it up better, and then jerked his head around as he realized what it was: the shrill cries of the songbird sentries. "*Raptors! Raptors! Take cover!*"

Love Bug looked up and was astonished to see hawks, falcons, ospreys, *eagles*, falling like hammers from the leaden sky. Dingus took up the alarm cry, his silvery voice ringing. And Wendy launched herself forward, running in a wide circle to gather her troops and shepherd them through the wide front gate of *Sans Gloire*.

Love Bug ran after her, his heart in his throat. Sometimes he wished she wasn't so brave. He did some rapid calculations as he ran. The local songbird sentries were not the highly trained aerial fighters of the *Armée Libre* Air Wing. Stan had taken all of those south to the Stone Stair to work on the birdball formation. So they would not be of much help with the surprise attack from these diving raptors.

Out of the corner of his eye, he could see Yasmin racing for the disassembled crossbows, yelling at the crews to see if any were operable.

Ahead, Wendy was shouting orders and head-butting stragglers as she pushed her people to safety. They were almost done with their sweep. Just a few more seconds and they would be back at the big gate. Love Bug, his bite blade flapping as he ran behind her, began to breathe a little easier. This was a shock, but they would get through it. They were resilient and—

Then a white shape dropped down in front of his eyes. It took him a moment to realize what it was: the wide spread of the tail feathers of an eagle, the largest raptor in the Known World. The yellow claws were reaching down, curved black talons shining. Wendy looked over her shoulder and her eyes widened in terror. She put on a burst of speed.

But the claws were already nearing her, then closing around her middle and plucking her from the ground. A metal circlet around the eagle's left ankle gleamed in the winter sun.

Love Bug heard a terrible sound come from Wendy that he had never heard before. Now her squat body was rising, and she was airborne, her wide paws flailing in the air. The huge brown wings of the eagle came down and blotted out the sun. It seemed like they were moving in slow motion. *Whoom. Whoom. Whoom.*

He knew she was just moments away from disappearing forever. Once she was out of reach, he would never see her alive again. A burst of adrenaline born of terror powered his back legs as he threw himself skyward. As he flew, he jerked his bite blade out of its sheath. An instant later, he was slicing across the right foot of the eagle, cutting through the leathery skin and flesh.

The eagle shrieked in pain and looked down, canting sideways as his right foot lost its grip, and all of Wendy's weight hung on his left. Then Love Bug was falling back toward the ground, hitting and rolling. Above him, Wendy's brown body wriggled like a dervish. She was trying to draw her bite blade, but the eagle's talon was caught in her neck strap and kept it pulled tight against her throat.

The eagle's head was darting down now, yellow and

black eyes glaring, ready to kill the struggling prey. Love Bug launched himself upward again, his bite blade slashing, and managed to drag it across the eagle's face.

With a loud *skree!* of rage, the eagle threw Wendy aside and seized Love Bug as he was falling back. The left foot gripped his shoulders strongly, and the bloody right foot weakly held his hindquarters. A moment later, he was rising, and Wendy was falling away from him as the raptor climbed. Then Dingus was racing into his field of view, pointing upward and chattering, already getting smaller.

Love Bug had his bite blade in his mouth, but he couldn't move enough to get at the legs. The head came down for the *coup de grâce*, the great yellow hooked beak slashing at his head. He jerked up his bite blade and the eagle's killing strike sheared off to the side. He knew he had just a few seconds to make something happen. Once rabbits vanished into the sky, they never came back.

From the side of his eye, he could see the long brown spiky shoots of the poplar tree going by as the raptor gained altitude, huge wings thumping the air. And incredibly, it seemed as though he could hear Dingus, close at hand, shouting.

The beak came down again, and Love Big twisted his body, slashing the air near him, using the razor edges of his bite blade to create a zone of threat around his head. He realized that while the eagle was distracted with him, he had slowed his climb. He could see that the branches of the poplar tree were no longer racing past.

Now it seemed as though the voice of Dingus was actually *above* him. How was that possible? Love Bug stole a moment to look away from the eagle and saw Dingus racing up the poplar tree, his sling and a bag of stones over his shoulder.

A moment later, and Dingus was out on a branch end, fitting a stone, and whirling the sling. Love Bug could hardly believe what he was seeing. Then Dingus released the stone and it flew wide, missing the eagle by several feet. The raptor did not even notice. Dingus threw the sling over his shoulder and clambered upward.

Love Bug glanced down. They were quite high now, half the height of a tree. A new fear surged into him. If he were dropped now, it would be fatal. But he could see that Dingus was going to try again. Thinking rapidly, he could see that the best he could hope for was for the eagle to be injured and forced into a crash landing, which would allow Love Bug to survive the descent.

He could see Dingus at the tip of another branch, sling whirling around his head. So he lunged sideways, curving his body, trying to get his teeth around one of the claws of the right foot, so he could hold on even if he was dropped. The eagle, startled, looked down again and slowed his ascent, hovering for a moment.

Without his bite blade in his mouth, Love Bug was vulnerable, and the curved beak came toward him and struck his forehead, tearing open a gash. Love Bug groaned in pain and terror.

Then he caught just a glimpse of Dingus firing another stone. The stillness of the eagle must have helped, because it struck a glancing blow to the side of his neck. The eagle jerked his head around, yellow eyes scanning, clearly aware of this new threat. Already enraged from the unexpected fight with the rabbits, he looked ready to tear this new problem to bits.

Even with the blood running into his eyes, Love Bug could see Dingus racing upward through the tangle of bare branches, gaining height. In a few seconds he had reached the crown shoot, the lone flexible tip at the top of the tree. Hanging on to it with his back feet, he pulled out his last stone. It was larger than the others, and the weight of it in his hand bent his body forward. His pouch flapped empty on his shoulders.

A moment later, he fitted the stone into his sling and began swinging it in great arcs around his head. The eagle was accelerating toward the squirrel, yellow beak outstretched. His great wings struck the air like a hammer. *Whoom.*

Now the weight of the stone was bending the crown shoot, so the orbits of the sling were increasing with each revolution. In Love Bug's terrified state, the motion crawled before his eyes. The squirrel's stone swung in a circle five feet across. Then eight feet across. Then ten feet. Dingus fought to control the sling, both hands above his head, back feet slipping towards the tip of the shoot, which swung further out with every turn. The huge wings thrummed. *Whoom.*

The springy shoot came around again. A twelve foot arc. The sling was cutting through the air like a scythe. The squirrel's black eyes were locked on the eagle, now just moments away. The dark wings were driving the killing beak forward. *Whoom.*

Then Dingus released the stone, and it flew across the shrinking space between the animals, striking the eagle dead in the center of his forehead. Love Bug heard a sharp *thuk!* as it connected.

At first, the eagle seemed impervious. And then suddenly the claw holding him began to loosen. The next beat of the wings was weak. Love Bug felt himself begin to drop, even though the claw was still around him.

The eagle was above the poplar tree now. Dingus was racing down the crown shoot. The great raptor seemed dazed. It fell clumsily into the scree of small branches. Love Bug's bite on the bloody right foot was knocked free. The left claw opened and suddenly he was plunging downward, slipping through a welter of twigs and shoots that slapped at his face and knocked the breath from him. It was a terrifying succession of blows, but they kept him from entering free fall. And a few moments later, he fetched up suddenly in the fork of a major branch, breathless and dazed, with blood running in his eyes.

He saw the eagle fumble his way out of the tree and limp off through the winter air, flying erratically, calling weakly, clearly just wanting to be away from these strange monsters.

Love Bug lay without moving, amazed to be alive. There was a scurrying sound near him, and he looked up to see Dingus rushing down the trunk with his sling in his teeth. As soon as he came near, he used the sling to bind Love Bug to the tree limb so he could not fall further. Then Dingus lay on the branch, breathing hard, eyes closed, his hands and feet hanging limp.

Love Bug lay his head on the branch, still catching his breath. "I was wrong," he said, after a moment. "You ... are ... magic."

Anastasia

The pups were newly energized after their meal of sausages from the carrion bush, and they romped around the island, play fighting, practicing the new game of tag, and sometimes stopping to howl just for the fun of it.

Anastasia sat under the palm trees in the middle of the island, smiling. She was so relieved that she would not have to be an assassin that she felt happy and relaxed for the first time in weeks. She was also inclined to indulge the pups, so when their rough-and-tumble play came near her, she let them swarm around her. The growls of their playfighting were close to her ear, but it did not scare her. All the fear and killing anxiety was gone. And even as their muscular bodies clambered over her and around her, she continued to feel a blissful serenity.

I am not the angel of death. I am just a bunny, waiting to go home.

Micah was the most aggressive, in his bright, puppyish way. He was wrestling with Tennyson, and the two rolled across the sand. In a moment, their wriggling bodies were tumbling over Anastasia, rolling her onto her back.

Micah made a playful lunge at Tennyson's throat, his jaws snapping eagerly. As Tennyson squirmed, Micah slipped and fell forward, and his jaws snapped shut near Anastasia's exposed throat.

In a previous time, at any other moment in the world, the jaws of a carnivore banging shut near a rabbit's most vulnerable place would have driven an instant plunge into the life-or-death adrenaline burn, followed by a race for the horizon.

But Anastasia was now so sure that these puppies would not harm her, and in fact adored her, that she felt nothing of the age-old terrors she had inherited.

"Well, aren't you fierce," she laughed, pushing them off

with her powerful back legs and swatting Micah on the nose with her forepaw.

He popped up and assumed a ferocious stance. "So big!" he shouted happily. "Look how fierce I am!"

Sephora shouldered into him from the side and bowled him over. Then the two of them rolled toward Anastasia and snuggled against her. A moment later, Tennyson joined them.

Anastasia felt a warm glow as the winter sun shone down on their comfy tangle. Yes, this little band of survivors was born of opposing gangs of blood enemies. But in their tiny world on the island, they had escaped from the endless death march and found their way toward something new.

They had striven together, shared the warmth of their bodies, found new ways of being, and forged bonds of deep affection. It was the peaceable kingdom made manifest.

Then a new song began to arc toward them, coming from somewhere high above. It sounded like the bright, ringy notes of a cardinal.

"*Pookie, we are on our way*
We will be there any day"

Chapter 19

The other animals call us dirty because the Dead Gods blamed us for their choices. I have never infected anyone, but sometimes I wish I had.
—*Rattus Rattus*
Book of Gnawledge

MABEL

Mabel's head was awhirl as the rat peddler's boat pulled up to the main loading docks at City of Oom. The area was a hive of activity. Large cargo ships crewed by raccoons were swarmed with burly *procyonine* stevedores unloading the bales of raw materials, bundles of craftwork items, and clusters of winter fruit piled high on their decks. Barges full of freshly caught fish drifting down from the City fisheries were being pulled toward shore. And out on the wide Shandy, the vessels of rat traders were driving upstream, spinnakers out to catch the prevailing winds blowing eastward.

As the peddler ushered Mabel and Sunbeam off his boat, he explained quickly about going to the Pass Board and getting passes. "I'll meet you there to vouch for you," he said. "The Queen of Sorrows asked me to." Then he pushed off, telling them he was heading for Dirty Town, where all the rat boats were assigned to unload.

As they made their way along the wharf, a two-masted yawl slipped into a berth, its decks filled with large, flat wicker shapes. A muscular golden wolf came striding through the crowd, chatting with a smaller, limping coyote, eyes eagerly fastened on the cargo.

Mabel, who had stood in the *Armée Libre* line at the Battle of the Narrows, facing down the charging Summerday Clan, shuddered and averted her face as she passed by. *Aliyah Summerday? I thought the golden wolves were done.*

Still, even with this news, they had their objective to pursue. After some flailing about, they found the office of the harbormaster, who was a rather irritable fox in a small kiosk covered with reliefs of black bass and crappie.

"Passage downstream?" he said. "Most big traders are headed inland now, for a last run before the spring floods. Might be able to get you onto a river trade scow, but it'll be a few days."

They left their names on a standby list and continued up the street, following the directions to the Pass Board.

In a few minutes, they came out into the main square. Mabel felt overwhelmed by the gigantic buildings, the mass of animals in motion, and the smorgasbord of goods and services on offer. And the proximity to all the killers made her heart race. This was like Hella Cozy to the *nth* degree.

Sunbeam ran hither and yon through the crowd, unfazed by the teeth and claws, nosing up to the small kiosks to see what was happening.

Mabel, wishing for some lotus leaves, tried to calm herself with the breathing she had learned from Dingus. *In, two, three, hold, out, two, three, four.* The words of the Queen of Sorrows rang in her ears. *You may learn something in the City. Maybe you can do something helpful.* Since they had to wait, she was determined to do just that, but she was not sure how.

She saw a group of hunters, gathered in a semi-circle, watching something intently. Her instinct was to shy away and go around it, but she pushed herself forward. *Be brave. Learn something,* she told herself. *That's what Newly Beloved would do.* She realized she had hardly thought about Dah recently. It was a fleeting thought.

On a small stage of everstone, there was a fox with white clay on her face, accented with black clay triangles above and below the eyes. She was silently acting out a battle performance before an enthralled audience, under the spreading boughs of an ancient oak tree. Then she seemed to be attacked by flying things that came from nowhere and injured her. Mabel nibbled a foreclaw. Sunbeam was restless. It was hard to tell exactly what was going on.

Out of the corner of her eye, she saw a rabbit on the other side of the crowd, with plush, creamy fur and dark ears. She recognized him immediately, since they had been at several South Shandy religious conferences together. It was Aiden, the one-time Rememberer of Bloody Thorn Warren. After the Battle of the Narrows, he had become a devotee of Newly Beloved and gone to the uplands to proselytize. She noticed the henna heart on his forehead, and a few seconds later, realized that there were many rabbits near him, all with similar hearts. So the proselytizing was going well.

She threw him the paw signs for *greetings, brother.*

He looked startled to see her, then signed back. *Greetings, sister.*

Then her attention was jerked back to the stage. The fox had just been joined by a white weasel with her face covered in a similar black and white clay pattern. Mabel stared. *Is that Saskatoon?* It was hard to tell; the clay made her look so different. A quick glance at Sunbeam showed her to be transfixed, her paws weaving small patterns on the air before her.

The fox and weasel fought together valiantly against an unseen foe, then the weasel was suddenly attacked by a mob of invisible opponents. The odds were greatly stacked against her. She fought valiantly and was almost killed, with many injuries to her face and neck. In the end, she narrowly escaped with her life.

After the performance, both animals came to the front of the stage and bowed. Then the weasel riffled the fur on one side of her face and down her neck, showing the scars of many stab wounds.

At this proof of suffering, a great "*Ahhhhhh,*" rose up from the rapt hunters. And Mabel was electrified. Another fox came forward and addressed the audience. "That was '*Lunchmeat From Hell,*' he said. "Please make some noise for Juliette and our new artist, Saskatoon! An exciting and authentic new voice!" The audience members drummed on the street and yelped supportively, while three young foxes trotted through the crowd carrying baskets in their mouths, collecting moneystones.

Mabel looked down so she would not be recognized. Sunbeam leaned in close to her cheek. "That's *her*."

"Ya," murmured Mabel. From the side of her eye she saw Aiden making his way toward her through the crowd. She felt a hot prickle run across her neck. Then she turned and whispered into Sunbeam's golden ear. "I think I just got an idea."

Anastasia

Anastasia had the three pups lined up, facing her, on the sand under the palm trees. Now that she had heard that Freddie was on his way, she knew her season of the wolf was drawing to a close.

"I have good news," she said.

The puppies perked up their ears. Life was already full of snuggles and sausages all day long. Could it even get any better?

"Rescue is coming." She smiled. "We will all be lifted to safety."

The pups looked shocked. "How?" asked Sephora.

"I'm not sure," said Anastasia. "My people will do it. They are clever."

The puppies looked at each other. In their short lives, they had spent two weeks with their birth mother, and then four weeks with Anastasia. After surviving one terrible loss, and then learning to love their current lives, the thought of more change was not at all welcome.

Micah began to inch forward. "And then what?" he murmured.

Anastasia assumed a bright and pleasing tone. "And then I will go back to my people. And you will go back to your people."

Micah caught his breath, and in another moment, an anxious whine escaped him. Soon the other pups joined him. "Please don't leave us," he whispered.

Sephora gazed at her with huge green eyes. "I want to stay with … *her*."

Tennyson crept forward and lay his head on her feet, his breath coming fast and thready.

Anastasia steeled herself. She had done her best to step up to the task imposed on her by Anima Mundi and *love these children.* They had entered a special time together, a visit to a world without killing. But now that time was over.

Once they left their miniature world, they would be going back to the place where wolves hunted and rabbits died. These wolf toddlers were happy to subsist on plant sausages now, but as they grew, that would change.

She had done the undoable thing. She had preserved the lives of young hunters who would grow up to be killers of her own people. Would that change everything? It was hard to see exactly how. Maybe in the distant future, one of these golden killers would step back from a killing when a memory of their dear old rabbit caregiver came to mind. Maybe they would rise to positions of power, and thread a world-changing idea through the society of killers. Maybe one day they would shine a light on a path out of this forever war. Maybe.

But as of today, their special time was over. To pretend otherwise was just too dangerous.

"You can't live with my people," she said gently. "That would never work."

"Why?" The question came from all of them, in their voices, in their eyes, in their drooping tails.

She stepped forward, nuzzling against their furry upturned faces. She spoke softly. "Because you're killers."

A terrible groan rose up from them, and their scent was thick with fear and loss.

Micah crawled toward her, weeping. "I would never hurt you, Mummy." The word stabbed at her. The sight of this crying child made her feel sick.

"I know you believe that now, darling," she said, striving to keep her voice from quavering. She kissed his forehead tenderly. "But the world says we must part ways." Her golden eyes took in Tennyson and Sephora. "And there's no arguing with that."

STAN

The densely packed ball of hundreds of songbirds rose over the edge of the Boreal Cliff and began to sweep across the lower end of the Braided Gorges. Stan the Air Captain was flying just ahead of the ball, so the other songbirds could see him and maintain their relative positions.

"Raptor attacks at *Sans Gloire* show that they're changing strategy and might show up anywhere," said Stan, as they flew fast and low, just above the tree tops, so they would not be silhouetted against the ashen-gray sky. "They want to knock us off balance. If we get a raptor strike, break formation and attack, other than that, stick to the plan."

They flew silently, tracking across the many gorges, hundreds of black and orange eyes scanning for a clump of red-leaved palms. In less than a minute, the first upland songbirds began to appear. "Dirty ones! Dirty ones!" they called, swooping toward the birdball and curving into large orbits. Clearly, they were unnerved by the size of this aerial monstrosity. So they weren't attacking, but their calls were drawing more and more upland songbirds to come and investigate. Soon, the birdball was trailing a long tail of loudly calling songbirds as it flew.

At a gesture from Stan, the *Armée Libre* songbirds began to peel off from the formation in groups of three. They rushed the following birds, pinioning their wings, closing their beaks with claws, and falling to earth with them. Their goal was to keep them still and silent for the few minutes the birdball was over the uplands, thus blunting the effect of the alarm calls.

The birdball had now traveled several miles and reached the far side of the Braided Gorges, so it turned and moved inland for a half a mile before turning back for another sweep across. Upland songbirds continued to arrive, and they kept on immobilizing them. It looked like their system was working. Of course, the longer they were up there, the more attention they would attract, and the more the *Armée Libre* songbirds would have to leave the birdball to silence alarm-raisers. So there was definitely a time limit for the maneuver.

The birdball reached the edge of the Braided Gorges and headed inland for another half-mile. Then it turned to make a third sweep across. Stan was feeling jittery now. They were well into hostile territory, and if they ran into a raptor patrol, it would be dicey to deal with both big predators and upland songbird zealots without getting cut to ribbons.

A small jumble of red caught his eye. He almost missed it, it was so small and far off. Then he did a double take and realized this could be it. He sped toward the red cluster of leaves, the bird ball close behind him. Soon he was nearing a loose grouping of five red-leaved palms growing at the edge of a deep slash in the earth.

Then he was dropping into a steep-sided gulch with long rust-colored smears on the bone-white walls. He saw a narrow island in a fast-rushing stream. There were coconut palms and scrubby pear trees. And as he came down to within a few dozen feet of the surface, with a cloud of whirling songbirds around him, her saw her. Anastasia came out from under the palms, looking upward with her forepaws spread, golden eyes wide open in shock.

"It's the Godmother!" he trilled. "We frickin' did it, *paisanos*!"

Then he saw the strangest thing he had ever seen. Three golden wolf pups came out from under the little pear trees, looking skyward at the birdstorm. Little flashes of silver flickered across their golden agouti fur as they stared upward, apprehension at this astonishing sight written on their faces.

Then they ran to Anastasia and snuggled against her flanks for comfort. She did not run, or even seem surprised. Instead, she rested her paws on them as she stood, looking skyward, smiling.

DEATH RAGE

Death Rage and Throat Punch had spent several days scouting City of Oom, learning as much as possible about how it worked. They were also trying to find out what the bears were likely to do in terms of attacking the Million Acre Wood. They had overheard enough scuttlebutt down at the docks to know that a series of shipments of large flat pieces of wicker were being delivered, all earmarked for the wolves and coyotes. So they knew something was happening in that realm but they weren't sure what. They had also gotten familiar enough with the City that they had started to split up and cover more ground.

On this day, Death Rage was ensconced in the dead leaves in Force Majeure's study, since they had noticed that he often held meetings there in the late mornings. Throat Punch was creeping around the central square, with occasional visits to the City Guardhouse.

Force Majeure was standing at his reading stone, looking at pieces of paperbark and dictating to his raccoon scribe. As the morning waned, the mouse saw Aliyah Summerday come through the door suddenly, with her coyote companion limping a few paces behind. Today he was wearing hellebore blossoms twined around his ears and tail and seemed in a playful mood.

Aliyah took a few steps into the chamber and bowed. "Counselor."

The bear, focused on reading a piece of paperbark that a racoon librarian had brought from deep in the stacks somewhere, answered without looking up. "*Salve.*"

Aliyah stood upright. "You sent for me?"

Death Rage was surprised to see that the coyote played a little percussion accompaniment on the floor with his paws when Aliyah spoke. She had no word for this, but a Dead God would have said it sounded like bongos.

Force Majeure looked up and seemed surprised to see the coyote there. "Yes," he said. "For you." Then he leaned forward. "Your passion and experience have not gone unnoticed. Atticus will be the field commander in the equinox attack, but I want you to captain the canids during the descent of the Stone Stair. That will be three hundred wolves and coyotes under your command. We leave the day after tomorrow."

Death Rage was electrified by this news. Finally, real information. This was their mission. Learn something. Strike if possible. Report back.

Aliyah bowed again. "I am honored, *Servus Populi*." The coyote again played his percussion accompaniment as she spoke. The grizzly looked slightly annoyed.

"There could be great things in the City for you," he rumbled, looking at Aliyah.

"It is a wonderful place," said the golden wolf carefully. *Bappity bap bap bap* went the coyote's paws.

The bear shambled to the side of his chamber and stood, combing through a pile of paperbark binders. "You know," he said casually. "It's clear you got off on the wrong foot with Atticus Peacemaker, but if you stopped treating him like a wayward puppy, you might find you enjoy his company."

Death Rage could see that Aliyah looked shocked. "What?" *Bappity bap.*

Force Majeure trundled back to his reading stone. Death Rage could see that he definitely looked irritated now. He indicated the coyote with one large paw. "Must you bring your little friend everywhere?"

"He's not my friend," said Aliyah.

City of Oom

Bappity—The coyote stopped playing and now it was his turn to look shocked. His tail drooped and Death Rage's keen ears picked up just the quietest groan from him.

"Ah," growled the grizzly, with a slight smile.

The golden wolf paced over to the coyote. She touched noses with him, then turned and looked at Force Majeure. "He's my mate."

Mabel

Mabel trembled as she stood on the edge of one of the small stone stages in the public square in City of Oom, her new City visitor's pass earring in her right ear. *You are a party girl,* she reminded herself. *You are good at this.* Then she stepped out onto the performance space and addressed the crowd of animals gathering to see a new show.

"*Mesdames et Gentilschasseurs,*"[37] she said. "You have been hearing stories of late about lunchmeat gone bad. And yes…" She sat down at the edge of the stage and smiled, then leaned on one paw like a lounge singer, and said, "We can be very … *very* … bad."

There was a little chuckle from the audience of mostly hunters.

"I want to tell you a story about the worst lunchmeat of all." She preened her black-and-white fur for a moment and let her eyes drift lazily across the watching faces. Then she began to sing, improvising a bluesy, legato melody.

---

[37] Ladies and gentlehunters.

"The Rabbit Witch-Queen comes out of the wild and into a lovely town."

Then she began a cycle of stories in which the Witch-Queen arrived from seemingly nowhere, and slowly began to challenge the local powers. They were enraged and decided to kill her.

While she was singing, Aiden and his acolytes stepped onto the stage wearing triangular cottonwood leaves over their long ears, so they looked like the ears of canids. They stalked her as she sang, creeping closer and closer. Mabel moved about the stage, staying focused on the audience as the faux hunters trailed her.

Then one of them rushed forward to make the kill. Mabel turned and fixed him with her dark eyes, and the roiling pattern of black and white fur on her forehead caught for a moment in a shaft of sunlight. And she sang:

"The Rabbit Witch-Queen sings songs of love and lays the hunters down."

She draped a garland of flowers around the stage hunter's neck. He stopped and rubbed his cheek with his paw, then bowed down at her feet. Mabel could see that some audience members were struck by this performance, while some looked skeptical, and others were openly scoffing. Time to unleash the next phase.

She looked to where Sunbeam was standing in the crowd and gave her the eye. Then, as Mabel continued with her next story, Sunbeam moved noiselessly through the audience. She took a position behind a brown fox. When Mabel reached the climax of her tale, Sunbeam slipped a braided chain of flowers over the fox's head and tightened it around his neck.

The fox yelped in surprise, then spun around, snarling. Sunbeam stood without moving, holding her flower garland, a mischievous sparkle in her green eyes. Her broad smile plainly said, *welcome to the cabaret.* The fox shook himself, then laughed nervously. The other members of the audience chuckled. The golden bunny collected her flowers and stole away.

Over the next few minutes, as Mabel told more stories, and more onstage hunters joined the array of adoring hunters around her feet, Sunbeam skulked through the crowd with her floral braid wound around her forepaws. At the next story climax, she dropped it over the head of a wolf pup, which elicited some startled barks. And the time after that, it was a northern goshawk, which precipitated some furious thrashing and squawking. Every time, the audience laughter got louder.

Then it was close to the end of the show. As Mabel began her last story, she spotted Saskatoon walking up to the edge of the crowd, gazing around curiously. It looked as though she hadn't seen anything that had happened so far. Mabel made sure Sunbeam had seen the weasel, and then spun her story out a little longer, so she had time to get into position.

As Mabel leaned into her story crescendo, the golden bunny slipped up behind Saskatoon and threw the floral garrote over her head, pulling it tight against her neck. Instantly, the weasel exploded into a squall of snarls, forepaws clawing at the flower garland and tearing it to pieces. Sunbeam stood with a sweet smile on her face as the white weasel rounded on her, spitting and screeching. The laughter of the crowd was bright and mocking.

Saskatoon stepped up to Sunbeam, head high and long neck undulating like a snake. Her lips were drawn back to reveal a mouthful of white spikes. It was her full threat posture. "You *murderer*," she snarled. This caused a fresh burst of laughter from the audience, who had only seen the flower garrote, not the wire one.

Sunbeam actually leaned forward a bit, chin out, as though daring her to strike. Mabel felt her heart in her throat for a moment. They had learned when they received their City passes that anyone with a City earring was protected by Ursine Law, but Saskatoon's rage was white hot.

The weasel turned to the crowd of mostly hunters, many of whom were still chuckling. "Don't you know who they are?" she shouted. "They're monstersss! They kill innocent hunters like us who are only living as the Goddess commands." She started to push through the crowd. "Their Witch-Queen doesn't sing songs of love, she sings songs of *death*!"

The crowd looked uncertain. Was this part of the show? Mabel heard a wolf in the front row murmur to a companion, "Wow, that weasel is really *good*."

"*Total* commitment," said a coyote. "I can't look away."

"They're coming for you," raged Saskatoon. "These killer rabbits and their murdering goonsss. They're unnatural! And they'll make you crazy, because they don't do what rabbits do. And their queen is the worst. She will *unwolf* you. *Uncoyote* you. *Undo* you."

Sunbeam clasped her forepaws together and stood with a

small concerned smile on her face, the exemplar of the harmless, eager-to-please drama nerd. Which only made Saskatoon seem more like a lunatic.

"You think I'm nutsss?" she was racing though the crowd now, using her claws freely. "*I was there.* I've got the scars to prove it!"

A passing City Guard patrol of four wolves happened by and noticed that Saskatoon was starting to draw blood on City citizens as she caromed through the packed audience.

"Mushroom overdose," said the wolf captain. Then all four wolves stepped forward, and Saskatoon was quickly and quietly escorted away, with jeers of "Go sleep it off!" coming from the crowd.

Aiden's bunny acolytes took off their leafy predator ears and ran forward with baskets to collect moneystones from the excited, talkative crowd.

"That was *The Witch-Queen Cometh,*" said Mabel. "We'll be here for a few days. Tell your friends."

Sunbeam joined her on stage, looking as innocent as can be, and the two shared a discreet paw bump. Mabel leaned over and whispered, "Good job, you little monster."

FREDDIE

"She wants *what*?" said Freddie, feeling his eyes bug out a little.

Stan, who had just arrived at *Sans Gloire* with the news of finding Anastasia, hopped back and forth impatiently as he talked. "She wants us to bring out these three golden wolf pups that are in the gulch with her."

"But you can't lift out wolf pups via Songbird Air," said Freddie slowly, frowning in spite of himself. Learning that the birdball had found Anastasia was wonderful. Suddenly having to deal with Anastasia's demands was perhaps less so.

"Of course not," snapped Stan. "Way too big."

Nicodemus looked up from the earthsketch where he and Freddie had just been working on the design of the slings. "*Golden?*" he said. "Must be Summerdays. Why would she want to do that?"

Stan shrugged his little bluebird shoulders. "It's the Godmother. Why does she want anything?"

Wendy came lumbering over from where she was putting teams of squirrel slingers through their paces as part of the weapon redesign. "Go in on ground? How cross gullies?"

Love Bug followed after, with several slings hanging over his shoulder. "I've done quite a few runs along the edge of the Gorges now," he mused. "I think there might be a way to do it. Only thing is"—he shrugged apologetically—"we'll need raccoons."

Chapter 20

Reed is humble, yea
Asks little, grows much, roots deep
At last, all is reed

—*Seven Haikus to Victory*
Reed Mouse Colloquium

DEATH RAGE

Death Rage found Throat Punch at their meeting place in the central square and told her what she had learned about Aliyah Summerday leading the attack on the Stone Stair. They stepped out of the traffic and huddled in a spray of gorse growing through the pavement.

"We *have* to stop her," said Death Rage. "She's the only wolf up here who's learned to really fear crossbows. She might get them past the Stair defenses and out into the Million Acre Wood."

Throat Punch nodded "With her, they could win. Without her, they're naked."

Death Rage chewed on her claws and lashed her tail in frustration. "But we can't just attack her. We'd be killed in a second. It has to be sneaky. It has to be…" She trailed off as she started to pace. " … from a distance."

"It has to be quiet," said Throat Punch. "Unexpected."

Death Rage snapped her tiny fingers. "What about that reed weapon you blow into? By the wicker mice? It's all those things."

"You asked before, and got a pretty clear *no*," said Throat Punch.

"Well, let's try again," said Death Rage. "If we don't do *something* to help Free Nation, a lot of people will die."

"If we get it, who's going to do it?" said Throat Punch, running her fingers over the tip of her greatsword.

Death Rage looked at her for a long moment. "We'll have one chance. Should be our best fighter."

Throat Punch nodded. "It should be you," she said quietly. "I bungled our last two fights." She cleared her throat and looked down. "Sorry I'm such a weak partner."

"Don't even say that," said Death Rage. "You're just new at this."

They headed out for the Wicker Flats Reedcraft shop. On the way over, they agreed to sound casual and not reveal too much. In a few minutes, they were there. It was late in the day and they could see Poison Wind inside sweeping up. After a moment, they went in and introduced themselves, reminding the reed mouse that they had met before.

"Yea, I make you travelers," said Poison Wind, blowing through his fluttering fingers. "I see you made it to the City."

City of Oom

"Yea, Master Wind," said Throat Punch. "And we have a question for you."

Death Rage cleared her throat. There was no way to make this ask that did not signal intent. They hadn't been able to come up with any tricky talk-arounds, so she just blurted it out. "We'd like to ask if we could rent your dreamstick for a few days."

Poison Wind stepped back and stroked his chin. "For what, friend?"

Death Rage took a deep breath. "It will benefit many, many mice," she said. She yearned to reveal the truth, to make an open and honest plea. But everything she had learned about the world told her that would be foolish. Finally, she said, "More than that, it's better that you don't know."

Poison Wind stepped to the shop door, looked up and down the street, and then locked it. "This is a busy time for us, strewth," he said. "And yet, we are always ready to make reed while the sun shines, as we are just two years out from the great sunflower seed famine that crippled our people."

"Thank you, Master Wind," said Throat Punch.

"I must tell you that the dreamstick may not be rented, but it could be freely loaned to a Friend of the Flats," said Poison Wind, his scent oily and ambiguous.

Death Rage felt a grim smile creep onto her face. *Here it comes.* "And how might one join this very select group?"

Poison Wind nibbled a foreclaw judiciously. "A small contribution to our music school might suffice," said Poison Wind. His eyes flicked up to hers. "A thousand pence."

Death Rage felt as though she had been kicked in the gut.

"Any room to move on that figure?" She waved her fingers back and forth. "You know, speaking mouse to mouse?"

Poison Wind rubbed his hands together. "That includes the mouse discount, I'm afraid."

Death Rage forced a smile. She was traveling with funds from the Free Nation treasury, but that was far more than she had. And of course, the local bank was out of the question. "And that could be delivered at a later time…?"

Poison Wind clucked sympathetically. "Yea, that would be a wonderful world, wouldn't it?" Then he shook his head sadly. "Moneystones on delivery, friend."

Death Rage fell silent, racking her brain for some answer. Throat Punch piped up. "How many darts come with the dreamstick?"

"I have three with me," said Poison Wind. "One for practice. Two that are tipped with dreamjuice. Together, they will kill a small animal." His eyes were dark and unreadable. "Or put a medium-sized animal to sleep for a day." He leaned forward. "And you must bring the darts back. We will require surety."

"Thank you, good master," said Throat Punch. She looked at Death Rage and jerked her head toward the door.

A moment later, the two mice were standing in the cold twilight. Death Rage was furious. "Why does everyone have to grab as much as they can?" she shouted. "Why can't we just do what is right and good?"

Throat Punch looked alarmed and put her paw over Death Rage's mouth. "Hush, he'll *hear* you."

"There's no way we can come up with that amount," hissed Death Rage. "Or even come near it." Her hand flickered to her rapier grip. "I could …. maybe I should…"

Throat Punch leaned into her. "There are many ways forward," she said softly. "I'm going to try something. Tell Poison Wind I'm going to come back with the moneystones, so you can start practicing with the dreamstick."

Death Rage stared at her. "Don't even tell me what you're going to do," she said. "I'm sick of the sleaze."

"You and me both, sister," said Throat Punch. "But I'm not afraid of it." And then she was gone.

THROAT PUNCH

Throat Punch had by now been to the Speakeasy in Dirty Town many times, so when she asked the barkeep where Bricabrac was, he just jerked a paw towards the back room. It was the dice room for high-rollers, and Bricabrac was there with a coterie of other finely dressed rats, throwing a set of classic chewystone dice while servers hovered around, dispensing top-shelf fermented fruits and the finest spiced seeds. His new vest featured accents of aluminum foil that gleamed like fire by the light of the bioluminescent mushrooms.

"What up, lil doe?" he said lazily, as he took a big bite of winterfruit and threw himself onto a comfy moss chaise lounge. "Got spiritual needs?"

Throat Punch took on his expansive gestures and draped herself on the couch next to him. "Rattus Rattus is smiling on all his pups," she said. "For a limited time, it will delight your god to turn a loan of ten dollars into *fifteen* dollars for the brightest son of the morning."

Bricabrac's eyes flicked to a stack of moneystones near him. There was a burst of cheering from the players as the dice clacked against the backboard. "That's big money," he said, sounding suddenly more serious.

Throat Punch reached across him, plucked a fermented berry out of a bowl, and took a bite of it. "And you're a big rat." She smiled.

Bricabrac studied his nails. "Guaranteed by … ?"

"The Killer of Blessed," said Throat Punch. "The Harbinger of Apocalypse. The Most Loving Auntie."

The rat looked up at her. "Of course, it doesn't matter what it will be used for."

Throat Punch lay back and looked at the ceiling, smiling. "Oh, wonderful things," she said. "Rainbows and muffins and presents for orphans." She turned and looked at him. "The same thing dark money is always used for." She rested her chin on her forepaw. "Love."

A half-smile crept onto Bricabrac's face. "You're a tough cookie, aren't you, Punchy?"

Throat Punch sat up. "Rattus Rattus would like to know if his gift will be honored."

The dice rattled against the backboard again, and there were cheers and groans from the players. Bricabrac steepled his fingers. "If someone takes ten loonies from that stack by the wall, I'll be helpless to stop them."

Mabel

After checking with the Dockmaster for available spots on downriver ships, as she did every day, Mabel headed back to the main square. They had been doing their *The Witch-Queen Cometh* shows for several days now, and attendance had boomed after the dust-up with Saskatoon had generated great word of mouth.

As Mabel came near to their stage, she saw Sunbeam conferring with Aiden and some of his Newly Beloved acolytes. Then she saw that the competing show with Saskatoon was just getting started. It looked like they had revamped it. No longer a mime show, now it had the white weasel and the fox telling stories and acting them out.

As she drew near, she could hear the fox declaiming, "Oh, what a glorious day to be a fox. I am strong and happy and free!"

And now Saskatoon: "The life of the hunter is the only true life." There was an ominous jangle of chimes off stage. "And surely those rumors I've been hearing mean nothing."

"Ha ha!" cried the fox. "Stories of the Rabbit Witch-Queen are just lies, put about by scoundrels."

Another audience was gathering, and as usual, it contained many wolves and coyotes from the nearby City Guardhouse. Mabel smiled. *Newly Beloved says, 'Songs of love are coming for ya.'*

Then she noticed a familiar figure huddled under the freelance crafter job board, speaking quickly and earnestly with a companion. Splash of white on the back. Bottlecap helmet.

"*Death Rage!*" she called, her heart leaping. She ran to her and the two exchanged warm nuzzles and many affectionate murmurings. After all their travels, it felt so extraordinary to see a familiar face in this foreign land.

Soon, she had collected Sunbeam, and the four travelers from the Million Acre Wood repaired to a nook under a squat juniper bush to share all that they knew. They also shared their plans, including Death Rage shooting Aliyah Summerday with the dreamstick.

"The equinox is tomorrow," said Throat Punch. "So the City attack force will be leaving early in the morning. We have one more day to get ready."

Sunbeam, who had been gazing at Death Rage intently, suddenly asked, "Where's the Kiss of Death?"

"I had to give it as a surety to borrow this weapon," said Death Rage, tapping the blowgun. "So they can be sure I'll bring it back."

"But your rapier…" Mabel nuzzled her head, murmuring. "I can't imagine you without it."

Death Rage stepped back and looked at Mabel with her dark eyes. "If I don't come back, I won't be needing it."

DEATH RAGE

It was early morning on the day of the equinox. Death Rage was clinging to a low tree branch growing out over a narrow everstone street. On one side of the street was a wall covered with vines, and on the other was the Shandy River, dark winter-grey with floating chunks of dirty ice. They had learned that the *Pax Legio* would come down this passage on its way out of the City.

Down below, Throat Punch was hidden at the foot of the wall in a pile of dead leaves, blending in with her gray succulent leather and lichen cloak which made her look like a stone. The darts had no barbs, and would fall out as soon as they had delivered their poison. It was her job to see where the darts fell, run out, and pick them up as soon as it was safe.

City of Oom

Death Rage fumbled the dreamstick as she put a dart in place. If she stuck herself with a point, she would black out and fall. To calm her trembling, she murmured a hymn to The One Who Makes The World.

"I see you
You see I
In my tree
Up so high

Now we will do
I and you
One thing that
Makes the world."

A hundred yards away, she saw the *Pax Legio* make the turn onto the street. They were in luck: Aliyah Summerday was leading, bright in her golden armor. Behind her was a mass of wolves and coyotes, with many murders of crows swirling overhead. And they were singing their war chant as they came. A broad rumble of low voices from the wolves rolled down the street in an open fifth harmony, while above them intertwining melodies from the coyotes told tales of victorious battles past as the crows cawed a marching cadence.

Death Rage held the dreamstick to her mouth and sighted along its length. The tiny points would be defeated by the thick fur of any wolf, let alone an armored one. She needed to aim for exposed skin. That meant the nose or the narrow swath of pink inside the ears. She had spent many hours practicing, but of course, with a new weapon, thousands of hours would have been ideal.

Aliyah was getting closer. She was walking at a measured pace, head high. The ears were a much bigger target, but it would be hard to hit the inside from above. Death Rage scrambled to the underside of the branch and clung to a twig to get a better angle of attack.

Even at this slow gait, the golden wolf was closing in quickly. Her window of opportunity to get off two shots would be measured in moments. She lined up the reed sights, saw the pink in the left ear and *pffft!* sent the dart flying. For a moment, she was not sure if she had hit, but then she saw Aliyah shake her head slightly, as she would if bothered by a gnat. *Good. Now the next one.*

Aliyah was just a few feet away from being directly under her now. It would have to be the nose. Her hands shook as she fumbled with next dart, straining to keep the point away from her skin. The fletching caught on the edge of the reed. She shifted her grip and tried to force the dart into place. Then suddenly it was slithering along the edge of a leaf, half hanging over empty space. Her breath caught. This was her only chance to strike a blow for Free Nation. She lunged at the dart and was relieved to get her fingers around it.

It took her a moment to realize she was falling.

Throat Punch

Throat Punch felt a wordless cry leave her body as she saw Death Rage plunging downward. Then the little auburn body with a white splash on the back struck the hard everstone pavement and lay without moving.

Throat Punch felt her heart start to hammer. She took a step out of the safety of the leaves, and then froze. Her body was telling her that running out in front of the great golden wolf was suicide.

She felt time grind to a crawl. She saw Aliyah's eyes track downward to this curious furry lump that had just fallen into her awareness. *Maybe the first dart's already working*. Maybe she would be slow to respond. Throat Punch knew she was telling herself this to overcome the voices of many mouse ancestors who were shouting at her not to rush headlong into mortal danger.

She took a hurried breath and darted forward. In a moment, she was grabbing the dreamstick and snatching up the dart which lay nearby. Being so near Death Rage's still form caused a wave of grief to roll through her, but she let it flow out through her fingers and disappear.

The golden wolf loomed over her. The head was dropping now, jaws opening, bright green eyes locked onto her. Throat Punch raised the dreamstick. In the past battles, she had been overwhelmed by fear and turned into a bumbler, but now there was no Death Rage to figure everything out and do the right thing.

She stuffed the dart into the dreamstick and raised it to her lips. The ears seemed far away. It would have to be the nose. The lower jaw was falling open, lips pulling back, coming toward her like a scoop edged with yellow spikes. The upper jaw rose. The nose was suddenly out of reach, way up on top of the muzzle. Bad angle. Throat Punch trembled so violently her small body shook like a leaf in a storm. Then her eyes opened wide as she saw her way out. A shiny expanse of mottled pink and brown. *Hit the gums*. She took a quick breath and *pffft!* the dart leaped across the small space between them, burying its tip in the wet pink flesh around the lower fangs.

The jaws stopped sweeping forward for a moment as the wolf felt the tiny pinprick. Throat Punch seized Death Rage's front paws and began to drag her to the side of the road. Out of the corner of her eye, she saw the great grey-pink tongue explore the spot where the dart had struck and then fallen out. And behind the golden form, the massed ranks of gray wolves were coming, a wall of death.

The tongue withdrew, and the jaws came near to her again, gaping wide. Something was making her head vibrate and she realized it was a snarl. But even then, she did not leave Death Rage to her fate. She let go of one of her paws and drew her broadsword, yanking it up and out of her back scabbard awkwardly as she crouched.

As the teeth lunged toward her, she pulled hard on Death Rage's still form with one hand and whirled her great blade around her head with the other one.

"Thank you for your donation!" she shouted.

Then, just as she was about to go *mano a mano* with the largest wolf in the Known World, the jaws suddenly slewed away as the great golden dragon staggered sideways, rolled out a rumbling growl, then crashed onto the everstone pavement and lay like the dead.

Love Bug

Love Bug had taken command of the rescue, as his scouting had given him the most experience with the edge of the Braided Gorges.

City of Oom

So now several platoons of the *Armée Libre* were trekking along the edge of the Boreal Ciffs, surrounding a command group that included Wendy, Freddie, and ten raccoons. Adderall and several other raccoons were carrying saws from the bunker that had been fitted with an extra handle to make them two-person affairs, capable of ripping through tree trunks relatively fast. Wellbutrin and Lorazepam had long coils of ropes over their shoulders. The day was unseasonably warm. Some of the raccoons were sweating.

Up above, the birdball hovered, absorbing upland songbirds as they appeared, then sending them groundward with teams of three songbirds keeping them quiet.

Love Bug's eyes swept over the group. Freddie seemed almost giddy with the knowledge that he would soon be seeing Anastasia again. Wendy was getting in his hair a bit. The raccoons mostly seemed cranky. So all was normal.

They reached the first ravine. A number of different trees were growing along the edge. Love Bug pointed to one of the older palm trees with rough bark and said, "This one."

Wendy, accustomed to being in charge, galloped up to the edge of the drop-off and indicated another tree, saying, "This one better, eh?"

Love Bug shot her a glance. "Been here before. This is the best one." He waved his paw and Adderall and another racoon sawyer approached. "Lay this one right down there, so it falls between those two boulders on the far side." He gestured with his forepaw. "That'll keep it steady."

Adderall worked with a will, pulling the saw toward himself with vigorous strokes. After a few moments, he said, "Crazy about those young wolves, huh?"

"Let's just get in and get out," said Love Bug evenly, eyes

scanning the distant trees for possible signals from Dingus or his other squirrel scouts. "We can argue about it later."

Throat Punch

Throat Punch was rushing up the street away from the river road, with Death Rage's arm around her neck. She stumbled as she half-dragged, half-carried the other mouse along. Death Rage seemed to be coming to, and groaned whenever she put any weight on her left leg.

Behind her, Throat Punch could hear that the sound of the wolves' war chant continuing, moving toward the west gate. Its vast rumble rose out of three hundred throats and swirled over this side of the City.

After a few blocks, the mice reached Wicker Flats Reedcraft. Throat Punch left Death Rage tucked under a friendly camelia bush and ran inside with the dreamstick and the two darts she had collected. She traded them for the Kiss of Death, which Death Rage had left as a surety. And a moment later, she was back under the camelia with Death Rage, pressing her rapier into her hands.

"Your friend is back," she murmured.

Death Rage groaned appreciatively. "Thank you," she whispered as she embraced it. "Friends are good."

They took off again, with Throat Punch again supporting her companion, and soon reached the main square where she saw Mabel and Sunbeam. "What happened?" asked Mabel, eyes wide and anxious as she nuzzled Death Rage, kissing her gently as she lay on the ground.

Throat Punch quickly filled her in.

"Did it work?" asked Mabel.

"Iunno," muttered Throat Punch, waving her forepaws helplessly. "Aliyah's down but they're still *going*. I thought they would stop without her."

"Need to warn Anastasia," said Sunbeam, nosing up a bone fragment laying in the street.

"Of course! But how?" said Throat Punch.

Sunbeam looked up. "Tricky, tricky rat," she said.

Throat Punch chewed her lip. "That's the best chance we got," she said.

Mabel gently picked up Death Rage by the thick scruff of fur behind her neck, carrying her like a kitten. Throat Punch embraced her companion and then took off for Dirty Town, with the two rabbits following.

A few minutes later, they were at Bricabrac's workshop, where he was stripping some copper wire out of a smashed toaster. He looked surprised to see the two rabbits, and then shocked to see Mabel lay Death Rage gently on the floor.

As Throat Punch blurted out their story, he ran to Death Rage and knelt down. "Another anonymous criminal?"

Death Rage opened her eyes and looked at him. "Gonna steal your rat crap and fade into the night," she said, a pained smile coming onto her face.

He patted her paw. "I'm calling the Guard right now, you faceless thug."

She tried to sit up and groaned. He ran his hands over her legs, then clucked his tongue. "Her left leg is broken."

The others gathered. "Are there any healers in Dirty Town?" asked Throat Punch.

"Don't have time for that," gasped Death Rage. "Need to warn Loving Auntie."

Bricabrac chewed his lip. "She needs…" He looked up at the animals gathered around him. "Go outside," he said suddenly. "I'm about to do something horrible and I don't want any witnesses."

The other animals went out. Throat Punch peeked through a crack in the door. When Bricabrac's workroom was cleared, he scampered around gathering two stiff twigs and several lengths of agave fiber yarn. Then, with Death Rage moaning quietly, he quickly bound the twigs to her leg, splinting it to protect it from further injury. He dug through his crates and came back with some willow bark. He gave her a piece to chew on, and tucked the rest into her backpack. Then he gently kissed her forehead.

When he was done, he picked her up and carried her outside, carefully laying her down near the others.

"Let's wrap this up," he said. "This has the smell of *co-conspirator* all over it."

"One last thing," said Throat Punch. "How can we get to Loving Auntie?"

"And *we* have a message for her, too," said Mabel. "From the Queen of Sorrows."

Bricabrac whistled. "Two rabbits, two mice? That's a lot to carry." He nibbled his forepaw. "And after that clusterflap at *Sans Gloire*, most big flyers are not going to cooperate."

Then he stood up and walked away from them, looking up toward the Great Hill in the Center of Oom. "Look, this is a war. I'm not taking sides and you can't suck me in," he said. "But I am scum. And I know other scum like me, who will do anything for money, war or no war." He flicked his tail over his shoulder and rubbed it against his cheek. "If I was a criminal, I would go to the far end of Raptor Heights and find a big black condor. Total thug. Stinks like death." He flicked his tail away. "Now get out."

Force Majeure

The crippled coyote stood over the still form of Aliyah Summerday, nuzzling her and whispering fiercely as tears ran down his dirty-gray muzzle. "My love, my love. Come back to me. All is good."

Force Majeure and Atticus Peacemaker stood nearby, gazing at her intently. The *Pax Legio* continued its march out of the City, with the crows and Civil Raccoons following. In the moments of confusion after her collapse, the grizzly had sent them on with a jerk of his head. Today was the equinox. There was no time to waste.

Force Majeure turned to the wolf commander. "You didn't see *anything*?"

Atticus shrugged. "I was close to the back, to give her space." His eyes flicked to Force Majeure. "As you requested."

The bear frowned. "Right."

"She just stumbled and fell," said Atticus. "Wasn't much to see." He sucked his teeth. "One of my captains mentioned a mouse or two, but that doesn't mean anything."

Force Majeure nodded to his scribe raccoon, who hovered at a discreet distance. "Go get the healers. She may yet be saved." The raccoon darted away.

The grizzly looked at Atticus. The confusion around

Aliyah had already cost them valuable time. "We cannot miss this day," said Force Majeure. He dipped his paw into his carrying pouch and came out with a pawful of *go leaf*, and they each tucked a wad into their cheeks. "Time to run."

The two sprinted after their army. Behind him, he could hear the anguished sound of the coyote's mourning howl rise up.

Chapter 21

Without bear, chaos.

—Ex Cathedra
General Counsel

Throat Punch

After several weeks scouting the City, Throat Punch knew it much better than the rabbits, so she ended up leading their small party up to Raptor Heights. Death Rage was riding in Mabel's backpack, and groaning quietly as the rabbit lollopped. They moved as quickly as possible through the tall trees, with the many birds of prey looming overhead. And she took them on a wide berth around the star plaza and the tumbledown chapel where the grizzly bear seer was known to live.

As they reached the far end, they saw a huge dark bird sitting on a single branch close to the ground, protruding from a stump. As they came up closer they could see that his head and neck were utterly bald, covered by wrinkled pink skin. A jagged scar lay across his bald pate and his eyes were a bloody amber. The smell of carrion was strong.

Throat Punch forced herself to walk toward him. "Pardon me, Master Flyer," she said, bowing. "Are you a condor?"

The great bird looked at her without moving. His eyes crawled over the group for several long moments. Finally, he said, "Who wants to know?"

"Bricabrac sent us, and said you may be—"

The bird interrupted her with a breathy grunt that might have been a laugh. "What a lovely ... little rat." A long hiss flowed from his beak. "He always sends me the plumpest ... passengers."

Throat Punch could not stop herself from exchanging an anxious glance with the others.

The condor rolled out a hissy chuckle. "Nothing to fear. I only eat ... dead animals."

"Do you make them dead?" asked Sunbeam.

"Nah. Too much work," said the condor. A slimy, orange tongue crept out and slipped up and down his beak. "I do like a bit of fresh radish and a ... hint of zest. Really brings out the *gamey*."

Throat Punch nodded. *Well, if he was going to kill us, Bricabrac wouldn't have sent us here*, she told herself. It almost made her feel better. "Could you carry two rabbits and two mice all the way to the Stone Stair at the Boreal Cliffs? We have moneystones." She jumped up and down to make them jingle.

The condor unfurled his wings and Throat Punch crouched

as they loomed over her like a black cloud, fully nine feet from tip to tip. His raspy grunt came forth again. "*Many* small creatures have traveled in my claws." Then he shifted on his perch, and for the first time, Throat Punch noticed that a white strip with a dark line running through the center circled around the condor's right foot and kept him tethered to the branch. The condor dipped his head apologetically. "But right now, I'm a guest of the City for another ... five days," he said, with a long yodeling grunt. "You know the bears love their *rules*."

Mabel and Sunbeam came forward, bringing Death Rage with them. They all stood, with their paws over their noses at the awful carrion smell, peering up at the raptor's feet.

"That looks like chewystone," said Throat Punch. "Why don't you just peck it apart?"

"It has a bone in the middle," said the condor. "My beak won't cut it."

Sunbeam squinted. "That's wire," she said.

Throat Punch took a deep breath and shinnied up the stump and out onto the branch where the condor towered over her like a pterodactyl. She looked closely at the chewystone strip with its wire center. Then she pulled her greatsword up over her head with both hands and began to hack at it. Her heavy blade cut quickly through the plastic. The wire center was much tougher, and every stroke made the sword vibrate painfully in her hands. But she kept at it, and in a few minutes had hacked it through.

The condor immediately leaped skyward and took off in a long sweeping circle around the area, cackling. Then he headed back and dropped down onto the ground where Throat Punch had joined the others. "Good little mousie," he said.

"I'll put you on my Yes Fly list." A ghastly smile that he probably assumed was a genial expression spread across his face. "Name?"

"Throat Punch."

"I'm Scirocco," the big flyer gurgled in a friendly way. "Ask for me wherever vultures are having a yak."

Then he beat his wings and hovered over them, his long gray talons reaching for his passengers. Throat Punch ran over to Death Rage where she lay in Mabel's backpack, fussing over her and making sure she was safely ensconced for the air journey. As she fiddled with the strap, Death Rage groaned a little and touched her paw. "Thanks," she said. "For everything." Her usually fierce eyes looked a little wet.

Throat Punch embraced her, and for a moment her mouth was near Death Rage's ear. "Proud to be on your team," she whispered. Then she turned and dashed over to Sunbeam and climbed into her backpack.

A moment later, Scirocco seized the rabbits and began climbing, his long wings undulating in the air like tree branches in a storm. "Okay, little morsels," he grunted. "Buckle up."

Anastasia

She could hear something going on above. Then a wonderful moment came when Freddie's round black-and-gray face appeared over the edge of the cliff top and he shouted, "I love you!"

"I love *you*!" she called, feeling warm all the way down into her toes.

Suddenly, the swirling mass of the birdball swept into

view above his head and began making a slow circular sweep of the area. Wendy and Love Bug appeared, looking down.

"Play time over," grunted Wendy. "Time for work."

Love Bug frowned and elbowed her. "Loving Auntie!" he shouted. "So happy to see you!" Other rabbits and several raccoons were popping up over the edge now, peering down into the canyon.

"So glad you're still biostable, honey!" called Lorazepam as she and Wellbutrin performed the traditional Rochefarian hand gestures of blessing.

"Thanks for coming for me, wonderful friends!" she called. Then she touched both paws to her chest and spread them wide. *I love you all.*

Love Bug spoke over the rising clamor. "We need to be quick," he said, as two raccoons threw down a long double rope with a tangled harness at the end. "Who will come up first?"

"I will," said Anastasia.

The pups, who had been suddenly shy at the appearance of all the *Armée Libre* commotion above, now crept out from under the little pear trees. "Remember what I told you," said Anastasia. "Be on your best behavior. Don't scare anyone. No rough housing." She quickly touched noses with all of them, then licked her paw and smoothed the fur on their faces. "My people are saving your lives. Show them respect."

All the pups nodded, their eyes large.

"After me, Sephora, then Micah, then Tennyson," said Anastasia. She turned and wriggled into the rope harness. When she was ensconced, she called up, "Ready!" and she felt the tension of the ropes get taken up. Then she was lifted with a jerk. Soon she was at the level of the ledge where she had heard the songbirds singing. Then she was higher still, looking down at the tiny island, seeing all the smudged and blurred tracks of their weeks on the sand.

The tiny golden wolf pups looked very small. So vulnerable. Once she might have taken the easy way out and just left them there. How much simpler for her. Just like something her mother, Olympia, would do. She saw an image in her mind of herself and her people running free over the grass, going back to their homes, with everything just as it had been before.

But she knew she was no longer that rabbit.

In a few more moments, Wellbutrin and Lorazepam were pulling her up over the edge. After a quick nuzzle of joyful greeting, she dashed to Freddie and pressed her lean body against his thick soft fur, rubbing her cheek against his. He kissed her forehead tenderly, entwining his long gray and black ears around hers, and they shared a moment of sweet and joyful tears.

"I wasn't sure I would see you again," she murmured.

"I knew I would find you," he whispered fiercely.

Then the two of them were surrounded by the warm bodies of her people, kissing, touching, murmuring their affection. Love Bug nuzzled against her neck. Dingus squirmed through the crowd and rubbed her toes. And many other small paws touched her and petted her. Even Wendy bulled her way through the scrum for a quick nose touch. For several long moments, no one said anything, as they were all lost in expressions of their love that were far deeper than words.

Then, as they lay there in a big snuggle pile, Love Bug started to explain about the trail of palm tree bridges that would bring them across several gorges and back to the open grassland atop the Boreal Cliffs, near the Stone Stair. She could hear the pride in his voice. *Look what we did for you, Loving Auntie.*

Suddenly, Adderall spoke, his voice cutting through the warm reunion vibe like a rusty blade. "This is great, but bringing these wolves out is *nuts*."

A moment later, the other raccoons started pulling the harness off her.

She had known this was coming. "Having a good relationship with some wolves will be helpful to Free Nation," said Anastasia. "I helped these little orphans when they were defenseless. They will always remember me kindly."

Now the ropes and harness were dropping back into the chasm.

Adderall stared at her, his eyes fierce in his dark mask. "These aren't just any wolves. Look at them! They're *golden*. These are Aliyah Summerday's *children*."

"Don't you think I know that?" snapped Anastasia.

The raccoon team started hauling up the ropes.

"This is our chance to wipe out the Summerdays for *good*," said Adderall, standing tall, his eyes sweeping the other animals. "We should leave them to starve. Or better yet…"

"No," said Anastasia.

"We should take care of this ourselves, right now. We have the weapons."

"*No*," she said again, turning her face way.

Sephora's golden fur and green eyes came into view as Welly and Pam heaved her over the edge of the cliff. Everyone froze for a moment as the reality of what they were doing hit home. Humoring Loving Auntie's zany ideas was one thing. Welcoming a living breathing killer into your group was another.

Adderall pointed at the pup with his dark paw. "This thing stinks of *wolf*!" he hissed. He came near to Anastasia and ran his nose over her. "And so do you."

Sephora stood uncertainly at the edge of the cliff as Wellbutrin pulled the harness off her and threw it down for the next pup.

"She's not a *thing*," said Anastasia. Then to the pup, she said, "Just lay down. We're going to get out of here together." Sephora lay down and put her chin on her paws, her green eyes huge and anxious.

Everyone could see the rope jiggling as the next pup below climbed the harness. Then the raccoons started to pull.

"Stop!" shouted Adderall. "We need to do this one at a time." His eyes raked the others. Then he ran to the rabbits, peering into their faces one by one. "Do you want another Summerday wolf pack growing right here, on our doorstep? They're pups *now*. In a month they'll be hunting you. In a *year* they'll be fully grown." He stepped up to the raccoons. "*They broke the Truce.* Killed our people by the *hundreds*. Are we going to let these killers slaughter us *again*?"

His voice was a hot ripsaw of accusation, insistent, unstoppable. Most of the other raccoons and rabbits were looking at Anastasia. She glared at Adderall. She knew this argument. It had been in her ears for weeks. It was the voice of experience, the voice of the ancestors, and it was hard to argue with.

At last Wendy raised a paw to stop Adderall's jeremiad.

City of Oom

Her midnight-black eyes were locked on Anastasia. "Is he wrong?" she rumbled.

Anastasia stared at her. There were dozens of trained rabbit fighters here, all with bite blades. The cutting tools the raccoons carried could easily become weapons. Even the squirrel scouts were carrying their usual thorn rapiers on their backs.

A burly rabbit with a scar on his neck took a step toward the golden pup. Then a raccoon inched forward, dragging his shiny-bladed saw with him. A squirrel moved, hand lightly touching the grip of her rapier. Then others did the same. And after a few moments, with many scattered steps here and there, the animals slowly began shuffling toward Sephora, now crouched down with her back to the sheer drop of the cliff edge. It looked like no one had really decided to do anything. But the voice of a million years was strong. It pulled them forward without intention. Without planning. Without thought.

Anastasia shot a glance at Love Bug, captain of this expedition. He was looking down, fiddling with his gear. Next to him, Freddie looked torn, his face anguished. Now Adderall was talking again, his voice a high and insistent litany of terrors and complaints. All of which were true.

Anastasia heard a small cry escape from Sephora, so soft she almost missed it. "*Her...*"

Her eyes flicked to the wolfling. She looked terrified. She was whimpering and her green eyes were wet.

Anastasia knew what it was like to be the lone creature terrorized by a group. A sharp memory of her own fear arced through her, setting her nerves on fire. With a sensation of walking through quicksand, she found herself moving toward the wolf pup and taking a position facing the rest of her people.

And suddenly Freddie was standing next to her. He faced the others as he pressed against her side. "If the Loving Auntie wants to help wolves now, then so do I," he said. His forepaw came up and rested against the scabbard of his bite blade. "If we haven't learned to trust Anastasia yet, then what is the matter with us?"

She sat up tall and spread her paws, glad to feel Freddie's warm fur against her, striving to keep her voice calm and authoritative. "Here is what we will do. We will bring up the other two pups, and we will walk out of here over the palm tree bridges you created. And we will do it together." She shook out her Dragon Claw and held it high over her head. In the warm late afternoon sun, it shone with a golden fire. Then she dropped forward into her fighting stance, shoulders high and jutting, head sweeping back and forth like a snake, steel blade gleaming, daring them to come at her. "Because in the Free Nation that I love, *we don't ... kill ... children.*"

Mabel

Scirocco was moving lazily through the sky, more than five hundred feet above the old forest interspersed with meadows that grew near the Boreal Cliffs. It seemed as though the condor's wings barely moved at all, but Mabel could tell by the wind on her face that they were traveling at great speed. She could feel Death Rage moving around a bit in her backpack.

As they passed over the next section of meadow, the top of the Boreal Cliffs came into view in the distance, on the far side of a large ridge. A flickery kind of motion below caught her eye. She looked again and saw that it was hundreds of crows flying across the space, fast and low to the ground. And her breath came short as she realized that just beneath them were *hundreds* of wolves and coyotes, running, carrying shields. And behind them came the bulky water-in-motion shamble of a grizzly bear, moving at speed.

"Oh, Dah, they're *right there*," she said, pointing.

The others looked where she was pointing and a chorus of groans erupted.

"We have to find Loving Auntie *now*," said Throat Punch.

They all began to crane their necks, looking ahead to the grasslands along the edge of the Boreal Cliffs, searching for the top of the Stone Stair. Mabel heard and felt Scirocco grunt in surprise as they crested the ridge.

"Huh," he said. "That's weird."

"What?" asked Mabel.

"Lots of little lunchmeat ... walking along the cliff tops." He gestured with his beak. "About two miles from the Stair."

Mabel felt a little *zing!* run across her nervous system. Probably some kind of *Armée Libre* party. Anastasia was likely with them. She looked but her weaker eyes could not make out what he was talking about. "Can you fly over?" she asked.

"Ya, sure," said the condor. He banked and took them in that direction. Soon they were coasting along the edge of the cliff, two hundred feet above the ground. A light dusting of cottonwood fluff was eddying through the treetops. In the distance, she could see dozens of rabbits, moving in military formation, with squirrel scouts in a perimeter dashing through the scrubby trees and bushes that dotted the grassland. A jittery round shape hovered a few feet above them. *What?* She squinted. It looked to be a ball of small birds.

There was something else there. It didn't quite make sense. As Scirocco dropped lower, she saw what it was. Golden wolf puppies. Not attacking. Just running with the rabbits. Around her, she heard exclamations of surprise. Even the condor seemed startled.

"Guess it's true what they say about the downlands," he muttered. "Everything's backward."

As they came in lower, she saw familiar faces. Freddie. Wendy. Love Bug. *Anastasia*.

"Land, land, land!" Throat Punch shouted. The rabbits on the ground were looking up now. Some of the squirrels mixed in with them started to whirl long strings around their heads. Then Love Bug yelled something and they stopped suddenly.

A few moments later, they were landing, the small animals spilling out of Scirocco's claws, Sunbeam and Throat Punch running to the Loving Auntie. Mabel felt Death Rage squirming in her backpack. She had the presence of mind to stop and dig out the coins to pay for their flight.

By the time she reached Anastasia, Throat Punch had already been yelling about a City army coming over the ridge, and most of the small animals in the area were converging in a scrum around the Loving Auntie and the newcomers. Mabel shoved past Dingus to get in close to her ear. She started blurting out Clytemnestra's message, ending with "They're not just afraid of you changing the world. They're afraid of you changing *them*." As she was jostled away from Anastasia, she called out *"Be the witch."*

Chapter 22

Then Newly Beloved kissed them and said, "Of all the weapons you may wield, the blade that cuts the deepest is love."

—*Book of Secrets, 5:27–28*

Anastasia

Anastasia's head was whirling. Wendy was roaring orders. Love Bug was shouting. Freddie was trying to get close to her. And the wolf pups were squirming through the packed mass around her, desperate to be near the only familiar face they knew. Above, the bird ball was a roiling mass of uncertainty, filled with raucous noise and small hurtling bodies.

It was late in the day. The sun was behind them, casting long shadows that amplified their every move. With an army of over three hundred canids about to break over the ridge, it was too late to make a run for the Stone Stair. She knew she could activate her emergency escape with the songbirds, but everything within her rebelled at the thought of leaving those she loved at the mercy of their enemies. What to do?

Be the witch.

What was this power? How could she activate it? She raked through her memory. Was there some option she was missing? Was there some wisdom she was overlooking? What had Anima Mundi said?

When you do what no one else will, it changes everything.

What did that even mean? She felt her usual flash of rage at Anima Mundi's gnomic pronouncements. As her rescue team struggled for some semblance of a defensive strategy while the largest army in the Known World thudded toward them, she beat her paws on the ground in frustration.

Suddenly, she felt herself at the edge of the largest threshold of her life. The gateway was right in front of her, rising out of the dirty snow, although no one could see it but her. The gateposts were tall and glowing. She was moved to sing an entry couplet:

"*Did I hear the robin sing?*
Let there be a song of spring"

Then she stepped through. And immediately felt her burdens lifting. She looked up into a bright light that the others could not see and raised her forepaws. She was seized by an urge to turn, then turn again. Soon, she was twirling under an invisible spotlight, her mind struggling to absorb the vortex of information and ideas coming at her.

The squirrel scouts on the furthest perimeter were racing

City of Oom

toward the cliff edge now, blasting a wave of frantic chatter about the wolves about to reach the top of the ridge three hundred yards away.

It seemed like every single person was shouting, except for the wolf pups, who were frozen in place, green eyes racing from one person to the next.

Anastasia came back to herself, breathing *out, two, three, four*. Then she stood up on her back legs and shouted, "*Silence!*" It was a testament to her power that she still had the ability to exert control, but she knew it could not last forever. Then she called urgently, quietly, almost softly, "*Hide*."

The songbirds dropped out of their birdball and disappeared into a thicket of juniper. The rabbits and raccoons threw themselves behind the holly and camelia bushes that dotted the grassland. The squirrels froze in their tracks, melding with the splaying branches of dogwood and cherry trees.

Anastasia's forepaws were flickering with signs. *Stop. Hush. Be silent. Eyes on me.* "Follow my lead," she said with her voice and paws.

A riffle of paw signs fluttered among the bushes and scrub like an army of butterflies. *Yes. I will follow. We are one. Vive la Sans Gloire.*

Then she ran to the pups. She could see that they had not fathomed what all the shouting was about, had no idea that an army of their own kind was about to appear. She nuzzled them all, one at a time, starting with Sephora, kissing their faces and murmuring to them. They pressed against her, licking her. She had been the only caregiver they had known for many weeks, more than half of their short lives. She knew that for them, Aliyah was slipping into the gray space of baby

361

memory, inchoate, distant, already wispy. They wanted nothing more than to have Anastasia stay with them and care for them, always.

"My darlings," she said. "Let's play tag." She kissed Micah's forehead. "You're it."

Then she dashed out into the open grassland.

Pax Legio

The great grizzly Force Majeure stood on the top of the ridge, panting after his hard run. An upland songbird had come to the *Pax Legio* and told them she had seen some of the rabbit army, with its infernal leader, on the top of the cliffs. So they had changed course away from the Stone Stair and sprinted all the way here.

Spread out on each side of him, a hundred wolves and two hundred coyotes stood in a line, breathing hard, looking down through the light scrub toward the grasslands along the cliff edge, their wicker shields resting at their feet. Atticus Peacemaker had held the crows back, in order to keep the element of surprise. So they had no advance scouts.

At first, he saw nothing. The sun was low in the sky, dropping toward the clifftops before them. So they were looking into the sunset, and every plant and rock cast a long dark shadow that stretched toward them, rippling over the ground. Maybe they had come to the wrong place? Songbirds often garbled what little they knew.

Then he saw a lean rabbit running across his line of vision, near the edge of the cliff. The golden sun made it a silhouette. A few seconds later, he saw a wolf pup running after it. The rabbit put on a burst of speed. The wolf pup followed closely after. It was clearly not an expert at this, but ran with a will.

The canids on the ridge saw this scene exactly the same way the Dead Gods would have seen a toddler at a picnic wrestling with a hot dog. It was an *awwww* moment. A sign that all was right with the world. Even when crazy rabbits were tearing down the traditions everyone lived under. Even when terrified killers were telling stories of new kinds of death entering their lives. Even when rumors of witch queens whispering spells could be heard on the lips of your closest friends, the world was still knowable.

Rabbits run. Wolves chase. It has always been his way, and always will be. Their dark shapes flickered along the edge of the cliff.

Force Majeure looked around. He traded a glance with Atticus. *Not much going on here.* The wolf commander shrugged. It was a false tip. Best to get moving back to the Stone Stair and start their attack. He threw a signal down the line.

Then the pup caught the rabbit. The wolves paused for a moment, waiting to see the sweetly sentimental finish. Waiting to see the toddler scarf that hot dog.

But then the thing that never happens suddenly happened. The wolf touched the rabbit with its nose. And the rabbit started chasing the wolf pup. Force Majeure blinked, his violet eyes narrowing. He and Atticus looked at each other, and then back at the rabbit. It was running hard after the pup. Their shadows were stretched out by the low sun, gliding over the flat grassland, making their every movement huge. Like a magic lantern the size of the world.

The pup zigzagged like a prey animal. The rabbit came hard after. The pup stumbled and rolled over a few times on the grass. Then they heard a breathless, happy yelp from the little wolfling. "*I love you, Mummy!*"

And a moment later, the rabbit called out, in a warm contralto, "*I love you, baby!*" Then the rabbit nose-bumped the baby wolf, and took off running.

Force Majeure stared and shook his head. He drew the back of his massive paw across his eyes. He could hear shocked grunts and harsh exhalations rippling along the line of canids. The rabbit was galloping away at top speed, and it leaped into the air, whirling its forepaws in a complex pattern. Suddenly, he realized he was hearing the distant sounds of laughter.

Now there were more wolf pups, bounding across the grass in the late afternoon sun. And more rabbits running among them, leaping and somersaulting. It was a frolic. Wolves chasing rabbits, rabbits chasing wolves, all in silhouette against the golden sun. A light dusting of breathy giggles floated toward him.

Force Majeure's breath came short. He was very aware of the animals nearby looking at him, awaiting his response. He felt like there was a great weight on his chest. Wolves and rabbits were *playing*. Was there no end to this novelty? Was there no end to this world without precedents? The shadows of the cavorting animals were long. They stretched all the way to his toes.

He swatted at the dark shapes without thinking. He had a job to do. He would do it. But when he cast a hasty glance down the line of wolves on either side, he saw their stunned, worried eyes.

They were looking at wolf puppies, the future of their tribe, gone soft. Rolling in the grass when they should be tearing their meal apart. Somehow *unhuntered, unwolfed, undone*. Would they themselves be next? A whine began and spread from wolf to wolf. Force Majeure growled. Atticus ran along the line, shouting. "*On my mark, charge! Three, two, one, go!*"

Some of the canids seized their shields and took a few steps forward, and then stopped when they realized that the others were not with them. Others began to mill around. A terrible groaning began. Fear was in their eyes. The crows, initially silent, began to roil and screech as the terror of their wolf family clans flowed through their lifelong bonds and set their amygdalae on fire.

"Go!" roared Force Majeure, and the inescapable rumble of his earth-deep voice made the head of every canid vibrate. His glaring eyes burned a hot red-violet. But the *Pax Legio* did not move forward. Some canids began to fight with each other. Some fell on their bellies and cried. Suddenly, they were not alpha killers but fearful animals, asked to do the undoable thing. Run into the unknown and kill that monster.

Because they could see that down by the edge of the cliffs, the poison rising up from the downlands was strong. Going there meant unbeing a wolf. If you went there, you would lose your birthright. You would become a *dog*. Or less than a dog, a *pet*. A neutered *always-child.* You would play with *bunnies* and lick the hand that held the leash tied to the collar around your throat.

Force Majeure roared and smacked the earth. He had a strong

urge to start picking up wolves and throwing them. Atticus set off on a charge by himself, to shame the others into joining him, but when he had gone a hundred feet he realized no one was following him. He stood shouting, and then lost his ability to speak and his voice became a long, splintered howl leaping across crazed, chaotic intervals. Instantly, dozens of howls joined his.

Abruptly, a lone squirrel flickered into existence at the tip of a cherry tree branch and stood, back feet together, right front paw held high. It was the stance of the herald. A silvery voice arced out across the field, piercing the ears of the animals of the *Pax Legio*, now snarling, weeping, and pawing at the ground while the cottonwood fluffs fell around them.

"Behold, it is the unchosen one."

The voice was cool, bright, uncompromising. It sliced through the howling and everything went silent. The squirrel was framed by the bright disk of the setting sun. Force Majeure could not rest his eyes on it for more than an instant. The voice came at the hunters again, falling like a silver hammer on their frantic tumbling and driving a great stillness

"Unblessed. Without glory. Unloved by angels. Called by no god."

The wolf pups and rabbits had stopped playing now. They stood on the crest of the cliffs, with the wide ocean behind them turned a glowing crimson by the setting sun. In the center, the lean rabbit sat tall, looking straight at him, framed by the wine-dark sea. The wolf pups gathered near her and nuzzled into her fur. The other rabbits leaned against the wolves, panting after their game.

The squirrel began again. The voice was penetrating, relentless, inescapable.

*"Adored by hunters. Worshipped by killers.
Exalted by murderers. Loved by all that is you."*

Force Majeure could hear the terrified whine rising above the wolves like a storm of panic. Their scent was a bright, acrid cloud of fear. The unearthliness of it was crushing them. Their paws beat a frantic drumbeat of uncertainty and fear.

The squirrel spread both his hands wide in a gesture of benediction. A puff of wind brought forth new seed fluffs from the trees nearby, and they floated like a blessing on the newly warm air, a harbinger of a new world. The pups looked up at the lean rabbit adoringly. She kissed their heads.

The fabric of the wolves' world strained and tore. One turned and ran. Then another. Then many. And soon, their line was collapsing. The crows were reeling. The world was changing.

Force Majeure felt the hot fire of rage rolling over him, his eyes blazed a bright magenta, and he yearned to use his great body to destroy everything about this moment. But he held himself back. Even if he killed every animal he could see, news of his defeat would still spread far and wide.

The silver voice came at him again, striking against his ears like a stinging lash.

*"Hear her name. Hear her name. Hear her name.
She is Anastasia Bloody Thorn, Mother of Wolves."*

Thank you

Thank you so much for reading *City of Oom!* It's wonderful to have the opportunity to share these animal stories with you.

I'd be very grateful if you would leave a review of *City of Oom* at the store where you got it: you can find the link at books2read.com/cityofoom

Would you like to stay up-to-date on new books and audiobooks in the *War Bunny Chronicles*? Let's connect!

- Join the mailing list: christopherstjohn.com/join-email-list
- Instagram: @christopherstjohnwriter
- Facebook: christopherstjohnwriter
- X: @stjohnwriter

Book 4 is currently in development. I'll send out information to the mailing list when it's published.

Thanks again!

Acknowledgements

I would like to thank the animals who served as models for some of these characters. Rescue bunnies all, they've come to have a profound impact on my understanding of who counts as a "person." Anastasia and Freddie came from SaveABunny in Mill Valley, California. Love Bug and Wendy came from RabbitEARS in Oakland, California. Mabel was rescued from a California fur farm and lives with a friend.

I'd like to thank my sisters, Catherine McKenzie and Julia Singer Presar, who have spent many hours talking through ideas with me.

I'd like to thank the beta readers who provided wonderful and astute feedback, pointing out lots of ways *City of Oom* could be better, greatly enriching the story. A heartfelt thank you to Teryl Mandel, Chantal Comeau, Nancy Gage, Caitlin Throckmorton, Marisa Sterling, and Hannah Niklaus.

The team at Harvest Oak Press has spared no effort to make *War Bunny* the best it can be. It was wonderful working with editor Laurel McKenzie. Belle McClain's evocative cover art is the perfect match for this story. And artist Manolis Karavidas did a splendid job on the classic pen-and-ink map. Thanks for all your hard work!

Christopher St. John

And I must offer oodles of thanks to my wife, Gayle Paul, who this year, and every year, wins the Grand Slam Award for Being The Super Duperest Number One Very Tiptoppy Most Bestest Of All Da Bunniez.

Characters

RABBITS

Warren *Sans Gloire*

Anastasia – Loving Auntie – Brown fur, golden eyes
Nicodemus – Elder Reader – Silver fur, splash of white on forehead
Wendy – Commander – Lop ears, brown fur, black eyes
Freddie – Maker of New – Black-and-grey harlequin fur
Love Bug – Captain – White fur, dark eyes
Yasmin – Captain of the Home Guard – Cinnamon fur, dark rim around eyes
Holly – Home Steward – Amber and white fur, missing a leg
Gregoire – Healer – Brown fur turning gray
Juniper – Healing Intern – Black fur splashed with gray

Tumble Stone Warren

Mabel – Remembering Acolyte – Black-and-white fur, witchy eyes

Sunbeam – Anastasia's Younger Sister – Golden fur, green eyes

Wandering

Aiden – Rememberer – Cream-colored fur, dark ears and feet

Coyote

Gaetan – Injured Coyboy – Dirty-gray fur

Wolves

Summerday Clan

Aliyah – Clan Mother – Golden fur, maple-green eyes
Sephora – Pup – Golden agouti fur, forest-green eyes
Tennyson – Pup – Golden agouti fur, maple-green eyes
Micah – Pup – Golden agouti fur, aquamarine eyes

Municipal Wolves, Peacemaker Clan

Atticus – Commander – gray fur, artic-blue eyes

Crows

Summerday Crows

Grammy Kark – Leader – Black feathers, elder

Raccoons

Wellbutrin – Dirty Apple Sales – Black-and-gray fur
Lorazepam – Fermentator – Black-and-gray fur, snaggletooth
Adderall – Dirty Apple Bro – Black-and-gray fur, white scar on face
Vicodin – Shandy Lift Operator – Black-and-gray fur, long fingers
Lunesta – Hella Cozy Proprietor – Black-and-gray fur, scar on back

Foxes

Isadore – Young Hubby – Red fur, white underbelly
Juliette – Young Wifey – Red fur, white underbelly, silver ear tips

WEASEL

Saskatoon – Killer – White fur, dark eyes

MICE

Death Rage – Warmouse – Auburn fur, splash of white on back
Throat Punch – Warmouse – Vermillion/rose fur, golden eyes
Poison Wind – Craftmouse – Tawny fur, dark eyes

SONGBIRD

Stan – Bluebird – Air Captain – Orange-breasted, blue wings, balding

RAT

Bricabrac – Craftrat – Dark brown fur, reddish underbelly

SQUIRREL

Dingus – Guru – Red-brown fur, white underbelly

Bears

Ex Cathedra – General Counsel – Dark bronze fur, dark eyes
Force Majeure – Counselor – Mahogany fur, violet eyes
Clavis Aurea – Seer – Chestnut fur, golden eyes

Les Enchantés

Clytemnestra – Queen of Sorrows – White hair, cerulean blue eye, many scars
Aeschylus – Soldier – White hair, sapphire blue eyes, many scars
Calliope – Healer – White hair, periwinkle blue eyes

Raptor

Scirocco – Condor – Dark feathers, pink neck and head

The War Bunny Chronicles

"A fierce and cozy adventure"
– *The Portalist*

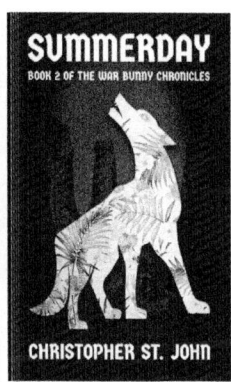

| BOOK 1 | BOOK 2 | BOOK 3 |

Available now at your favorite online bookstore!

War Bunny audiobook coming soon

Book 4 is currently in development

Sign up for the email list at www.christopherstjohn.com

HARVEST OAK
PRESS

Printed in Great Britain
by Amazon